A Short History of Africa

Roland Oliver was born in 1923 at Srinagar, Kashmir, and educated at Stowe and King's College, Cambridge. In 1948 he was appointed to a Lectureship at the School of Oriental and African Studies, in 1958 to a Readership in African History and in 1963 to a Chair in African History in the University of London, from which he retired in 1986. He has travelled in most parts of Africa and has held visiting appointments at the University of Ghana (1957), the University of Brussels (1961), Northwestern University (1962) and Harvard University (1967). In 1966 he won the Haile Selassie I Prize Trust Award for African Research. He has written *The Missionary Factor in East Africa*, 1952, *Sir Harry Johnston and the Scramble for Africa*, 1957, *A History of East Africa, Vol. I*, with Gervase Mathew, 1963, *Africa since 1800*, with A. E. Atmore, 1967, *Africa in the Iron Age*, with Brian M. Fagan, 1975, and *The African Middle Ages*, with A. E. Atmore, 1981. He and John Fage were the founding editors of the *Journal of African History*, 1960–73, and the general editors of *The Cambridge History of Africa*, 8 vols., 1975–86.

John Fage was born in 1921 and educated at Tonbridge School and Magdalene College, Cambridge. His interest in Africa was kindled during the Second World War when service with the Royal Air Force took him to various parts of the continent. In 1949 he went as Lecturer in History to the fledgling University of Ghana, where he rose to be Professor and Deputy Principal. In 1959 he joined Roland Oliver (whom he had known since the two of them were researching in African history at Cambridge in 1948) at the School of Oriental and African Studies, which he left in 1963 to become the first Director of the Centre of West African Studies and Professor of African History at the University of Birmingham. After becoming Pro-Vice-Chancellor and Vice-Principal, he retired from the University in 1964. He has held visiting appointments in African History at the University of Wisconsin, Madison, and at Smith College, Massachusetts. He was for many years Chairman of the Culture Committee of the U K National Commission for UNESCO. His publications include *A History of West Africa*, 1955; revised 1969, *An Atlas of African History*, 1958; revised 1978, *Ghana: A historical interpretation*, 1959, and *A History of Africa*, 1978.

A Short History of Africa

Sixth edition

ROLAND OLIVER
AND J. D. FAGE

PENGUIN BOOKS

PENGUIN BOOKS

Published by the Penguin Group
27 Wrights Lane, London W8 5TZ, England
Viking Penguin Inc., 40 West 23rd Street, New York, New York 10010, USA
Penguin Books Australia Ltd, Ringwood, Victoria, Australia
Penguin Books Canada Ltd, 2801 John Street, Markham, Ontario, Canada L3R 1B4
Penguin Books (NZ) Ltd, 182–190 Wairau Road, Auckland 10, New Zealand

Penguin Books Ltd, Registered Offices: Harmondsworth, Middlesex, England

First published 1962
Second edition 1966
Third edition 1970
Fourth edition 1972
Fifth edition 1975
Reprinted with revisions 1978
Reprinted in Pelican Books 1984
Sixth edition 1988
10 9 8 7 6 5 4 3

Made and printed in Great Britain by
Richard Clay Ltd, Bungay, Suffolk
Set in Monophoto Ehrhardt

Contents

List of Maps

Preface to the Sixth Edition

The first edition of this book was written in 1961. At that time the academic study of African history was less than fifteen years old. There were four named posts in the subject in Britain, of which we held two. The first learned journal devoted to the publication of the results of new research in African history had been founded in the previous year with ourselves as the editors. At the handful of universities then existing in Africa, teachers of general history, nearly all of whom were non-Africans, were pioneering degree courses in which African history was beginning to be a major component. What we hoped to achieve in this small book was to give some unity and shape to the history of a continent which had until very recently been studied mainly in bits and pieces, as parts of this or that European empire or sphere of missionary or commercial influence. Africa in 1961 was experiencing the full tide of decolonization, and it was clear that the first need of newly independent countries was to learn much more about their African neighbours. Outsiders too had to learn to think of the continent as a whole.

Since 1961 there has been a great advance in knowledge of the African past. And a quarter of a century rich in momentous events has been added to its span. Four times already we have revised our work in the light of the new literature and attempted to summarize the most recent events. This time the publishers generously offered to re-set as much of the text as we thought it necessary to re-write. We have therefore been more radical. Chapter 20 has been largely reconstructed, and Chapter 21 is entirely new. Chapter 8 has been considerably rewritten. Chapter 4, already much changed since the original version, has been still further revised. Throughout the text we have tried to correct what was wrong. What we have tried *not* to do is to change significantly the proportions. Largely as a result of the political situation in different parts of Africa, the progress of knowledge has been very uneven. To have taken full account of the research salients would have made havoc of our battle-line. We believe that the strength of the book has been in its general design, and we have tried to keep it so.

R.O.
J.D.F.

1 The Hunters

The first popular idea about Africa is also the first major misconception. The notion of Africa as the Dark Continent is a parochial European idea, which gained currency because Africa was the last of the continents to be opened to the gaze of the outside world, and because it was the last to experience that full impact of European people, ideas and techniques which was so marked a feature of world history from the sixteenth to the early twentieth centuries. At the beginning of this modern period of history, however, Africa was far from the most backward of the continents. The Australians, for example, when they were discovered by the Europeans, were still living as hunters and gatherers, and were using stone tools comparable with those of the Upper Palaeolithic cultures abandoned by most European and African peoples from six to nine thousand years before. Again, the more advanced of the sixteenth-century American Indians were neolithic or 'New Stone Age' cultivators, using polished stone tools. A very few of them were just beginning to learn the use of metals. But many more were still Mesolithic hunter-gatherers. The Africans of the same period, on the other hand, with few exceptions, were farmers equipped with tools of iron – and there were in consequence many more of them. Throughout the northern third of the continent most of them belonged to the urbanized civilization of Islam. Even in the southern two-thirds of the continent, most of the African peoples were organized into states and communities powerful enough to deter invaders and migrants from overseas until late in the nineteenth century. True, much of Africa was unhealthy and inaccessible, but not more so than Panama or Peru. The real reason why the Europeans did not go inland and seize the gold mines of western and south-eastern Africa, for example, was that the Africans there were already well enough organized to exploit these resources themselves and to keep the overland trade in their own hands. It was in large measure the progress already made by the Africans in earlier centuries that enabled them to resist the modern age for so long.

In historical times, therefore, the backwardness of Africa was always a backwardness relative only to the mainstream of human development in the more favoured parts of Europe and Asia. In *pre-historic* times – at least through all the long millennia of the palaeolithic or 'Old Stone Age' – Africa was not even relatively backward: it was in the lead.

Archaeologists today are increasingly confident that it was in Africa, and more specifically in eastern equatorial Africa, that man's ancestors became differentiated from other primates. Equatorial Africa is still the home of mankind's closest relatives, the gorilla and the chimpanzee. The fossilized remains of man's more immediate hominid ancestors, the so-called Australopithecines, have so far been found only in or near the highland savannas of eastern and southern Africa, in contexts dating from around 4 to 5 million years ago. The currently accepted distinction between man and other hominids is that man made and used stone tools. Judged by this test, the earliest men were, once again, East Africans, the earliest dated examples occurring around 2·5 million years ago. By about 1·5 million years ago the human species had attained the stage known scientifically as *Homo erectus*, with a cranial capacity about two-thirds that of modern man. It was probably only at this period that human populations spread northwards into Saharan and North African latitudes, and so across the isthmus of Suez into Asia.

The earliest stone tools, known as Oldowan after the famous sites at Olduvai Gorge in northern Tanzania where they were first excavated in large numbers by Louis and Mary Leakey, were made from rounded cobbles or pebbles, which were split and then chipped around the edges so as to give a cutting edge. Some of the chippings were further worked into sharp flakes for piercing skin and sinew, and into smaller tools for scraping. Essentially, it was a butchering outfit, one that marked man's progress from a vegetarian to a meat-eating diet, and from a way of life spent mainly in gathering roots, fruits and nuts to one increasingly dominated by hunting. Most of the sites containing tools of this description have been found in the highlands of eastern and southern Africa. Those few which have been found further afield, in Israel and Morocco, appear to belong to a considerably later period. Though some early men of the *Homo erectus* type are known to have lived in Indonesia and China, and to have used chopping tools faintly reminiscent of the Oldowan, their date is likely to have been well within the period of man's first expansion from the African cradleland.

Around 1·4 million years ago, the earliest human tools began to be superseded, in the East African heartland, by a radically new tool-kit known as the Acheulian, which was destined to spread all over the

1   Africa: principal geographical features and vegetation

western half of the Old World. Its most characteristic item was the mysterious pear-shaped stone implement, misleadingly called a 'hand-axe'. No one knows exactly what it was used for. Certainly it was not an axe. Professor Desmond Clark, after much practical experiment, has described it as an all-purpose skinning-tool and meat chopper. At all events, it was the most standard and the most characteristic of man's artefacts for more than three-quarters of a million years. It has been found all the way from India to Spain and from England to the Cape of Good Hope: of the parts of the globe inhabited at this period, only the Far East and Central Asia escaped its influence. The successive techniques employed for making the hand-axe have been named, in accordance with the perversity of archaeologists, after the two French villages of Chelles and St Acheul, where the 'type-sites' were established. But Europe was not the centre of these industries. The Chellean-Acheulian sequence is consistent in Europe, Asia and Africa, and there is little doubt that the centre of its development was in Africa. Far more hand-axes have been found in Africa than anywhere else, and the East African dates are by far the earliest. Two of the richest hand-axe sites in the world are at Olorgesaile, forty miles south of Nairobi, and at Olduvai Gorge, just across the Tanzania frontier from Olorgesaile. Only in East Africa, and at one site in Morocco, is it possible to observe the evolution of pebble tools and hand-axes as a single continuous process.

Throughout the million years or so during which men in the western part of the Old World were making Acheulian tools, they were themselves evolving from the 'erect' towards the 'sapient' stage. Here again there is little doubt that man in Africa was in the lead. It was not only that in Africa man had had a longer history. The carrying capacity for wild game of the human cradleland in eastern and southern Africa was about ten times as great as the most favourable environments found elsewhere, and this fact alone would account for a greater density of human population and therefore a more rapid evolutionary process. While the skeletal record of the earliest sapient forms is thin, there is no doubt that both of the more recent stages – *Homo sapiens neanderthalensis* and *Homo sapiens sapiens* – were reached much earlier in Africa than in Europe, by more than 100,000 years ago in both cases.

By this time, if not before, man had learned to control fire, and he was tending to abandon his former open-air camps for the comparative comfort and stability of caves and rock-shelters. These were but two symptoms of a much greater power of adaptation to different environments which was manifested also in the evolution of tools. Here, the changes which occurred at this period mark the transition from the lower to the middle palaeolithic. Everywhere the old Acheulian hand-axe and the rather indeterminate smaller tools that had accompanied it, gave way to one or other of a series of new tool-kits, each adapted to a particular range of environment. These kits were not exclusive: there was a great deal of overlap between one set and another. But in Africa it is possible to distinguish three broad, regional traditions. The first, comprising all of Africa north of the Sahara, is called, like its northern Mediterranean counterpart, Mousterian. The second was a heavier, woodland tool-kit, designed more for grubbing and grinding than for hunting. It is usually called the Sangoan, and it belongs to the woodland regions surrounding the equatorial forest, from southern West Africa to the Congo-Zambezi watershed. The third was an open-country tool-kit, the Fauresmith, used from northern East Africa to the Cape of Good Hope.

During most of the middle palaeolithic the characteristic tools from all these regional traditions consisted of stone flakes of various shapes and sizes, first struck from a large core and then retouched by chipping around the edges so as to produce tools appropriate for different purposes, such as the killing, skinning, chopping and scraping of meat, bone, skin and sinew, the grubbing and grinding of roots, and the working of wood and other materials. Much later on, towards the end of the middle palaeolithic, came the appearance of blades, produced by striking off slice after slice from a carefully prepared core. These marked a great advance in the efficiency of cutting tools, such as chisels and gouges, knives and razors. And this in turn led, round about 30,000 years ago, to the stage of material culture called upper palaeolithic, of which the most important characteristic was that most of the stone artefacts were microliths, that is to say, they were the small, sharp components of composite tools made of stone and wood and various kinds of ligatures. At this stage, tool-kits became even more closely adapted to particular environments, but the three broad traditions of the middle palaeolithic can still be detected. The Mousterian tradition had developed into the Aterian, the Sangoan into the Lupemban and the Fauresmith into the Stillbay. In all of them the increasing range and complexity of tools was accompanied by a decline in stone-shaping techniques, but with the new utilitarianism came an inventiveness which greatly enriched the scope of man's material and imaginative life. With the bone needle came the beginning of the tailor's art. With string there came the possibility of the bow: Aterian arrow-heads were perhaps the first to be used anywhere in the world. Again, it was in upper palaeolithic times that men and women used the first cosmetics, the tell-tale stains of red ochre witnessing to a self-consciousness and sophistication which might perhaps be equated with 'the knowledge of good and evil'.

It was during the period of territorial expansion and regional specialization represented by the Mousterian, the Sangoan and the Fauresmith traditions of material culture and their upper palaeolithic derivatives, that man's physical development in Africa, as in the rest of the inhabited world, was reaching the sapient stage. There is no need, today, to postulate any war to the death in which rival species of man were extinguished. Rather, we should visualize a long drawn-out process in which sapient characteristics spread by genetic means. However, at the same time as more fundamental differences were being eliminated, specialization towards particular environments was having its own genetic consequences in producing differences of a less fundamental kind, which can best be thought of in terms of 'race' or 'physical type'. Here, as with traditions in material culture, it always has to be remembered that there are no hard frontiers. Where races meet there are large areas of interaction, and the stereotypes merge into imperceptibility at the edges. Nevertheless, following this caveat, we can usefully distinguish four broad categories of African population which probably had their origin during the middle and upper palaeolithic. First, and most distinct from the others, there were the peoples living to the north of the Sahara and to the east of the Nile, whose nearest affiliations were with the peoples of south-western Asia – Arabia, Palestine, Syria and western Mesopotamia. Of medium height and brownish complexion, these peoples are referred to in the older literature (earlier editions of this book included) as

Caucasoid, but Afroasian is a much more accurate term. Second, there were the peoples of the sub-Saharan savanna and forest fringes, who during wet climatic phases penetrated northwards into Saharan latitudes. Tall, lightly built and dark of hue, with woolly black hair, these were the Blacks. Third, there were the peoples adapted to conditions of true forest. Short in stature and pale in complexion, these were the Pygmies. Fourth, there were the peoples of the eastern and southern savannas. Of medium height and yellowish, with hair growing in separate tufts, these were the Bushmen. Though very different from each other in outward appearance, the last three types have a very similar pattern of blood-groups, which are the most strictly genetic of all human physiological characteristics. They may therefore be thought of as three variants of a basic African stock which became divergently specialized towards different geographical environments. The Afroasians, although like the rest of mankind they were ultimately of African origin, had undergone much of their long evolution towards the sapient state outside the African mainstream: for this the existence at most periods of the Saharan desert zone is a sufficient explanation.

Nevertheless, the Afroasian peoples of Africa, despite their comparative geographical isolation, had an important role in African history as the main human link between Africa and the outside world. Obviously, this role was most significant during the exceptional periods when, for climatic reasons, the desert zone was at its narrowest, and when populations from the north and south of the desert could most easily meet and interact. Such a period did in fact occur towards the end of the upper palaeolithic, and during it the stage was set for the greatest of all economic revolutions, namely the transition from hunting and gathering to food production. This was the period when the monsoon rain-belt was shifting northwards into the African and Arabian deserts, converting them temporarily into parklands, rich in game and with streams and rivers flowing north and south from the mountain massifs of the central Sahara. Not only was it a period of unrivalled opportunity for the hunter; it also saw a great new development in one of the patterns of a hunting and gathering existence, namely fishing. Throughout the northern half of Africa, significant elements of population gathered along the river banks and by lake shores, and began to lead a kind of life that was almost sedentary – a life based upon fishing, in which hunting and gathering had become only marginal activities.

In these exceptional circumstances the river lines and sea coasts of northern Africa took on a great significance, and they were lines which provided easy communication between the Afroasian and Black populations, by which development in the new riparian way of life could spread across the whole region. The Red Sea coast offered one avenue, the drainage system of the Nile another. The eastward-flowing tributaries of the upper Nile were separated by a narrow watershed from the rivers flowing westwards to Lake Chad, at this time a vast inland sea covering most of the central part of the modern Tchad Republic and emptying westwards into the Benue and the Niger. At the peak of the wet phase, around 7,000 B.C., the Nile was probably connected by its Sobat tributary with Lake Rudolf and the northern lakes of the East African Rift Valley. In this last region, the sites of people who lived mainly by fishing are associated with a remarkable industry of blade tools known as the Kenya Capsian. The Capsian blade, especially when made of the natural, volcanic glass called obsidian, had a cutting edge as sharp as any steel knife or chisel. It was admirable for working bone, and bone harpoons soon became one of the hallmarks of late upper palaeolithic fishing communities all the way from the Kenya Rift Valley to the tributaries of the upper Niger. Somewhere along the line, perhaps in some central area such as the upper Nile valley, there occurred the stupendous invention of pottery – certainly the earliest pottery in Africa. This 'wavy line' pottery of early African fishing communities, like their bone harpoons, was made and decorated in a nearly standard pattern throughout the drainage systems of the Niger and the Nile, thus illustrating how easily new ideas and techniques could spread among communities which in other respects had very different material cultures and ethnic origins.

Seven or eight thousand years ago, therefore, at the end of man's purely parasitic existence as a hunter and gatherer, and at the dawn of the settled life of agriculture and stock-raising, Africa was already inhabited by the ancestors of the four main racial types recognized as indigenous in historical times – Bushmen and Pygmies, Blacks and Afroasians. Of these four types, the most widespread at the end of the upper palaeolithic was probably still the Bushman, who seems to have inhabited all the open savanna country to the south and east of a line drawn from Somalia to central Angola. In the forested country to the north-west of that line were the Pygmies, who were perhaps nearer to being forest-adapted Bushmen than forest-adapted Blacks. The black Africans at this period seem to have been essentially men of the woodlands and savannas to the north of the equatorial forest, from the Atlantic to the foothills of the Ethiopian highlands. It may indeed be that at this period the Blacks were more men of the open country than of the woodland, for some of their earliest identifiable remains have been found far out in Saharan latitudes, and it is significant that the waterside fishing variant of the hunting life which they favoured did not at this stage penetrate the forest reaches of the Congo drainage system or down the line of the great lakes. So long as the wet phase lasted, the most open frontier of Black Africa may have been that with the Afroasian peoples to the north and, especially, to the east. Certainly the Afroasians and the black Africans were geographically the best placed to profit from the stupendous developments that were to come with the domestication of plants and animals, and in this great mutation the black African's apprenticeship as a fisherman-hunter-gatherer and a maker of pottery was to give him a huge advantage over peoples living further to the south.

2 The Farmers

As we have seen, it was some 4 or 5 million years ago that man's ancestors became recognizable as hominids practising a hunting and gathering economy, and some hundred thousand years ago that they were approaching the stage of physical development known as sapiency. In contrast, it was only some 10,000 years ago that sapient man at last began to cultivate, and thus started the third great revolution in human history. Food production – the deliberate selection and cultivation of edible plants previously merely gathered or grubbed in their wild state, and the taming and breeding of certain animals which had till then run wild – made possible the settled life of the village as opposed to the hunting-camp. It made possible the accumulation of material equipment on a scale which would have been merely embarrassing to the nomadic hunter or gatherer. Above all, it made possible for the first time population densities expressible in terms of men to the square mile rather than square miles to the man. This, of course, does not mean that the food-producing revolution was everywhere a sudden one. In Egypt it certainly was so. We now know that the dynastic period in Egypt was reached little more than a thousand years after the first food crops were planted; but this was due to the unique potentialities of the flood-plain of the Nile. Elsewhere in Africa the transition was much more gradual, and the beginnings of agriculture and stockbreeding were for a long time an alternative to, rather than a replacement for, the older hunting and fishing economies. All the same, there can be little doubt that in Africa, as in the rest of the Old World, it is from the spread of the food-producing revolution that the basic population patterns of the historic period derive.

The food-producing revolution seems to have affected Africa in three main stages. Beginning in the seventh millennium and gathering momentum in the fourth, it was responsible for the emergence of a really dense and mainly Afroasian population in the lower Nile valley. Secondly, south of the Sahara, beginning perhaps in the fourth millennium B.C. but probably gathering momentum only during the second and first, it brought the black Africans decisively into the lead all the way along the savanna belt between the desert and the equatorial rain forest. In the third stage, which seems to be linked with the beginnings of agriculture in forest clearings and forest/savanna mosaic, Black populations originating in the West African savanna expanded into Africa south of the equator and became the main populations of those regions also. We must now look at these three stages more closely.

Archaeologists today are tending to take a longer view than they did previously of the approach to food production, which consisted in the intensive gathering and more or less unconscious selection of wild food plants and the incipient domestication, through feeding, of certain animals. In a sense, therefore, every region that had reached the stage of intensive gathering indicated by the presence of neolithic reaping tools was on the road to food production. By the second millennium B.C. this had come to include almost all of Africa north of the equator.

It is recognized that at sites in the Wadi Kubbaniya near Aswan intensive food gathering dates from as early as 16,000 B.C. This region lies more or less astride the borderline between two climatic and botanical zones – that of winter rainfall to the north and that of summer rainfall to the south. The natural vegetation includes some items from both zones. In these circumstances it seems no longer reasonable to maintain that food production was invented to the north of the Sahara and redeveloped to the south of the desert after a time-lag for the domestication of new plants. The message of the Wadi Kubbaniya sites is that the preparation for food production was taking place more or less simultaneously, as a marginal activity, on both sides of the Sahara. It was merely the final stages of exploitation that came about somewhat earlier to the north than to the south.

On present evidence, the achievement of full food production, by the cultivation of wheat and barley and the herding of goats and cattle, at the site of Tell es-Sultan in the Jordan valley near Jericho is still earlier by some 2,000 years than the earliest comparable occurrence anywhere in Africa. Nevertheless, in the Nabta basin in the Western Desert of Egypt, close to the Sudan frontier, cattle were herded and two types of barley cultivated in the late seventh millennium B.C., so that the chronological discrepancy is not so great. It would seem that the domesticated animals at least must have been introduced from western Asia, since no wild ancestors of the domestic stocks existed in Africa.

It is perhaps significant that the earliest Egyptian food producers had their settlements not on the valley bottom, where swamp and jungle would still at this period have presented great difficulties, but on the high terraces at the edge of what is now desert and was then dry steppe, especially beside the courses of the tributary *wadis*, now dry but then seasonally flowing. The classic early neolithic sites at Deir Tasa, Badari, Merimde and al-Omari are all situated on the margins of the valley and the Delta, and not in the flood-plain itself. The most revealing of all the early sites yet excavated are those of the northern Fayum, a natural depression once connected with the Nile valley, with a lake-covered floor, its sides showing a series of former shorelines falling from nearly 300 feet above the present level. The steadily falling lakeshores were occupied by palaeolithic hunters, and they continued to be occupied off and on until Roman times; there is no question, therefore, of the earliest neolithic sites having been overlooked. Neolithic men built their first settlements by the lake when it stood 180 feet higher than it does today. By the radiocarbon method, their occupation has been dated to the early fifth millennium B.C. The surviving tools include ground stone axes and serrated stone sickles set in wooden shafts, while sunken silos lined with straw matting contain grains of barley and emmer wheat. The elaborate storage arrangements show that the communities were permanently settled. Hunting was practised with bow and arrow, and the remains of bone fishing-tackle recalls that of the Sudanic wet phase. The neolithic people of the Fayum used a coarse undecorated pottery and could weave linen. They imported shells from the Red Sea coast and amazonite from the borders of Libya to make pendants and beads. That they were an intrusive group is shown by the fact that upper palaeolithic hunters continued to frequent the depression after their arrival. Eventually the two elements fused, the newcomers taking to some of the flake tools and tanged arrow-heads of the hunters, who in their turn adopted the cultivation tools of the food producers.

It is clear from all the sites that the early Egyptian cultivators of the valley margin soon began to suffer from the steady desiccation of the climate during the late fifth and early fourth millennia. It was the encroaching drift sand of the desert which stimulated the Tasians and Badarians of middle Egypt to move down and clear the flood-plain, with results so startling for the history of the world. From that moment onwards the remains of the pre-dynastic period indicate a phenomenal growth of population; 20,000 people would probably be an extreme estimate of the population of hunter-gatherers that the Egyptian section of the Nile valley could have supported at the end of palaeolithic times. The population of the Old Kingdom 2,000 years later has been variously estimated at from 3 to 6 millions. The physical types found in pre-dynastic and early dynastic burials are remarkably consistent, and show that the ancient Egyptian cultivators were of a short and rather lightly built race indistinguishable from the modern Beja of the Red Sea hills or from the Danakil and Somali of the Horn of Africa. Their language, we know, was of the Hamito-Semitic or Afroasiatic family, which includes the Berber languages of north-west Africa on the one hand and the Cushitic languages of north-eastern Africa on the other. The increase in population which followed was essentially a natural increase of the pre-existing Afroasian population of North and East Africa, an increase due to the fantastic growth of food supplies made possible by wheat and barley, and also by the perennially rejuvenated soil of the Nile flood-plain.

Along with wheat and barley, domesticated goats, sheep, pigs and cattle existed in Egypt from the earliest neolithic times, and also flax and various vegetable and forage plants. It was the wheat and barley, however, which certainly exercised the most revolutionary influence; and it was upon the exploitation of alternative cereals to wheat and barley, suited to more tropical conditions of climate, that the spread of the food-producing revolution to the rest of Africa really depended. The Nile valley alluvium, however, had no equivalent elsewhere.

Westwards from Egypt, it would seem that the pastoral element in Egyptian food-production spread to Libya as early as the sixth millennium, and to Tunisia, Algeria and Morocco by the fifth. Sheep and goats were the first animals to be herded. Cattle followed anything up to a millennium later. Throughout this area, however, the tools of the earliest food producers were clearly of local origin, having developed from the indigenous Capsian tradition. There is thus no need to postulate that any large migration of new people accompanied the domestic stock. Moreover, there was a long delay before the introduction of agriculture. Pastoralism was practised along with hunting, which remained the predominant element in the economy until at least the second millennium B.C.

Moving up the Nile into black Africa, it is clear from the carbon-dated site at Shaheinab near Khartoum that the riverside communities of the upper Nile were by the early fourth millennium making neolithic tools similar to those of upper Egypt, but at the nearby and contemporary site of Kadero cattle and sheep were being herded in large numbers, while sorghum, eleusine and panicum millets were in regular use. Further west, it was certainly in the form of pastoralism that the practice of food production crossed the central Sahara. The evidence of this comes mainly from rock-shelters, painted and engraved with pastoral scenes, and the associated deposits dating to the fifth and fourth millennia B.C. This was towards the end of the Saharan wet phase, and by the late fourth millennium pastoralists were migrating southwards into the sub-Saharan savannas. Almost certainly the pastoralists had been familiar with domesticated cereals in the north and began to experiment with the wild cereal grasses which they encountered to the south of the desert.

The oldest cereal crops of sub-Saharan Africa were the millets,[1] but in West Africa west of the great bend of the Niger there was also the rice *Oryza glaberrima*. All these grains are native to sub-Saharan Africa and, more narrowly, to the light woodland savanna which stretches from the Senegal to the upper Nile and thence southeastwards into northern Uganda and parts of Kenya. There are those who would argue the case for an original and independent invention of agriculture in this sub-Saharan region, but taking the long view of the domestication process, such considerations have lost much of their earlier significance. What we can say is that the emergence of truly

1. Especially the many species of *Sorghum* (guinea corn or great millet), *Pennisetum* (bulrush or pearl millet) and *Eleusine corocana*.

food-producing communities came later in the western part of the Saharan region than in the eastern part. In Saharan latitudes there were pastoralists present from the fifth millennium, but the earliest evidence of agriculture in the sub-Saharan belt dates from the early second millennium in the central part of modern Ghana, and from the later second millennium in northern Nigeria and southern Mauritania. The only well-developed agricultural civilization that was once thought to have originated in neolithic times is that associated with the so-called 'Nok culture' of northern Nigeria. The first archaeological finds came from much disturbed deposits resulting from the tin mining on the Jos plateau and appeared to show neolithic tools in association with terracotta sculptures of high artistic quality. More recent research in undisturbed sites in the Taruga valley to the south of the plateau has shown conclusively that the 'Nok culture' was wholly an Iron Age phenemenon.

The sub-Saharan savanna, however, though it stretches from the Atlantic in the west to the Ethiopian highlands in the east, forms a belt seldom more than 600 miles wide which is transitional between the aridity of the desert to the north and the high humidity of the equatorial region to the south. Only in northern East Africa, where highland plateaux traverse the equatorial belt from north to south, is there a narrow corridor of open country connecting the northern savannas with those to the centre and south of the subcontinent. In this corridor archaeologists have so far identified with certainty only one set of Stone Age food producers, the originators of the Pastoral Neolithic cultures of the eastern Rift Valley. These people occupied parts of the Lake Turkana basin during the second millennium B.C. and had spread southwards into the Western Highlands by a millennium later. Probably they spoke Cushitic languages from the south-eastern branch of the Hamito-Semitic family. We do not know how far south into East Africa the Pastoral Neolithic people may have penetrated, but it seems likely that from central Tanzania southwards the main populations were still hunter-gatherers of Bush stock.

South of the Sudanic belt, however, and west of the East African plateau lay the equatorial forest with its fringes of humid woodland, where the problems of food production were entirely different. Here there was not enough sunlight for the Sudanic cereals, while trypanosomiasis and lack of fodder prevented the keeping of domestic animals. Here, therefore, the transition to food production depended on vegeculture rather than agriculture, on planting rather than sowing, on roots and fruits rather than grains, on clearing rather than hoeing, and on the combination of these activities with fishing rather than with hunting. In these circumstances the beginnings of food production, being almost indistinguishable from gathering, probably antedated in some sense the beginnings of agriculture and stock-raising in the north and east. However, progress towards a mainly food-producing way of life seems to have become noticeable only during the first millennium B.C., and even then to have been severely handicapped by the limited range of indigenous forest food crops. Several species of small yams were undoubtedly indigenous; also the oil-palm, the shea-butter tree, the kaffir potato and various kinds of beans and peas. But it is a remarkable fact that all the really important forest food plants of modern Africa orginated in other continents. The staple crops of the Guinea and Congo forests and their humid fringes are today maize and cassava, both of which came to Africa from South and Central America during the sixteenth and seventeenth centuries A.D. These late arrivals from the New World were preceded in the same areas by those of South-East Asia – the banana, the Asian yam (*Dioscorea*) and the Coco-yam (*Colocasia*). It is unlikely that these South-East Asian plants reached Africa much before the beginning of the Christian era. Thus, in West and West-Central Africa the coming of food production seems to have been a fairly precarious development until it was fortified, perhaps almost simultaneously, by the introduction of the South-East Asian food plants and by the coming of the Iron Age. In East-Central and Southern Africa, from southern Tanzania, Moçambique and Malawi to Zambia, Zimbabwe and South Africa, the food-producing revolution seems to have been, from beginning to end, an event of the Iron Age.

These conclusions about the spread of food production not only reconcile the existing views of archaeologists and botanists. They are also in some important respects consistent with the findings of comparative linguists about the relationships of different groups of African languages. These show that, apart from the Hamito-Semitic languages of the Afroasian peoples of the north and north-east, and the Khoisan languages of the Bush peoples in the east and south, there

were two main categories of languages spoken by the Blacks: those
formerly called Western Sudanic, but nowadays usually Niger-Congo;
and those formerly called Eastern Sudanic, which today may be called

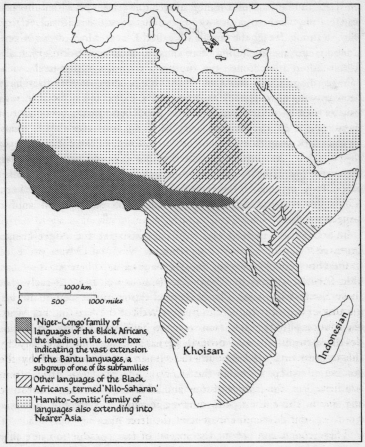

'Niger-Congo' family of
languages of the Black Africans,
the shading in the lower box
indicating the vast extension
of the Bantu languages, a
subgroup of one of its subfamilies

Other languages of the Black
Africans, termed 'Nilo-Saharan'

'Hamito-Semitic' family of
languages also extending into
'Nearer Asia'

Khoisan

Indonesian

2   Simplified distribution map of language families in present-day Africa

Note: The scheme is essentially that proposed by Professor J. H. Greenberg,
but there have been departures from his terminology so as to suit a historical
text. Greenberg adds a small group of languages in Kordofan (not shown
above) to 'Niger-Congo', and thus arrives at the term 'Congo-Kordofanian'
for this major family.

Nilo-Saharan. Most of the Niger-Congo languages are spoken in West Africa between the Senegal and Cameroon, although one Niger-Congo subgrouping has spread across the same latitudes as far east as the Uele, while part of another subgrouping has spread south-eastwards from Cameroon across the whole of sub-equatorial Africa: this part includes all the languages called Bantu. Most of the Niger-Congo languages, including often those spoken in adjacent areas, are widely differentiated one from another – so much so that in the view of many linguists it would be reasonable to suppose that they have been growing apart for at least 5,000 years, that is to say for at least as long as their speakers have been food producers. In sharp contrast to these ancient differences, however, the Bantu languages spoken today by the black peoples over most of Africa south of the equator are so closely related to each other that they are generally agreed to have been growing apart for a very much shorter period. This applies particularly strongly to the Bantu languages of eastern and southern Africa, for which a dispersal period of 2,000 years would appear quite possible.

The linguistic pattern certainly suggests that the Niger-Congo languages were originally concentrated in West Africa west of Cameroon from where they have expanded at the expense of the Nilo-Saharan languages to the east of them, as well as south-eastwards across the Bantu sphere. The likely implication would seem to be that the black peoples living in the western half of the Sudanic belt were more successful in the transition to food production in moist woodland conditions than those living in the eastern half, and so were able to press with expanding numbers into a wide zone to the south of the second group. Probably the basis of this population growth was established on the fringes of the Guinea forest by the domestication of the yam and the oil-palm during the third and second millennia B.C. With the development of near-neolithic clearing tools made of roughly ground and polished stone, it became possible to carry this means of livelihood deeper into the forest, especially by following river lines and ocean coasts, which offered a source of protein to the fisherman. It is thus possible to envisage an initial dispersal of Bantu-speaking populations from the region of Mount Cameroon both eastwards along the northern fringes of the Congo forest and southwards into the forest itself.

Since the second phase of the Bantu dispersion seems to have coincided closely in time with the coming of the Iron Age to Africa south of the Sahara, it is natural to ask how far the two events were connected. There are, for example, undoubted resemblances between the earliest Iron Age potteries of much of eastern and central Africa which would be consistent with the very sudden expansion of an early Iron Age population formerly concentrated within a much smaller area. It now looks more and more as though early Bantu-speaking populations must have been established both in the Congo forest and around its northern edges before the end of the Stone Age, and as though the knowledge of iron-working reached them in time to assist in their southern expansion from there. The distribution of the Bantu languages over Africa south of the equator is so complete that it must be assumed to be the result of population growth by a successful intrusive group rather than of conquest. The main significance of iron-working was probably, therefore, in the improvement of clearing tools, such as axes and hoes, although iron weapons were doubtless important in hunting and in war. On the whole, it would seem from the distribution of the earliest Iron Age sites as though the early iron-using farmers had preferred moist environments, making their settlements along river banks, lake shores and ocean coasts, and also in mountain valleys. Fishing certainly played a large part in many early Iron Age economies, and it was probably combined with the cultivation of sorghum millet, yams and various kinds of beans and peas. The earlier populations of late Stone Age hunter-gatherers, as also the late Stone Age hunter-pastoralists of the eastern Rift Valley, seem often to have been left in undisturbed possession of the drier savanna lands with their teeming herds of wild game. It was only piecemeal, as the hunters were attracted first to trade with and then to settle down alongside the iron-using cultivators, that linguistic and cultural absorption began to take place.

Some hundreds of radiocarbon dates are now available from early Iron Age sites in Africa south of the equator, and it is clear enough that the knowledge of iron-working spread over most of this vast area between the first and the fifth centuries A.D. It is only in the inter-lacustrine region, around the western shores of Lake Victoria and in the adjacent highlands of Rwanda and Burundi that significantly earlier Iron Age dates have been obtained. Some of these appear to go

back into the first half of the first millennium B.C., and so to antedate
the earliest known Iron Age occurrences in any other part of Africa.
If so, this could only mean that the whole complex process of mining,
smelting and working iron was independently invented in tropical
Africa. But this is not yet generally accepted as a safe assumption:
more dates from a wider area need to be assembled. At the very least,
however, the interlacustrine region must be seen as that from which
the knowledge of iron-working spread to the rest of the subcontinent,
following a period of several centuries during which an iron-using
and Bantu-speaking population had been building up its numbers in
this uniquely fertile and favourable environment.

Thus, by about the fifth century A.D. nearly the whole of Africa
had begun the transition to Iron Age farming, and by about the tenth
century the process was complete in the sense that most of the initially
surviving enclaves of hunter-gatherers and hunter-pastoralists had
been absorbed into the societies of their agricultural neighbours. One
large region, however, was still an exception. It stretched over the
south-western corner of the continent, from southern Angola across
Namibia and Botswana to the Cape Province of South Africa. Most
of this region was too dry to be attractive to Bantu cultivators. There
was within it one small area of good rainfall along the southern coast,
but here the rain fell at seasons different to the summer rainfall
pattern to which Bantu agriculture was adjusted. For these reasons
the south-western corner of Africa remained as the last surviving
homeland of hunter-gatherers and hunter-pastoralists, speaking the
old Khoisan languages, thin upon the ground and lacking iron
weapons. The existence of this power vacuum in the immediate hinterland of the Cape peninsula was to be very significant in later African
history.

3   The Townsmen

It was only in one small corner of Africa that food production led directly to urbanization. When the Tasians and Badarians moved down into the flood-plain of Middle Egypt, probably in the late fifth millennium, they quickly became the inhabitants of permanent villages such as those revealed by the excavations of Flinders Petrie at El Amrah and Naqada. The cemeteries there already reveal a revolutionary growth in population. Villages were fortified and the paintings on Amratian pots show captives with their hands tied behind their backs. They also show large papyrus boats, which were probably used for comparatively long-distance trading and raiding. It is certain that the Amratians imported gold and copper from the Red Sea hills, as well as obsidian, which perhaps came from as far away as the Ethiopian highlands. Jars and vases of carved alabaster and basalt make it likely that there were already full-time specialists and craftsmen. The dead were buried with a wealth of grave-goods, showing an acute preoccupation with the problem of the afterlife.

By the middle centuries of the fourth millennium, when the Amratian civilization was succeeded by the Gerzean, the larger villages were already growing into small towns, and rectangular houses with mud walls and strong wooden doors and window-frames began to resemble those of many a modern Middle Eastern town. The trade relations of Gerzean Egypt were very extensive. The Nile valley was probably in steady contact with the other rapidly developing centres of civilization in Mesopotamia. Metals like silver and lead were regularly imported from the Aegean islands. Shipwrights were building vessels for sixty oars. Gerzean cemeteries show that great differences in wealth had developed. A specialist stone-worker might now spend a whole year grinding out a single

vase in polished porphyry to adorn a rich man's house or to furnish
his tomb.

It is clear that in density of population, as in economic and artistic
achievement, pre-dynastic Egypt of the late fourth millennium had
already travelled further than almost any other part of Africa was to
travel during the next five millennia. In a sense, therefore, much of
the history of ancient Egypt is irrelevant to that of Africa as a whole.
What is least irrelevant, however, is the body of politico-religious
ideas which developed with startling suddenness at the beginning of
the dynastic period. Widely opposing views have been held about
where those ideas originated. It is significant that none of the excavations carried out at Gerzean sites has revealed anything that can be
regarded as ancestral to the dynastic royal tomb. On the other hand,
the latest chronological evidence places the earliest royal dynasties of
Mesopotamia in a period contemporaneous with the Fifth Dynasty of
Egypt: there are thus great difficulties in the theory of Asian orgin,
of which Flinders Petrie, for example, was an ardent exponent.

It seems on the whole most likely that the Egyptian idea of kingship
emerged in Egypt itself, and that it developed very rapidly following
the political unification of the country by the First Dynasty. This
would seem to be the clear lesson of the archaeological record. The
earliest dynastic tomb – that of Narmer at Abydos – was a brick-lined
shaft measuring twenty-six feet by sixteen by ten. Even so, it was a
striking development on the wealthiest Gerzean tomb, especially in
that the body of the Pharaoh was accompanied by those of human
victims killed and buried with their master in order that they might
continue to serve him in the next life. The First Dynasty tomb of the
Pharaoh Zer contains half as many burials as a whole public cemetery
of Amratian or Gerzean times. The Third Dynasty tomb of Zozer,
with 10,000 stone vases, was more elaborately furnished than any
pre-dynastic town cemetery. And with the Fourth Dynasty, the great
pyramid of Gizeh, built for the Pharaoh Khufer only about 500 years
after the reign of Narmer, was 481 feet high and consisted of some
2,300,000 stone blocks of an average weight of 2·5 tons, and cost,
according to the credible tale of Herodotus, the labour of a hundred
thousand people for twenty years.

It would accordingly seem to be the organizational triumph of the
early Pharaohs that was mainly responsible for the elaboration of

3 The Nile valley

divine kingship, Egypt's eventual legacy to so much of the rest of Africa. It has been estimated that Egyptian peasants of the third millennium B.C. may have been able to produce perhaps three times as much as their own domestic requirements. Under a harsh system of servile exploitation, the surplus could be turned to impressive account not only in public building but also in the support of large noble, priestly and official classes, the leaders of which developed an increasingly elaborate court life around the person of the living Pharaoh and around the tombs of his predecessors. Political unity was the final and vital stage in Egypt's amazingly rapid development from a jungle-filled, swampy valley to the scene of a complex and coherent society comprising several million people. It is surely at least possible to infer that politico-religious ideas and practices, which later became very widely distributed, had their origin and growth in this uniquely fertile soil. Later, much later, they would be exported, directly to Nubia, and, at tens and hundreds of removes, to more distant parts of Africa, where one petty dynasty after another would try, usually by borrowing from its neighbours, to apply some already greatly modified form of the Egyptian idea of the state. So it would come about that 4,000 years and more after the Old Kingdom had reached its peak, a Monomotapa ruling to the south of the Zambezi would marry his 'Queen Sister', or that on his accession an Omukama of Bunyoro in western Uganda would ceremonially 'shoot the nations' by firing arrows to the four points of the compass. At the time when these customs were evolved in Egypt, Uganda and Zimbabwe were still uncultivated by any tool more advanced than the primeval grubbing-stick, and human societies must have been far too small and dispersed to need any leadership more extensive than that of the family patriarch.

The relevance of ancient Egypt to Africa is thus something fundamentally different from its relevance to Europe. It is something which can only be studied in the light of the historical and archaeological evidence about Egypt's relations with the lands to the south. The earliest contacts were certainly those of trade. As we have seen the exploitation of Nubian gold from the hills between the Nile and the Red Sea was already in progress in predynastic times. From the beginning of the dynastic period at least, there was regular contact with the coasts of Eritrea, Somalia and southern Arabia, where grew the incense which was burnt in such prodigious quantities in the temples of Egypt. From the end of the third millennium occasional large expeditions went by sea; but the land routes through Nubia were certainly much older, and these, using the valleys of the Nile and the Atbara, already touched the land of the Blacks. Certainly by early dynastic times. Egypt had exhausted its own supplies of ivory and hardwoods and had to seek these and other raw materials from the black south. An inscription of about 2,275 B.C. tells how one Herkhuf, a servant of the Pharaoh Merenra, made four great expeditions to the south, from the last of which he returned with 300 asses, laden with incense, ebony, ivory, skins and boomerangs, and even with a pygmy to delight the heart of his master. Probably, therefore, he had ascended the Blue Nile into what is now southern Ethiopia; just possibly, he had followed the White Nile and the Bahr-al-Ghazal to the confines of the Congo forest. The boomerang, or throwing-stick, is still the characteristic weapon of the ancient black stocks living both east and west of the White Nile above Khartoum.

Trading expeditions such as those of Herkhuf doubtless had their effect upon the material culture of a wide region. Probably the Egyptians took with them both animals on the hoof and vegetable seeds to sow in the rainy season. Domestic animals may also have been used as items of exchange, and so have helped to accelerate the growth of food production to the south of the Sahara. Probably even at this stage an Egyptian musical instrument, or a piece of decorated basketry, would be bought and copied by those who came to exchange a tusk or a leopard-skin at the traders' camp. The deeper influence of Egyptian beliefs and social organization was, however, certainly confined to those parts of Nubia which became progressively the scene of something more like direct Egyptian colonization. At Buhen, near the Second Cataract in Lower Nubia, there existed by the mid-third millennium B.C. a fortified town where copper ore from the desert to the west of the Nile was brought for smelting and export down the river. Early in the second millennium there emerged the independent but highly Egyptianized kingdom of Kush, with its capital at Kerma, just above the Third Cataract. Kush was inhabited by people with a strong Black element, who spoke a language belonging to the Nilo-Saharan family. Kush was important to Egypt on account of its control of the southern trade-routes, which used the river and were especially liable to interception by raiders in the cataract regions, where boats had to be manhandled around the rapids. By the later second millennium B.C., Egyptian influence over Kush had been extended into direct imperial rule. The capital of Egypt itself was by this time at Thebes, the modern Luxor; and the Pharaohs of the Eighteenth, Nineteenth and Twentieth Dynasties, finding their traditional lines of expansion into Asia threatened by the growth of the Hittite empire, were turning their attention increasingly towards the south. Nubia, between the First and Third Cataracts, was fully occupied, and according to one calculation its mines were yielding 40,000 kilograms of gold a year, an amount which was never again reached in world production until the nineteenth century A.D. And to the south of the Third Cataract, along the Dongola reach of the river, there was now a whole series of Egyptian towns, each with its temple and priestly hierarchy, including an important offshoot of the Theban temple of Amon at Jebel Barkal near the Fourth Cataract. It was probably from the high-priestly family of Jebel Barkal that there sprang the dynasty of independent, albeit highly Egyptianized, kings that was to rule Kush, first from a capital at Napata and then from Meroe, for more than a thousand years – indeed, until the middle of the fourth century A.D.

Egypt by the beginning of the first millennium B.C. was in full decline. To the north the Assyrians were succeeding the Hittites as the chief Asian power. Lower Egypt was increasingly a prey to its Libyan mercenary troops, who established a series of short-lived dynasties in the Delta. In the far south excavations by Reisner and Dows Dunham at Napata have shown that the earliest royal cemetery there came into use early in the ninth century B.C. A century later these rulers of Kush had become strong enough to conquer Egypt, where five of their number are remembered as the Twenty-fifth Dynasty of Pharaohs. For a brief period Napata became the capital of the ancient world, and Sudanese kings intrigued with Tyre and Sidon, Israel and Judah in a vain attempt to stem the growing might of Assyria. In Egypt the end came swiftly. In 676 B.C., in the reign of the Pharaoh Taharqa, the Assyrians under Esarhaddon occupied Lower Egypt. In 666 under Ashurbannipal they pressed into Upper Egypt, and a few years later carried out the first terrible sack of Thebes. Taharqa retreated southwards into Kush, where the Egyptianized kingdom survived. While Egypt proper fell a prey successively to the Assyrians, the Persians, the Greeks and the Romans, its former dependency, Kush, retained practically undiluted a sturdy remnant of Egyptian civilization. According to the traditional viewpoint of western historians, it was ancient Egypt running downhill to an inglorious and too long protracted conclusion. According to the very different perspectives of African history, it was ancient Egypt moving nearer to black Africa, at a period when at least part of black Africa was more capable than it had ever been before of experiencing the influence of an urban civilization.

Throughout its long period as an Egyptian colony, and also during the first two or three centuries of its independent existence, Kush was an essentially riverine state, populated by farmers and fishermen who seldom penetrated beyond the narrow confines of the river valley. Around the sixth century B.C., however, Kush began to extend its frontiers southwards beyond the desert, into what was then the well-wooded country at the northern margin of the summer rains. The capital was moved south from Napata to Meroe, a little above the confluence of the Nile and the Atbara. The triangle between the two rivers, known today as the Butana, once cleared of its tree-cover, made ideal pastureland, so that in its new setting the state commanded a much wider basis of food production, and also, for so long as the woodland lasted, a source of fuel for the iron industry which grew up in Kush at this time. The Kushites had, it would seem, learned the techniques of iron-working from their Assyrian enemies, whose iron weapons had driven them out of Egypt. While Egypt had neither iron ore nor fuel with which to smelt it, and while northern Kush had ore but still no fuel, the southern region of Kush had both commodities in abundance. Equipped with the iron spear and the iron hoe, Meroe was able not merely to provide for its own subsistence, but to trade and conquer far and wide in the Sudanic belt of Africa.

From the archaeological evidence unearthed by Garstang and Dows Dunham, it appears that the great period of Meroe stretched from the middle of the third century B.C. until just into the Christian era. It corresponded more or less with the rule of the Ptolemies in Egypt, and was probably connected with the revival of trade which came when Persian influence was superseded by that of Hellenistic Alexandria. Probably Meroe grew rich by exporting to the outside world the traditional African products – ivory, slaves, rare skins, ostrich feathers, ebony and possibly gold – drawn from a wide region of inner Africa which may have extended from the Ethiopian highlands on one side to the Niger on the other. At all events, this period was the most prolific in monumental building. It saw a revival of Egyptian sculpture and a return to funerary inscriptions in Egyptian hiero-glyphs. It saw also the invention of the cursive Meroitic script, which has not yet been properly deciphered. The iron industry was now very fully established: one of the most important temples of the period stands upon the top of a hill of slag. Not only Mediterranean but also Eastern influences were present. Fragments of cotton cloth appear in the tombs. Tanks and reservoirs point to influence from at least as far away as south Arabia. The sculptured relief of a king of Kush seated on an elephant suggests the presence at Meroe of at least one Indian artist. The basic inspiration of Meroitic civilization remained, nevertheless, that of ancient Egypt. The gods worshipped in the temples of Meroe were the Egyptian gods. Its kings continued to call themselves the kings of Upper and Lower Egypt, and to lead the dedicated high-priestly lives of Egyptian Pharaohs, marrying their Queen Sisters, honouring their Queen Mothers, leading their people in the ceremonies of seedtime and harvest, honoured as gods by their subjects and expected to behave with the capricious absolutism thought to be characteristic of divinity.

It is clear that by the middle of the first century A.D. the material basis of the Meroitic civilization was in decline. Of the score or so of kings who had still to reign before the extinction of the kingdom, only ten had architects literate enough to transmit the royal names to posterity, while the last six sovereigns lacked even the masons to encase their little brick pyramids with a thin façade of stone. The reason for Meroe's poverty was almost certainly the rise of a rival trading empire, with its centre at Axum in the northern corner of the Ethiopian highlands. The origins of the kingdom of Axum are still unclear. Probably, it was just the most successful of a series of city states which had grown up among the Semitic-speaking population of the northern part of the Ethiopian plateau since about the fourth century B.C. It was first mentioned in an Alexandrian sailors' guide, *The Periplus of the Erythrean Sea*, written about the early second century. By then it had become the greatest ivory market of North-

East Africa. Its capital was growing into a city of splendid stone monuments – including palaces, temples and carved stone obelisks. Its king traded with the Greeks of Alexandria, spoke their language and ate from gold and silver plate. Armed with imported iron weapons, his hunters and caravaneers were already penetrating beyond the Nile in the latitude of Khartoum. During the second and third centuries the power of Axum rose steadily. In the middle of the fourth century its rulers became Christians, and at just about the same time its armies made their last and decisive invasion of Kush, burning the town of Meroe and causing the final break-up of the kingdom. Already before the Axumite invasion, however, the kingdom of Kush, deprived of the prosperity built on its external trade, had fallen prey to the Nuba, a population of Nilo-Saharan-speaking nomads from the hilly country to the west of the middle Nile which still bears their name. The Nuba had come in several waves, from which there were eventually to emerge three kingdoms, successor states to that of Meroe, which were converted to Christianity in the sixth and seventh centuries. It was upon the chaotic beginnings of the Nuba conquest that the Axumite blow fell, and it is likely that its purpose was mainly pre-emptive, to warn off the Nuba from attempting any conquests further to the east. In this it was successful. The Nuba kept to the Nile valley, and Christianity eventually came to them from Egypt. Axum, meanwhile, had engrossed the trade of the whole western coast of the Red Sea as far as the Egyptian frontier. It was to be the dominant power in north-eastern Africa until about the ninth century.

It remains to ask what may have been the influence of the kingdom of Kush upon the neighbouring regions of Africa during the thousand years of its rule over the northern and central Sudan. Here, after all, in a part of Africa extending well to the south of the Sahara and inhabited very largely by black people, a great and powerful kingdom carried on the traditions of the Pharaohs into a period when there was at last beginning to be a population of agriculturalists and stock-raisers spread out across the sub-Saharan savanna, to which the state-craft inherited from Egypt by Meroe was no longer quite irrelevant. It was formerly proposed by the pioneer archaeologist and historian of the Sudan, A. J. Arkell, that, following the defeat by Axum, the royal family of Meroe had retreated to the west, to Kordofan and Darfur, where Meroitic styles of pottery and brick buildings were said to exist in sites yet to be excavated, and where even the royal property marks survived in the camel brands used by the pastoral nomads of that region. Darfur remains unexcavated. Meanwhile, however, the progress of knowledge would no longer seem to demand any such concrete transfer of complete systems from one region to another. It is enough that Meroe, especially following its expansion into the great plain of the Butana, had become a state that included large and prosperous communities of pastoral nomads, with a mobility much greater than that of the cultivators of the Nile valley. Through such communities political ideas could flow freely, adapting themselves to a variety of situations and circumstances. An idea or an institution found useful by the banks of the Nile could be transmitted through a myriad permutations to the banks of the Niger and the Senegal, or even southwards into Bantu Africa.

4 The Sudanic Civilization

Stretching right across sub-Saharan Africa from the Red Sea to the mouth of the Senegal, and right down the central highland spine of Bantu Africa from the Nile sources to Zimbabwe we find the axis of what we shall call the Sudanic[1] civilization. The central feature of this civilization was the incorporation of the various African peoples concerned into states whose institutions were so similar that they must have derived from a common source. At the head of such states there were kings, to whom divine honours were paid and to whom divine powers were attributed. Typically, the king led a life sedulously secluded from the common people: he gave public audience from behind a curtain; not even the most intimate of his courtiers might see him eat or drink. Each year the king hoed the first plot of farming land and sowed the first seeds. Upon his physical well-being depended the fertility of the land and the regular flow of rain. The divine king could not die a natural death. Whether in serious illness or in extreme old age, his end had to be hastened by poison or by ritual suffocation. After death the royal corpse was embalmed; funeral ceremonies often involved the sacrifice of human victims; relics, such as hair and fingernails, were preserved as part of the cult of the royal tomb. The great rituals of these divine kingdoms tended to be associated with the new moon, and sacred fire was almost everywhere kept burning and carefully guarded as the main symbol of the king's life and authority.

The subjects of a divine king might number anything from a few thousand to a million or more. Most kingdoms, however, were small,

[1] The German ethnographer H. Baumann termed it the '*neo*-Sudanese' civilization, in order to distinguish it from the older civilization of the first black farmers, which he termed the 'palaeo-negritic' civilization.

and it is a fair assumption that the few larger ones had become so through a long process of successful conquest and absorption of weaker neighbours. Kingdoms tended in fact to form in clusters, with one or more larger units towards the centre of the cluster and a host of smaller ones scattered around the periphery. Even the smaller kingdoms, however, contrasted sharply with the loose family or lineage institutions of those societies which had never been organized in this way. The 'Sudanic' state was not feudal. It was not based on the hereditary position and power of great families. It was in origin a kind of theocracy organized under a priest-king and his ritual assistants. And, as it grew and evolved, the successful 'Sudanic' state tended to become something nearer to a bureaucracy – a bureaucracy without paper, ink, desks or telephones – in which power was wielded by officials who held their offices during the king's pleasure and who could be transferred from post to post, promoted, demoted and even destituted by a nod of the divine head or a syllable from the divine mouth. Around the royal person circled a galaxy of titled office-bearers, as numerous as the economic organization of each particular state was able to support. The pre-eminent offices were nearly always those of the Queen Mother, the Queen Sister and of a limited number of titled 'great wives' of the ruler. At the head of the administration were a few high officials, often four in number. From these depended a descending hierarchy of provincial and district chiefs, often re-cruited from the pages, sons or nephews of the great, who had been educated at the royal court. The main concern of such administrations was the raising of tribute for the support of the king and of the semi-urbanized inhabitants of his capital – on the one hand, articles of consumption such as wives and labour, beer and foodstuffs; on the other, the materials of long-distance trade, such as ivory, skins, gold, copper, salt and kola-nuts. External trade was always in some sense a royal monopoly. Artists, craftsmen and other specialists were located at the royal capital and were an important attribute of the royal power; there was, indeed, a tendency for the rulers of such states to be themselves identified at least with the mysterious craft of the smith.

In many ways, the 'Sudanic' state looked like a superstructure erected over lineage groups rather than a society which had grown up naturally out of them. Working from his ethnographic data, Baumann, for one, had no hesitation in saying that these parts of Africa had been overrun by later comers of a higher culture than the original societies of peasant cultivators. It must be said at once, however, that the ethnographic method of comparing the political institutions of a large number of states founded at widely varying periods, on the basis of descriptive information of variable quality obtained for the most part at a late date in the history of the states concerned, is one that must be used with great caution. Such a method can only provide the first diagnosis of a problem to which history has to find an answer, so far as it can. The historian cannot be content to postulate vague notions about 'waves of conquest'. The problem must be approached through the known history of the states concerned and chronological evidence must be sought wherever it is available. Judged by this test, most of the 'Sudanic' states which had achieved large dimensions and elaborate political structures at the time when they were first described by literate observers can now be shown to have grown from comparatively insignificant nuclei within the previous few centuries. Nevertheless, there would seem to be evidence that in at least three regions widely distant from each other, 'Sudanic' states had reached a fairly developed stage by the end of the first millennium A.D. The kingdom of Ghana, with its centre some 500 miles to the north-west of its modern namesake's nearest boundary, was first mentioned in writing by an Arab author of the ninth century, al-Fazari. Two centuries later, when Ghana was well known to the Muslim world by its export of gold to North Africa, the Moorish geographer al-Bakri of Cordoba described what was still a sturdily pagan kingship ritual:

The audience is announced by the beating of a drum which they call *dubā*, made from a long hollow log. When the people . . . approach [the king], they fall on their knees and sprinkle their heads with dust, for this is their way of showing respect . . . The religion of the people of Ghana is paganism and the worship of idols. When their king dies, they build over the place where his tomb will be an enormous dome of *saj* wood. Then they bring him on a bed covered with a few carpets and put him beside the dome. At his side they place his ornaments, his weapons and the vessels from which he used to eat and drink, filled with various kinds of food and beverages. They also place there the men who had served his meals. They close the door of the dome and cover it with mats and furnishings, and then they assemble the people, who heap earth upon it until it becomes like a large mound. Then they dig a

ditch around the mound so that it can be reached only at one place. They
• sacrifice victims for their dead and make offerings of intoxicating drinks.

The kingdom of Kanem, lying to the north-east of Lake Chad, was
mentioned, together with its Zaghawa rulers, by al-Yaqubi, writing in
the ninth century, while the tenth-century writer, al-Muhallabi, made
it quite clear that this was a divine kingdom of the 'Sudanic' type:

> The kingdom of the Zaghawa is a great kingdom among the kingdoms of
> the Sudan. It borders in the east on the kingdom of the Nuba, who dwell in
> the upermost part of Upper Egypt, there being between them a distance of
> ten days' travelling. They are many nations. Their country is fifteen stages in
> length by the same in width, in continuously inhabited lands. Their houses are
> all reed huts as is also the palace of their king, whom they exalt and worship
> instead of Allah. They imagine that he does not eat any food. There are
> persons who have charge of this food secretly and bring it to his house. It is
> not known where it is brought from and if it happens that one of his subjects
> meets the camels carrying his provisions, he is killed instantly on the spot. . .
> He has unlimited authority over his subjects and he enslaves from among
> them anyone he wants. His wealth consists of livestock such as sheep, cattle,
> camels and horses. The greater part of the crops of their country is sorghum
> (*dhura*) and cowpeas (*lūbiyā'*) and then wheat (*qamh*). Most of his subjects go
> naked, wrapped [only] in skins. Their means of subsistence is crops and the
> ownership of livestock. Their religion is the worship of their kings, for they
> believe that they bring life and death, sickness and health.

And finally the great traveller and geographical writer al-Masudi
of Baghdad, who himself journeyed by sea from the Persian Gulf
down the east coast of Africa to Sofala in modern Moçambique in or
about A.D. 922, clearly recorded the existence of a substantial trade in
gold and ivory, which was shipped from Sofala to Oman and thence
to China and India, and which originated in a large African state in
the hinterland of modern Moçambique. The king of this state bore
sublime titles such as 'son of the great master, the god of the earth
and the sky', and was the foremost of all the African rulers known to
the Arabs who frequented the east coast. It is highly probable that
Masudi was referring to the state whose rulers were later responsible
for the earliest stages of stone building at Great Zimbabwe, currently
attributed by archaeologists, on the basis of carbon-dating, to approxi-
mately the eleventh century. It is very clear, from Portuguese descriptions of the societies they found in this region five centuries

later, that although political fragmentation had set in, political structure was uniform and showed most of the typical features of 'Sudanic' divine kingship.

The geographical spread of the 'Sudanic' states, for which we happen to have documentary evidence stretching back into the first millennium A.D., makes it highly improbable that they were the only states of their kind to exist even at this early period. Archaeological evidence, valuable as it is in relation to material culture, does not often tell us much about ideology or institutions. Nevertheless, where institutions are clearly associated with, for example, a characteristic pattern of urban settlement, as in the Hausa-speaking region of northern Nigeria or the Yoruba-speaking region of south-western Nigeria, it is perhaps permissible to infer the existence of the institution from the carapace in which it was housed. In both these cases archaeology provides us with some dates in the first millennium A.D., and there are many other similar examples. It may be that the existence of small town sites along the western arm of the Niger bend, with dates going back as far as the third century B.C., can be taken as an indication of the possible antiquity of the 'Sudanic' state in the Sahelian zone of West Africa. In Bantu Africa there is no widespread tradition of town building. Only in Zimbabwe and the Transvaal has the availability of surface stone in convenient sizes led to the development of a kind of prestige architecture which may reasonably be connected with the earlier stages of 'Sudanic' kingship known otherwise mainly from much later reports. The origins of this prestige building may be placed around the tenth century A.D., and it is a fair speculation that by about the same period small states of the 'Sudanic' type would have been emerging in the better-populated parts of eastern and central Africa, the rulers of which would have inhabited capitals made of less permanent materials. In the interlacustrine region to the west of Lake Victoria, the emergence of a pattern of small states seems to have come about as the result of interaction between Bantu cultivators practising an early Iron Age culture and mixed farmers of Nilotic origin who had introduced a superior iron-working technology. The best chronological evidence for this transition comes from Rwanda and Burundi, where it can be dated to about the eighth century A.D.

The essential conclusions that emerge from this brief survey would thus seem to be, first, that the formation of states, in sub-Saharan and in Bantu Africa alike, was a process which involved the deployment of a considerable fund of common political ideas; secondly, that the earliest lines of deployment seem to have been interior lines, running out in two long arms westwards and southwards from a common point of origin in the upper Nile valley; thirdly, that this fund of common ideas was pre-Muslim and pre-Christian, in the sense that the basic ideas of the system ran sharply counter to the tenets of both these religions, and therefore that if the Nile valley was the point of departure, they must have started to disperse outwards from that region before either Christianity or Islam became firmly established there. Islam did not seriously begin to penetrate the Nilotic Sudan until the eleventh century. Christianity, however, spread from Egypt to Nubia in the late sixth century, and by the seventh was strongly enough established there to resist the southward spread of Islam for more than four centuries. In our search for the sources of the 'Sudanic' civilization, we are therefore driven back to the history of the Sudan during the first six centuries A.D. At the beginning of that period the Meroitic state was still at the height of its power, and there can be little doubt that the ideas of ancient Egypt, percolating through the Meroitic filter, formed the basic element in the 'Sudanic' civilization. This, however, is certainly not the whole story. With the third and fourth centuries came the economic and political dominance of pagan Axum, which may account for further elements; but by the end of the fourth century Axum was beginning to be a Christian state, possessing strong political as well as religious links with Byzantine Egypt, and increasingly directing its expansive energies across the Straits of Bab-el-Mandeb into southern Arabia. It is in this direction that we must seek the third main series of elements in the 'Sudanic' civilization.

It cannot be entirely without significance that over large stretches of the central and western Sudan traditions ascribe the foundation of early dynasties to pre-Islamic immigrants from the Yemen. It is true that such traditions always come from areas where the 'Sudanic' civilization has been overlaid by Islamic influences, and that the form in which they are preserved clearly shows the influence of Arabian Muslim traditions about the pre-Islamic period. There can, in fact, be no doubt that these traditions as we know them today represent hypothetical explanations suggested by early Muslim *literati* for the situation which they found in the Sudan. Nevertheless, there are strong reasons for thinking that for several centuries before the great overspill of newly Islamized Arabs into Africa in the early seventh century, South-West Asia in general and Arabia in particular had been emptying its surplus populations across the Red Sea and the isthmus of Suez. The advent of the camel into Africa – which can be clearly traced in classical sources for the frontiers of Roman and Byzantine North Africa during the first five centuries of the Christian era – was almost certainly accompanied by human migrations, augmenting and culturally modifying the nomadic populations of the Libyan and Saharan deserts. Again, the period of Axumite conquest in the Yemen during the sixth century is associated in early Muslim traditions with a time of special famine and hardship, symbolized by the bursting of the great dam of Mahrib some time in the third quarter of the sixth century which is said to have caused a great emigration of sedentary Yemenite cultivators across the Red Sea into the Sudan. Next, it must be remembered that the Yemenites finally rid themselves of the Axumite occupation by calling in the help of Sassanian Persia, and that the Sassanid rulers Chosroes I and II responded to the appeal not only by occupying Arabia but also by conquering Egypt from the Byzantines. In Egypt their rule was confined to a brief ten years, but it may well be a fact of decisive significance for the 'Sudanic' civilization that the rich 'X group' culture, which succeeded the Meroitic in northern Nubia and which, for example, contains the first iron bits and bridles found in any Sudanese sites, also shows definite traces of Sassanian influence.

Thus, while it is not possible to give any definite or precise account of the origins of the 'Sudanic' civilization, there is nevertheless enough circumstantial evidence of the various influences at work in the Meroitic and immediately post-Meroitic Sudan to account for most of the elements involved. There were mud-built towns inhabited by divine kings, their nobles and priests, merchants and craftsmen. There were riverside farmers producing fish, grain and vegetable foods. There were herders pasturing cattle and camels, sheep and goats. There was an iron industry producing tools for farmers and weapons for hunters and soldiers. There were horses and horsemen, slave-raiding and slaves. Where a modern interpretation would differ most strongly from one of fifty years ago would be in the ways envisaged for this civilization to spread. To scholars living in the first half of the twentieth century it seemed obvious that civilizations were transmitted by conquest. Today, taking into account all that we have learned of more recent African history, theories of widespread conquest appear anachronistic for the first millennium A.D. Infiltration looks much nearer the mark, and particularly the infiltration of riverside or lakeside farmers by pastoralists seeking to exploit the drier savanna country between the river lines. In these circumstances pastoralists and agriculturalists needed to accommodate one another. They needed a political authority which encompassed them both. The institutions by which this was achieved were probably more often borrowed than imposed. The scale of the earliest accommodations might be small indeed. An early 'Sudanic' state might include no more than a riverside settlement of a few hundred people who lived by fishing and cultivation of the seasonally deposited alluvium, and the nearby herders nomadizing towards the river valley in the dry season and spreading out over the surrounding countryside after the rains. The products of both communities needed to be exchanged, and the rights to land, water and manure needed to be regulated. When, later, a successful state began to expand into the territory of its neighbours, a more complex, more hierarchical political model might need to be borrowed from a little further away.

Despite all the uncertainties, and they are many, one conclusion at least about the spread of the 'Sudanic' civilization would seem to be irresistible. If we chart the regions of Africa where no 'Sudanic' states ever existed, and if we add to them the regions where the known history of 'Sudanic' states is shortest, there can be no reasonable doubt that it was in the central regions of the continent, and not on any of the peripheries, that the basic ideas of the 'Sudanic' state were forged. It is this fact that gives the history of Africa a certain unity, which it would have lacked if all the main motive forces had reached it from the outside.

5 Mediterranean Civilization and its links with West Africa

In the two previous chapters some account has been given of the possible influence of ancient Egypt on black Africa, more particularly of its undoubted influence on the kingdom of Kush in the Nilotic Sudan. The external influence of Egypt was, however, by no means limited to the Nile valley. Egypt had regular contacts through maritime trade with the lands to the north, notably with Syria, Cyprus and Crete, and thus Egyptian influence contributed powerfully to the rise of civilization in the Mediterranean. This is a story beyond the scope of this book, but African history cannot neglect the fact that for nearly 1,500 years, from the foundation of the first Phoenician colonies in North Africa in about the eighth century B.C. until the Arab conquest of the seventh century A.D., nearly all the Africans living to the north of the Sahara belonged in some sense to this Mediterranean civilization. These peoples, of course, were not black. They were the fair-skinned Afroasians whom the ancient Greeks called Libyans, and whom they distinguished from the 'Ethiopians', the men with 'burnt faces', as they called the Blacks. The Libyans spoke languages of the Hamito-Semitic family and their purest descendants today are some of the more isolated Berber groups in the mountain regions of North Africa. Nevertheless, that the Libyan Berbers lived so long within the fringes of the Mediterranean world was not without its significance for the black peoples south of the Sahara.

It was the westward expansion of Phoenician merchants from the seaports of Syria, prosperous from their domination of the trade in the eastern Mediterranean basin, which first brought the young Mediterranean civilization to North Africa. At first the Phoenicians were probably more interested in the rare metals of the Iberian peninsula

4 North Africa and the Sahara in ancient times

than in African trade. But because they preferred to sail only by day and within sight of land, they were led to establish staging-posts at short intervals along the North African coast. Of these Carthage became by far the most important. This was partly a consequence of its position, which enabled it at once to command the gateway to the western Mediterranean, through the Sicilian narrows, and to dominate the Tunisian plains, the largest area of cultivable land in North Africa outside of Egypt. When the mother cities in Syria finally lost their independence during the sixth century B.C., and when from the seventh century onwards the coast of Cyrenaica was planted with Greek colonies, Carthage became the metropolis of a series of towns stretching along the North African shore from the Gulf of Sirte to the Atlantic coast of Morocco.

Many of the original Phoenician settlements did not far outgrow their first status of maritime staging-posts, and the number of original Phoenician colonists in Africa was probably not great. Nevertheless, Carthage and her satellites came to exert a considerable influence on the life of the native Berbers. Two categories of Carthaginian in- fluence may be distinguished: a general influence throughout those parts of North-West Africa which were accessible from the coast, and a specific influence on the Tunisian plains. Since the Phoenicians were quick to develop any opportunities of trade which came their way, and since their mercantile skill was backed by advanced agri- cultural techniques, even the smallest coastal settlement tended to become a local metropolis where Berber tribesmen could gain some knowledge of a more ordered and settled mode of living. Where there was a sizeable area of arable land available, or where the opportunities for trade were more than merely local, even more influential cities developed. The growth of Carthage herself was phenomenal. This was largely a consequence of her imperial responsibilities, which were greatly heightened by the needs of her wars with Rome, first for the mastery of Sicily and then for sheer self-preservation. Her population at its peak may have reached half a million. Such a city could only be provisioned and defended by the extension of direct rule over its hinterland; thus the fertile northern half of the Tunisian plain became a Carthaginian estate, while its tribesmen were converted into agri- cultural labourers.

Thus while throughout North-West Africa the Phoenician language, Punic, became the *lingua franca* of trade, administration and civilized life, and while there was a general encouragement of agriculture and peaceful development, in and around northern Tunisia these processes were greatly accentuated. Here, and to some extent in other coastal regions as well, an influential class of Punicized Berbers had emerged. Two particular aspects of this Punicizing process merit especial notice. By the end of the Carthaginian period, independent Berber chieftains in the Numidian mountains adjacent to the Tunisian plain had begun to organize their semi-nomadic tribesmen into settled agricultural kingdoms. Secondly, since from the earliest times people whom we should now call Jews had been involved in Phoenician colonization, some elements of Judaic religious beliefs had been assimilated even by tribal Berbers, and especially, it would seem, by the tribes of southern Tunisia and adjacent Tripolitania.

In Sicily and elsewhere in the northern half of the Mediterranean, Greek colonies were soon competing with the Phoenicians, but the Carthaginians successfully kept them out of North Africa west of the Gulf of Sirte. It was therefore only in Cyrenaica and Egypt that Greek civilization was able to secure a footing in North Africa. Egypt, indeed, became the major channel for Greek influence on Africa, especially after its conquest by Alexander the Great in 332 B.C. Alexander died ten years later, and the world empire he had established was shattered. But his dream of fusing the civilizations of the east and the west survived in the intellectual life of the city he had founded by the Canopus mouth of the Nile, Alexandria. Under the dynasty established by one of his generals, Ptolemy, Alexandria became the greatest of all Greek cities. The Ptolemies became wealthy, like the Pharaohs whose place they had taken, by taxing the unique agricultural wealth of the Nile valley. They grew richer still by developing and then taxing the trade in luxuries between Asia and Europe. But above all, in Alexandria the Greek civilization, its culture, philosophy and science, was penetrated and stimulated by the eastern cultures. Not the least of these was the Semitic. While Egypt became progressively Hellenized, its capital, Alexandria, with almost as many Jews as Greeks among its 300,000 citizens, became a forcing-bed for religious and philosophical debate, a role which it was to retain for the rest of the Hellenistic period and also through the vital first three centuries of the Christian era.

When, in the middle of the second century B.C., the citizens of the upstart Roman republic finally humbled mighty Carthage, they had little thought of establishing an empire in Africa. They tore down the city of Carthage and ploughed its very foundations into the earth. But they appreciated the value of the Tunisian plains as a granary for the growing population of their own metropolis; and they found that to make their hold on them effective they had also to control the neighbouring territories. The Numidian kingdoms were soon conquered, and the Romans also quickly occupied the whole of the coastal strip westwards to the Atlantic plains of Morocco. But there remained the difficult problem of the semi-nomadic tribes, always seeking to encroach upon the area of agricultural and civilized life. Ultimately, the only solution lay in the extension of direct Roman rule over the tribes as far as the edge of the Saharan steppes. Thus when during the first century B.C. both Cyrenaica and Egypt also came directly under Roman control, the Romans possessed an African empire reaching from east to west for nearly 3,000 miles and encompassing all the cultivable land north of the Sahara.

This Roman empire in Africa had no meaning or unity of its own. It was essentially no more than the southern limit of the Mediterranean world which the Romans had mastered. Within it, however, there were two areas of particular interest to the Romans: the provinces of 'Africa' (equivalent to modern Tunisia and the adjacent coastlands of Tripolitania) and Numidia (roughly the eastern half of modern Algeria); and Egypt. In 'Africa' and Numidia, the work begun by Carthage of converting the Berbers to a settled agricultural way of life was greatly extended. Nearly fifty of the seventy or more Roman towns whose sites are known in North-West Africa were in this region, and the bulk of their inhabitants were not colonists but Romanized Berbers. In Egypt, the effects of Roman rule seem to have been less beneficial. Though more efficient than the later Ptolemies, the Romans adapted themselves far less to the Egyptian scene. They remained foreigners in Egypt, and by ruthlessly exploiting the country in the interests of Rome and her proconsuls, they ended by exhausting an agriculture which initially they had done much to revive.

The greatest contribution of the Roman empire to Africa was a largely incidental one: by bringing northern Africa so positively within the sphere of Mediterranean civilization, it greatly facilitated the spread of Christianity. The two great centres of the new religion were Alexandria and Carthage, and in both places, as throughout the Mediterranean world, the Jewish communities provided most of the early converts. Alexandria, traditionally the see of St Mark, was the native city of both Arius and Athanasius, whose doctrinal disagreements resulted early in the fourth century in the formulation of the Nicene Creed, still used by all the major branches of the Christian Church. The greatest of all the early Christian fathers, St Augustine, was a Libyan Berber brought up and educated at Carthage. When, however, in the fourth, fifth and sixth centuries of its existence, Christianity became increasingly the state religion of the Roman empire, opposition to Roman rule both in Egypt and in the provinces of 'Africa' and Numidia, sought expression in doctrinal or sectarian divergences. In North-West Africa in the fourth century, Donatism was less a heresy than a movement marking the resistance of many tribal Berbers, especially in Numidia, to the encroaching pressures of Roman rule. In Egypt, after the Council of Chalcedon in 451, the native Egyptians attached themselves wholeheartedly to the condemned Monophysite view of the nature of Christ, and developed a deep loyalty to their own 'Coptic' church in opposition to the orthodox 'Melkite' church supported by the Byzantine officials. In the sixth century, both churches sent missions to the Nubian kingdoms which had developed out of the heritage of ancient Meroe in the Nilotic Sudan. The Monophysites were the more successful, converting the kings and courts of Nubia in the north and Alwa in the south, while the Melkites seem to have succeeded only in the middle kingdom, Makurra (which at some later date seems to have been merged with Nubia in a single state ruled from Dongola). Ethiopia, having been converted by Egyptian and Syrian missionaries, also followed the Monophysite path.

By the fourth and fifth centuries, in Africa as in Europe, Roman power was already shrinking. In Africa the process was hastened by the introduction of the camel from Asia during the early centuries of the Christian era. In the hinterland of Tunisia and Tripolitania, there emerged an ominous new grouping of the nomadic Berbers of the Saharan steppes. These were the Zanata, and it is possible that they gained some of their new political coherence from the assimilation of some traits of Judaism. It is certain that they quickly appreciated the opportunities offered by the camel for the development of a predatory life based on the dry fringes of the desert, from which they were able to raid the settled communities of the Roman provinces. As a result, the area under ordered administration decreased, and the whole trend of the preceding Carthaginian and Roman periods was reversed. Nomadic pastoralism began to expand at the expense of sedentary agricultural civilization. This incipient disintegration was hastened by the invasion of North Africa from Spain by the Vandals in the fifth century and its subsequent reconquest by the Byzantines in the sixth. The Vandals, a Germanic tribe who were Arian Christians, were at first welcomed by the Donatist Berbers as deliverers from Roman oppression. But their coming initiated a period of religious persecution and civil anarchy which continued into the Byzantine period, to the advantage of none but the camel nomads.

The decay of the old Roman empire marks the beginning of the end for the 'Mediterranean period' of North African history, and this is the point at which to consider briefly how significant it was for Africa south of the Sahara. It must first be emphasized that neither Carthaginian nor Roman rule ever reached across the desert. The Carthaginian empire was not territorial but commercial and maritime. The enigmatic account which has survived of the voyage of Hanno in the fifth century B.C. suggests that the Carthaginians at least prospected the possibilities of trade southwards down the Atlantic coast of Africa. Interpretations of the extent of Hanno's voyage vary widely; but it is clear that in general the Carthaginian galleys were unsuitable for Atlantic navigation, and this, combined with the long barren coastline of the Sahara, prevented the extension of their regular pattern of trade and settlement anywhere south of Morocco. The Romans, if only because of their need to defend their territorial empire against the nomads, were concerned with the northern parts of the Sahara. But the evidence is that the oasis of Djerma (the ancient Garama) in the southern Fezzan marks the extreme limit of their direct occupation.

There can be no doubt, however, that indirectly the two worlds of the Mediterranean and the western Sudan were in touch throughout ancient times. The size and evident prosperity of the Roman city of Leptis Magna, close to the modern Tripoli, can best be explained by supposing that it lay at the head of a major trans-Saharan trade-route running southwards through the Fezzan. It has similarly been suggested that the Carthaginian settlement of Lixus, on the Atlantic coast of Morocco, was the terminus of a trade-route across the Mauritanian desert. Herodotus, writing in the fifth century B.C., reported that the Garamantes, the Libyan Berber pastoralists of the Fezzan, were in the habit of raiding the 'Ethiopians', that is to say, the Blacks, in four-horse chariots. His report is amply proved by the discovery in recent years of numerous rock-drawings of horse-drawn vehicles, aligned essentially in two bands running across the desert towards the great bend of the Niger, one from the Fezzan and the other from southern Morocco. These bands correspond to two of the major caravan routes of later times, when wheeled vehicles had been superseded in the Sahara by riding and pack animals, the camel especially. Chariots would have been used for raiding, not trading, but the one can easily lead to the other. Moreover, the distribution of the drawings does tend to confirm that the contact they represent led to the emergence of major trans-Saharan trade routes focusing on Leptis Magna and Lixus.

The agents of this contact were undoubtedly the Berber pastoralists of the desert. The Berber contact with black Africans was a very old one, which long antedated the Mediterranean civilization. It had probably been continuous since the wet phase of the seventh to the fourth millennia B.C., when much of the Sahara was grassland, and the hunting-grounds of Afroasiatic and black peoples overlapped. During the subsequent desiccation the Saharan Blacks tended to withdraw southwards, but this was also the period when some Afroasiatic pastoralists likewise moved southwards with their herds, so that today the black peoples in large parts of modern Niger and northern Nigeria speak the Berber-related Chadic languages. Eastwards, in the Tibesti mountains and the highlands of Ennedi, Black populations seem to have made a successful transition to food production within desert latitudes, with the result that Nilo-Saharan languages remained dominant in this region. In all these circumstances, trade contacts of some kind were probably maintained throughout the dry period. As in historic times, the main exports of the western Sudan would have been gold and slaves, ivory, ostrich feathers and rare skins, but the southwards traffic in salt and dates would scarcely have been possible until the advent of the camel. It may be that, as in the southern hinterland of Axum, domestic cattle were important in the trade from north to south. It is particularly significant that both of the ancient chariot routes led to that part of the Sudan where there were deposits of alluvial gold, which the local peoples were certainly working by the beginning of the Islamic period and which they were presumably working many centuries earlier.

Ghana, the earliest of the 'Sudanic' states known to history, lay just north of the gold-bearing river valleys of the upper Niger and Senegal, a region which became known to the Arabs as Wangara. When exactly Ghana came into being is not known, but al-Fazari's statement that it was known in Morocco as 'the land of gold' suggests that both Ghana and its links with North Africa were well established by the time he was writing, in the ninth century. It is certain that the wealth of Ghana, and of its successor empires in the western Sudan, stemmed from control of gold exports to the north and of the distribution of salt and other imports in the south. Trade was thus a vital element in the development of these states.

It would seem, moreover, that the northern influence was not always limited to trade. It is unquestionable that the bulk of the population of ancient Ghana were Soninke, northern members of the great Mande-speaking group of black peoples. By the eleventh century at least, and probably much earlier, its kings were equally black. But chronicles compiled from traditional sources by Sudanese scholars in seventeenth-century Timbuktu report that the first kings of Ghana were what they called 'white men' from the north. This story is not an isolated one. Thus the legends of the origin of the Hausa of northern Nigeria, and, less clearly perhaps, those of Kanem-Bornu to the east and of the Songhai to the west, suggest that their states were the results of immigration from the north, from the desert, as well as from the east, from the direction of the Nile valley.

A definitive interpretation of these and other comparable legends is not easy at the present time, when there is little positive archaeological evidence available. But two points must be considered: first, the nature of this northern influence; and, secondly, the question of its relation to the development of the 'Sudanic' states in west Africa.

It may be said at once that although the growth of trade with the

Mediterranean was important for the states of the West African savanna, and particularly so in the extreme west, the cultural influence which entered from the north was not Mediterranean but Berber. While economic currents generated by the Mediterranean civilization crossed the desert, generally speaking the Mediterranean culture did not extend beyond the limits of agriculture in North Africa. Indeed, the general effect of the expansion of Mediterranean civilization was to intensify the traditional distinction between the sedentary Berbers of the plains and valleys of North-West Africa and the nomadic Berbers of the steppes and desert. This distinction was further enhanced by the introduction of the camel and by the coming of Islam. By the beginning of the Muslim period, the Berbers of the desert were becoming recognizable as the people now known as Tuareg. Their tribal links with the sedentary Berbers were still evident; thus the Arab historians recognized both the western Tuareg and the sedentary Berbers of the Kabyles in eastern Algeria as members of the Sanhaja tribal group. But the Tuareg retained the matrilinealism which was being extinguished in the settled areas, and they alone retained (or perhaps developed) the indigenous Berber script, Tifanagh. While both the social and the political organizations of the sedentary Berbers were fundamentally democratic, those of the Tuareg were hierarchical, with distinct castes of nobles, vassals and slaves. A major distinction of the nobility was that its menfolk were veiled, never revealing their faces below the eyes, and its principal criterion was birth, with children by non-noble women excluded. The slaves – the cultivators and artisans of the oases – seem always to have been black. With the passage of time the vassal class seems to have become increasingly black also.

Today the Tuareg survive only in the central Sahara, roughly in the triangle Ghadames–Timbuktu–Air. On either side of this triangle the desert tribes have been Arabized. Before this occurred, however, there can be no doubt that the tribes to the west, the *mulethlemin* or 'veiled Sanhaja' of the early Arab historians, were Tuareg. It is probable that the Zaghawa tribes dominating the eastern Sahara were fundamentally not dissimilar, though distinguishable from the other desert tribes because their proximity to the Nile valley seems to have occasioned some degree of influence from its civilization and its divine kingship.

It is evident that when the legends of the western and central Sudan ascribe the origins of their dynasties to northerners, it is to ancestors of the Tuareg or to the Zaghawa that they refer. Thus we are told by al-Bakri in the eleventh century that the royal succession in ancient Ghana was matrilineal (though the name he gives for the king in his day seems certainly a Soninke one). Evidence of matrilineal influence may also be found in traditional Bornu dynasties, while some of the Hausa legends of origin even suggest something approaching an early period of royal matriarchy. A residual veil survives as a distinguishing mark of the nobility of Hausaland and Bornu, while Bornu tradition states that between about the eleventh and the thirteenth centuries, when the state was centred in Kanem, their kings took care to marry only noble women from the north.

In fact it is clear that for centuries pastoral tribes from the Sahara, whose culture was essentially Libyan-Berber, were drifting into the western and central Sudan. It is likely also that on more than one occasion their warrior nobility, toughened by desert living and controlling the supply of camels and good horses, were able to seize political power and to found important dynasties. But this is a very different thing from arguing, as some European writers have done most persuasively, that kingship in the western and central Sudan originated from a patron and client relationship between 'white' pastoralists and black peasants.

Kanem-Bornu and Hausaland have in effect two separate sets of traditions for the origin of their states. From these it may be deduced that desert pastoralists infiltrated into a land whose black peoples were already organized along divine kingship lines though their kingdoms would seem to have been of small size. Military superiority and their initial independence of local ties helped the newcomers to enlarge the scale of political organization, but culturally they could not escape becoming submerged in the earlier tradition of Sudanic kingship with its agricultural and (in this case) highly urbanized society. A similar pattern can be made out for the Yoruba to the south-west (whose society is also highly urbanized), and also, though less clearly, for the Songhai on the Niger to the west. Further west still, it would appear that the Mossi-Dagomba states of the upper Volta basin were founded by men in whom the two traditions were already fused.

As far west as ancient Ghana, however, the picture may well be different. We know little of ancient Ghana other than the accounts given of it by Arab authors towards the end of its history. If, for instance, one looks in al-Bakri for evidence of divine kingship, it can be found, as has been seen. But there is a marked difference between Arab accounts of Ghana and of Kanem. It is not only al-Muhallabi who stresses the divine kingship element in Kanem. Right up to Maqrizi in the fifteenth century, the strange nature of the Kanem monarchy continues to be a dominant theme in the Arab writings. The emphasis for Ghana, or for that matter for its successor state of Mali, which was better known to the Arabs, is quite different. The Arabs who wrote about Ghana were quite as much impressed by its commercial wealth and its links with the north by way of the desert Sanhaja as they were by its pagan constitution. Thus Ibn Hawqal in the tenth century remarks that he saw a draft made out by a Sudanese merchant to a colleague in Morocco for the equivalent of as much as 20,000 gold sovereigns. Al-Bakri gives details of the tolls levied by the Ghana king on the salt, copper and general merchandise entering or leaving his country.

It is possible that this is no more than a Muslim view of a state that had already been subjected to at least two centuries of Muslim influence. Al-Bakri, for example, remarks that most of the Ghana king's ministers were Muslims, and tells us of the large stone-built Muslim city, with its twelve mosques, close by the mud-built native capital. On the other hand, however, the evidence suggests that the kings of Kanem became Muslims before those of Ghana. It seems, in fact, as though the differences observable between the Arab assessments of Ghana and of Kanem were due to the much greater strength of pre-Islamic northern influences in Ghana. Indeed, the chariot-drawings in the desert provide considerable evidence of the great antiquity of the western-most Sudan's contacts with the Saharan peoples, attracted doubtless by its gold. Such an attraction did not exist further east, and it would seem that the Saharan influences did not enter the central Sudan until after its Negro kingdoms were well established. But as far west as ancient Ghana, it would seem that the type of state which had emerged by the tenth century may have represented a more even balance between Sudanic and Saharan traditions.

6 The Arab Empire in Africa

In A.D. 639, the first Muslim Arabs entered Egypt. By the beginning of the following century they had overrun all Africa north of the Sahara and were invading southern Europe. North Africa was severed from the Mediterranean influences of the previous 1,500 years of its history, and within a few centuries its peoples had become firmly part of the new world and culture of Islam. This first wave of Arab conquest did not cross the Sahara. Arabs did not begin to penetrate the desert in the east until after the collapse of the Nubian Christian kingdom of Makurra in the fourteenth century. In the west the Arabs did not begin to enter the Sahara in significant numbers before about the twelfth century, and the western Sudan was never theirs. But if the Sahara served as some check to actual conquest, the religion and culture the Arabs had brought spread persuasively from the firm base established in North Africa deeply into the Sudan, so that the whole Sudan eventually became part of the Islamic world.

The seventh-century Arab invasion of Africa was one of a series of great outpourings of peoples from Arabia into the neighbouring lands which had occurred at intervals throughout history. The ancestors of both the Phoenicians and the Jews had been part of one of the earlier emigrations. The fundamental cause of these movements was over-population, since except for its south-eastern fringes the greater part of Arabia is desert. The seventh-century emigrants in fact were typically Beduin, that is desert Arabs. Some of these could supplement their meagre pastoralism by carrying or harrying the trade passing between the horns of the Fertile Crescent which enfolded the desert to the north, or by mercenary service in the armies of the empires that arose there. Periodically, however, the desert became too small to contain the numbers and the jostling energies of its tribes, and they would overflow to join in the exploitation of the lands of the Fertile Crescent and to contribute to its population.

The particular outpouring of peoples from Arabia which began in the seventh century was notable not only because it was to reach further afield than usual but also because it launched Islam as one of the great world religions. Few single sentences can have had a greater impact on world history than the message preached by Muhammad to the Arab tribes between A.D. 622 and 632, the message which became the foundation of the Muslim creed – *lā ilāha illa'llāh muhammadun rasūlu'llāh:* 'there is no god but God; Muhammad is the Messenger of God.' In the doctrine of the one God and the paramountcy on earth of his Messenger, the Arabs found a brotherhood to transcend the divisions and conflicts among their tribes; and the Koran, the direct revelation of God to Muhammad, crystallized and symbolized a belief that Arabic was a perfect vehicle for the expression of true knowledge, wisdom and beauty. Islam canalized the energies of the Arab tribes and enabled them to explode into the outside world with a vital new unity of purpose.

Shortly after the death of Muhammad in 632, Arab bands began a series of increasingly bold excursions into the territories of the two great world empires of the time, Byzantium and Sassanid Persia. These may at first have been no more than raids, but the desert warriors quickly appreciated their ability to defeat even the greatest military concentrations that could be brought against them. The Byzantine and Sassanid armies had superiority in numbers, in arms and in technical organization, but their conscripts could not match the compelling inspiration Islam had brought to the Arab tribesmen. Moreover, the imperial lines of communication were dangerously exposed to the hardy mobility which desert life had engendered in the Arab tribes. The Arabs who had come to raid and plunder stayed to rule and exploit in the name of Allah and his Messenger. The *jihad*, the war against the infidel, became almost as much as prayer, alms-giving, fasting, pilgrimage and the profession of faith in Allah and his Messenger, a binding obligation upon the true Muslim.

Once Syria had been overrun (634–6), a permanent occupation of the fertile wealthy lands on either side was feasible. In the east, the Arabs conquered Mesopotamia and Persia, and were ultimately to reach the Indus and the Oxus. In the west was Egypt, whose wealth

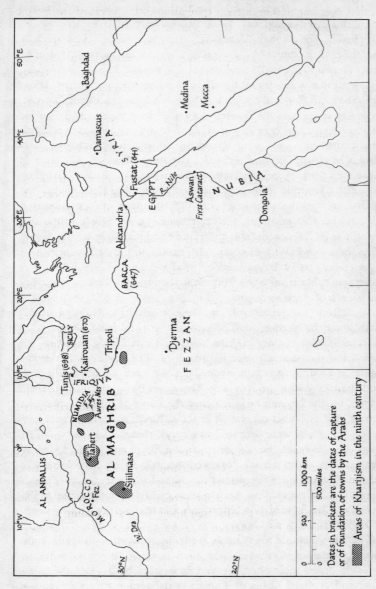

5 The Arabs in North Africa

made it a natural target. Furthermore, the Arab position in Syria and in Arabia itself could not be secure so long as Byzantine forces, supplied by sea through Alexandria, remained on their flank. In 639, therefore, 'Amr ibn al-'As, jealous of the victories and profits won by other Arabs in the east, came with a few thousand men to prospect. The conquest was simple, for the Byzantine rulers of Egypt, aliens exploiting the land and people for their own and their empire's profit, were not supported by the native Copts. Once the main Byzantine army in Egypt had been defeated (640), 'Amr was able to conclude a treaty with the Copts, who agreed to pay regular taxes to the new-comers in return for freedom to practise their Christian religion, and protection for their goods, lands and water-rights. In 641, Babylon, the great Byzantine fortress at the head of the Nile Delta, fell to the Arabs, and in the following year the Byzantine forces evacuated Alexandria. This great city, the capital of Egypt for nearly a thousand years, was too Hellenistic, Mediterranean and maritime for the Arabs. They began to build a new capital, Fustat, close by Babylon, which lay at the heart of Egypt's agricultural wealth and which also was more accessible from Syria and from the Arabian desert where lay the source of Arab strength.

With Lower Egypt firmly in their hands, the Arabs soon re-established the historic southern frontier at the First Cataract, garrisoning Aswan against Nubian raids. To check this nuisance, an expedition was sent into Nubia in 651–2. The northern Makurran capital at Dongola was bombarded, but the Arabs then quickly concluded a treaty with the Nubians. Their own historians indicate their respect for the Nubian bowmen, and the terms of the treaty suggest that as long as Nubia continued to act as Egypt's source of gold and slaves, the Arabs were prepared to let well alone. The treaty, which eventually governed the relations between Egypt and Nubia for some six centuries, did not make Nubia tributary to the Arabs. Nubia was to send Egypt regular supplies of slaves, and to guarantee freedom of access and of worship to Arab traders, while in return the Arabs agreed to respect Nubia's independence and to supply its requirements of foodstuffs, cloth and horses.

The Arab attitude towards the lands in the west, *al-Maghrib*, took longer to define. Cyrenaica was soon overrun, but 500 miles of waterless desert intervened between its western border and the cultivated and civilized plains of Tunisia, a dangerous advance even for the Arab camelry, particularly while the Byzantine fleet survived to command the narrow road along the coast. Furthermore, as early Arab raids revealed, the temper of the Berber tribes was very different from that of the Egyptians. The conquest of the Maghrib entailed more than merely defeating Byzantine armies. As Donatism had shown, many of even the sedentary Berbers were still hostile to foreign interference, and behind them there were the nomad pastoralists, ready to take advantage of any slackening of government in the agricultural lands. In the Zanata, indeed, the Arabs faced a foe comparable to their own Beduin in hardiness and mobility and in the tenacity with which they would fight to maintain their tribal integrity. This is probably the explanation of a story told by 'Abd-al-Hakam, the earliest (ninth century) historian of the Arab conquest of North Africa. Following his Egyptian success, 'Amr ibn al-'As apparently suggested to the Caliph 'Umar that he should continue his conquest westwards into Ifriqiya (the Arabic version of the old name 'Africa'). But 'Umar is said to have replied 'This country should not be called Ifriqiya, but rather "the treacherous land beyond the frontier". So long as I am alive, I forbid that anyone should go near it or make an expedition against it.' Ultimately, it was a nephew of 'Amr's, 'Uqba ibn Nafi', who took the first effective step towards the conquest when, in 670, he established in southern Tunisia an advance base for further operations, Kairouan. But when, in 681–3, he ventured out on a long expedition further to the west, he and his men were trapped and overwhelmed by a coalition of sedentary Berber tribes. For a time Kairouan was lost, and the Arabs suffered a further disaster when the Byzantine navy landed troops to cut the coast road from Egypt. By the end of the century, however, both the sedentary tribes and the Byzantine armies had been overcome. With the eclipse of Byzantine naval power by the new Arab navy,[1] Carthage was captured and the new Arab city of Tunis began to rise in its place. Hitherto, the pastoral Berbers had stood aloof from the fighting, doubtless hoping to benefit from its aftermath. But the tribes of the Aures mountains had combined together under a redoubtable woman leader known as Kahina ('the priestess'), and shortly after the capture of Carthage in 695 they swept down against the Arabs on the plains below. Much bitter fighting was necessary before the Arabs were

---

[1] The need for this had been evident to the Arabs in 645, when the Byzantines' command of the sea had enabled them to reoccupy Alexandria for a short time.

again in control. Not until 705 was it finally possible for them to incorporate Ifriqiya, the most settled and valuable of the North African territories, as a regular province of their empire. But only in the Tunisian plains, which the Arabs now ruled from Kairouan, with their long tradition of agriculture and settled government descending from Carthaginian times, was the situation at all comparable to that in Egypt. Numidia, always a centre of opposition to alien influences, continued to resist assimilation for many centuries. Elsewhere in the Maghrib, however, many Berber tribes must have surprised the Arabs by the facility with which they took to the faith and enthusiasm of Islam, quickly grafting it on to their ancient beliefs, fundamentally pagan but already prepared for Semitic monotheism through the ancient influence of Phoenician Carthage and centuries of Judaic and Christian infiltration. The Muslim conquest of the Iberian peninsula, begun in 711, which was to round off the conquest of the Maghrib, was undertaken as much by Berbers as by Arabs.

By this time, however, the Arab empire, in Africa as elsewhere, was beginning to suffer strain. It had been begun in the first flush of enthusiasm occasioned by the rise of Islam; but once the Arabs started to settle down and to enjoy the fruits of their conquest, their basic tribal divisions and animosities began to reappear. Sometimes, indeed, these were magnified by the larger stage on to which they had been projected. Islam was no longer the unifying force that it had been at its outset. Differences of opinion arose naturally enough when after the death of Muhammad it became necessary to define his teaching. Moreover, since Islam had become a world empire as well as a world religion, Muhammad's death also occasioned disputes over where power in the Islamic community should reside and how it should be passed on.

Some of these early divisions within Islam became of considerable significance in Africa, but a full explanation of them lies outside the scope of such a brief history as this and belongs properly to works primarily concerned with the beliefs and history of Islam.[1] Here only the crudest of outlines can be given. At first, then, Islam was governed by four 'orthodox' Caliphs who had been among the original Companions of Muhammad. The third of these, 'Uthman, was weak and nepotic, and resentment against him arose on several sides. 'Uthman

1 See 'Suggestions for Further Reading', p. 265.

was murdered in 656, and his successor, 'Ali, who had married Muhammad's daughter Fatimah, never won complete acceptance. In particular he was opposed by the governor of Syria, Mu'awiya, and his army. In 657 Mu'awiya tricked 'Ali into an arbitration of their differences. The result was unfavourable to 'Ali, and from 659 Mu'awiya was effectively Caliph, establishing the Umayyad dynasty which ruled Islam from Syria until 750.

While most Muslims, the orthodox Sunnis (though divided into a number of schools on matters of interpretation), accepted the Umayyad succession, two major groups stood out against it. These were the Shi'ites and the Kharijites. The Shi'ites were originally no more than the political supporters of 'Ali. Among them, however, there eventually developed a doctrinal basis for their opposition to the Umayyads – the idea that the rightful rulers of Islam could only be Muhammad's lineal descendants through 'Ali and Fatimah (hence the terms 'Alids' and 'Fatimids'). Following the Umayyad victory, Shi'ism went underground and became increasingly mystical, claiming that 'Ali's descendants, though denied temporal power, were 'hidden *Imams*', retaining true spiritual supremacy. Some Shi'ites, indeed, borrowing perhaps from Christianity, developed the doctrine of the Mahdi, the great leader who would manifest himself in due time to prepare for the day of judgement. The Kharijites were 'the seceders', a group of nomad tribesmen who were also originally supporters of 'Ali but who broke away because they rejected the process of human arbitration by which he was superseded as an action contrary to the will of God. Kharijism thus came to represent a puritan fanaticism, which Islam as a whole had rejected, but which has often attracted closely-knit tribal groups within it.

In the middle of the eighth century, the Arab empire experienced a second great crisis, which ended in the replacement of the Umayyad Caliphs by the 'Abbasid dynasty. The 'Abbasids ruled not from Damascus, the strategic heart of the empire in Syria, but from a new city, Baghdad, built in one of its richest provinces, Mesopotamia. Firmly based on Mesopotamian agriculture and commerce, the 'Abbasids brought the empire to the peak of its civilization and sophistication. But in the process, while remaining Muslim, it ceased to be exclusively or, in time, even predominantly Arab. Exploitation rather than conquest now provided the basis of wealth; power now lay not with the Arab tribes but with professional soldiers and administrators, who were usually chosen from among the Turkish slaves of the Caliphate.

The eastward shift of both the centre and the spirit of the empire had significant results in Africa. The western provinces began to break away. Spain was never effectively part of the 'Abbasid domains; from 756 it had an independent Umayyad government of its own. In the African Maghrib, independently minded Berber groups began to make use of the divisions in Islam to express their own particularisms. Many of the tribes on the borders of the settled country, pastoralists and traders with the Sudan, became Kharijites. In this way they could be at once Muslim and independent of external authority, much as earlier Berbers had found in Donatism a way of being Christian without being Roman. Around Sijilmasa, the great caravan centre in southern Morocco; to the south of Tripoli and Tunisia; and above all, perhaps, around Tahert in the central Maghrib, Kharijite communities and even states flourished during the eighth and ninth centuries. Some Berbers went even further and made use of rifts in the Muslim and Arab firmaments not merely to mark a negative tribal independence but to develop larger intimations of statehood. Thus an Alid refugee, Idris ibn 'Abd Allah, was accepted as Imam shortly after 788 by a Moroccan Berber tribe, and with its support he began to carve out a sizeable kingdom in the western Maghrib. Although the Idrisids failed to establish a lasting dynasty, the forty years of their rule provided Morocco with its first native capital city, Fez, and sowed a seed which was later to germinate into the idea of a united Moroccan kingdom.

The political changes in Ifriqiya and in Egypt were less startling. Arabs continued to rule in Ifriqiya, but in 800 the governor of the day succeeded in making his post hereditary within his family, the Aghlabids, who became independent of Baghdad in all but name. The situation in Egypt was more complex. Here the governorship became the perquisite of Turkish favourites at the 'Abbasid court. By the end of the ninth century, however, the nominees whom these favourites sent to govern in Egypt had tired of passing on its surplus revenues to their masters in Baghdad. They began to convert them to their own use, developing the splendid new palace-city of al-Askar alongside the older Fustat, and building up an army of Turkish and black African slaves with which they sought to establish personal empires in Syria and the Hejaz and to withstand the armies of Mamluks (Turkish slaves) sent against them from Baghdad. By 935 Egypt had been finally lost to the 'Abbasids, but it can hardly be said that the Egyptian people had thereby gained their independence. They remained subject to the rule of foreigners, for whom the good governance of Egypt and the proper development of its resources were apt to be overshadowed by the struggle to maintain their position against threats from Asia and the attentions of rivals jealous of their power at home. In the event they proved incapable of establishing a regime able to survive the ambitions of its slave ministers and generals. The Tunisians, on the other hand, were more fortunate. The Aghlabids were able to keep power firmly in their own hands and those of their Arab kinsmen. As a result they were able to reconstruct much of the agriculture and the economic life they had inherited from Rome within a new Islamic frame which, though never as splendid as that of Egypt, nevertheless possessed a distinct intellectual brilliance of its own.

Although the Arab conquest of northern Africa did not give rise to a lasting political empire, it nevertheless wrought a remarkable and permanent social change. Christianity, the last and greatest legacy of the Mediterranean civilization, both as a religion and as a way of life, had been eclipsed by Islam. In Egypt, Christianity managed to survive only as the religion of a minority living in an entirely Muslim world, but in the Maghrib its eclipse was total. Some explanation of this lies in the very partial assimilation of Christianity by the tribal Berbers. With them, the Christianity which succumbed to Islam was as much a set of local religions as it was part of the universal Church. But this cannot explain its disappearance in the towns, especially since the Jewish communities there did manage to retain their identity. It seems that the cause of Christianity had been weakened by the Donatist schism and by the ensuing persecutions, first from the official Roman church, then from the Arian Vandals, and finally from Byzantine orthodoxy. Possibly the persecutions helped to destroy the native Donatist church without strengthening the position of the Catholics.

Certainly the position in the Maghrib was in strong contrast to that in Egypt, where the people were so accustomed both to Hellenistic influences and to alien oppression that once they were presented with the opportunity of having a church of their own, they took to it wholeheartedly. The Coptic church became an integral part of the popular life and the channel through which a new national language was fashioned out of the ancient Egyptian tongue. The term 'Copt' in fact was synonymous with 'Egyptian'. Both materially and intellectually the Coptic church was poor compared with the official Byzantine church, but it was the latter, not the former, which virtually disappeared following the Arab conquest. If the majority of the Egyptians eventually became Muslims, this was less the result of the failure of their church than of the pressures to which they were subjected. Deliberate persecution was at most intermittent; perhaps Christianity would have been stronger had there been more. But the majority of the Copts could not withstand the steady stream of Arabs, soldiers and clients of the innumerable governors, sometimes whole tribes, which flowed into Egypt from nearby Syria and Arabia. Inevitably more and more Copts became in one way or another involved in the new regime. Finally, during the 'Abbasid period, when to be an Arab was no longer to be automatically a member of the conquering and ruling caste, the greater part of the Copts began almost imperceptibly to fuse with the Arab settlers into the modern Egyptians, Arabic in speech and Muslim in faith.

Only a sturdy minority of Christians remained as evidence that for centuries all Africa north of the Sahara had partaken of Mediterranean civilization. Now the southern fringes of the old Mediterranean world were firmly part of the new world and culture of Islam. In the Maghrib, the way of the Arabs and Islam had been prepared by Phoenician Carthage. In outlook and language the Arabs were closer to the Berbers than the Greeks or Romans could ever be; they were therefore more capable of enfolding them in their own civilization. The civilization of Islam thus became much more deeply rooted in North Africa, and much more capable of expanding southwards into black Africa, than had been that of the Mediterranean. All the same, within the Muslim culture of North Africa there were still elements of the Mediterranean civilization. The Arabs themselves had learnt much from the Mediterranean empires they had overrun, particularly in Egypt, and the agents for the expansion of Islamic culture to the south were not so much Arabs as Muslims who had been Mediterranean North Africans.

7 Northern and Western Africa during the Great Age of Islam

The greatest achievements of Islam in Africa came after the break-up of the Arab empire. Indeed, they dramatically reveal the ability of African peoples to assimilate and develop for their own purposes a set of new ideas of worldwide significance. The period from about A.D. 800 to about 1300, when Islamic civilization was unrivalled anywhere in the world for the quality of its thought, art, science and government, was also a time in which there flourished some of the most notable of all African states. The North African Berbers played a major part in the history of the western world and of nearer Asia, while behind them, south of the Sahara, lay some of the greatest and most magnificent of all the 'Sudanic' kingdoms, where Islam also had a significant role to play.

For the origins of these dramatic developments, it is necessary to go back to the major schisms in Islam. It must be appreciated that the 'Abbasids had risen to power with Shi'ite support, but that once they had established themselves as Caliphs of all Islam, they had kicked away this ladder in the fear that others too would seek to climb it. The Shi'ites who survived their persecution naturally redoubled their clandestine efforts against the establishment. At the end of the ninth century, one of their missionaries was sent from the Yemen to the Maghrib. There he was so successful among the Kutama, a Berber tribe of the Kabyles who had always been hostile to settled administrations, that Ifriqiya was overrun and its Aghlabid government overthrown. The Mahdi of the time soon himself arrived from the Yemen to exploit the situation. In 910 his proclamation as Caliph made it clear that he wanted much more than the leadership of a mere Berber tribal movement. The aim of the Fatimids, as the new dynasty was called, was nothing less than the mastery of all Islam. To aid in this purpose, the Fatimid capital was soon moved from Kairouan to the eastern-looking coastal fortress of Mahdiya. Early expeditions against Egypt, however, proved premature. In order to secure a military and naval power sufficient for their purpose, the Fatimids needed to compel the support or the quiescence of the tribes throughout the Maghrib, and in this the Kutama were the first to suffer. Egypt was at length conquered in 969, and shortly afterwards both Syria and the Hejaz, the homeland of Muhammad, acknowledged the Fatimid Caliph, al-Mu'izz, who in 973 arrived at al-Kahira (Cairo), the new capital built for him alongside al-Askar and Fustat. The move was clearly meant to be permanent, for al-Mu'izz brought with him not only his court and treasure but even the coffins of his ancestors.

The Arab conquest of the Maghrib had now been spectacularly reversed. Not only were Berber governors and soldiers ruling Arabs in Syria and even in parts of Arabia, but Berber merchants for a time took an important part in the Levant's trade with further Asia. All the same, there was to be no united Berber empire of North Africa. Fatimid Caliphs continued, at least in name, to rule in Egypt until 1171, but, as will be seen, Egypt and the Maghrib soon parted company. Under the Fatimids and their successors, especially the Ayyubids, Egypt entered upon one of the more glorious periods of her history. The revenues of the state were efficiently organized; trade flourished, with markets and shops renowned for their organization and for the excellence of their goods; and Cairo developed into a royal city in which the Caliph had some 20,000 well-built brick houses to let. One of the most notable buildings was the new mosque of al-Azhar, under the arches of which a great theological school was to develop. If the heterodoxy of the Shi'a Caliphs initially somewhat discouraged scholarship, it proved a great stimulus to literature and the arts, bringing in rich influences from Persia and Byzantium.

Although the power of the Fatimids rested largely on African troops, initially Berbers from the Maghrib and later blacks from the Sudan, theirs was essentially an oriental regime embroiled in the affairs of nearer Asia, as was inevitable with their claim to supremacy throughout the world of Islam. This was ultimately to prove their undoing, both for internal and for external reasons. Internally, the Fatimids withdrew within their own rich world of Cairo, entrusting the exercise of power to viziers and generals who were often recruited from Asia. Ultimately, one of these, the great Salah al-Din Yusuf ibn Ayyub (Saladin), a Kurd, was to take the title as well as the reality of power, initiating the new dynasty of the Ayyubids. Externally the Fatimids' main preoccupation was with Syria, a part of their empire which was never secure. The people were hostile to Shi'ism, and at first there was danger from Byzantine armies seeking to reconquer their empire. Syria was then invaded by the Seljuq Turks, who swept over the old Islamic empire from the east, took Baghdad in 1055, and entered Damascus in 1076. Finally, in 1096, the European Crusaders appeared on the scene. Ultimately, Syria became a separate Muslim state controlled by the armies of Turkish or Kurdish generals, who were Sunnis. These naturally sought to control Egypt also, especially when the Crusaders there tried to turn their southern flank.

Saladin first came to Egypt as the lieutenant of one of these Syrian kings. But he was able to win the confidence of the Egyptians in a way that his Shi'a predecessors had never done, and under the Ayyubids the cultural movements initiated by the Fatimids reached their greatest glory. But he spent most of his reign campaigning outside Egypt, in Syria and elsewhere, and the regime he inaugurated confirmed that Egypt's main service to Africa was one of shielding the continent from foreign invasion. The Ayyubids lasted only until 1250, but their role was more than adequately assumed by the Egyptian Mamluks, a remarkable self-perpetuating military aristocracy recruited from the slave markets of central Asia. Originally mainly of Turkish descent, though later possessing a dominant Circassian element, the Mamluks gave an appearance of legitimacy to their regime in 1261 by inviting an 'Abbasid refugee from Baghdad to set up as Caliph at Cairo. This puppet Caliphate remained in Egypt until after the Turkish conquest of 1517. Under Baybars (1260–77) and Kala'un (1279–90), the Mongol hordes were kept away from Africa and the Crusaders were finally expelled. Egypt reached a peak of military power not to be approached again until the time of Muhammad Ali in the nineteenth century. From about the end of the fourteenth century, however, though the Mamluk regime maintained its outward splendour, its real power decayed. Their ceaseless struggles for office so occupied their attention that the irrigation and agriculture on which Egyptian wealth and power depended sank into ruin. Moreover, the country's role as a focus of international trade was severely damaged by Mamluk exactions and commercial monopolies.

In the Maghrib, the grand Fatimid conception of empire had held no meaning for the bulk of the Berber tribes, and did not survive the removal of the Caliph and his army to Egypt. The Sanhaja chieftain to whom Al Mu'izz had entrusted the vice-royalty soon declared his independence, but in so doing he lost control of his own homeland in the Kabyles to a rival branch of his family. The Fatimid answer to the emergence of these independent Sanhaja kingdoms was to send against them a number of Beduin tribes who had been giving them trouble in Upper Egypt. With the Banu Hilal at their head, the Beduin began to arrive in the Maghrib in 1061. Their advent marks a new departure in the region's history. Hitherto, the Arabs in the Maghrib had been a relative handful, a thin and essentially urban upper crust of the population, which had been increasingly permeated by the native Berbers. Though Islam had become the religion of most Berbers, and classical Arabic the language of education, culture, administration and trade, the vast mass of the people were still tribesmen loyal to their own Berber dialects. But the Hilalian invasions were a mass movement of predatory, pastoral and indeed primitive Arab tribesmen, who possessed little of the Islamic culture which had already made its mark on a Maghrib veneered by earlier civilizations. Ibn Khaldun, the greatest of Arabic historians, who was Tunisian born, described the Banu Hilal and the other Beduin invaders as 'a swarm of locusts destroying all in their path'. The Sanhaja kingdoms were reduced to coastal principalities, and the civilization and agriculture of the Ifriqiyan plains were severely damaged. A new lease of life was given to the Zanata, but as more and more Beduin arrived, their tribes were penetrated and Arabized, so that Berber society began gradually to disintegrate from the east into a congerie of competitive quarrelsome Arab–Berber tribal groups. The Berber life which managed to survive in mountain strongholds like the Kabyles and the Aures was narrowly tribal in outlook. If the Maghrib was to be saved for civilization, it could only be from the west, from Morocco, where the Idrisids had already planted the idea of a larger Berber state. And here in fact a new initiative did develop, though not originally among the

Moroccans themselves but among some of the Tuareg of the western Sahara.

The early contacts between the Arabs and Islam, on the one hand, and the peoples of the Sahara and the Sudan outside the Nile valley on the other, are little documented. But during the Umayyad period, parties of Arabs had raided or reconnoitred into the Fezzan and to the south of Morocco. We know also that by the ninth century the Arabs had made contact with both Ghana and Kanem, and that two centuries later the Kanem kings became converts to Islam, almost certainly as a result of their links with Ifriqiya and Egypt. But before the Hilalian invasions, the Arabs in the Maghrib were not numerous enough to attempt direct control of the Sahara. Like the Romans and the Carthaginians before them, they tended to leave the desert and the direct responsibility for desert traffic to the Tuareg Berbers. By the eleventh century, however, in the western Sahara at least, Islamization had proceeded far enough among the members of the Sanhaja Tuareg tribal confederation which dominated the Morocco-Ghana caravan route to make it possible for them to give birth to a puritan revivalist movement. This was to have great consequences both in the Maghrib and in the western Sudan.

The traditional story related by Ibn Khaldun and other Muslim authorities starts with the pilgrimage of a desert Sanhaja chieftain to Mecca. This led him to appreciate the debasement of his people's Islam, and when he came home he brought a Muslim divine from near Sijilmasa, one Ibn Yasin, to undertake a reforming mission. The Sanhaja Tuareg at first did not take well to Ibn Yasin's puritan principles. But after initial difficulties he was able to train a religious and military élite capable of enforcing his disciplines throughout the confederacy. This was the beginning of the Almoravids (*al-murabitun*, 'people of the *ribat*' [1]). Once the Almoravid doctrine had been established among the Sanhaja tribesmen, they swept out from the desert to conquer both north and south. Ultimately the movement split. One wing, under Abu Bakr, moved south into the black empire of Ghana, and its fortunes will be followed later in this chapter. The majority,

1 The normal meaning of *ribat* is a fortified monastery in which pious Muslims receive military as well as religious training. However, it seems doubtful whether in this instance there was such an establishment in any physical sense. *Al-murabitun* would therefore mean something like 'the body of men committed to the fight of establishing true Islam'.

led ultimately by Ibn Tashfin, went north to Morocco and by 1069 had altogether overrun the region. They then continued east to the borders of the Sanhaja kingdoms in the eastern Maghrib. In 1086, Ibn Tashfin responded to an appeal for help from the Muslims of Spain, then hard pressed by the Christian *reconquista*, and by 1103 the whole of Muslim Spain was also under Almoravid control.

Significant though the religious impulse in the rise of the Almoravids undoubtedly was, the movement cannot be regarded simply as the triumph of a fanatical Islamic sect over effete Muslims in the Maghrib and pagan Blacks in the Sudan. It must be viewed in relation to the political and economic pressures enveloping the western Sahara at the time. Morocco was in a disturbed state. The Fatimid invasions, though militarily successful, had not really conquered the country, partly because of the innate hostility of the tribes to any alien rule, and partly because they had provoked intervention from the Umayyads of Spain. The real victors were neither the Fatimids nor the Umayyads, but the westward-moving Zanata nomads. The Zanata infiltration was significant in two respects. First, much of their expansion was at the expense of Sanhaja chiefdoms in southern Morocco, and a call for help went out from these to their Tuareg kinsmen in the Sahara. Secondly, the coming of the Zanata disrupted the economy of the Moroccan terminus of the trans-Saharan trade which the Tuareg Sanhaja conducted. At the same time, these Saharan Sanhaja were being hard pressed by the growth of Ghana, which by the end of the tenth century had succeeded in imposing tribute on Awdaghost, their principal southern centre and trading entrepôt. Thus the ultimate response to Ibn Yasin's mission can be seen as a reaction to developments prejudicial to Sanhaja interests both in Morocco and the Sudan.

In the Maghrib, the Almoravid achievement was considerable. Presenting themselves as liberators of the people from corrupt rule, taxes unsanctified by the Koran and alien Zanata invasions, they were able, from their new city of Marrakech,[1] to build up a magnificent and remunerative empire over the western half of the Maghrib. In so doing, however, they began to lose the simple faith and the military energy and cohesion of their desert days. They began to appear to many Moroccan tribes as foreigners restricting the liberties of the

1 From Marrakech, incidentally, derives our word 'Morocco'.

natives and fattening themselves on their tribute. The preachings of a southern Moroccan divine, one Ibn Tumart, against the Almoravids, claiming that in their later preoccupation with self-interested administration they were subverting the unique oneness of God, found ready ears among the Berbers of the Masmuda tribes scattered through the Moroccan Atlas. These were ancient foes of the Sanhaja but had hitherto lacked unity. About 1125, Ibn Tumart established a *ribat* and proclaimed himself the Mahdi. The Almoravids failed to act against him swiftly or firmly, and the movement he had inspired, the Almohads (*al-muwahhidun*, 'monotheists'), gained increasing support among the mountain tribes hostile to the Sanhaja. By 1147, his successor, 'Abd al-Mumin, a Zanata, was installed in Marrakech as master of all Morocco, with the title of Caliph.

Although the Almohads soon superseded the Almoravids in Spain too, 'Abd al-Mumin appreciated that the greatest danger to his regime came not from the Christians of the north but from the east. Here were Sanhaja states naturally hostile to his Masmuda-Zanata alliance, and here too was the insidious destruction of Berberdom by the advancing Beduin. By 1159 'Abd al-Mumin had conquered as far east as Tunis and had brought the whole Maghrib under one Berber government. The Maghrib was now a major force in the Islamic and Mediterranean worlds. The Almohads created a professional civil service, which they recruited from the educated classes throughout the Maghrib, especially from Spain, while Marrakech, Fez, Tlemcen and Rabat became beautiful and cultured cities. To pay for this and for their professional army and navy, they had the land throughout the empire surveyed, and levied regular taxes on its assessed productivity. But in doing all this the Almohads were intensifying an already apparent distinction between the original members of their confederation, who as it happened belonged mainly to the Masmuda and Zanata tribes, and all other Berbers. As their first reforming zeal began to be submerged in the legalities of an orderly administration, this distinction became increasingly dangerous. Despite their great achievements, then, the Almohads were unable to inspire any common idea of statehood among the multiplicity of Berber tribes, and this failure gravely weakened their attempts to deal with the major difficulties facing their empire: the maintenance of an orderly succession to power, the problem of Spain and the menace of the Beduin.

The problem of the succession reproduced in miniature the problem which had faced early Islam: was power to pass to the founder's Companions or to his descendants? 'Abd al-Mumin proved sufficiently strong and successful to set up a hereditary succession, and until 1213 the Almohad caliphs all proved capable rulers. But as a Zanata family they were bound by their very success to incur the enmity of most other Berbers. This became especially dangerous when the empire was threatened by renewed activity both from the Christians in Spain and from the Beduin in the central Maghrib. In an attempt to deal with both threats at once, the Caliph Muhammad an-Nasr (1199–1213) divided his government, appointing a Viceroy from the Hafsids, one of the outstanding families in the Almohad administrative service, to command the east from Tunis. Unfortunately for the Almohads, however, the Hafsids were all too successful. The Beduin were defeated, but the wars against them intensified the destruction of the central Maghrib and extended it westward towards Morocco. Northern Tunisia, under the capable Hafsid administration, became an island of relative stability and prosperity cut off from the west. By 1230 an independent Hafsid monarchy had emerged, able to conclude commercial pacts with European trading states and to attract much of the trans-Saharan trade to its profit.

In the west Almohad prestige suffered greatly from the resounding Christian victory of Las Navas de Tolosa in 1212, which marked the beginning of the end not only for the Moorish power in Spain but also for the Almohad regime in Morocco. Their kingdom disintegrated into its tribal parts, and in the confusion the Zanata nomads triumphed. One Zanata group, the 'Abd al-Wadids of Tlemcen, were by 1235 dominating the eastern approaches to Morocco. Another, the Marinids, based in the Saharan marches, gradually extended their power over the Moroccan heartland, finally establishing themselves at Marrakech in 1269 as the successors to the Almohads and what was left of their administration.

The great days of Berber empire were over. The unity imposed on the Maghrib had now dissolved, and the three divisions which were to mark its subsequent history were already apparent. In the east the well-established Hafsid kingdom continued until 1574, prospering from what could be recovered of Tunisian agriculture, and from its

6 West Africa in the Great Age of Islam

Approximate boundaries of African
empires at their greatest extents:

—F— Fatimid empire (c. 973)
—AR— Almoravid empire (c. 1100)
—AH— Almohad empire (c. 1200)
—GH— Empire of Ghana (c. 1000)
—MA— Empire of Mali (c. 1350)
—S— Songhai empire of Gao (c. 1520)
—K— Kanem empire (c. 1250)
- - - - Major trans-Saharan trade routes

trade with southern Europe and the Sudan. In the west was Morocco, where first the Marinid dynasty and then the Wattasids (1465–1554) strove to secure the ideas of a central monarchy and a regular administration against the inroads of tribesmen from the mountains and steppes, and also against foreign invaders. In the centre lay what was eventually called Algeria, where the 'Abd al-Wadids, themselves of nomad stock and unsupported by the wealth or by the tradition of ordered government available in Tunisia or Morocco, proved quite powerless to check the almost complete destruction of civilized society at the hands of the Beduin.

In the western Sudan the traditional story is that the Almoravids began to campaign against ancient Ghana about 1062 but met with considerable resistance and did not enter its capital until 1076. However, recent research has questioned whether there was ever a military conquest. What does seem to be the case is that there was constant infiltration by the Muslim nomads from the desert which led to substantial Islamization, and possibly also to a change of dynasty, but that the 'Sudanic' concepts of kingship and empire were not destroyed. But post-Almoravid Ghana was not the power that it had once been. The trans-Saharan trade, so vital to the economic strength of the empire, had been sadly disrupted by the Almoravid outburst. Moreover, in the dry Sahel lands surrounding the ancient capital, agriculture was unable to recover from the damage done by the desert nomads and their flocks. With its economic cohesion thus weakened, Ghana's empire began to break up into its component tribal units. But the idea of empire did not die in the western Sudan. It had been merely pushed further to the south, into better agricultural land more remote from the desert and the possibility of attack from its destructive pastoralists. The heritage of ancient Ghana was eventually assumed by the leader of one of the Mande clans in the upper Niger valley. Under Sundiata, who reigned from about 1230 to 1255, an even greater Mande empire, that of Mali, began to rise.

It would appear that Sundiata rose to power as a pagan, but he and his successors seem to have been quick to appreciate the political and economic advantages for themselves and their state in the adoption of Islam. As has been seen, in their later days the Ghana kings had depended to some extent on Muslim advisers, but it is likely that at least initially these were strangers from the north. But one result of the Almoravid conquest was greatly to stimulate the growth of Islam among the Sudanese themselves. Sundiata seems to have been at least a nominal convert, and during the great period of Mali history, up to the end of the fourteenth century, his successors as *Mansa* (emperor) were all undoubtedly Muslims, many of whom made the pilgrimage to Mecca. From this time on, the major states of the western Sudan were usually ruled by kings who professed an allegiance to Islam.

One advantage of Islam for the states of the black peoples of the West African savanna was that it gave them an assured status with the governments and merchants of North Africa, whose goodwill was so necessary for the prosperity of the states of the Sudan. By about the thirteenth century onwards, the merchants of the Sudan itself were usually Muslims too, and, ranging further afield than the lands under the direct control of their kings, they became the great propagators of Islam throughout the western Sudan. Thus, for example, it was Mande merchants of the fourteenth century who introduced Islam into Hausaland.

Islam and Islamic culture also provided a useful tool in attempting to solve the major internal problem facing the 'Sudanic' empires. A king or emperor could legitimately claim the allegiance only of his own kinship unit or clan, and of such other related kinship units as could recognize his descent from an original king whom the whole group acknowledged as a great founding ancestor. But many rulers, especially those of Mali, and of the Songhai who eventually succeeded to their power, extended their dominion very much wider than this. Ghana had shown how rich and powerful a monarchy could become if it could impose its control over all the trade of a given area in the Sudan. Mali and Songhai in effect tried to control as much of the Sudan as they could. The further afield their armies could impose one system of law and order, the more their peaceable production and trade would grow. The flow of trade and tribute, clients and slaves to their capital would correspondingly increase, providing the means for even further extensions of their power.

The more widely an empire was extended, however, the more alien its emperors appeared. Local chiefs could not be trusted to remain faithful vassals; they tended instead to become rallying points for local resistance to imperial rule. This situation could be met to some extent by an emperor sending his own men, supported by an adequate number of his own soldiers, to rule outlying territories in his name. But this still did not solve the fundamental problem of securing loyalty from other kinship units. At best a provincial governor might do no more than transfer local allegiance to himself, and if he were a kinsman of the emperor with some claim to the imperial succession, this could be extremely dangerous. Accordingly, provincial governors were often chosen from among the slaves rather than from the family of the emperor.

For the continued maintenance of a large empire, it was therefore necessary to establish an impartial central administration, with sufficient continuity and a good enough system of communication to secure a proper control over all that was happening throughout the empire; and secondly to find some principle of allegiance which might transcend the one based on kinship. Islam could help with both. With the growth of Muslim schools and colleges in the Sudan, there emerged a class of educated, literate and even scholarly men who could organize imperial government and trade efficiently. Such men were not dominated by their kinship allegiances; their own interests were in fact closely tied to the maintenance of the imperial administration and peace. On the other hand, before the nineteenth century at least, Islam does not seem to have penetrated sufficiently deeply into the lives of the mass of the people to have affected the second purpose to any very great extent. Whenever the central power was weak or divided, a Sudanese empire always tended to dissolve into its basic pagan kinship allegiances.

It must be emphasized that both Mali and Songhai were considerable empires by any standard. During the fourteenth century the writ of the emperors of Mali ran from their upper Niger valley capital of Niani westward to the Atlantic over all the land north of the forest, and east along the Niger valley to the borders of Hausaland. Among its principal vassals were the kings of the Songhai, who monopolized fishing and canoeing activities along the middle Niger. Control of the Songhai was essential if Mali's merchants were to have access to Timbuktu and Gao, which by the thirteenth century were becoming important southern bases for the trans-Saharan trade, and beyond them to the Hausa states. But the Songhai kings did not take kindly to subordination to Mali's interests, and were continually trying to regain their independence. Eventually a king emerged, Sunni Ali (*c.* 1464–92), who was able to mobilize the traditional pagan energies of the Songhai to defeat Mali and, with the help of men experienced in its armies and administration, to begin to convert its eastern dependencies into an empire of his own. His successor, one of his Mande generals, the *Askia* Muhammad (1493–1528), completed his work by more than restoring the Muslim influences which Sunni Ali, in the first flush of Songhai imperialism, had tended to destroy. The final result was an empire even greater than that of Mali. Its capital was Gao, on the Niger bend, some 700 miles east of Niani, and the area of its power in the west was accordingly less. But it reached northwards to the Saharan salt mines and almost to the confines of Morocco, while eastwards it reached almost to Bornu.

The power, wealth and good order of these empires excited the admiration of Muslims from more central parts of the Islamic world, who, confident in their own achievements, were not lightly wont to praise those of others. Thus the great traveller Ibn Battuta, whose earlier journeys had taken him as far as China, after a tour through the Mali empire in 1352–3, wrote that its Blacks

> are seldom unjust, and have a greater horror of injustice than other people. Their sultan shows no mercy to anyone who is guilty of the least act of it. There is complete security in their country. Neither traveller nor inhabitant in it has anything to fear from robbers or men of violence.

He was continually noting evidence of the prosperity of agriculture and trade, and remarked on the ease and safety with which traders and foreigners could travel, after little advance preparation, because they could always be sure of buying food and of finding good lodging for the night. A few years before Ibn Battuta's visit, *Mansa* Musa, probably the greatest of the Mali emperors and certainly the best known, like many of his predecessors had made the pilgrimage to Mecca by way of Cairo. He created a most favourable impression in Cairo, and he had brought so much gold in his train that the value of the metal in Egypt was quite appreciably debased. This journey of *Mansa* Musa placed the western Sudan squarely on the map of the great states in the world of the time; quite literally, for Mali and its 'Lord of the Blacks' appear on the very first map of West Africa ever drawn in Europe (in 1375). Doubtless it was his success that inspired

Askia Muhammad of Gao to attempt an even more magnificent display when he went to Mecca in 1495–7.

Without losing their distinctive 'Sudanic' character, the great states and cities of the western Sudan became definitely part of the Islamic world. Their mosques and schools were able to attract divines and scholars from other parts of this world, those of Timbuktu being especially famous. They even maintained their own hostels for their students and travellers in Muslim centres like Cairo. But of course it was trade more than anything else which linked the Sudan to North Africa, and there would seem to be an interesting correlation between the course of events in the Sudan and those in the Maghrib during the centuries following the Almoravid explosion. At the beginning of the Muslim period, most trade seems to have taken the western trans-Saharan road between Morocco and Ghana. Doubtless this was because the most accessible Sudanese gold lay just south of Ghana, while there were also major salt mines immediately south of Morocco. But by about the fourteenth century Mande merchants had begun to open up a gold trade with lands to the south-east, in the Black Volta valley and beyond, and the extension of Mali power down the Niger and the subsequent rise of the Songhai empire mark eastward shifts in the centres of power in the western Sudan. The region's exports too began to flow east down the Niger to new centres like Timbuktu and Gao before crossing the desert along more central routes. It seems possible that this eastward shift of political and economic power in the Sudan was due first to the disruption of the old western trade routes by the Almoravids, and secondly to the fact that (after the brief flowering of the Almoravid and Almohad empires) the most stable power in the Maghrib was that of the Hafsids of Tunis. It may also be significant that the peak of power reached by the Kanem kingdom in the central Sudan during the thirteenth century, when its influence was felt as far north as the Fezzan, was also broadly contemporaneous with the build-up of the Hafsid state.

8 North-East and East Africa in Medieval and Early Modern Times

In North-East and East Africa the rise of Islam did not produce the same swift and catastrophic results as it did in Egypt and North Africa. Even the Christian kingdom of Axumite Ethiopia, which had been the oppressor of South Arabia until the eve of the Prophet's birth and was the nearest organized state to the source of the Islamic expansion, was left substantially in peace for many centuries. In the seventh century Arabian Muslims profited by a temporary weakness of the Christian kingdom to seize the port of Massawa and the neighbouring Dahlak Islands; but we know from the Arabic writers of the ninth and tenth centuries – Yaqubi and Ibn Hawqal – that at this period the Ethiopian state still dominated most of the Red Sea coast opposite the Yemen, and that its influence stretched round the shores of the Gulf of Aden as far as Zeila on the northern coast of Somalia. The coastlands, especially the ports, were occupied by communities of Muslim traders, but all these paid tribute to the king of Ethiopia, and the Muslim world did not regard Christian Ethiopia as being subject to the *jihad* or holy war.

Thus, although it may be true that the rise of Islam was the turning-point in Ethiopian history, it was so only in a remote and long-term sense. The new world of Islam cut off Ethiopia from its former Mediterranean allies. It resulted in the substitution of Muslim Arab traders in the Red Sea ports for the Egyptians, Greeks and Jews who had been there before. But for six or seven centuries at least it did not result in permanent hostilities between Christians and Muslims as such. There was no eastern parallel to the pattern of *jihad* and Crusade which forms the medieval history of the Mediterranean. In large measure this was because the Ethiopian Church had followed its Syrian and Egyptian teachers into the Monophysite heresy, condemned by orthodox Christendom at the Council of Chalcedon in 451, and had thus benefited from the settlement with the Egyptian Copts effected by the Arabs. Throughout the Middle Ages, therefore, even during the Crusading period, Ethiopian bishops were consecrated in Cairo, and Ethiopian pilgrims, thousands at a time, marched through Egypt on visits to the Holy Land, with drums beating and flags flying, and with regular halts for the celebration of Christian worship. In fact it was Saladin, the greatest opponent of the western Christian Crusaders, who gave the Church of the Invention of the True Cross to the Ethiopian Christians as their religious centre in Jerusalem.

The real crisis of medieval Ethiopia came not from the Muslims to the north but from the pagans to the south. Of the details of this crisis we are almost completely ignorant. One surviving letter from an Ethiopian king of the very late tenth century to his brother monarch, George of Nubia, tells the pitiful tale of a kingdom in ruins through the invasions of a neighbouring pagan state, which is probably to be identified with the Agau kingdom of Damot, lying in the great bend of the Blue Nile. The Christian kingdom's recovery must certainly have been the most heroic period in Ethiopian history, though the least known. A new dynasty of kings, the Zagwe, who were not Semitic-speakers like the founders of Axum but Christianized Agau from the central region of Lasta, led the renascence, leaving as their main monument the magnificent rock-hewn churches of Roha. Christianity triumphed, not through the sedentary propagation of a learned faith but rather (as in fifth- and sixth-century Ireland) as a Church of ascetic monks and hermits who established their influence by personal sanctity and denial of the world. Through two and a half centuries the political and religious frontiers were pushed southwards, the fertile plateau of Shoa in the region of modern Addis Ababa being occupied by Semitic-speaking Christian Amhara from the region to the east of Lasta. By the mid-thirteenth century these pioneers had become the most dynamic element in the kingdom, and in 1270 power was seized by a Shoan dynasty claiming descent from King Solomon and the Queen of Sheba and the old Axumite line of kings. The early 'Solomonid' rulers proved great conquerors. Leading the hard life of military commanders in peripatetic, tented capitals, they extended their rule over Gojjam and Damot to the west of Shoa,

7 East and North-East Africa, seventh to eighteenth centuries and then turned their attention south-eastwards to the valley of the Awash and the great trade-route that led down it to Zeila on the Gulf of Aden.

In all this latter region the Christian Ethiopians had been forestalled by Muslim traders and clerics, in origin mostly Afar from the vicinity of Zeila. The traders had built up a network of commercial influence among the little independent states of Ifat and Dawaro and Fatejar and Hadya which lay across the route to the rich, gold-, musk- and slave-producing lands of Enarea and Kaffa in the south-western highlands. The key to this trade was the salt of the Aussa depression, where the waters of the Awash are trapped and evaporate before they can reach the sea. The Afar carried it up the escarpment by camel and then transferred it to donkeys for distribution over the highlands. The merchants also brought up horses for use in slaving expeditions, and married the daughters of the local ruling families which supplied the trade. Clerics followed in the wake of the traders, and so a process of conversion was set in train. The Christian Ethiopians impinged on this scene mainly as conquerors demanding tribute. They did not seek to overthrow the local dynasties or to change their faith. But in the long run the effect of Christian military intrusions was to cause these rulers to think and act as Muslims rather than as traders, and to organize rebellions based on religious vows of victory or martyrdom.

The first result of revolt was that Christian Ethiopia blotted out the leading Muslim state, that of Ifat, pursuing the fugitives as far as Zeila and capturing and killing the Ifati king in 1415. Northern Ifat was incorporated under the direct rule of Ethiopia, which now enjoyed for more than a century the most brilliant period of its history. Church and state flourished hand in hand. A system of standing militia was recruited to guard the frontiers, and royal intendants were established in every province to ensure the loyalty of the local lords. Tribute was regularly raised from a wide semicircle of states beyond the eastern and southern frontiers. Only the leading Muslim elements of the former Ifat kept alive the spirit of opposition by migrating to the Chercher highlands on the eastern side of the Rift Valley, where they began to build up the new state of Adal, with the *jihad* against Ethiopia as its real unifying force. When, therefore, in the early sixteenth century the Ottoman Turks succeeded the Mamluks in

Egypt and brought the use of firearms and artillery down the Red Sea ports and into southern Arabia, they found in Adal a united Muslim community ready to use these weapons against the Christian kingdom. Adal produced a military genius, Ahmad bin Ibrahim, who in 1529 inflicted a shattering defeat upon the Christian armies at the battle of Shimbra Kure. He followed it up with a systematic conquest and plundering of the whole kingdom. Every church and monastery was burned and every bit of accumulated wealth carried off. Only Ahmad's attempt to stay and govern Ethiopia through renegade Christian officials was less than successful. Opposition built up around the royal family, and it was aided in the nick of time by a small force of Portuguese musketeers sent from Goa, with whose help Ahmad was at last defeated and killed in 1543. During the century and a half that followed, Christian Ethiopia was able to effect a considerable recovery, but only by shifting the centre of the kingdom far to the north-west, to the region of Gondar. The worst result of the Adali conquest had been to break down the frontier defences to the south and east of the old kingdom, thus allowing the pastoral and warlike Oromo (Galla) to infiltrate the southern and eastern provinces on a scale that proved irreversible.

To move now around the sharp point of Cape Guardafui, the medieval history of eastern Africa has until very recently indeed been presented mainly in terms of the urban settlements, assumed to have been those of foreigners, which straddle the coast and the offshore islands from Mogadishu in the north to Sofala in southern Moçambique. Today the emphasis has shifted to the indigenous people of eastern Africa, and the starting-point is seen to be the penetration of the whole region by Iron Age and Bantu-speaking peoples spreading in on a broad front from the west and gradually absorbing the Late Stone Age populations of Cushitic and Khoisan speakers who preceded them. We have already seen that the Iron Age reached north-eastern Zaire, Rwanda, Burundi, southern Uganda and north-western Tanzania at a period which must have been as early as the second or third century B.C., and may have been considerably earlier. From there it spread eastwards and southwards, reaching the coastal regions of Kenya and Tanzania by about the first or second centuries A.D. and those of Moçambique and Natal by the third or fourth centuries.

Inland, southern Zaire, Zambia, Malawi, Zimbabwe and the Transvaal were similarly affected by about the fourth or fifth centuries. Throughout all this region the coming of the Iron Age coincided with the transition from hunting and gathering to food production. It was, therefore, a revolution of the most fundamental kind.

It is against this background that sources for the history of the Indian coast have nowadays to be considered. First, *The Periplus of the Erythrean Sea*, probably attributable to the early second century A.D., with its picture of South Arabian merchants sailing regularly down the coast to the approximate latitude of Dar es Salaam, in search of ivory and tortoise-shell and rhinoceros horn. Secondly, the *Geography* of Claudius Ptolemy, belonging in the form we know it to the late fourth century, which indicates that the Alexandrian traders of this period knew of the existence of Mount Kilimanjaro and also of the great lakes in the interior where the Nile had its sources. Thirdly, the evidence from finds of Roman coins, which show a heavy concentration in the fourth century. It thus looks as though the commercial penetration of central East Africa, doubtless in the interests of the ivory trade, was far deeper at this remote period than it was to be at any later time up until the eighteenth century. But although we know that the occupation of the coastal belt by Iron Age peoples must already have begun, the classical sources give us no real help in identifying them. Moreover, from the fourth century until the ninth East Africa disappears entirely from the historical record. Even the references to 'Zanj' slaves in Arabic and Chinese chronicles of the seventh and eighth centuries have been shown to refer to people from the Red Sea hinterland rather than the eastern coast. The absence of information does not, of course, mean that nothing happened. One event in particular which must have occurred during this 'dark age' was the planting of an Indonesian population on Madagascar, which had been till then uninhabited. The Indonesian contact must certainly have extended in some form to the mainland, and must have bequeathed an important legacy of South-East Asian food plants, such as the banana, the Asian yam, the coco-yam, the coconut, rice and citrus fruits. But it is only with the revival of the Arabian trade from the Persian Gulf during the 'Abbasid caliphate that evidence begins to flow in a continuous stream.

The earliest Islamic site so far known from the east coast is that on Manda Island, in the Lamu archipelago, near the modern frontier of Somalia and Kenya. Here a community of foreign traders, apparently from the eastern side of the Persian Gulf, built a small settlement of some 45 acres with sea-walls and some other features in cut blocks of coral rag some time in the ninth century. Their neighbours were the north-easternmost of the Bantu-speaking peoples, and significantly it was here that the ancestors of the Swahili and Comorian languages were originally spoken as ethnic tongues. The main implication of this important fact is that these Bantu people learned enough about ships and the sea both to take charge of the local coasting trade and to form trading settlements in their own right down the coastline of modern Kenya, Tanzania and Moçambique, as well as on the offshore islands of Pemba, Zanzibar, Mafia, Kilwa, the Comoros and northern Madagascar. Some foreigners, including Arabs, Persians and Indians, later came and settled in all these places, sometimes supplying local dynasties and contributing significantly to their Islamic culture, and especially to their architecture. From Masudi's travels we can probably conclude that there was an Omani settlement on Pemba in the tenth century. A Kufic inscription from Zanzibar refers to the building of a mosque at Kizimkazi in the twelfth century. The so-called Shirazi period of Kilwa, responsible for the Great Mosque and the rich palace site at Husuni Kubwa, has been dated to the beginning of the thirteenth century. But it seems likely that all these settlements were originally founded by Swahili, that is to say, by north-eastern Bantu farmers and fishermen who had made a speciality of the local maritime trade in ivory, mangrove poles, dried fish and agricultural products which helped to supply the intercontinental trade of the foreign merchants.

In sharp contrast with the scarcity of remains for the first five centuries of the Muslim era, it is obvious from the archaeological evidence that from about the middle of the thirteenth century until the coming of the Portuguese at the end of the fifteenth the East African coast enjoyed a period of quite remarkable prosperity. All the way down the coastline of Somalia, Kenya and Tanzania, there sprouted urbanized Islamic communities, building in stone or coral rag and wealthy enough, for example, to import such luxury goods as Thai stoneware and the porcelain of late Sung and early Ming

China. The Kilwa sultans of this period even minted their own silver and copper coinage in the earliest mint to be established anywhere in Africa south of the Sahara. There does not seem any satisfactory explanation for this prosperity in terms of the discovery of new resources in East Africa itself. Kilwa, like its northern predecessors, lived on the Zimbabwean and perhaps the Katangan trade, placing its governors in the gold-port of Sofala and levying large duties on seaborne traffic in both directions. Malindi and Mombasa had been known at least since the twelfth century for their mines of highly concentrated iron ore, which was exported to India for the manufacture of steel blades for swords and daggers. Mogadishu had its weaving industry, producing coarse cotton goods and camel-hair cloth for the Egyptian market. Slaves and ivory were no doubt, as always, the staple exports of all the smaller settlements along the coast.

What happened economically in the thirteenth century, therefore, seems to have been mainly an intensification of the already established lines of commercial exploitation. The material improvement was impressive, but it seems that the main significance of this thirteenth-century revival was cultural and religious. This was the period when from one end of the Indian Ocean to the other, Islam was stretching outwards on its second great wave of expansion. The thirteenth century saw the first serious Muslim penetration of India. In Indonesia it saw the Islamization of the Hindu town cultures in Malaya, Java and Sumatra. In East Africa it marked what was probably the first real incorporation of the coastal region within the world of Islam. Earlier Muslim settlers had been few, and communications with the rest of Islam had been so tenuous that most of their descendants had probably lost the faith. With the thirteenth century, the bulk of the Indian Ocean trading system passed into Muslim hands, and all its participants acquired a new solidarity. In East Africa it is from this time onwards that religious monuments such as mosques and tombs are found all along the coast.

From the evidence at present available, it seems highly unlikely that there existed any long-distance trade links between the Islamic civilization of the central part of the east coast and the interior of East Africa. North of the Bantu sphere there are some indications that the coastal Somalis, particularly after their adoption of Islam, traded inland with the Oromo peoples to the south of the Ethiopian kingdom. And again, to the south of Kilwa, land and sea routes linked the coast with the gold-producing regions of Zimbabwe and probably with the Luba copper-mines of Katanga. There do not seem to have been any corresponding connexions between the Zanzibar coast and the region of the great lakes, which even at this period was probably the most populated part of East Africa and where the evidence of tradition and archaeology shows that organized states were already in existence at least by the thirteenth and fourteenth centuries. At Bigo in western Uganda the excavation of the great earthwork site, which was probably built in the fifteenth century, has not yet yielded a single coastal import – not even a bead.

The reason is, doubtless, that between the coast and the lake regions there lies a wide belt of the driest and least cultivable land in eastern Africa, which at this period was probably occupied only by sparse groups of Cushitic and Nilotic warrior pastoralists, who lacked both the inclination and the organization to supply and protect caravans. It seems that it was only in the eighteenth century that expanding Bantu populations from western Tanzania pressed into the southern part of this region as cultivators and opened the first long-distance trade-routes between the coast and the interior. It is in the second half of the eighteenth century that the traditional history of the Buganda kingdom on the north-western shores of Lake Victoria records the first large-scale imports of cotton cloth and other luxury goods from the outside world.

By this time the Portuguese occupation of the Zanzibar coast had come and gone. Even on the coast it had left no deep mark, and in the interior, none at all. Throughout the Indian Ocean the aims of the Portuguese were essentially commercial and maritime: their object was to supplant the pre-existing network of Arab seaborne trade. Initially, in the early years of the sixteenth century, this carried them not only to India and the East Indies but right up the east coast of Africa to the mouth of the Red Sea and into the Persian Gulf. In this sector they planted their first bases at Sofala, Kilwa, Socotra and Ormuz. In 1542 a small Portuguese expeditionary force intervened decisively to prevent the overrunning of the Christian kingdom of Ethiopia by the Turkish-armed Somali state of Adal; and for nearly a hundred years afterwards, Portuguese missionaries laboured unsuccessfully to bring the Ethiopian Church into obedience to Rome.

This, however, was the only Portuguese venture on the East African mainland to the north of the Zambezi. Their other settlements were virtually confined to the offshore islands – Moçambique, Zanzibar, Pemba, Mombasa and the islands of the Lamu group. Their positive interests in East Africa were limited to the gold region of the Zambezi, and to the island base of Moçambique, from which the East India convoys sailed direct to Goa.

The diversion of the gold trade into European channels removed the linch-pin of the East African coastal commerce: within a few years of the Portuguese occupation, Kilwa had withered to an unimportant village. North of Kilwa, the Swahili settlements on the mainland maintained furtive links with Arabia and the Persian Gulf. In 1593, in an effort to contain the political disaffection of the coast, the Portuguese built and garrisoned the great citadel of Fort Jesus at Mombasa; but already the north-east corner of the Indian Ocean was slipping from their grasp. In 1622 they were finally ejected from the Persian Gulf. By mid-century the seafarers of the maritime state of Oman were regularly raiding as far south as Zanzibar. In 1700 they finally cleared the Portuguese out of Fort Jesus. By the eighteenth century the East African coast north of Cape Delgado had in large measure resumed the late medieval pattern of its external relationships. The wider commercial connections with India and Indonesia, which had given their special lustre to the late medieval culture of the coast, were now only indirect connections. The important Zimbabwean element of the East African trade was still in Portuguese hands; but the essential cultural and commercial contact with the centre of the Islamic world had been re-established. The eighteenth century saw the re-emergence of Swahili city states, mostly under dynasties owing a nominal allegiance to the Ya'rubi Imams of Oman. It was from these bases that the first serious penetration of the central part of the East African interior was to be undertaken.

9 The States of Guinea

We have already seen how in response to two external stimuli, one the arrival from the east, from the Nile valley, of the political concept of the 'Sudanic' state, and the other the expansion from the north, from across the Sahara, of international trade, the black communities of the western and central Sudan formed such considerable states as ancient Ghana and Mali, the Songhai empire, Kanem-Bornu and the Hausa kingdoms. Both the formation and the existence of such states were bound to affect the black peoples living further south, in and near the great tropical forest region of West Africa which is usually termed Guinea.[1]

The early history of Guinea is necessarily more obscure than that of the Sudan. It lay beyond the limits of knowledge of the Arab authors who wrote about the Sudan between the eighth and the fifteenth centuries. From the fifteenth century onwards, European writings become of increasing value; but it was not until the nineteenth century that European observers began to penetrate inland to any significant extent. In so far as the earlier records mentioned events in the interior, it was from hearsay. The historian must therefore rely heavily upon orally maintained traditions whose historicity cannot always be clearly established. However, in some instances archaeology has been able to confirm these traditions (and even occasionally to lengthen their meagre chronological indications).

It is clear, however, that at least by the thirteenth century the

1 The term 'Guinea' was borrowed by the Portuguese from the first African tongue known to them, that of the Moroccan Berbers. Strictly speaking, *Akal n-Iguinawen* means the same in Berber as the Arabic *Bilad as-Sudan*, namely, 'land of the Blacks'. But in modern geographical usage, Guinea is reserved for the forested southern half of West Africa, just as the Sudan is reserved for the savanna northern half.

Dense tropical forest

Land over 3,000 ft (900m)

Approximate lines of major internal trade routes

500 km.

300 miles

L. Chad KANEM

BORNU

Adamawa Highlands

R. Benue

Katsina

Kano HAUSA Zaria

(Nok)

NUPE

Old Oyo YORUBA

Ife Benin

R. Niger

Gao SONGHAI

R. Volta

Timbuctu

Djenne MOSSI

GONJA BANDA Bono AKAN Gold Coast

(Liberia) IVORY COAST

Kumbi Saleh (Ghana)

WANGARA MANDE

Niani (Mali)

R. Niger

R. Senegal

R. Gambia

10°W

0°

10°N

0°

10°E

8 The states of Guinea

Blacks of Guinea had begun to develop states similar in pattern to those of the Sudan. The Guinea states to the west of the Volta river had affinities with the 'Sudanic' states of the upper Niger, with ancient Ghana and Mali. Those to the east of the Volta, on the other hand, had affinities with the states between the Niger and Lake Chad, mainly with Kanem-Bornu and the Hausa kingdoms. The legends of origin for the eastern Guinea states, and the marked similarities in their political structure, indicate that the idea of the 'Sudanic' state spread south and west from the region of ancient Kanem. According to the traditions of the Jukun people living along the Benue, and to those of the Yoruba and kindred peoples now inhabiting the forests of western Nigeria, their states were founded by immigrants from the Nile valley. Such legends are hardly to be taken at their face value, however. They would refer at most to small conquering minorities of the same kind as those who founded the state of Kanem. Moreover, it must certainly not be assumed that such migrants were responsible for all the more civilized aspects of Nigerian art and culture. The probability is that any immigrants from the eastern Sudan came to a region which already possessed an advanced culture. The whole of this Nigerian region south-west of Lake Chad seems to have been one in which agriculture, pottery, metal-work and sculpture had been leading the rest of sub-Saharan Africa since the time of the Nok culture in the first millennium B.C. The magnificent naturalistic sculpture of Ife, though its practitioners may conceivably have learned the technique of metal-casting, for example, from comparatively recent immigrants, nevertheless in its basic inspiration stems from the Nok tradition. The Nile valley influence, therefore, operated primarily in the sphere of political ideas.

Further west, the traditions of origin for the Akan peoples of Ghana, for example, point due north towards the upper Niger. Here, therefore, the idea of the 'Sudanic' state would appear to have come not directly from its eastern source but indirectly from the 'Sudanic' states established in the western Sudan, and here too the 'Sudanic' tradition was subject to the same modifications as in the states to the north.

It would seem reasonable to suppose that the agricultural skill of the peoples of the Sudan, together with their subsequent success in establishing states capable of ruling and trading over wide areas, brought about an appreciable increase in the population of the savanna. It would equally be reasonable to suppose that this growth of population in the Sudan led to a steady infiltration of the forest-lands. The botanical evidence, however, suggests that the occupation of the forest by anything like its present densities of population (which, from Cameroon to the eastern Ivory Coast, are today among the highest in all black Africa) was not feasible before the introduction of the South-East-Asian food-plants. Certainly it is these, together with still later introductions from tropical America, which provide the greater part of the staples of West African forest agriculture today. Early infiltration from the Sudan must therefore have been limited to small groups. The movement seems to have intensified with the growth of states in the Sudan, and to have proceeded fastest in the area between the lower Niger and the Ivory Coast, where the belt of really dense forest is thinnest.

Many of the earliest-known states of peoples like the Akan and the Yoruba, whom today we think of as typical forest-dwellers, in fact originated either north of the true forest or in its northern fringes. The earliest Akan states were Bono and Banda, founded in the orchard bush to the north of the Gold Coast forest, probably about the thirteenth century. The first southward expansion of the Akan from this region seems to have avoided the forest as far as possible by an eastward sweep to the Volta valley, which took them through the forest at its narrowest point and so into the coastal grasslands. The forest itself does not seem to have been directly penetrated to any great extent until about the fifteenth century. Ife, the traditional dispersal-point of those who founded the Yoruba states, and also of the great historic dynasty of Benin, is situated within the Nigerian forest but close to its northern edge. Oyo, the Yoruba state which from the seventeenth century onwards held the political paramountcy, had its centre to the north of the forest and (like the states of the Sudan) employed cavalry, quite unsuited to forest warfare. Horses were likewise at least a ritual symbol of power for the rulers of Benin, whose capital was separated by the whole breadth of the forest from any country where cavalry could have been useful. This suggests that the founders of even the most typically forest states came originally from the savanna. The coherently preserved traditions of Benin indicate that its dynasty was founded by immigrants from Ife some three centuries before the coming of the Portuguese. Modern archaeology has indeed confirmed that Benin City was extant by the thirteenth century, and that the urban culture of Ife goes back to at least the eleventh century.

In common with the states of the western and central Sudan, the society of the Guinea states was markedly urban in character, especially in the east. Though their economy was based on agriculture, there was little of the pattern of dispersed homesteads so common elsewhere in black Africa. The people lived in compact settlements around the houses of their kings and elders, and sallied forth to their fields by day. The settlements varied in size from simple villages, the geographical representation of the basic kinship units, to large towns where members of many kinship units lived in distinct wards around the royal palace, and where there were also quarters set aside for stranger peoples. In the eastern states, most notably among the Yoruba, the geographical pattern was similar to that of the Hausa states further north. The nucleus of the state was a town surrounded by a wall, which enclosed an area large enough to shelter and sometimes possibly even to feed the whole population during an emergency. Most of these Guinean towns lay beyond the sphere of European observation until the nineteenth century. Benin, however, was an exception, and it is quite clear from the accounts given by sixteenth- and seventeenth-century visitors that they regarded it not only as a great city but also as one which might quite fairly be compared with the major European cities of the time. Thus in 1602 a Dutch author observed:

The town seemeth to be very great; when you enter into it, you go into a great broad street, not paved, which seems to be seven or eight times broader than the Warmoes street in Amsterdam; which goeth right out and never crooks . . . it is thought that that street is a mile long [this is a Dutch mile, equal to about three English miles] besides the suburbs. At the gate where I entered on horseback, I saw a very high bulwark, very thick of earth, with a very deep broad ditch . . . Without this gate there is a great suburb. When you are in the great street aforesaid, you see many great streets on the sides thereof, which also go right forth . . . The houses in this town stand in good order, one close and even with the other, as the houses in Holland stand . . . Their rooms within are four-square, over them having a roof that is not close[d] in the middle, at which place the rain, wind and light come in, and therein they lie and eat their meat; but they have other places besides, as kitchens and other rooms . . .

The King's Court is very great, within it having many great four-square plains, which round about them have galleries, wherein there is always watch kept. I was so far within the Court that I passed over four such great plains, and wherever I looked, still I saw gates upon gates to go into other places . . . I went as far as any Netherlander was, which was to the stable where his best horses stood, always passing a great long way. It seems that the King has many soldiers; he has also many gentlemen, who when they come to the court ride upon horses. . . . There are also many men slaves seen in the town, that carry water, yams and palm-wine, which they say is for the King; and many carry grass, which is for their horses; and all this is carried to the Court . . .

The two main southward-flowing streams of influence from the Sudan corresponded in historic times with two major systems of long-distance trade linking the Sudan to Guinea. The dominant traders in the east were the merchants of the Hausa states, whose activities were supplemented towards the south-west by the Yoruba. In the western half of West Africa, Mande merchants were dominant. The two trading systems met at the edge of the forest, north of the Gold Coast, and some idea of their antiquity may be gained from the traditions relating to the trade with this region. It would seem that Mande merchants from Djenne, the metropolis for the trade of the western Sudan to the south, were already visiting Bono, primarily for gold, by about the middle of the fourteenth century. The trade from the north-east seems to have developed slightly later, with Hausa merchants beginning to go to Gonja, north-east of Bono, in the fifteenth century.

Before the appearance of Europeans on the scene, there was thus a network of trade routes linking towns and villages throughout almost the whole of West Africa between the Sahara and the coast. Regular markets were held, often arranged in daily cycles so that neighbouring markets would not compete with one another. Although much trade was doubtless purely local in character, for example the exchange of foodstuffs for local manufactures within a particular area, the operations of the Mande, Hausa and Yoruba merchants were truly international.

It is evident that this long-distance trade was closely connected with the existence of organized states. The regions untouched by the itinerant traders were for the most part difficult country such as marshland and mountain in which simple kinship groupings had escaped the attention of the state-builders. By far the largest of these regions seems to have been the particularly difficult and thinly populated forest of what is now Liberia. However, the correlation between long-distance trade and statehood was positive as well as negative. The staples of the trade were for the most part luxuries rather than necessities. In the first place, most West African communities could grow or manufacture enough to supply their own basic needs. Secondly, the cost of transport was high. This was particularly so in the forest, where head-loading was the rule because animal transport was inhibited by the lack of fodder and the presence of tsetse. It was therefore economic to carry over long distances only commodites whose value was high in proportion to their bulk. A demand for luxuries, of course, implies the existence of a wealthy class. This first existed in West Africa in the shape of kings and their courts, and the specialized professions – administrators, soldiers, artists, metal-workers, court musicians, remembrancers and the like – which they were able to support from their control of the surplus wealth produced by their subjects. This surplus flowed into each court essentially in the form of tribute, and it was doubtless accumulations of tribute in such widely desired commodities as gold or kola-nuts which made the initiation of international trade possible when outside demands arose.

Generally speaking, as has been seen, states developed in the Sudan before they did in Guinea, and this explains the dominating position in the Guinea trade of merchants from the Sudan. The Mande and Hausa merchants doubtless first moved southwards in response to demands coming from the north, across the Sahara, which their own states were able to satisfy only inadequately or not at all. But trade breeds wealth, and so more trade, and Sudanese merchants were soon trading to Guinea to satisfy the demands of their own growing wealthy class, of which, indeed, they themselves were becoming significant members. Nor was this all. The Guinea states also began to trade for their own enrichment, though – with the possible exception of the Yoruba – their trading remained for the most part a royal enterprise. Their merchants were at least as much agents of the kings as members of an independent class doing business on its own account.

The principal exception to the long-distance trade in luxuries alone was the trade in salt, carried into the forest both from the sea and from the Sahara via the Sudan. There was also a trade in cattle and in horses, from the Sudan into Guinea. The principal Guinea exports were gold-dust, which reached the Sudan and ultimately the Mediterranean from workings in the Gold Coast region and the earlier workings in Wangara; kola-nuts, one of the few stimulants tolerated by Islam and therefore valued throughout the Sudan, which also reached the Maghrib; and ivory, though the ivory trade was nothing like as important as it became in European times, when part of the Guinea coast west of the Gold Coast became known as the Ivory Coast. Goods which travelled mainly in the other direction, from north to south, included – besides horses and cattle and some of the salt – beads, trinkets and other small items of metalware such as cutlasses; scarce and therefore valuable base metals such as copper and its alloys; cloth; and cowrie shells. These last, brought all the way from the Indian Ocean via Egypt, serve to remind us that West Africa had well-developed systems of money, as also of weights and measures. In addition to cowries, gold dust, blocks of salt, and pieces of iron, of copper or even of cloth were also recognized mediums of exchange. Not all the beads and cloth traded in Guinea, however, were imports. Some or perhaps most of the cloth had been woven in the Sudan or in North Africa, and some of the beads came from the Mediterranean region; but there was also trade in stone and glass beads and in cloth which had been manufactured in Guinea itself; Yorubaland in particular seems to have exported both.

In view of later developments, there is one striking omission from the list of commodities featuring in the early Guinea trade, namely slaves. This does not mean that slavery and serfdom were unknown. There was little or no surplus free labour in a situation where almost all men were subsistence farmers and land was abundant. The success of any major political or economic enterprise therefore depended on the extent to which a ruling group could force other men to become its servants, retainers, soldiers, craftsmen, labourers, carriers and clients. But this equally meant that there was little desire to dispose of labour for sale, at least until needs developed for other commodities which were equal to or greater than the need for men. In the West African Sudan, this situation may have been reached by the ninth century. The first Arabic reference to trans-Saharan trade in black slaves is of this time; from the twelfth century, such references are common. In the Guinea coastlands it seems clear that it was only with the growing European demand, from the sixteenth century onwards, that the large-scale slave trade developed. The other trades, however, were already well developed by the time of the European arrival on the coast. Thus, when Europeans reached the Gold Coast towards the end of the fifteenth century, they found that Mande merchants were already there, and that among the goods in local demand were Moroccan cloth, and beads and cloth exported from Benin but probably for the most part manufactured by such adjacent peoples as the Yoruba, Ibo and Nupe.

It was this universality of trade in cloth and other luxuries which, together with the largely urban pattern of settlement, chiefly distinguished the Guinea region from all other parts of Africa south of the 'Sudanic' savanna belt, at least during late medieval and early modern times. In the whole of Bantu Africa, imported cotton cloth was known at the time of the first Portuguese contacts only in the urban settlements of the eastern seaboard and in a very limited inland region around the gold-producing area south of the Zambezi. But at the same period in Guinea practically every village was linked by trade of some sort with the Muslim civilization of the Sudan and of North Africa. And when Europeans arrived on the Guinea coast by sea, they accordingly found a fertile field for their commercial activities. In time, however, the entrance of long-distance trade to West Africa from the south was to bring radical changes both to its economy and to the balance of power among its states.

10   The Era of Firearms and the Slave Trade: (1) North and West Africa

As a consequence of the Arab invasions and of the ensuing spread of Islam over most of the northern third of the continent, a larger area of Africa than ever before in historic times had been brought into the mainstream of human history. At the same time, however, the Mediterranean, originally a fertile meeting-place for African, Asian and European peoples and their ideas, had been converted into a political and ideological frontier in constant dispute between the forces of Islam and Christendom. Probably Africa lost little from this; from the eighth to the fourteenth centuries she almost certainly gained more from her partial inclusion in the civilization of Islam than she lost from lack of contact with Europe, then passing through a dark age redeemed only by the surviving light of Christianity. In any case, the Mediterranean frontier was not a complete iron curtain. The Crusades, carried to their objectives by the ships and seamen of the Italian city states, led to the development of a mutually profitable trade between southern Europe and Egypt and the Maghrib. The European side of this trade became increasingly engrossed by Venetian merchants, who proved ultimately far more successful than their rivals in establishing good relations with the Muslim powers. Thus African exports, including West African gold, and Asian luxuries too, via Egypt, continued to filter into Europe, while in return North Africa received valuable iron and timber as well as slaves and manufactures.

In the fifteenth and sixteenth centuries, new and dynamic forces, which were to affect Africa vitally, emerged from this Mediterranean combination of economic cooperation with political and military warfare. Africa north of the Sahara ultimately became much more of a dead frontier-land than before. Other parts of the continent, however, were introduced to the new European demand for African slaves, and received in return from both Europeans and Turks a new weapon, the firearm, which was ultimately to lead to considerable upsets in the balance of power in many parts of Africa.

First of the new forces was the vanguard of the new nation-states of western Europe, Portugal and Spain. Having tempered themselves in the long struggle to free the peninsula from Islam and the Moors, these nations began from 1415 onwards to follow the foe across the Straits of Gibraltar into Morocco. Despite early successes on the coast, the Iberians ultimately failed in their bid to conquer Morocco. Indeed, by the close of the sixteenth century, the principal result of their attacks seemed to have been to consolidate the Moroccan tribes in support of the Sa'did dynasty (1554–1659). Their early involvement in the Maghrib, however, gave the Portuguese new knowledge and new ambitions.[1] They learnt that across the Sahara lay Guinea, a land of gold which was beyond the control of their Muslim enemies. They also learnt that the sphere of Arab navigation included the East African coast, and that Arab geographers believed the whole of the continent to be surrounded by sea. This knowledge, with the promptings and the technical and financial assistance of mariners and merchants from those Italian cities which were being shut out of the Mediterranean trade by Venice, suggested to the popular Aviz dynasty, particularly perhaps to that prince whose name is remembered as Henry the Navigator (1394–1460), a grand design of outflanking Islam by circumnavigating Africa. In so doing Portugal would gain new strength from the gold of Guinea and from cooperation with African Christendom, the power and the extent of which were then commonly exaggerated. She would also break into the Muslim-controlled system of Indian Ocean trade. By importing valuable Asian commodities, especially spices, directly and in bulk, at prices which the Venetians could not match, Portugal would gain immeasurable wealth to further the expansion of Christendom in general and of her own power in particular.

This great enterprise got under way shortly after 1415 and gradually

1 Until 1492, the Spaniards were still to some extent preoccupied with the reduction of Granada, the last Moorish emirate in the peninsula. Thereafter, of course, their external energies were mainly directed to the New World, discovered for them by Columbus in the year when Granada fell.

increased both in momentum and in scope. Portuguese mariners, who had already learnt to master the ocean in the hard school of the Atlantic fisheries, made their first contacts with black Africa in 1444–5, when they reached Cape Verde and the mouth of the Senegal. Shortly afterwards Portugal began to colonize the Cape Verde Islands as a base for trade leading inland towards Mali. By 1471 the Portuguese were at the Gold Coast. They found it so rich in gold that in 1482, at Elmina, they began the first of a series of coastal forts designed to exclude the other European seafarers, now following in their wake, from its profitable trade. By this time, at Benin and at the Congo mouth, they were also in touch with two powerful 'Sudanic' states that seemed to offer considerable opportunities for the expansion of Portuguese trade and influence. In 1488 Bartholomew Diaz rounded the Cape of Good Hope, and this, together with the explorations of Pedro da Covilhan, who had reached India and Ethiopia by the traditional routes, made possible Vasco da Gama's triumphal voyage up the East African coast to India and back again in 1497–9. Egypt and Venice quickly combined to mount a naval assault on the Portuguese in the Indian Ocean, but with the summary defeat of their fleet off Diu in 1509, Portugal's grand design seemed complete. She had gained complete freedom to penetrate sub-Saharan Africa at any point she chose from the Senegal to the Red Sea, and she seemed also to have mastered the whole trade of the western Indian Ocean.

This mastery, however, was soon disputed by the appearance in the Indian Ocean of the Ottoman Turks, who during the fourteenth and fifteenth centuries had built up a formidable military power in Asia Minor, and who in 1517 occupied Egypt. Possession of Egypt enabled the Turks to advance both west to the Maghrib and south-eastwards down the Red Sea; and from the seamen of their Greek coasts and islands, whose own ambitions for booty more or less coincided with the Turkish interest, they were able to derive a seapower which at first seemed almost as formidable as their power on land.

In the east, Turkish fleets ultimately failed in their bid to crush the Portuguese in the Indian Ocean, but they effectively denied them entry to the Red Sea, while (see Chapter 8) their control of the Red Sea's African coast brought guns and fresh energy to its Muslim peoples, endangering the survival of Christian Ethiopia. In the west, the bold advance of their corsairs gained them the control of the whole North African coastline as far west as Morocco. Here the Sa'dids, with the weight of the Moroccan tribes behind them, proved as successful in checking Turkish invasions as they were in containing the ambitions of Spain and Portugal; but Tripoli, Tunis and the new corsair centre of Algiers all became pashaliks of the Ottoman empire. Had the formal seapower of the Turks not gone under to the Christian fleets at Lepanto in 1571, it is possible that North Africa might have become more effectively Turkish than it did. As things were, however, the Ottoman empire there soon became merely nominal. Pashas were regularly sent to Cairo, but the reality of power in Egypt soon reverted to the Mamluks. Bypassed by the main stream of east-west trade, whose diversion to the oceanic route round the Cape of Good Hope was finally confirmed by the Turkish naval defeats, and with its agriculture still at a low ebb, Egypt sank into insignificance until such time as Europe once more sought to open up the direct road to Asia. The Turkish soldiers who had pushed beyond Egypt up the Nile as far as the Third Cataract soon settled down and became no more than a ruling class among the local Sudanese. The rest of the Nilotic Sudan was left to the Beduin tribes and to the Funj Sultans of Sennar, who had succeeded to the power of ancient Alwa.

At Tripoli, the pashalik eventually became the hereditary possession of a local clan. At Tunis and at Algiers, power resided not with the Turks as such but with self-perpetuating cliques descended from the Greek corsairs and the Anatolian janissaries [1] who had originally conquered them for the Ottoman empire. In Tunisia the conquerors gradually merged with the local people. By the eighteenth century (though Tunisia was nominally still subject to Constantinople) a national monarchy, the Husainid Beys, had emerged, able to resume the Hafsid policy of commercial links with the Sudan and with Europe. Between Tunisia and Morocco lay what became known as the Regency of Algiers; and here the position was less happy. In 1711, the Dey, the autocrat elected by the janissaries, finally took over the pashalik, but it can hardly be said that the Regency had a government. The Dey and his soldiers and seamen were rather a band of licensed

---

1 The janissaries were the professional élite of the Ottoman army, composed at this time of forced levies of youths from among the Christians within the Ottoman empire, who were subjected to a rigorous military and Muslim training.

brigands seeking to make profits, on land by periodical predatory raids against the interior tribes, and on sea by corsairing, which had now come to mean the capture of Christian ships and their goods, with the enslavement or holding to ransom of their passengers and crews.[1]

With the control of affairs in North Africa still in the hands of Muslims, largely incapable, except at first in Morocco and later in Tunisia, of maintaining the old ties with the Sudan, and with the Mediterranean after Lepanto dominated increasingly by the navies of the western European states who were developing the oceanic trade routes, the new forces of power politics and trade did not easily reach into black Africa from the north. Nevertheless, by the later sixteenth century, firearms and Turkish military instructors had passed from Egypt to Bornu with considerable consequences. During the fourteenth century, the old dynasty of Kanem had been forced to shelter in Bornu, the province of its empire to the south-west of Lake Chad, following the overrunning of Kanem by the Bulala. These were a people comparable to the Zaghawa, who were themselves being pushed to the west by Beduin tribes overspilling from the Nile valley. The availability of musketry enabled *Mai* Idris Alooma and his immediate successors of the old Kanem line not only to make Bornu the dominant power south and west of Lake Chad but also to assert its suzerainty over the Bulala to the north and east. Furthermore, in Bornu itself, the monarchy was now powerful enough to insist that Muslim concepts of law and government should penetrate directly into the lives of the ordinary people.

At the same time, the Sa'dids of Morocco, at the peak of their power after victories over both the Portuguese and the Turks, sought from 1590 to 1618 to take advantage of dissensions within the Songhai empire in order to secure control of the western Sudan's gold trade for themselves. Small forces of soldiers experienced in musketry and hardened in the Mediterranean wars – many of them were in fact Christian slaves or renegades – proved capable of surviving the Saharan crossing and of defeating the massed levies of the Songhai *Askias*. But with its central government destroyed, the Songhai empire

---

1 Seamen from other parts of the Maghrib also engaged in corsairing during the seventeenth and eighteenth centuries, but it never became such an essential part of the economies of Tunis, Tripoli or Morocco as it did of Algiers.

dissolved into tribal kingdoms, which the Moroccans lacked the strength to police or govern for themselves. The resultant chaos upset the flow of gold and other trade into the commercial cities on the Niger – Timbuktu, Gao and Djenne – which alone they were strong enough to hold, and where their descendants, independent of Morocco after 1660, remained, a futile and increasingly Sudanized military aristocracy. The western Sudan became a battleground in which considerable gains were made by the Tuareg nomads, encroaching from the desert, and the Fulani, black pastoralists infiltrating from the west. The only possible focus of stability lay in the growing kingdom of the Bambara of Segu, which had inherited some at least of the great tradition of its Mande ancestors, and which by about 1670 had imposed its suzerainty on Timbuktu and the other Moorish towns. In the eighteenth century, however, Segu was beset by internal divisions, which finally resulted in the establishment of a rival Bambara kingdom in Kaarta.

One consequence of this disruption of organized government in the western Sudan was to confirm the primacy of the trade routes across the central Sahara to Tunis and Tripoli. After the seventeenth century, when the power of Bornu began to weaken, the southern termini of these roads became firmly fixed in the Hausa states, which, with Kano and Katsina at their head, now entered upon the period of their greatest prosperity and influence. With the principal exception of the trade in slaves to North Africa, however, the trans-Saharan roads were now becoming less significant as major arteries of international commerce, for the trade of Guinea, if not of the Sudan, was being diverted more and more towards the European traders at the coast.

Initially the coming of the European sea-traders had had little effect on the Guinean trade. West Africa, and indeed Africa generally, had less to interest the early European merchant adventurers than either of the other two continents into which they were then breaking. Pre-industrial Europe's requirements from overseas were essentially either luxury manufactures, such as silks, drugs and perfumes, or specialized tropical crops, like spices and sugar. Unlike many Asian peoples, Africans were not organized to produce these for export. On the other hand, unlike the American Indians, such was the density of their population, especially in the richer agricultural

9   West Africa, fifteenth to eighteenth centuries

areas, that, when the problems of climate, disease and communications were also added, the Europeans were prevented from entering Africa to produce what they wanted for themselves. The plantation system was tried in West Africa during the fifteenth and sixteenth centuries, but only on its accessible and manageable off-shore islands. Indeed, it was from the Canaries that the Spaniards transported the system to the West Indies, and from the Cape Verde Islands and from the islands of the Gulf of Guinea, particularly São Tomé, that the Portuguese introduced it to Brazil. Initially, of all the commodities for which there was a steady demand in Europe, West Africa could offer little more than ivory and gold. By the eighteenth century, the supply of the first was greatly diminished; the latter came principally from the Gold Coast, which until the middle of the seventeenth century was the principal focus of European interest to the neglect of other areas. Early Portuguese interest in Benin, for example, waned in part because Portugal was able to get better pepper more expeditiously from Asia.

In the seventeenth century, however, this situation began to change with the rapid growth of the demand for labour by the European plantations in tropical America. The early Spanish colonies there had been supplied with African slaves, mainly through the Portuguese, from about 1510. But it was not until the competitive irruption into the West Indies of the Dutch, French and English in the seventeenth century, when there was a rapidly growing European demand for sugar – a crop making heavy demands on labour – that the transatlantic slave trade began to dominate European activities in West Africa. Compared with an estimate of some 275,000 black slaves landed overseas by 1600, the seventeenth-century figure is thought to be at least 1,340,000; the figures for the eighteenth and nineteenth centuries seem to have been at least 6,050,000 and 1,900,000 respectively. The new development was pioneered by the Dutch, who by 1642 had permanently ousted the Portuguese from the Gold Coast. The success of the Dutch provoked English and French hostility, and by the eighteenth century it was the traders of these two nations who were the principal competitors in the international trade, though the Portuguese continued with a private slave trade of their own, from Angola and São Tomé to Brazil. In terms of trade alone, victory went to Britain. By the end of the eighteenth century, her ships were carrying nearly half the slaves taken to America. This was in part a reflection of the growing maritime and commercial ascendancy of Britain in Europe, but it was also due to the fact that British activities became concentrated from the Gold Coast eastwards, on the shores of the most thickly populated and economically most developed region of Guinea. The coast between the Gold Coast and the Niger Delta, in fact, was soon known as the Slave Coast. The main area of French activity was in the Senegal–Gambia region, and though the French penetrated some 300 miles up the River Senegal, the results were disappointing, since the westernmost Sudan was now relatively poor both in population and in trade.

The French penetration up the Senegal was exceptional. The normal practice was for the Europeans to stay at the coast – in forts like those erected in large numbers on the Gold Coast during the seventeenth century, in hulks moored in river mouths such as those of the Niger Delta, or in factories [1] in or close to the African towns which developed on the coast as a consequence of the trade. Invariably the Europeans bought their slaves from African kings or merchants. This explains the early concentration of European slave traders on the Gold Coast, for it was there that the African taste for European imports – cloth, hardware and metals, spirits and firearms – was probably better established than elsewhere, while the African traders who were already accustomed to supplying the Europeans with gold were willing to supply slaves too when the demand for these developed. The persistent growth of the demand led to the extension of the trade, principally eastwards, towards the Niger Delta and beyond, rather than towards the less economically developed and more thinly populated western coasts. The early slave trade was largely a catch-as-catch-can affair, but after *c.*1650, as the demand for slaves increased, and as Europeans provided increasing quantities of firearms in exchange, it became a big business organized in their own interests by a series of large new kingdoms which developed close to the Guinea coasts.

During the eighteenth century, the export slave trade began to have revolutionary effects on the West African scene. It does not, however, seem to have occasioned devastation and depopulation on

1 This is the original use of the word factory, namely 'a merchant company's foreign trading station', the place where their factors (i.e. merchants) did business.

the scale produced in other parts of Africa, like Angola or, much later, East Africa. The reasons for this have not been unequivocally established, but it would seem that the loss of manpower from Guinea, which in the eighteenth century may have averaged 44,000 fit young men and women a year, was not a crippling rate of loss in relation to the total population.[1] Moreover, in a purely *economic* sense (if in no other), it would seem that much of this loss was made good by the increase of wealth brought to the more advanced Guinean communities through their trade with Europe. In both respects, the Angolan and East African situations were different; populations there were relatively thin, and the indigenous economies often not far removed from the subsistence level, so that even a small loss of productive manpower could be disastrous.

The general effect of the Atlantic slave trade was, indeed, to move the centres of wealth and power in West Africa away from the Sudan and towards the coast. The direct European share in this was negligible. The French, firmly established on the lower Senegal and at Gorée, and the British, Dutch and Danes, who occupied the Gold Coast forts, hardly possessed extensive political influence. Even the Gold Coast forts, impressive architectural monuments to the bitter European competition of the seventeenth century, were built on land leased from the local African states. In the last resort their lonely garrisons were unable to withstand determined opposition from the Africans of the towns which came to cluster round them. However, a community of interest existed, which came to ally the Europeans with their African neighbours when both were threatened by the growth of new states in the immediate hinterland, and from this, in the nineteenth century, the seeds of colonialism could grow.

The most impressive development of the seventeenth and eighteenth centuries was the growth of African states just inland from the coastlands. Initially the only major kingdom near the sea was Benin. But Benin, reacting to early Portuguese attempts to infiltrate its society, took little part in the new trade before the eighteenth century.

---

1 This estimate for the eighteenth century represents a higher rate of loss than that suggested by the overall estimates given on p. 101. But the latter are for slaves *landed overseas*, and allowance must be made for the mortality on the voyage across the Atlantic, which could be high, and must, on the average, have been at least 16 per cent. A further allowance should be made for the loss of life caused by slaving operations in Africa, but this is quite impossible to evaluate.

The new centres of power were somewhat further inland. An early development was the short-lived empire of the Akan state of Akwamu, which between about 1680 and about 1730 expanded parallel with the eastern Gold Coast and the western Slave Coast in an attempt to engross the whole trade of their hinterlands with the south. Akwamu, however, failed to find a principle of administration capable of securing an enduring allegiance from its Ga and Ewe subjects, and its place as the major Gold Coast power was soon taken by Ashanti. In the early eighteenth century, Ashanti, learning from Akwamu experience, began to expand to the north, incorporating or making tributary states like Bono, Banda, Gonja and Dagomba. Then, with the trade of the interior profitably secured, she turned south to seek direct contact with the European traders. Further east, the relatively new kingdom of Dahomey among the Aja began to advance to the coast early in the eighteenth century, conquering other Aja states such as Allada and Whydah, whose political structures had been weakened by the growth of European influence on the Slave Coast. But Dahomey itself was forced to pay tribute to Oyo, the most northerly of the Yoruba states, which was its neighbour to the northeast. Oyo had begun to feel the pull of trade with the Slave Coast early in the seventeenth century. Eventually it embarked on policies of military and political expansion which led, in the following century, to the establishment of an Oyo paramountcy over more southerly Yoruba peoples, and also to the diversion of much of the local slave trade from the coast of Dahomey to more easterly ports like Badagri and Lagos.

By the end of the eighteenth century, then, over three centuries of European trade on the coasts of West Africa had led to little penetration of European influences. The Christian missionary effort in Guinea had been negligible; only the early Portuguese had been at all interested in the expansion of Christendom. Their early mission to Benin was soon withdrawn to Warri, where it lingered into the seventeenth century, but they were even less successful in creating a native Christian state here than in the Congo. Their other principal field of mission activity was in the coastlands opposite the Cape Verde Islands; here the best that could be achieved was the creation of a doubtfully Christian class of half-caste traders. With hardly another exception, the Europeans who had gone to West Africa were interested solely in exporting its produce, and in effect only in the slave trade. Permanent European settlement on the coast, as on the Gold Coast and at the mouth of the Senegal, did tend to produce a thin layer of coastal Africans who were partly European in their outlook and even, sometimes, in their formal education. But the vast mass of West Africa and its peoples remained untouched by direct European influence. The principal effect of the coming of European traders to the coast, of their demand for slaves and their introduction of new goods, of which firearms were the most influential, was to stimulate in Guinea a potent new coastwards-looking manifestation of the well-established 'Sudanic' civilization.

11 The Era of Firearms and the Slave Trade: (2) From the Congo to the Zambezi

When the Portuguese discovered the estuary of the Congo in 1482, they found themselves in contact with one of the largest states in Africa south of the Sahara, and with one of the very few large states situated anywhere near the coastline. This was the kingdom of the *Ba*kongo, a Bantu people whose king, the *Mani*kongo, had his capital at *Mbanza*kongo, the modern São Salvador in northern Angola. The Kongo kingdom was a typical 'Sudanic' state, the nucleus of which had been founded, probably in the late fourteenth or early fifteenth century, by a conquering group from the little state of Bungu on the north bank of the lower Congo. The founders were sufficiently numerous to introduce the Kongo language and gradually to subject and assimilate an indigenous population, most of which previously spoke Mbundu. The Bakongo founders were remembered especially as clever smiths. On this account they had been formidable both as hunters and as warriors, and in the Kongo kingdom smiths were always afterwards treated to chiefly honours and privileges. Most of the kingdom was directly administered by the Manikongo through a hierarchy of appointed chiefs and subchiefs. It was bounded by the Atlantic, the Congo, the Kwango and the Dande, and its population was estimated by a seventeenth-century missionary at 2.5 million. Around the directly administered provinces were clusters of smaller states which formed part of the same complex. Between the Congo estuary and the Kwilu Niari, the next big river to the north of it, were the three kingdoms of Ngoyo, Kakongo and Loango, which had likewise been created by Kongo-speaking conquerors from Bungu. To the east and south were large regions, such as Okango, Matamba and Ndongo, where scores of small indigenous kingdoms paid fitful tribute to the Manikongo in order to avoid the attention of his raiding armies. At the time of the first Portuguese contacts the most important of many small rulers in the Ndongo region was one with the hereditary title Ngola, whence the name of the Portuguese colony.

From the end of the fifteenth until the last quarter of the sixteenth century, however, the Portuguese concentrated their efforts not upon Angola but upon the main Kongo kingdom. Missionaries were sent in 1490, with masons, carpenters and other skilled artisans. The Manikongo, most of his family and some of his great chiefs were converted; the capital was rebuilt in stone; and many young Congolese were removed to Europe for education. As was only to be expected, most of the early converts proved not very serious; but concerning one of them, at least, there was never any doubt. Nzinga Mbemba, baptized as Afonso in 1491, succeeded to the throne in 1507 and ruled as an ardent and enlightened Christian until his death in 1543. It was his wholly sincere wish to remodel his kingdom along the lines of those of western Europe, and had the Portuguese been able to sustain the partial altruism of their early contacts, he might have gone far towards succeeding. Unfortunately, the extension of the slave trade soon began to loom larger in Portuguese aims than the creation of a Christian state in Africa.

There had been slavery in Kongo, as in every other part of Africa, long before Europeans began to export slaves overseas; and even Afonso, though he made clear his dislike of the trade, was willing to pay in slaves for the European goods and services which he regarded as essential. The demand for labour in Portugal's transatlantic colony of Brazil, however, was soon such that it could be supplied only by more warlike means than Afonso and his successors were prepared or able to employ. Though a handful of missionaries continued to work in the Kongo kingdom, Portuguese 'aid' soon dried up; and in 1575 Paulo Dias de Novais was sent as a *conquistador* to inaugurate a new phase in Portuguese relations with West Central Africa. Paulo Dias made his base at Luanda, a little to the south of the Kongo frontier, and thence initiated a century-long war of conquest against the Ngolas of Ndongo. Officially, relations with the Manikongos remained peaceful. But the new Portuguese method of colonization, aimed principally at supplying the slave trade, was to train and arm bands of native 'allies' to make war on the peoples all round the slowly expanding frontier of the colony; and naturally it was not long before the Kongo kingdom's southern provinces became a favourite target for such forays. Early seventeenth-century Manikongos, all of whom were still Christian in name, and some so in practice, addressed pitiful appeals

10 Africa from the Congo to the Zambezi

to the Holy See through their missionaries. Several Popes showed a personal concern in the situation, and stern letters passed from Rome to Lisbon, but the Portuguese government declared itself powerless to control its subjects in Angola. Finally, in 1660 the Bakongo turned to war – with disastrous results. Defeated by the Portuguese and their allies in a series of battles, the Manikongos were left too weak to maintain the internal unity of their kingdom. Peripheral provinces broke away, rival dynasties competed for the throne, even the missionary contacts with the outside world broke down; so that by the end of the eighteenth century Christianity was but a memory, and the former kingdom had shrivelled to a few villages around São Salvador.

Angola remained the supply-base for the Brazil slave trade, and during the seventeenth and eighteenth centuries was converted into a howling wilderness. The Kongo kingdom, as we have seen, was near enough to the storm to be torn apart by it. More interesting, and far less destructive, were the indirect effects of the Portuguese presence upon the peoples living in the far interior, where no Portuguese ever penetrated until the eve of the nineteenth century. The utter limit of direct Portuguese penetration in Angola was the valley of the Kwango – the first of the great northward-flowing tributaries of the Congo. Beyond the upper Kwango, between it and the upper Kasai, and eastwards again to the Lualaba, lived the Lunda. They were matrilineal Bantu peoples, not very unlike the original inhabitants of Angola and the Kongo kingdom before their conquest by the Bakongo. From traditional history it seems that the Lunda had no large states or powerful chiefs until there appeared in their midst, perhaps towards the end of the fifteenth century, a small group of Luba ivory-hunters who proceeded, by diplomacy and prestige as well as by force, to build up a 'Sudanic' state whose kings later took the dynastic title of Mwata Yamvo. Moreover, as with other conquest states of this kind, the Mwata Yamvos' kingdom was soon surrounded by a mushroom growth of Luba-Lunda satellites, which by the middle of the seventeenth century covered a very large area indeed of the present southern Zaire, western Angola and northern Zambia.

Almost from the start of its existence, the Mwata Yamvos' kingdom was in indirect commercial touch with the Portuguese in Angola, and in this way was receiving firearms and powder, as well as cloth and other luxuries, from overseas. It is difficult in fact not to conclude that the larger state-building operation in this instance had an economic motive. The immediate perimeter of the Portuguese colony was dominated by the slave trade, and here warfare and destruction were the main result. Beyond this perimeter the main commodity of value for export was ivory, the hunting and handling of which, though highly lucrative, required large-scale organization of a political kind. This political and economic know-how already existed in the Luba region of northern Katanga. It looks very much as though it was mainly in response to the economic stimulus provided by the Portuguese opening of the Atlantic coast that the extension of state-formation into the vast area of Luba-Lunda domination was carried out.

The last large extension of the Luba–Lunda system was a south-easterly movement from the Mwata Yamvos' kingdom undertaken during the early eighteenth century, which established the important kingdom of the Kazembes, with its capital in the Luapula valley a little to the south of Lake Mweru. The Lunda of Kazembe, who established this new state with the aid of guns which came ultimately from the Portuguese in Luanda, were soon trading their ivory to the Portuguese stations on the Zambezi. In this sense it may be said that Portuguese influence was indirectly felt from coast to coast of Africa.

South of Angola lay the parched lands of South-West Africa, with their sparse hunting and pastoral communities of Herero and Khoisan. The Portuguese did not settle there, nor yet at the Cape of Good Hope, which seemed to them to answer better to its earlier name, the Cape of Storms. It was only in the middle of the seventeenth century, when the Dutch had discovered how to sail east on the trade winds, taking wide sweeps across both the South Atlantic and the south of the Indian Ocean, that the Cape acquired its unique position as the 'half-way house to the Indies'. For the Portuguese, who crossed the Indian Ocean on the monsoon from Moçambique to Goa, the Cape was merely an obstacle across their path, one apt to be the scene of shipwreck if storms were encountered on the return journey.

Most of our early information about South Africa comes, in fact, from shipwrecked Portuguese who trekked to safety across parts of the Transkei, Pondoland, Natal and southern Moçambique. Their accounts show that at this time, contrary to the beliefs of most present-day white South Africans, South Africa was by no means empty of Bantu inhabitants. The Cape Province west of the Kei was inhabited only by Khoisan hunter-gatherers; but east of the Kei, peoples who can be identified as Xhosa and Tembu and Pondo and the Nguni ancestors of the Zulu lived very much where their descendants were living when they were overtaken by the Great Trek of the Boer frontiersmen in the 1830s and 1840s. Long before there were any white South Africans, the Bantu had in fact occupied the only parts of the subcontinent with a climate and rainfall suited to intensive agriculture. They had left the high and dry Karroo of the central plateau, like the deserts to the west of it, to the pastoral Khoi and San hunter-gatherers. These, therefore, were the immediate neighbours of the small Dutch colony planted at the Cape in 1652 in order to supply fresh food for the passing Indiamen. It was not until over a century later that the expanding colonists first encountered the Bantu, near the Fish River, some 500 miles to the east of Cape Town.

Apart from Zaire and Angola, the other principal scene of early contact between black and white was in the region of the Lower Zambezi. Here, as we have seen, the Portuguese tried to take over a trade in gold and ivory which had been the main attraction of East Coast traders since the tenth century at least, and perhaps a little earlier. When the Portuguese took over control of Sofala at the beginning of the sixteenth century, they soon learned that the leading power in the interior was that of the Vakaranga, one of the Shona-speaking peoples of Zimbabwe, whose ruler was known by the title of *Mwenemutapa* or, as the Portuguese usually wrote it, Monomotapa. At this period the capital of the Karanga kingdom lay a hundred miles or so to the north of modern Harare, at the nothernmost edge of the Zimbabwean plateau, which here drops away northwards to the Zambezi valley in a steep escarpment of nearly 3,000 feet. This sixteenth-century capital thus lay nearly 200 miles to the north of the main gold-bearing areas in the east and centre of the plateau. It also lay nearly 300 miles to the north of the area of stone ruins, which coincides with the belt of boulder-topped granite hills in the southern sector of the plateau, where the land begins to fall gently towards the

Limpopo in the south and the Kalahari in the west. According to their own account, however, the Vakaranga had moved north, under their Monomotapa dynasty, owing to the exhaustion of their salt supplies, only towards the middle of the fifteenth century. They remembered that in their former country the royal capital, or *zimbabwe*, had been made of stone. In some sense, therefore, the Monomotapa dynasty was a descendant of that which had occupied the earliest stone-built royal capital and hill 'temple' at Great Zimbabwe, which archaeologists today attribute to a period from about the eleventh till about the fifteenth century. According to the latest interpretations, Great Zimbabwe was the capital of a dynasty whose wealth was ultimately derived from the control of gold exports from the central Zimbabwean plateau but whose main investment of that wealth consisted in the accumulation of large herds of cattle, the cattle being pastured on the southern slopes of the plateau and moved up and down hill in a system of transhumance which followed the seasonal advance and retreat of the tsetse fly. As the system developed, it spread to the northern slopes of the plateau, where the exportable wealth consisted in the copper and ivory of the Zambezi valley. On this showing, the Monomotapa dynasty was merely the most successful of several Karanga lineages which had moved north to exploit this opening. By the late fifteenth century it had consolidated a very large area indeed under its suzerainty. It ruled the Zambezi valley for about 700 miles of its length, from the Kariba gorge to the sea. It ruled the northern and eastern parts of the plateau, and the lowlands of southern Moçambique between the Zambezi and the Limpopo. The region which it did not succeed in ruling was that from which its ancestors had sprung. Great Zimbabwe, abandoned in the fifteenth century, passed under the rule of another successor dynasty, that of the Torwa, with its centre at Khami, near modern Bulawayo. This was the kingdom of Butwa, to which the Portuguese never penetrated, the trade of which descended the Zambezi to their entrepôts. As with the Lunda kingdoms, the stimulus of indirect trade contacts was happier in its effects than the direct Portuguese influences experienced by the Kongo kingdom and by that of the Monomotapas.

The first Portuguese contacts with the lands of the Monomotapas were with the tributary kingdoms lying in the hinterland of Sofala, and there is little doubt that Portuguese influence helped to loosen their bonds with the parent state. The next Portuguese moves were up the Zambezi, where they founded (or took over from Arab and Swahili traders) the river-ports of Sena and Tete. Here they were in territory directly ruled by the Monomotapas. Tete, occupied in 1560, was only four or five days' march from the capital. The first Portuguese to go there was a missionary, Gonzalo de Silveira, who baptized the Monomotapa but was immediately murdered at the instigation of the king's Muslim advisers. A series of military expeditions over the next fifteen years brought the Monomotapas into treaty relations with the Portuguese, and in the early seventeenth century this dependence was further reinforced when later Monomotapas required assistance against their over-mighty subjects. In 1629 the Monomotapa Mavura declared himself a Portuguese vassal, and thus heralded his kingdom's final decline. On the one hand his dominion in the lower Zambezi valley was eroded by the establishment of Portuguese *prazos*, private slave-run concessions. On the other hand, more and more of his up-country subjects defected to the Changamires, a subdynasty reigning on the high plateau, which refused to bow to Portuguese overrule. In a campaign lasting from 1693 till 1695 the Changamires finally drove the Monomotapas off the plateau, leaving them to rule a tiny remnant of their former territories in the valley between Tete and Zumbo, as puny puppets of the Portuguese. From there the Changamires went on to conquer the state of Butwa, establishing their capital at Dhlo Dhlo (Danangombe). The later history of the Changamires' kingdom has yet to be recovered by studying the traditional history of its surviving remnants. The short answer, however, is that it was brought to an end by the great Zulu warrior emigration from Natal during the second quarter of the nineteenth century, which will be described in a later chapter.

Viewed simply as an exercise in European colonization, the Portuguese achievement in Africa from the end of the fifteenth century until the end of the eighteenth was not great or constructive. Some of their missionary work was heroic; much more of it was mere time-serving by clergy unwanted at home. Some of its individual fruits were astonishing and impressive, but nowhere were adequate foundations laid to ensure the transmission of a faith very alien to earlier African beliefs and customs. Portuguese colonization was hardly more successful on the material plane. Angola was a mere shambles, in which the criminal classes of Portugal were employed in inciting the native peoples to make war on each other in the interests of slave labour for Brazil. Moçambique, based on gold rather than on slaves, was a shade less bloody but hardly less vicious. The effect of the two penetrations into the African mainland was almost wholly injurious to the African societies with which they came into direct contact. The presence of the Portuguese was an advantage only to those who were fortunate enough to be a little further removed from them. Trade is always a valuable stimulus to those who take part in it: ideas are exchanged along with goods, the discoveries of one set of people are transmitted to another. It was not only that the Portuguese placed some of Africa in touch with the outside world; through the opening of new long-distance trade routes, different African societies were also placed in touch with each other. Of the imports into Africa from the outside during these three centuries, the most important were certainly the new food plants which the Portuguese introduced from South America. Three of these at least – cassava, maize and sweet potato – made a tremendous difference to food supplies, especially in the more humid equatorial regions. It seems likely, indeed, that the depopulation caused in some districts by the slave trade was more than offset by the growth of population through these new means of subsistence in tropical Africa as a whole. Viewed as a period in African history, the three centuries in which Portugal was the dominant external influence were by no means insignificant.

12 The Turn of the Tide in Europe

For as long as the commercial relations between Africa and the outside world remained centred upon the slave trade, it was inevitable that contact should be slight and influence indirect. The maritime slave trader had no incentive to go inland from his coastal forts or hulks, and his operations did not make it easier for others to do so. To the inevitable difficulties of climate, disease, terrain, supplies and insecurity, the slave trade always added the hostility of the African middleman communities, who bought cheap inland and sold dear at the coast, and were therefore quick to suspect potential competitors. Even more seriously deterrent, however, was the influence of the European slave-trading interest upon those in their own countries who might otherwise have attempted to make contacts of another sort. The slave trade was profitable enough to discourage almost all attempts to develop other kinds of commerce. Moreover, even though the absolute wickedness of slavery was a late discovery of the Christian conscience, the actual practice of the slave trade was so manifestly ugly, even to those who took part in it, that the prying eyes of the disinterested observer were very actively discouraged. In the older Portuguese colonies missionaries existed on sufferance, and the government of Portugal took the most active measures to prevent the Popes from sending to Africa missionaries who were not under its own control. Not until the anti-slave-trade movement had won a decisive victory in Europe itself was it practicable to organize from Europe any other kind of contact with Africa.

The slave-trading interest suffered its first serious reverse in Britain, mainly perhaps because it was there that it most obviously overreached itself. In the mid-eighteenth century, the West Indies with their slave-produced sugar were described as the richest jewel in the English crown. Had the West Indian planters confined their use of slave labour to the Caribbean, it might have been much longer before they were attacked. When planters began to bring their domestic slaves back with them to England, however, they presented an obvious target for the attack of the more radical Christians, and despite the owners' care for the interests of property, the courts were eventually forced to declare that there was no such thing as slavery in English law. Lord Mansfield's famous judgement on a test case in 1772 was the first victory for a small pressure group composed mainly of evangelical Christians, who proceeded to organize a relentless campaign against the British slave trade, and later, with equal success, against the institution of slavery in Britain's overseas territories. Eventually Parliament was prevailed upon to pass a law in 1807 which made the slave trade illegal for British subjects, and to follow this up four years later with another Act imposing very heavy penalties on any who continued in it. As a result, it may be said that from 1811 Britons ceased to engage in the trade.

Nothing better illustrates the exclusive character of the slave trade than the fact that having once abandoned it, Britain immediately proceeded to attack its continued practice by other nations. This was not done out of pure philanthropy or even self-righteousness but for sound commercial reasons. Since the trade in slaves was easier and more profitable than any other African trade, it had to be internationally suppressed before what was called 'legitimate' commerce between Africa and Europe could develop. The Danes had anticipated the British abolition by three years; the slave trade became illegal for the United States in 1808; and the Dutch outlawed it in 1814. Under British pressure, most of the other maritime nations followed suit after the Napoleonic wars, though at first Portugal and Spain (where the slave trade had only *become* legal in 1789) could be induced only to limit their slave trade to the seas south of the equator.

By about 1842 the carriage of slaves across the Atlantic was technically an illegal activity for the seamen of almost all European and American nations. But this did not mean the cessation of the trade. In the first place, only Britain had both an adequate will and adequate naval means to enforce her laws on the high seas, though at times, and especially from the 1840s onwards, both France and the United States contributed some naval effort to the anti-slave-trade cause.

Britain therefore engaged in a second diplomatic campaign, to persuade other nations to grant British cruisers the right to arrest slaveships sailing under their flags. This campaign not unnaturally aroused considerable resentment abroad; little Portugal was virtually forced to comply, but France and the United States, ancient naval foes of Britain, steadfastly refused to give her the powers she sought. Secondly, while in the ancient sugar colonies of the British and French West Indies the slave interest was dying or dead, in the United States, Brazil and Cuba it was rapidly expanding over virgin lands to meet new demands for cotton or sugar. As long as there was a profitable market for slaves in the Americas, men could be found to defy their countries' laws and to risk the British naval patrols. Though the naval measures against the slave trade began to have some effect after the 1840s, Britain became involved in yet a third campaign, to persuade or force African rulers to outlaw the export of slaves from their territories. France also acted similarly from time to time, but it was much more typically a British activity. In this way an important new element in the contacts between Europe and Africa began to develop. The presence of naval patrols made it possible for legitimate traders to operate, even in competition with slave traders, and from 1849 onwards, in addition to the cruisers there were consuls with the task of aligning African communities on the side of legitimate commerce. Ultimately, however, it was not any action in Africa which finally extinguished the slave trade but the cessation of the demand on the other side of the Atlantic. The victory of the North over the slave-owning South of the United States in 1865 was rounded off by the final abolition of slavery in both Cuba and Brazil in the 1880s.

In Britain especially, the anti-slavery movement remained intimately linked with the religious enthusiasms of its founders. Protestant Christianity had in general been slow to recognize its duty of preaching the gospel to every human being. For the first two or three centuries of their existence, the various reformed Churches had been almost exclusively occupied with the problems of their own survival. Towards the end of the eighteenth century, however, in pietistic circles of both Lutheran and Calvinist tendency, there swept over northern Europe a concern, almost unprecedented since the early centuries of Christendom, for the conversion of the non-Christian peoples of the world. The earliest manifestation of this movement was perhaps the formation in 1722 of the Lutheran sect later called the Moravian Brethren, every member of which regarded himself as a potential missionary to the heathen. In England the Baptists were the first to be affected and to found a Missionary Society in 1792, with British India as its primary field of operations. They were soon followed by independent and mainly Congregationalist groups who founded the London Missionary Society, which was to work first of all in the Pacific and in South Africa. In the Society for the Propagation of the Gospel, the Anglican Church already had an organization originally intended to minister to Anglican emigrants overseas, and this was to become increasingly concerned with missions to non-Christians, especially in southern Africa. In addition, in 1799 Anglicans of evangelical views founded the Church Missionary Society, which was to develop important fields of work in both West and East Africa. The early nineteenth century saw the foundation of many other Protestant missionary societies, of which the most important for Africa were the Methodist Missionary Society, with missions in West and South Africa; the Basel Society, with missions in West Africa; the Berlin Society, with missions in South and later in East Africa; the Universities Mission, a high Anglican society, with its field in the central part of East Africa; and the missions of the Scottish Presbyterian Churches in South Africa, West Africa and East Africa.

To the Roman Catholic Church, the idea of missions to the heathen was, of course, not a new one. Nevertheless, the missions undertaken during the sixteenth and seventeenth centuries in Asia, Africa and the Americas had been to a very large extent indeed undertaken by Portuguese and Spanish clergy, and in the eighteenth century the ecclesiastical effort of the Iberian countries declined along with their secular energies. In 1622 the Holy See had attempted to centralize the direction of missionary work in Rome by creating the Sacred Congregation of the Propaganda, but because of vested interests the Spanish and Portuguese colonies were excluded from its jurisdiction, and it was more than two centuries before any really fresh impetus occurred in Roman Catholic missions to Africa and the East. The most vital of these nineteenth-century movements began in France; and for Africa, by very much the most important was the refoundation in 1848 of the Congregation of the Holy Ghost, whose members worked in West Africa, in Gabon, in the Lower Congo, in South-West Africa and in the coastal regions of East Africa. A later development, again French in origin, was Cardinal Lavigerie's foundation in 1868 of the Society of Our Lady of Africa, commonly known as the White Fathers. From their original base in Algeria, the White Fathers were to undertake missions all over the centre of the continent, both in the interior of West Africa and on both sides of the Great Lakes, from Uganda in the north to northern Zambia in the south. Both of these great new orders, and their counterparts for women, were to become international in membership and in due course be joined in Africa by contingents from the older orders and congregations – Benedictines, Franciscans, Dominicans, Jesuits – as well as by those of many newer foundations such as the Society of the Divine Word and the Mill Hill Society of St Joseph.

The foundation of a great missionary society, even more than that of a government department or a great commercial company, is something which takes time to get under way. Recruits have to be found and trained for many years. Financial support has to be developed through a wide network of worshipping congregations. The setbacks arising from the first and inevitably costly ventures into the unknown have to be overcome. Half-way through the nineteenth century, the missionary movement into Africa was still only beginning to gather momentum. Not until the seventies did it acquire any really impressive geographical spread. But the existence of the movement in embryo from the end of the eighteenth century onwards was one of the great new factors in the relationship between Europe and Africa. It was perhaps through the actions of their missionary representatives as much as through the actions of their governments that the people of Europe, and later of America, were to make their influence felt among the peoples of Africa. And missionary action, unlike that of governments, was not confined to the narrow circle of the colonial powers.

Before any of these new influences, whether missionary or commercial, could play directly or strongly upon the African scene, there had to be an end to the outside world's almost total ignorance of Africa. To late-eighteenth-century Europe, Africa was little more than a coastline, a coastline not very representative of the interior. North Africa was a part of the Muslim world, which was still almost closed to Christians from the west. The Barbary states, famed for piracy, were known mainly through the accounts of the few Christian slaves who had been captured by the corsairs and been fortunate enough to escape or be ransomed. A handful of Europeans disguised in Arab dress had travelled up the Nile from Cairo. One or two, including the Scottish laird James Bruce, had penetrated to the Ethiopian capital at Gondar or to that of the Funj kingdom at Sennar on the Blue Nile. Among the other great rivers of Africa, the Zambezi was known for some 700 miles from its mouth, and the Congo for less than a hundred. No European had yet seen the Niger, the very mouth of which was unknown. Following the mistake of Leo Africanus in the early sixteenth century, it was widely believed to flow from east to west. The only African societies known to eighteenth-century Europeans were those of the forest regions of West and West Central Africa. Despite the writings of Leo Africanus, and despite the seventeenth- and eighteenth-century probings up the Senegal by the French, it was scarcely appreciated that behind those forests to the north there lay open country where peasants grew grain crops and pastured cattle, and where Muslim town-dwellers traded their manufactures on camelback to Egypt and the Maghrib. It was certainly unsuspected that behind the forests to the east the spine of Africa consisted of high plateaux, 4,000 or 5,000 feet above sea level, all the way from Ethiopia to the Cape.

The European exploration of inner Africa was in large measure yet another manifestation of the humanitarian movement which was attacking the slave trade and seeking to put Christianity and legitimate commerce in its place. The geographical movement started just before the end of the eighteenth century, and it took about seventy-five or eighty years for the main facts to be established. The first probings were made from the north and west, under the auspices of the Association for the Discovery of the Interior Parts of Africa, a small group of wealthy Englishmen of whom some were prompted mainly by scientific and others mainly by humanitarian interests. It was the 'African Association' which financed the notable first journey of Mungo Park in 1795–7 to the upper Niger, an expedition which established that the river flowed eastwards. It was the influence of some members of the association, notably Sir Joseph Banks and Sir John Barrow, which succeeded in implanting in the British government the idea that African exploration was a proper subject for official expenditure. It was in British government pay that Park returned to Africa, to sail down most of the course of the Niger in 1805–6; that Denham and Clapperton explored Bornu and Hausaland after crossing the Sahara from Tripoli during 1823–5; that the Lander brothers traced the course of the lower Niger to the sea in 1830; and that the great German explorer Heinrich Barth undertook his meticulous explorations in the central and western Sudan during 1850–55.

Until the eve of their great political expansion in the 1870s, the French contributed surprisingly little to the exploration of western Africa, in view of the extent of their previous involvement in the slave trade and of their earlier penetration of the Senegal. Only the great 1827–8 journey of René Caillié, from the Rio Nuñez to Timbuktu and across the Sahara to Tangier, really compares with journeys such as those of Park or Clapperton, and this was a private initiative unsupported by government. In view of developments after 1883, however, it is worth recording the not inconsiderable part taken by German-speakers in the European opening-up of Africa, both as explorers and as missionaries, though sometimes, like Barth, they found their opportunities under British auspices. Early German activities were by no means confined to western Africa. The pioneers both of missionary work and of the exploration of the interior on the East African mainland were two German members of the Church Missionary Society, Krapf and Rebmann, who in 1847–9 were the first Europeans to see the snow-capped peaks of Kilimanjaro and Mt Kenya. Beyond 1862 and 1869, Gerhard Rohlfs made very extensive journeys in the North African Sahara, and his work was later extended by other Germans, notably Gustav Nachtigal, who in 1870–74 explored the Sudan between Lake Chad and the Nile. During 1860–72, Karl Mauch was the first European in modern times to explore the region of the ancient Monomotapas. The Moravian Brethren were the first Protestant missionaries to Africa, arriving at the Cape in 1792; the Basel Mission was the first on the Gold Coast in 1828, and was followed there by the Bremen Mission in 1847, the year in which the Rhenish Mission was the first to be established in South-West Africa.

On the whole, however, it may be said that Europe's interest in the exploration of southern and eastern Africa began only when the geo-

graphical problems of West Africa were approaching solution, and
that the initiative here again was a British one. It is significant that
despite the existence of a colonists' frontier in the south, it was the
missionaries who at every stage of nineteenth-century South African
history lived farthest north; and it was a missionary, David Livingstone, who in 1853–6 travelled from the south overland to the
Victoria Falls and thence westwards to Luanda and eastwards again
to the mouth of the Zambezi. Livingstone published his explorations
under the title of *Missionary Travels and Researches*, and it was as a
missionary that he aroused the enthusiasm of Victorian England for
the opening of this side of the continent to the 'Christianity and

0   1000 km.

0   500   1000 miles

Regions generally known to
Europeans before *c.* 1790

Regions where first explorations
took place *c.* 1790 – *c.* 1857

Regions where first explorations
took place *c.* 1857 – *c.* 1873

Regions where first explorations
took place *c.* 1873 – *c.* 1900

Regions still largely unknown
to Europeans in 1900

11   The progress of the exploration of Africa by Europeans

commerce' which were to relieve its inhabitants from ignorance, famine and disease, and from the attentions of the East Coast slave-trader. The 'African Association' had by this time developed into the popular and powerful Royal Geographical Society, subsidized by the government and with presidents who had easy access to ministers and departments of state. It was the Royal Geographical Society which sent Burton and Speke to Lake Tanganyika in 1858, and Speke and Grant to the Victoria Nyanza and down the Nile in 1862–4. It was the influence of the Society which procured Livingstone a consulship and the expenses for his Zambezi expedition of 1859–64, in the course of which Lake Malawi was discovered. Livingstone's last six years of journeying, in 1867–73, mostly around the upper reaches of the Congo, were undertaken at his own expense. His books had made him into a rich man, and his popularity was so great that an American newspaper proprietor was able to start the young war correspondent, H. M. Stanley, on his career as an African explorer by sending him on an expedition to find Livingstone. Stanley's famous phrase – 'Dr Livingstone, I presume' – was the climax to the scoop of the century.

Stanley's next African journey, in which he crossed the continent from Zanzibar to the Congo mouth, marked the point at which the exploration of Africa became involved in schemes for its political annexation. On his return to Europe, Stanley was met at Marseille by the representatives of King Leopold of the Belgians, with results which will appear in a later chapter. Up till then the exploration of Africa had, in mid-twentieth-century terms, been something between the world refugee problem and the conquest of space. Not in Britain only, but all over Europe and America, unknown Africa was the field in which heroism was best displayed. And yet it was a heroism deeply dyed in philanthropy, because it was a firm belief both of the explorers and of their public that the object of the exercise was the regeneration of the black African race and its adoption into the mainstream of human progress. During the classic period of African exploration, it was seldom imagined that this process of redemption was one which would involve the taking of political power. This was the age of *laissez-faire*, and it was generally assumed that the Christian gospel, combined with the natural propensity of man to traffic and exchange, would prove a sufficient stimulus. Missionaries would teach the Africans both to cover their nakedness and to obey the moral law. Traders would supply the means to satisfy the first requirement in the shape of bales from the mills of Lancashire, which would be exchanged for the primary produce grown by industrious, thrifty, Christian, African peasants. Tribes would combine into federations for the better advancement of commerce, and so the nations of the future Africa would be born.

Governments, in their wisdom, were perhaps a little less starry-eyed than the general public. Governments knew that in West Africa the palm-oil trader would not have superseded the slave-trader without the aid of the gunboat. Governments knew that nowhere outside eastern Nigeria was there the unique combination of an economic crop and a network of natural waterways by which it could be conveyed to the coast. Governments knew that in most parts of Africa beasts of burden, if they were introduced, died within a few weeks, and that the real opening of the African interior to trade would have to await the building of railways. Governments, had they thought about it, might well have doubted whether developments on this scale could be carried through without radical changes in political control. But governments before the middle seventies of the nineteenth century did not think these things through to their logical conclusion, because they had no intention at all of allowing themselves to be drawn into policies of territorial expansion in Africa. The whole trend of European thought was against such expansion, and certainly there seemed to be no economic wealth in Africa which could possibly justify the expense. In fact, the eyes of European governments were as always mainly concentrated upon each other, even within the African theatre. Each was content with informal and overlapping empires of 'influence', so long as the others exercised a similar restraint. The situation was nowhere vastly different from what it had been in the eighteenth century. Europe had now definitely turned its gaze upon Africa, and Africa was changing under its influence; but Europe was not yet even sharpening the sword of formal empire, and for the first three-quarters of the nineteenth century the history of Africa is by no means synonymous with that of Europe in Africa.

13 The Nineteenth Century: North and West Africa

Towards the end of the eighteenth century, the uneasy balance of power between Christian Europeans and Muslim North Africans which had survived in the Mediterranean since medieval times began at length to move decisively in favour of Europe. While generally this was due to the growing material might of western Europe, compared with the relative stagnation of the Islamic world since the fifteenth century, it was particularly occasioned by a revival of European interest in the direct route to Asia through the Levant. Initially, following the Portuguese and Spanish example, the growing commercial and imperial energies of Europe had been diverted outwards into the Atlantic. But during the great war of 1793–1815, the global eighteenth-century struggle for oceanic power between Britain and France had been finally resolved in favour of Britain, with the result that the French were attracted to the old road to Asia through Egypt. In 1798, British naval power frustrated Napoleon's expedition to Egypt (as it was also to frustrate French ambitions in the Omani realm in the Persian Gulf and East Africa), but on land Britain thought it politic to recall to Egypt her nominal suzerain, the Ottoman Turks. The splendid medieval anachronism of Mamluk power could not survive the impact of modern arms, and by 1811, despite British interference, control of Egypt had passed to the Albanian troops of an Ottoman army commanded by Muhammad Ali.

Muhammad Ali (Mehemet Ali) was a man of quite remarkable ability, ambition and vision. When, as a failing man of seventy-five, he handed over power to his son and lieutenant Ibraham in 1847, he had gone far towards transforming the medieval province of the Ottoman empire to which fortune had brought him into an independent modern state. He had been least successful in his foreign policy.

Ibrahim's military successes in Syria, intended to secure the complete independence of Egypt from Constantinople by restoring her traditional empire, had been undone by European and particularly British diplomacy, which preferred that the gateway to India should remain under the weaker Turkish power. Egypt therefore stayed technically part of the Ottoman empire; Muhammad Ali was able to secure no more than the recognition of Egypt as an autonomous province under the hereditary rule of himself and his heirs (who in 1867 were granted the title of Khedive). Nevertheless, the Nilotic Sudan had been conquered, and the reality of Turkish power in the Red Sea had been made firmly Egyptian. Within Egypt itself, irrigation, land tenure, revenue and administration had all been drastically overhauled, and cotton, indigo and sugar had been developed as export crops by a system of state monopolies. The interests of European traders were to some extent protected by the institution of new non-Muslim courts, and European experts were brought in to promote educational and health reforms, and above all to help train a new Egyptian army. Muhammad Ali's regime was entirely autocratic, but the disbandment of his Albanian regiments (whose jealousy and untrustworthiness were soon manifest) and their replacement by Egyptian conscripts sowed the seeds for the growth of Egyptian nationhood in the future. Once Egyptian officers had risen to the command, ultimate power in Egypt would be in Egyptian hands, a thing which had not been known for 2,000 years.

Immediately, however, the future of the new Egypt depended entirely on the personal qualities of its rulers, and Muhammad Ali's absolute power descended to heirs who could not match his drive and purpose. Foreign merchants, concession-seekers and money-lenders were permitted to exploit the new economy. The British, concerned with passing mails and men quickly to India, gained a significant foothold in the 1850s with their construction of the railway from Alexandria to Cairo and on to Suez. In 1854 a concession was granted to a former French consul, de Lesseps, to build and operate the Suez Canal. This was eventually completed by 1869, in the teeth of formidable diplomatic and financial obstructions created mainly by the British, who were incapable of foreseeing that developments in steam propulsion would soon totally outmode the old sailing route to India by the Cape, and mistakenly supposed that the canal would mainly benefit France. The cost of the canal to Egypt was great. The terms of the concession involved her in the loss of lives, land and revenue, while (as Muhammad Ali had foreseen in resolutely opposing earlier projects) Egyptian independence was now at the mercy of the European maritime powers who were the canal's principal beneficiaries. The truth of this became manifest in 1879 when the Egyptian government became bankrupt, largely because of the Khedive Ismail's reckless policy of pledging the revenue to secure foreign loans (on terms which favoured only the foreign capitalists and their agents in Egypt) which were then spent on sometimes splendid but often unremunerative modernization schemes. Eventually, Turkey was prevailed upon to depose Ismail, and control over the Egyptian revenue and hence ultimately over its government was given to British and French nominees.

The containment of French ambition in Egypt in 1798–1801, and Muhammad Ali's subsequent achievement there of virtual independence from Turkey, produced a chain of reactions elsewhere in Mediterranean Africa. In 1830, with no British fleet to frustrate it, and with a government anxious to secure overseas the success denied it at home, a French force occupied Algiers. The most reasonable of the various pretexts for this action was the need finally to extirpate corsairing, which had tended to revive during the years between 1793 and 1815 when the European navies were principally engaged with one another. Algiers was more vulnerable than other Maghribian states which had engaged in corsairing. In 1835–6, the Turks, frightened both by Muhammad Ali's achievement in Egypt and by the French action at Algiers, took steps to restore their authority at Tripoli, and they were kept out of Tunis only by French naval demonstrations.

The Tunisian Beys were quick to appreciate the significance of these events. They had already taken steps to outlaw corsairing, and they now proceeded to westernize their administration. In 1857 they were in fact the first Muslim rulers ever to grant a constitution to their people. Had it not been that the Husainids' programme of modernization was accompanied by financial extravagances similar to those of the Egyptian government, it is possible that Tunis might have remained independent longer than it did, for French ambitions there were to some extent checked by rival Italian interests. But the financial embarrassment of the Bey's government eventually gave France the opportunity to proclaim a protectorate over Tunisia in 1881. Moroccan independence, however, was preserved into the twentieth century – not by her own efforts, for tribal anarchy had steadily gained ground since the great days of the Sa'dids, but by the mutual jealousies of the European powers. Her strategic position at the gateway to the Mediterranean was such that neither France, nor Britain, nor nearby Spain dared interfere in Moroccan affairs for fear of antagonizing the others.

For most of the nineteenth century, then, direct European intervention in North Africa was confined to the activities of the French in Algeria. But although it had been easy for the French to seize the town of Algiers and the person of its Bey, and then to occupy the other major ports of the territory, it was by no means easy to decide upon subsequent policy. No French government was prepared to surrender a conquest won by French arms; the question was rather how far the French were willing to go in subjugating the Arab and Berber tribes of the interior. In 1832 these showed their hostility to the foreigner by rising in a *jihad* inspired by 'Abd al-Kadir, the son of a *marabout* (holy man). The tribes' attacks made impossible any idea of occupying only the coastal plain. Eventually, in 1840, General Bugeaud embarked on a policy of relentlessly expelling the tribes and replacing them by European colonists. But even this drastic policy could not provide a final answer to the problem facing the French, because it was clearly impracticable to push all the Algerian tribes into the Sahara. It became necessary for the mountains and steppes to be systematically occupied by military posts and swept by flying columns. Despite the capture and exile of 'Abd al-Kadir in 1847, Algerian resistance did not cease until about 1879, when the French army had effectively subjugated all the tribes between the sea and the desert.

By this time the French had to think of what to do with the vast territory which 150,000 soldiers and perhaps as many pioneer colonists had died to make French. Those parts of the northern plains which received regular winter rains (the *Tell*), and which had been largely cleared of the tribes, could be colonized and assimilated to the civil government of metropolitan France. For the rest, the French were forced to recognize what Napoleon III had seen, that Algeria was not only a French colony but also 'an Arab kingdom'. Muslim tribesmen could not be quickly assimilated. The system of *bureaux arabes* initiated by the army had to be adapted into an enduring system by which French officials ruled the people through their tribal chiefs and councils. Even with this compromise, the future of *Algérie Française* was by no means assured when in 1879 military government finally gave way to civil administration. There was no clear reason why Frenchmen should want to emigrate to Algeria, where land, disease and native peoples were all hostile, and there to try to produce crops which would only compete with those grown by established farmers in Mediterranean France. In fact, of the 350,000 Europeans who were living in Algeria by 1880, nearly half were not French at all, but Spaniards, Italians and Maltese. Moreover, the more successful the foreign settlers and capitalists were in creating farms and dams, in building roads and railways, schools and hospitals, the more they were bound to incur the envy and suspicion of the native population, shut away in the poorer lands and, under the peace imposed by France, steadily increasing in numbers.

France sought compensation in West Africa also for the loss of her old empire, which had been finally destroyed by the British during 1793–1815. On the coast, however, the pace was increasingly set by the British, who exhibited a much firmer commercial purpose than the French, and who were thoroughly committed to the campaign to oust the slave trade and to replace it by new trades and a new order. Over most of the interior, until the 1870s, the initiative still lay with the African peoples. In the Senegal valley, however, France had an inheritance from her old empire which she could seek to develop. In the seventeenth and eighteenth centuries, the Senegal had been remunerative merely as a highway to the trade of an independent Sudan. Attempts to create a plantation colony having failed, it was left to a young army officer, Louis Faidherbe (who in Algeria had acquired both military experience and some understanding of Muslim society) to show what might be made of the Senegal. Appointed governor in 1854, Faidherbe undertook the systematic conquest of the Senegal basin and the conversion of its inhabitants into farmers producing crops, notably groundnuts, of value to France. When he left the colony ten years later, it was already a sure base for the later French conquest of the western Sudan with Senegalese soldiers. Indeed, the French were already matching their strength against the empire of al-Hajj 'Umar, the westernmost representative of a remarkable new recrudescence of Muslim power in the region.

Islam had initially been brought to and spread through black West Africa by merchants. These had little incentive to subvert the societies with which they traded. In the Sudan, as was seen in Chapter 7, kings and courts often saw advantages in professing the new religion, but both the fundamental organization of society and the means used to control it remained essentially pagan. However, the Moroccan destruction of Songhai power opened the Niger bend to domination by pastoral tribes from the Sahara. Following their conquest of the Maghrib, some Beduin had entered the western Sahara, and a number of its Berber tribes had become not only Muslim but thoroughly Arabized. These tribes provided a path for the establishment in West Africa of brotherhoods (*tariqa*) of divines who were committed to the achievement and expansion of a wholly Muslim society; if persuasion and education were not sufficient to this end, then *jihad* could be preached. The rulers of the major Sudanic kingdoms to the east and west of the Niger bend, the kings of the Hausa and the Bambara Mande, were obvious targets for this new breed of clerics who were both learned and militant. In their eyes these rulers were pagans or as good as pagans.

The major agents in changing this state of affairs proved to be the Fulani, the only West African people to practise pastoralism. This fact, together with a number of physical traits which tend to distinguish the Fulani from other West Africans, has led to conjectures that they were originally of Saharan origin. But their language is indubitably a Niger-Congo language, belonging to a West Atlantic subfamily along with languages like Serer, Wolof and Tukulor; indeed it is hardly distinguishable from the latter. When first met with in history, the Fulani pastoralists were living with the Tukulor, the people of the ancient Senegalese kingdom of Takrur, Ghana's contemporary and western neighbour, which had been Islamized in the eleventh century. By about the fourteenth century, however, the Fulani were beginning to spread eastwards through the Sudan as pastoralists, infiltrating themselves and their herds between the agricultural villages. By the sixteenth century they were strongly estab-

12 West Africa in the nineteenth century

lished in Massina, upstream from the Niger bend, and were penetrating Hausaland to the east of it. Two centuries later some of them
were settling in Adamawa in northern Cameroon. Most of the
Fulani remained pagan herdsmen (*Fulanin boroje*) who managed their
own affairs quite independently of the peoples among whom they
lived. But some became not only Muslims but also some of the most
devout and learned of Sudanese clerics. There were probably a
number of reasons why this was so. The Fulani maintained kinship
links with the long-Islamized Tukulor. Some of them settled in the
towns of the Sudan, doubtless as agents for their pastoral brethren,
and in this alien environment, where strangers were commonly Muslims, it would not be easy for them to maintain their traditional
pastoral pagan practices. Finally, some of those who remained in the
countryside as pastoralists must have felt an attraction to the *tariqa* of
the equally pastoral Arabized-Berber tribes, the more so as their
numbers and those of their cattle grew and so provided increasing
occasions for friction between them and the pagan societies who
held the land and sought to levy rent, taxes and services from
them.

From the middle of the seventeenth century onwards, Fulani in
the far western Sudan, in Bondu and Futa, began to wage *jihad*
against their neighbours and to establish new theocratic polities. But
the first large-scale *jihad* developed in the central Sudan. Here, at the
end of the eighteenth century, severe tensions developed between
Fulani clerics and successive kings of the Hausa state of Gobir. In
1804, an exceptionally learned and able cleric, Usuman dan Fodio,
saw no alternative open to him but to declare a *jihad* and to call on
true Muslims to rise against the Hausa rulers. Many Hausa com-
moners were not averse to the establishment of Islamic law to limit
and control the exactions of their kings and nobility, but what gave
the movement initiated by Usuman the single momentum which
enabled it to replace all the old Hausa dynasties with Fulani emirs
was the way in which the *boroje* rallied to the call of the Muslim
Fulani.

The Fulani conquerors met with effective resistance only in Bornu,
where the ancient but now effete Kanem dynasty was swept away by
Muhammad al-Kanami, who stoutly maintained that the Fulani possessed no monopoly of Islamic rectitude and so rallied the people

behind him. But Adamawa became part of the Fulani empire, and Fulani armies also swept southwards into Nupe and Yorubaland. The northern provinces of the Oyo empire and its historic capital were occupied, and, as the emirate of Ilorin, became a firm base for the steady spread of Islam among the Yoruba. Dan Fodio was a scholar and a divine more than a statesman, and the practical direction of the empire soon passed to a son, Muhammad Bello, who oversaw its larger eastern half from Dan Fodio's new city of Sokoto, and to a brother, Abdullahi, who controlled the west from Gwandu. Both these men, Bello especially, were also extremely competent scholars and joined with Dan Fodio in the epistolary wars which were waged against al-Kanami to justify the Fulani *jihad*.

The Fulani success in the central Sudan had important repercussions farther west. In Massina, a Fulani cleric, Ahmadu ibn Hammadi, was inspired about 1818 to lead a *jihad* against its Bambara overlords, and shortly another Muslim Fulani state had been created. Further west still, the standard of Muslim revolt was raised by al-Hajj 'Umar, a Tukulor who on his way back from his pilgrimage to Mecca had spent some time at Sokoto, where he had, indeed, married a daughter of Bello's. 'Umar followed the traditional pattern of training, in a *ribat*, an élite which he was able to equip with firearms secured from the coast. By about 1850 this force was ready to move out in a *jihad*. In the Upper Senegal it was checked by the French, but 'Umar's men quickly overran the Bambara kingdoms and also conquered Massina. By 1863, therefore, 'Umar possessed an empire reaching from the Senegal to Timbuktu. But, whatever his own original motives may have been, most of his followers seem to have been concerned as much with plunder as with the advancement of Islam, and there were numerous risings against him by both Bambara and Fulani. In 1864, 'Umar was killed while fighting one of these, and he left a very disturbed inheritance to his son and successor Ahmadu Seku.[1]

It is tempting to suppose that these new empires were at least in part a Sudanese reaction to the course of events elsewhere in West Africa. Considered together with the *jihad* of 'Abd al-Kadir in Algeria and of the later *jihad* of the Mahdi Muhammad Ahmad in the

---

1 And, also, it may be remarked, the nephew of Sultan Bello of Sokoto.

Egyptian Sudan (see Chapter 15), they certainly suggest that African Muslims were demonstrating their opposition to alien pressures. But in the case of the western Sudan it is not immediately obvious what these pressures were. A direct European menace can hardly have been felt outside the Senegal valley before about 1880. However, one of the principal directions of Fulani advance was south into Yorubaland, while al-Haj 'Umar's first attempts to expand were directed down the Senegal. Although there is no evidence for any decline in the Sudan's trade with North Africa across the Sahara before the 1880s, it does seem that there may have been increasing awareness among its leaders of the new commercial and other opportunities developing in the coastlands. As is perhaps most obvious in the case of the Oyo empire, the general growth of European trade and influence at the coast was leading to a fatal undermining of the established situation in Guinea.

The ultimate result, of course, was to bring the Sudan eventually into a fatal headlong clash with European strength. At first, however, this was more obvious in the case of France than in that of Britain.

Compared with the French conquests on the Senegal, there was for some time little formal advance of British power in West Africa. A new colony began to take shape around Freetown in Sierra Leone at the end of the eighteenth century, but this was initially a private venture of the anti-slavery humanitarians. These people had the dual aim of finding a home for a few unwanted black ex-slaves from Britain and North America, and of establishing a base from which legitimate trade could reach into Africa. In this latter purpose they were wholly unsuccessful, and their colony survived only with difficulty until 1808, when it was taken over by the British government as a base for its anti-slave-trade naval patrols. Until the close of the nineteenth century, British Sierra Leone comprised only a few square miles around Freetown, but it exerted a much greater influence on the course of West African history than either of the other two settlements of freed slaves which were made on the coast in this period.

Liberia began as a venture of American philanthropists in 1821. When it was formally constituted an independent republic in 1847, it consisted of only a few thousand black settlers, striving to maintain themselves and their ideals against the hostility of the native tribes, with little or no outside support. Its foster-parent, the United States, did not even formally recognize it until 1862. Libreville, established by the French on the Gabon estuary in 1849, was consciously modelled on Freetown, but it remained essentially stagnant until the eve of the European partition, mainly because France's naval activity against the slave trade was only fitful. Britain, on the other hand, maintained an anti-slave-trade patrol in West African waters continuously from 1807 until the 1860s, and one important result of this was that by the mid-century something like 70,000 blacks captured from slave-ships had been liberated and settled in Sierra Leone. Many of these freed slaves became assimilated to European ways, especially as a result of the educational work of the Protestant missions, who deliberately chose Sierra Leone for their first footing in West Africa. Some of the liberated Africans became considerable traders along the coast, while others augmented British resources by becoming priests, doctors, lawyers, administrators and clerks in the service of the British missions, trading companies or government. When, as some of them did, they returned to their homelands, especially to Yorubaland, they became agents for the further expansion both of Christian and of European influence. Sierra Leone had an even more direct influence in that its early governors soon became convinced that the most effective way of stopping the export of slaves from West Africa was by establishing British rule or protection over the principal slaving coasts. Thus, for example, in 1821 the British forts on the Gold Coast were transferred to the Colonial Office from the merchants who had hitherto controlled them.

This forward policy did not immediately bear fruit. For a Britain which was steadily moving towards *laissez-faire*, the cost of extending British rule in West Africa seemed disproportionately great in relation to the visible commercial or humanitarian benefits, and a number of early acquisitions, such as the Iles de Los (off modern Conakry), were eventually abandoned. The numbers of slaves carried more or less surreptitiously across the Atlantic in Brazilian, American and Spanish vessels hardly decreased before the end of the 1840s, and the British trade in other commodities soon appeared to be thriving best in the Niger Delta (then known as the Oil Rivers), where it had no official backing. And so when Britain became involved in war with Ashanti on the Gold Coast, and a governor of Sierra Leone was killed there (1824), official policy was reversed.

From 1830, however, an administrator nominated by the merchants, George Maclean, demonstrated how British trade and influence on the Gold Coast could increase with only negligible expenditure, through an informal jurisdiction over the coastal states coupled with a firm but peaceful attitude towards Ashanti, and in 1843–4 official British control of the Gold Coast forts was resumed. The lessons of Maclean's time were not wholly learnt, and trade declined. The fundamental explanation for this was a perpetual conflict of jurisdiction with Ashanti. Ashanti, like Dahomey, its neighbour to the east, was now a stable military state whose days of imperial expansion were largely over and whose interests lay in the development of its foreign trade. But unlike Dahomey, Ashanti had reached the coast only after European traders had become firmly entrenched there. While Dahomey succeeded in bringing the activities of foreign traders on the Slave Coast under its control and, for that matter, was able to continue to export slaves, on the Gold Coast the Europeans after some years of difficulty were able to maintain their independence. Indeed, the Europeans, the British in particular, tended to make common cause against Ashanti with the small coastal states which, in Ashanti eyes, were her subjects through conquest. Both the Danes and the Dutch, the only other Europeans still holding forts on the Gold Coast, eventually came to the conclusion that without the slave trade their connections with West Africa were hardly profitable. In 1850 and 1872 respectively they handed over their forts to the British and left. Their departure meant that it was now possible for the British to assert their direct rule over the whole Gold Coast. An attempt by the coastal states themselves to establish their own European-style administration was thwarted; Ashanti was warned off by a punitive expedition which sacked its capital, Kumasi; and in 1874 the Gold Coast was declared a British colony.

The growth of Britain's power on the Gold Coast brought her into closer touch with the increasingly troublesome affairs of the territories further east. Here, two apparently contrary tendencies were at work. On the Slave Coast, both the kingdom of Dahomey and the traders in slaves to Brazil and Cuba, who were for the most part Brazilians, were still thriving from the slave trade. Most of the slaves came from a Yorubaland where the Oyo empire was collapsing into civil war and anarchy. Around the mouths of the Niger Delta, on the other hand,

European traders – mainly though not exclusively British – were joining with African merchants and potentates in enriching themselves by the export of palm oil and kernels from the forests just north of the Delta. African city states on the coast were engaged in developing commercial monopolies in the interior, and were vying bitterly with each other and with the Europeans to secure the maximum profits from the trade.

Early British attempts to deal with these problems were fruitless. Diplomatic missions failed to persuade Dahomey to stop exporting slaves. In 1841 an official expedition up the lower Niger, attempting to use the Landers' experience and to by-pass the turbulent Oil Rivers by taking British trade and Christian missionaries directly into the hinterland, demonstrated only the hostility of the mosquitoes and of the established traders in the Delta, black and white alike. But the interests of British commerce, of the campaign to eradicate the slave trade and to replace it with legitimate trade, as well as the concern of the missionaries, who by the 1840s were following the Sierra Leone emigrants into disturbed Yorubaland, all combined to force some action on the British government.

In 1849 the British Foreign Office began to send out consuls to the Gulf of Guinea. These had the dual purpose of keeping an eye on the slaving activities of ports like Whydah, Badagri and Lagos, and of trying to bring some order to the Oil Rivers, where British merchants were all too ready to try to blast their way out of disputes with the numerous African governments by calling in cruisers of the British West African naval squadron. Some of these consuls, notably the first, John Beecroft, were forceful men, and with naval backing the consular jurisdiction began to bring results. Neither funds nor force were available for a direct assault on Dahomey, but in 1851 Lagos was captured and ten years later it was formally constituted a British colony. This action, together with later coastal annexations, including that of Badagri, put an end to the export of slaves from Yorubaland and permitted a virtually complete blockade of Dahomey. In the Oil Rivers, the work of the British consuls and navy in bringing the local kings within the realm of an informal British jurisdiction gradually paved the way for an eventual British administration.

But this still lay in the future. In 1879, the year in which the French began their advance into the Sudan from the Senegal, and

Goldie mobilized the British traders to force open the Niger waterway, West Africa was still largely free of European penetration. The Senegal was firmly French, and for strategic reasons the French had in 1857 also occupied Cape Verde.[1] Britain's flag had followed her trading or humanitarian interests to the mouth of the Gambia and to the coasts of Sierra Leone, the Gold Coast and the future Nigeria, but her power had hardly been felt inland. Ashanti was still the only major black African kingdom to have been invaded by a European army, and after 1874 she was left alone to recover her strength. The old commercial link between Europe and West Africa had been broken with the suppression of the Atlantic slave trade, which had been practically extinguished by the mid-1860s. But few new staples of trade had been found besides the two oil crops, palm kernels and groundnuts. The humanitarian interest apart, little had yet been done to bring West Africa into the European fold.

---

1 Thus acquiring an ideal site on which to build Dakar, eventually to be the metropolis of a vast French West African empire.

14 The Nineteenth Century: Southern Africa

Before the onset of the colonial fever in the 1890s, Europeans had already made substantial inroads into the southern third of Africa. During the first three-quarters of the nineteenth century, events there were dominated by the expansion of European settlement north-eastwards from the Cape of Good Hope. By 1880 this stream of settlement was already touching the Limpopo, over a thousand miles into the interior from its base at Cape Town. Indirectly its influence was being felt even further afield, with missionaries and traders from the South African colonies producing an impact as far north as the Zambezi. In particular, Livingstone's great transcontinental journey of 1853–6 was to have important consequences both for the Bantu peoples of central Africa and for the long-established zones of Portuguese interest in Angola and Moçambique.

When the Dutch East India Company had founded its refreshment station at the Cape in 1652, the last thing it intended was to become involved in the African interior. But to provide for the defence of its settlement, and to secure an adequate supply of cheap foodstuffs for its passing East Indiamen, the Company found it necessary to attract colonists to the Cape. Very soon, however, the settlement had outgrown its purpose. By the time the policy of encouraging immigrants was reversed, the colonists were already chafing at the restrictions imposed on their freedom of action by the Company, and were suffering from the inadequacy of Cape Town and its visiting ships as a market for the sale of their produce. During the course of the eighteenth century, as their numbers grew by natural increase, more and more settlers went to seek a new life in the interior, away from the control of the Company, hunting, trading with the Hottentots for cattle and eventually as cattle-farmers themselves.

Thus there came into being the Trekboers,[1] sturdy pioneers who had cut adrift from the mainstream of European development and adapted themselves to the hard business of wringing a livelihood from extensive grazing on the dry grasslands of interior South Africa, in competition with its native peoples, cattle-farmers like themselves. Ultimately their descendants were to call themselves Afrikaners; they differed from other Africans mainly in their individualism and in the seventeenth-century Calvinist beliefs and outlook which reinforced the conviction, born of the circumstances in which they found themselves, that they were an elect of God and that the heathen coloured folk had no natural rights against them or to the land they were taking for their own.

In this spirit the early Boers, moving east rather than north, towards the zone of higher rainfall in Natal, hunted down the San hunter-gatherers and overran or dispersed the Khoi herders until by 1779 they had encountered the vast mass of the strongly organized Bantu peoples, whose frontier then ran along the line of the Great Fish River. The result was the first of a series of 'Kaffir wars'[2] which were to prove a sore trial to the authorities at Cape Town for the next hundred years. At first it made little difference that during the Anglo-French wars of 1793–1815 the Cape passed from Dutch to British control. Like the Dutch Company before it, the British government valued the Cape simply for its strategic position, commanding as it did the entry to the Indian Ocean. The existence, as an appendage to the Cape, of a vast colony of dispersed settlement, reaching north to the Orange and east to the Fish River, was little more than a nuisance which the British sought to limit as best they could. In fact British rule on the frontier was more effective than that of the Company in its last years, and the independent Boer frontier republics of Swellendam and Graaff Reinet, which had been proclaimed at the very end of the period of Company government in 1795, were brought under control. In 1820, Britain planted some 5,000 settlers, ex-soldiers and their families, close behind the frontier, hoping in this way both to strengthen it and to provide a British leaven in the Boer mass.

1 Literally translated, the name means 'migrant farmers'.
2 'Kaffir' which is common usage by white South Africans for a black South African, is of course the Arabic *kafir*, 'infidel'. It would seem to have reached South Africa from the East Coast, where the Portuguese took it over from the Arabs, who had applied it to the Bantu.

13 Southern Africa in the nineteenth century

Initially the most important result of the collision between the advancing Boers and the Bantu was the production of considerable strains among the Bantu peoples. The great bulk of the Bantu had been settled for many centuries in the coastal plains between the Drakensberg and the sea. This region received monsoon rains from the Indian Ocean, and was therefore much more fertile than the dry veld of the interior plateau, where Bantu settlement, like that of the Boers later, had of necessity to be much less dense. As their population and their herds gradually increased, the Bantu had always so far been able to take up more land. The San and the Khoi had presented no more of an obstacle to them than they did to the Boers. The most profitable new lands naturally lay to the south-east along the coast. The arrival of the Boers, however, blocked this avenue for the future. The result was that tribes needing to enlarge their territory could do so only at the expense of their neighbours. By the beginning of the nineteenth century, the Zulu clan of the Nguni in Natal had produced a ruthless military genius, Shaka, capable of breaking this stranglehold. He formed the men of the younger age-sets in his patron Dingiswayo's kingdom into regular regiments living only for war, which they fought at close quarters in disciplined formations, using their assegais to stab and not in the traditional way as not very effective long-range throwing weapons. Thus trained and disciplined, Shaka's impis carried all before them, plundering the cattle of less warlike communities and incorporating the boys and young women they captured into their own society. After Dingiswayo's death in 1818, Shaka became the dictator of a new and inherently aggressive military nation, the Zulu. Shaka was assassinated by his half-brothers in 1828, but one of these, Dingane, proved just as powerful and ruthless as his predecessor. The Zulu homeland in northern Natal, especially to the south, became surrounded by a no man's land deserted by its inhabitants and turned into a Zulu grazing-ground.

The effects of the Zulu outburst were felt much more widely than this, however; indeed they were felt throughout southern Africa. Some of those attacked by the Zulu emulated their example and set out on careers of conquest or rapine of their own. Thus the Sotho leader Sebetwane took a small group, the Makololo, northwards to conquer and rule the Barotse kingdom on the upper Zambezi, while Mantatise's basically Sotho force struck out westwards towards Botswana on an ultimately self-destructive campaign of plunder. In two areas, unusually able chiefs were able to merge refugees from the Zulu wars with their local peoples into new nations strong enough to withstand Zulu pressure. Such was the origin of Swaziland, created by Sobhuza and his descendant Mswazi just north of Zululand. Such also was the origin of the modern Lesotho kingdom to the southwest, which was the creation of the great southern Sotho king Moshweshwe. In addition, some Zulu formations (often those whose leaders had quarrelled with Shaka) struck out on their own. Soshangane took his people, the Shangane, northwards into Gazaland, where they conquered and largely absorbed the native Tonga.

Zwangendaba and his warriors broke even further afield, sweeping destructively through the highlands between the Limpopo and the Zambezi until they eventually settled around Lake Malawi. Mzilikazi led his Matabele (more correctly Ndebele) across the Drakensberg to disperse the Transvaal Sotho westwards towards the borders of the Kalahari in Botswana and south towards Lesotho, the land of the BaSotho.

It was into this turbulent interior, from 1836 onwards, that a growing stream of Boers began to project themselves in the exodus from the Cape Colony known as the Great Trek. Trekking away from control by Cape Town was already part of the Boer tradition, and this more positive and final Trek was not occasioned by the imposition of British rule as such. So long as it gave them security against the Bantu on the frontier, while allowing them liberty to take land and to employ native labour on their own terms, British rule was neither worse nor better than Dutch rule. But from about 1825 the character of British administration in South Africa had begun to change in a way the Trekboers could only regard as inimical to their interests. In part this was a reflection of new currents in Britain herself. The old authoritarian tradition of government, and of empire as a weapon in a world struggle for trade and survival, was giving way before *laissez-faire*, free trade and a more liberal and humanitarian attitude towards subject peoples and the underprivileged, whether at home or overseas. But it was also a consequence of the establishment for the first time in South Africa of Christian missions to the native peoples, and of the success of one mission in particular, the London Missionary Society, and of its South African superintendent, Dr John Philip, in bringing pressure to bear on government and opinion at home in the interests of the South African native peoples, whose human rights had hitherto been ignored.

From 1825 onwards the British administration at the Cape began to introduce measures to give protection under the law to its non-European peoples. It also began to lose the essentially military character of its early years. Elements of democracy were introduced, and attempts were made to bring the revenue closer to the expenditure by reducing military commitments and by seeking to raise revenue from land, the only asset of an impoverished economy, by dint of regulating its acquisition and thus raising its value. The abolition of slavery throughout the British empire in 1833 did not greatly affect the frontier Boers, since most of the 20,000 slaves in the colony were in the settled districts near Cape Town (where they formed a vital element in the emergence of the Cape Coloured people – of mixed slave, Boer and Khoi ancestry). Two decisions taken in London shortly afterwards, however, did greatly affect the frontiersmen. In 1834 the Colonial Office disallowed a law passed by the new Legislative Council which would have undone part of the new legislation protecting non-Europeans. Then in 1836 it was decided that an area of the eastern frontierlands, recently annexed in the interest of security, should now be returned to the Bantu in the interest of retrenchment. Since it was already difficult for younger sons to find new farms of the 6,000 acres or so needed to support a Boer family on the veld, this denial of prospects constituted the final blow that determined many frontier Boers to band together in organized parties to trek across the Orange River. The greatest of their early leaders, Piet Retief, plainly declared the trekkers' purpose to establish new communities beyond the reach of British interference, where society could be organized on traditional Afrikaner principles.

Some Boers dispersed across the High Veld, clashing with the Matabele and forcing them north across the Limpopo to establish their hegemony over the Shona peoples, whose own political organization had already been badly shattered by Soshangane and Zwangendaba. But the main body of trekkers moved towards the area of rich grassland in Natal which had been depopulated by Zulu aggression. The Boers hoped for what Dingane at first seemed to promise, a peaceful occupation, and the ox-waggons of the Boer families rumbled over the Drakensberg to disperse over the promised land. But the Zulu nation could not tolerate such a permanent occupation of its preserves. Retief was murdered and the impis descended on the settlers. Then a new Boer leader, Pretorius, emerged to gather the families into laagers and to strike back with mobile commandos. The guns and the mobility of the Boers overthrew Dingane's power, and in 1839 Pretorius was able to proclaim the Boer republic of Natal.

The Zulu, however, were not the only enemy the Boers had to face. The British government took the line that in crossing beyond the Cape boundary the Boers had not thereby ceased to be British subjects. It refused to countenance an independent Boer regime which might control harbours injurious to its own Indian Ocean interests and whose expansive proclivities were certain to cause further Bantu pressures on the Cape frontiers. British troops were sent to Port Natal (the future Durban) and in 1845 Natal was formally annexed. Thus thwarted in their bid for independence, many trekkers began to move back across the Drakensberg.

The Boers were naturally opposed to restriction of their individual rights and interests. Widely dispersed across the High Veld, each little group tended to be a law unto itself. Nevertheless, the continuing need for cooperation against the Bantu made some central government essential, and the trekkers eventually came together in two major republics, the South African Republic (Transvaal) between the Vaal and the Limpopo, and the Orange Free State between the Orange and the Vaal. For the most part the sum of the popular wills was ascertained through the Volksraads (People's Councils), but in times of stress the presidents, who were also directly responsible to the all-white male electorate, possessed potentially dictatorial authority.

In 1852 and 1854 the independence of these two republics was recognized by Britain. Provided that their doings led to no serious trouble with the Bantu which would prejudice basic British interests, the British government had concluded that any advantages resulting from a further extension of its administration into Africa would be totally outweighed by the responsibility and cost, especially since both republics lacked a viable economy. While in the 1860s the economy of the Cape Colony began to expand through the development of sheep-farming, producing wool for the world market, and Natal began to achieve some prosperity from sugar-planting with indentured Indian labour, the two republics, lacking both an economic agriculture and any communication with the exterior other than the long ox-waggon trails, were poor even by South African standards. But the very poverty of the small republican communities (in the 1870s, the Transvaal had only some 40,000 whites, and the Free State some 30,000, compared with nearly 250,000 in the Cape) made them incapable of coping with the wars brought about by the continual tendency of their farmers to expand into African lands. In 1871 the integrity of the Free State and of the eastern frontierlands of the Cape was saved only by the expedient of bringing Lesotho under

British control. In the same year Britain annexed Griqualand West, which had suddenly acquired value with the discovery there of considerable diamond deposits. This was an area on the western boundary of the Free State, whose claim to it had long been disputed by its Griqua inhabitants, a people of mixed Khoi and European stock and culture possessing close ties with the Cape.

By this time the more far-seeing British officials, both locally and in London, had come to appreciate that the multiplicity of European governments and policies in South Africa was prejudicing any sane solution of the difficulties arising from the Great Trek. The Trek indeed, by throwing black and white together as never before, had demonstrated that South Africa was essentially one country. At the same time its results were causing deep instability among the Bantu peoples. Their land was being taken, and they were being left with little alternative but service in the European communities as individual labourers. Moreover, chieftainly authority was being undermined, so that the tribes could no longer be regarded as responsible units with which the British government could make treaties in definition of mutual interests, as it had tried to do in the 1830s and 40s. The ideal solution was obviously a federation of the British colonies with the republics. In 1872, the Cape Colony, whose wealth and European population were now rapidly increasing as a consequence of the trade engendered by diamond mining, was granted internal self-government, with ministers responsible to a parliament elected on a non-racial franchise. The further extension of this principle, it was hoped, would enable black and white to come together to deal with their problems throughout South Africa, thus enabling the imperial government to withdraw to its primary interest, the naval base at the Cape.

The ideal solution, however, proved impossible to achieve. The Cape Colony would have no share in it; its new rulers had no wish to see its growing wealth squandered for the benefit of the more backward communities. Nor did they wish to see the nice racial balance of their society (which had almost as many whites as non-Europeans) upset by the admission of tribal Bantu from areas like the eastern frontier or Natal, for which Britain had hitherto been responsible. The Free State, otherwise generally willing to cooperate with the Cape, had been bitterly antagonized by the annexation of Griqualand West. Since Natal was still directly under the Colonial

Office, this left the South African Republic of the Transvaal, and here, in 1877, an energetic British proconsul, Sir Bartle Frere, thought he saw a chance to force the whole issue. The republic was bankrupt and incapable of coping with the Swazi and Zulu on its frontiers. It was therefore annexed, in a bold bid for Boer cooperation. But the plan completely miscarried. Britain became involved in war with the Zulu (with whom she had hitherto had good relations) and failed to make good Frere's promise of local autonomy for the Transvaalers. The latter, taking heart from an early defeat of British regular soldiers by the Zulu impis, rose against the British and, after a signal victory of their own at Majuba, brought Britain to reverse her policy in 1881. The independence of the Transvaal was recognized, subject only to British overseeing of her relations with foreign powers and with Africans beyond her borders, as well as to a vaguely expressed claim of ultimate British suzerainty. All Britain had succeeded in doing in the ten years since 1871 was to revive and increase the antagonisms which had first led the Boers to make the Great Trek.

Meanwhile the mutual hostility that had developed between the missionary societies and the Boers, whose own Christianity could not encompass any equality between white and black, had led the former to concentrate their efforts beyond the borders of the Cape and Natal in areas which were untouched by trekkers. Indeed the work of the missions sometimes helped stiffen the Bantu resistance to Boer pressures. They made little headway among the Nguni until the final crushing of the Nguni military systems after 1890 (though Robert Moffat of the L.M.S. established a remarkable friendship with Msilikazi in the Transvaal, and this was later to give the Society entry to Matabeleland). Their influence in Lesotho and among the Griqua, however, was considerable. The establishment of the Transvaal republic limited further missionary expansion northwards to the narrow strip of Botswana between the Transvaal and the Kalahari, and here the Bamangwato king, Khama, unhappily sandwiched between Boers and Matabele, became a notable convert. It was along this 'missionary road' that during the 1860s hunters, traders and ultimately concession-seekers from the Cape began to penetrate into Matabeleland and even as far as Barotseland, and it was from the London Missionary Society station at Kuruman that Livingstone (who was Moffat's son-in-law) set out on his first journeys.

Livingstone's transcontinental journey with Makololo porters from Barotseland (1853–6) brought him into close touch with the Portuguese in both Angola and Moçambique. He disclosed to the outside world a chain of forts leading inland from the Angolan coast from which half-caste *pombeiros* ranged far in search of slaves and ivory, and of an even more disastrous slaving system feeding plantations on the lower Zambezi valley and in the Moçambique coastlands. From east and west, indeed, the activities of the *pombeiros* were reaching right across the continent. Livingstone soon realized that the consequent destruction of African society could not be stayed by an advance of Christianity and of civilizing commerce from the south, for the line of communication was too long and tenuous. But he failed to secure much more than missionary penetration up the Zambezi and Shire routes which he prospected during his second major expedition (1858–64), and then not until the 1870s. However, he did succeed in stirring Portugal to a recognition that attitudes to Africa were changing, and that in the nineteenth century *pombeiro* trading was an anachronism which would not justify Portugal's traditional claim to all the lands between the Angolan and Moçambique coasts. When, therefore, the British government in the 1880s and 1890s began to move in support of the missions in Malawi, where the Protectorate of Nyasaland was created, and the juggernaut of European settlement driven by Cecil Rhodes began to roll up the new railway lines which were spreading from the Cape to Matabeleland and beyond, they found Portuguese explorers, soldiers and officials hard at work across their path.

15 The Nineteenth Century: East and North-East Africa

In East and North-East Africa the main external factor during the first three-quarters of the nineteenth century was not European but Arab and Egyptian. In East Africa the first half of the century saw the consolidation of the arabized Swahili-speaking population of the coast from Cape Delgado to Lamu, and of the arabized town-dwelling Somali of southern Somalia, under the suzerainty of the al-Busaid dynasty of Oman on the western shores of the Persian Gulf. In theory this suzerainty had existed since the Omani liberation of the coast from the Portuguese at the end of the seventeenth century, but it was first made effective in practice by a single very gifted ruler, himself by origin a usurper, the Imam Seyyid Said, who reigned over Oman, or at least over its capital Muscat, from 1806 till 1856.

Having built up an efficient little navy, Seyyid Said asserted his claims, first to tribute and later to customs, upon the trading communities of the coastal towns. He chose Zanzibar as the base for his East African operations, and on the island itself he started a plantation industry in cloves, introduced all the way from the Moluccas, with such success that by the end of his reign Zanzibar was producing three-quarters of the world's supply. Under Said's influence Zanzibar soon became the commercial entrepôt for the whole of the East African coast, the rendezvous for all foreign shipping, the export market for the slaves and ivory of the mainland and the import market for cloth and beads, guns, ammunition and hardware from India, Europe and America. Said spent more and more of his time there, and in 1840 finally made it his capital. A class of wealthy Arabs settled round him as plantation-owners on Zanzibar and Pemba, while others with their fortunes still to make were encouraged by him to begin the direct commercial exploitation of the interior, using the

14 East and North-East Africa in the nineteenth century

credit of Indian merchant financiers to stock up trading caravans with which they would disappear up-country for years at a time.

The Zanzibar Arabs and Swahili were not the first or the only long-distance traders of the East African interior. As we have seen, it was the Nyamwezi people of West-Central Tanzania who had pioneered the routes which led down to the Zanzibar coast, and throughout the nineteenth century the Nyamwezi retained an important place in the developing commerce of the region. It was they who in the 1820s and 1830s opened the trade-routes as far west as the kingdom of the Lunda Kazembes in the southern Katanga. In all probability it was they who from the late eighteenth until the mid-nineteenth century organized the increasingly important trade with the large kingdoms to the west of Lake Victoria – Karagwe, Buganda and Bunyoro. It was especially as carriers that they were unsurpassed. European travellers described how from their tenderest years Nyamwezi boys would practise carrying miniature tusks. As adults they were capable of enormous marches, travelling very light. Their profits they invested in slaves, who tilled the land while their masters travelled abroad.

To the extent that the Zanzibari superseded them, it was probably because of their larger organization and better credit. Where the Nyamwezi had dealt in beads and cloth, the coastmen could afford the more costly trade goods, especially the guns and ammunition so eagerly coveted by the African rulers. To some small extent the Zanzibari established their own political organization in the interior. At a few key-points, like Tabora in the Nyamwezi country and Ujiji on Lake Tanganyika, there were regular commercial depots where they exercised what might be described as extra-territorial rights. And, especially to the west of Lake Tanganyika, there were cases where coastmen (and Nyamwezi also) conquered the local rulers and set themselves up as political paramounts. This, however, was exceptional. In general the Zanzibari obtained their ivory and slaves by trade and not by force. They armed the native rulers, and the native rulers did the rest. The result was a situation in which the strong became stronger at the expense of their weaker neighbours. In southern Tanzania powerful Yao chiefs preyed upon the defenceless peoples of the Malawi lakeshores. In Uganda the strong Kabakas of Buganda kept their armies raiding among the disunited Soga to the east and in the little Haya states to the south. They sold their slaves and ivory to the Zanzibaris for good prices, receiving in return weapons for their armouries and cloth with which to reward their soldiers, their courtiers and their state officials.

In Uganda, by the late 1850s, and early 1860s, the expanding sphere of Zanzibar commercial influence from the east coast was approaching a rival influence simultaneously expanding southwards from the north. This was the sphere of the Khartoum Arabs, or the 'Turks' as they were usually called. Turks they were, in the sense that the Sultan of Turkey was still in name the overlord of Egypt, while the Khedives, his hereditary viceroys in Egypt, also ruled the Sudan. Muhammad Ali invaded the Sudan in 1820, deposing the Funj sultans of Sennar and installing an Egyptian governor at the new capital of Khartoum. The main object of the exercise was to gain control of the White Nile slave trade and so to ensure a regular supply of slave recruits for the Egyptian army. Slave raiding was thus an official function of government, and during the next thirty years a series of expeditions ravaged the country southwards of Khartoum between the Blue and the White Niles, the homelands of the Dinka, the Nuer, the Shilluk and the Bari. As early as 1839 an Egyptian military post was planted at Gondokoro, close to where the White Nile cuts the modern frontier between Uganda and the Sudan. By the fifties and sixties Khartoum-based private enterprise had developed and taken over from the government not only the slave trade but the even more wide-ranging search for ivory; but the methods employed were still more military than commercial. Westwards along the Bahr al-Ghazal and its tributaries, and southwards among the Nilotic peoples of northern Uganda, heavily armed raiding parties rounded up the cattle and held them to ransom for ivory and slaves, as well as for supplies of food and drink. The Khartoumers were astonished, when they finally encountered their rivals from the east coast, to see how the Zanzibaris paid for their purchases in solid merchandise; this was something they could never hope to compete with, because of their much longer lines of communication.

After the Portuguese occupation in the sixteenth and seventeenth centuries, the first continuing European pressure to reach any part of this region came with the inevitable interest of the British government of the Bombay Presidency in the expanding Sultanate of Muscat and

Zanzibar. The British had made their first treaty with Seyyid Said's predecessor at the time of the Napoleonic threat to the Middle East and India, and strategically it suited them well that a friendly oriental power should extend its dominion down the western coast of the Indian Ocean: better the Arabs than the French. At the same time political unity would obviously make for good trading conditions and ease of diplomatic relations. The main difficulty in attacking the west-coast slave trade had been the very large number of political authorities with whom it had been necessary to do business. The hegemony of Seyyid Said offered the possibility of dealing with the east-coast trade, and at the same time of building up a paramountcy of British influence in the region, through a single local authority. In 1822, when Said was still at Muscat, the British obtained a treaty limiting the slave trade to the north-eastern corner of the Indian Ocean; this was to prevent the import of slaves into British India. When Said moved to Zanzibar in 1840, the first British consulate on the East African coast was established at his court. Five years later a second slave trade treaty further limited the trade to the Sultan's African dominions. Henceforward the naval squadrons were able to operate in the western Indian Ocean and to close in on the East African coast. In 1861, five years after Said's death, the Sultanate divided, one son taking Muscat, another Zanzibar. Finally in 1873, Sultan Barghash of Zanzibar, under the threat of a naval bombardment, signed a decree outlawing the slave trade throughout his dominions. The great slave market at Zanzibar was closed. A Christian cathedral arose on the site.

These fifty years of British diplomatic and naval effort undoubtedly had some effect upon the export of East African slaves to the former Asian markets. They had virtually none, however, upon East Africa itself. The slave trade into Zanzibar and Pemba, and into the coastal region of the mainland, was legal until 1873 and continued to be practised for many years afterwards, until the actual status of slavery was made illegal in colonial times. Moreover, even if the export trade in slaves was decreasing, that in ivory was growing year by year throughout the period. It was the search for ivory, rather than that for slaves, which took the coastmen annually further and further into the interior; but slavery and its attendant evils were almost inseparable from the ivory trade. The hunting of the elephant required arms and ammunition, which could also be used for warfare. The transport of ivory was by human porterage, much of it by slaves. These last might never cross the wide seas to an external market, but they were nevertheless removed by violence from their homes and ultimately sold, perhaps to a Nyamwezi chief in the interior, perhaps to a Swahili shopkeeper at the coast, perhaps to the Arab owner of a clove-plantation on Pemba or Zanzibar. There was in fact no East African equivalent to the palm-oil of West Africa. The European campaign against the seaborne slave trade, and the strengthening of commercial ties with Zanzibar, led merely to an intensified exploitation of the only other exportable commodity which could stand the cost of transport to the coast, with the result that the area of the coastmen's operation in the interior was vastly extended.

In the Egyptian sphere the same was true. In Egypt British pressure had to be much more discreetly exercised than in Zanzibar. Nevertheless, the three sons of Muhammad Ali who succeeded him as Khedive were all in some degree imbued with the humanitarianism of contemporary Europe, and they would have stopped the trade if they could. All three legislated against it, and the last of the three, Khedive Ismail, went so far as to employ first the explorer Sir Samuel Baker and later General Gordon as governors, in the hope of evolving a new policy. In fact, however, the only new policy anyone could recommend was that the whole vast region should be brought under closer control, and this meant finding the revenue with which to control it. In the long run such a revenue could only come after mechanized transport had provided the means for the agricultural products of the interior to be marketed overseas. In the short term it could come only from the ivory trade, which was at least as destructive in its effects upon the weak societies of the southern Sudan as the trade in slaves.

Baker tried, with very limited success, to control the operation of the ivory trade by carrying the Egyptian frontier still further southward, from Gondokoro into what is now northern Uganda. Gordon, who followed him as governor of this 'Equatorial Province', grasped the one essential fact about it, that it was far more accessible from the east coast than from the north. Ismail, at Gordon's advice, sent a seaborne expedition to occupy the east coast port of Kismayu, perhaps not realizing, or caring, that he was invading the dominions of Zanzibar. On arrival, however, his forces were persuaded by British diplomatic pressure to make a peaceful retreat. Meanwhile, in the interior, and at the end of an impossibly long line of communication, Gordon had utterly failed in his attempt to bring the large Bantu kingdoms of Buganda and Bunyoro under Egyptian rule. Egypt's drive to the south thus petered out, some four years before the revolution of the Mahdi in 1881 put an end to Egyptian administration in the Sudan as a whole.

It could be said that in the last analysis both the Egyptian and the Zanzibar spheres of influence represented the triumph of European-manufactured firearms over the African spear and bow. It was their possession of firearms which gave to both these kinds of Muslim the confidence to sally forth among the infidel blacks; and when they encountered a well-established political unit among the Africans, it was the presence of firearms among their trade goods which enabled them to succeed in competition with earlier and less well-provided traders.

Between the Egyptian and the Zanzibari spheres there grew up during the second half of the nineteenth century a third sphere – that of the Christian Ethiopians, who were no less successful than the Muslims of the north and east in exploiting the weakness of their pagan neighbours. The Ethiopian expansion began later than the other two, because the chaotic internal situation of the country had been growing steadily worse since the middle of the eighteenth century. By the middle of the nineteenth century the kingdom had almost fallen apart into its constituent provinces, and rival emperors had become a regular feature. Then Ras Kassa, a robber baron of the north-western frontier, managed in 1855 to secure coronation at Axum under the imperial name of Theodore. It was Theodore who laid the foundations of something approaching a modern army, and as a result he was able to turn the tide against the pagan Oromo, who had been steadily overrunning the kingdom's southern and south-western borderlands since the end of the sixteenth century. It was Theodore who thus started the reunification of Tigre and Amhara in the north with the southerly province of Shoa. It was also Theodore who, by his capricious treatment of two British envoys, provoked the first direct European interference in the region since the sixteenth century – the punitive expedition led by Sir Robert Napier in 1867 against the fortress of Magdala, in the course of which, abandoned by many of his vassals, Theodore shot himself.

The superiority of Napier's weapons made a deep impression, not only upon the succeeding emperor, John IV, a Tigrean chief who fought his way to the throne with arms obtained from the British in exchange for his help in the Magdala campaign, but even more upon his vassal the young king Menelik of Shoa, who made himself so powerful that in 1878 John was compelled to recognize him as his successor. Throughout the eighties, while he was awaiting his inheritance, Menelik was building up his stock of European weapons from every available source – and not least from the Italians, whom he was ultimately to defeat with them at Adowa in 1896. Meanwhile, but more systematically, he was doing what all the successful African rulers of his time were doing: he was using ivory to get firearms, and firearms to get more ivory. In the process, too, he was year by year expanding his kingdom eastwards, southwards and westwards, at the expense of the Afar and Somali of Harrar and the Ogaden, at the expense of the Oromo to the south, at the expense of Kaffa and the now Oromo-occupied ancient Sidama kingdoms to the south-west. Menelik of Ethiopia is commonly regarded by European historians as an exceptional case, as a scrambler for Africa who happened to be an African ruler. In fact, however, Menelik of Ethiopia grew out of Menelik of Shoa, who was not essentially different from Mutesa of Buganda, Kabarega of Bunyoro or Msiri of Katanga.

Such, then, in necessarily impressionistic outline, were the conditions in East and North-East Africa at the time when European explorers were making their journeys and publishing to the western world the first descriptions of this corner of the continent. Such were the conditions at the time when the first parties of Christian missionaries established their settlements at the coast and in the interior, gathering round themselves the small groups (often of freed slaves) who were to be their first converts, but also and inevitably playing a political role as the advisers of African chiefs, who looked to them as to the Swahili Arabs for their knowledge of the world outside East Africa. Such again were the conditions in which British and French consuls pursued their strictly limited aims of furthering their national influence and interests from their bases at Cairo and at Zanzibar.

There was nothing in any of these still very tentative European approaches which was consciously preparing or even implying the scramble and partition which were to follow; and it would be the greatest possible error to imagine that the second phase was a necessary consequence of the first. The international hysteria which led to partition was caused not by the few European powers who already had small interests in tropical Africa but by a sudden stampede of those powers who had previously had no interests there at all. But for this stampede, it is probable that the main patterns of pre-partition development would have been pursued for a considerable time to come. On the East and North-East African scene, there were already in existence a few societies capable of learning from the new influences without being submerged by them, and they could react positively enough to the nineteenth-century condition of half-penetration to turn it to their advantage. Had there been no direct intervention of European power, the influence of the Muslims would have consolidated itself not only on the east coast and in the northern Sudan but in the southern Sudan also, and in many parts of East Africa and Zaire. To some extent this would have been the result of deliberate colonization by alien ruling groups, but to some extent too commercial contacts and political influence would have led to the Islamization of local institutions, as they had done in much of the Sudan in earlier times. It is doubtful whether Christian missions, starting as late as they did, would have been in time to forestall an Islamic expansion once Muslims had political power firmly in their hands. Had full-scale European intervention been delayed fifty years, not merely the northern third of Africa but the northern two-thirds would have belonged culturally to the world of Islam.

16 The European Scramble for African Colonies

In 1879, despite the steady increase in the power of the western European nations compared with that of other peoples in the world, only a small proportion of the African continent was under European rule. Algeria was French, but elsewhere in North Africa it was only in Egypt and in Tunis that there existed even the beginnings of European control. In West Africa, where Europeans had had commercial dealings with the coastal peoples for four centuries, it was only in French Senegal and on the British Gold Coast that there were colonial administrations ruling any considerable number of Africans. Only in the Senegal had European rule penetrated more than a few dozen miles inland. The British colonies of the Gambia, Sierra Leone and Lagos were no more than small enclaves in a political world still dominated by African governments. In the region which was to become Portuguese Guinea, there was Portuguese influence but hardly Portuguese rule. South of the Bight of Biafra, the French colony on the Gabon estuary consisted of little more than the small naval station and freed-slave community at Libreville. Apart from five or six coastal towns, Portuguese Angola and Moçambique were hardly colonies in the modern sense, but rather ill-defined trading preserves reaching towards the interior.

North of Moçambique even the coast was still virtually untouched by European political power. British diplomatic influence was strong in Zanzibar. The French had occupied the Comoros and also had a foothold in Madagascar. On the mainland, however, it was only in the extreme north-east that any European flag had yet been planted. This was a consequence of the Suez Canal, the construction of which had led France to seek a counterpoise to the British coaling station at Aden by establishing a base on the inhospitable Somali coast at Obok.

The only really deep penetration of Africa by European governments was in the extreme south, but here the position was complicated by the hostility between the British colonies on the coast and the Afri-kaner communities in the interior.

Two decades later, however, at the beginning of the twentieth century, European governments were claiming sovereignty over all

15 Africa in 1879

but six of some forty political units into which they had by then divided the continent – and of these six exceptions, four were more technical than real. This partition of Africa at the end of the nineteenth century was by no means a necessary consequence of the opening up of Africa by Europeans during the first three-quarters of the century. Very few indeed of the explorers of Africa had been sent by their governments to spy out the land for later conquest. It is probably safe to say that hardly any missionaries had ever imagined themselves as serving in the vanguard of colonialism. In so far as there was an economic motive for partition of the kind suggested by Marxist writers, it was a motive which appealed to those European powers which had no colonies and little commercial influence in Africa, rather than to those whose influence was already established there. The partition of Africa was indeed essentially the result of the appearance on the African scene of one or two powers which had not previously shown any interest in the continent. It was this that upset the pre-existing balance of power and influence and precipitated a state of international hysteria in which all the powers rushed in to stake claims to political sovereignty and to bargain furiously with each other for recognition in this or that region.

The first of these new factors to enter the African scene was not strictly speaking a power. It was a European sovereign acting in his personal capacity, though using his status as a sovereign to manipulate the threads of international diplomacy in pursuit of his private objective. King Leopold II of the Belgians was a man whose ambitions and capacities far outran the introverted preoccupations of the country he had been born to rule. His interest in founding an overseas empire had started in the 1850s and 1860s when, as Duke of Brabant, he had travelled in Egypt and had also scanned possible openings in places as remote as Taiwan, Sarawak, Fiji and the New Hebrides. Succeeding to the throne in 1865, he bent most of his great energies to the study of African exploration. Ten years later he was ready to act. His cover was the African International Association, created in 1876 to found a chain of commercial and scientific stations running across central Africa from Zanzibar to the Atlantic. The stations were to be garrisoned, and they were to serve as bases from which to attack the slave trade and to protect Christian missions. The first two expeditions of the Association entered East Africa from Zanzibar in

1878 and 1879, and attached themselves to mission stations of the White Fathers at Tabora and on Lake Tanganyika: From this moment, however, Leopold's interests switched increasingly to the west coast of Bantu Africa. Stanley, who in 1877 had completed his coast-to-coast journey by descending the Congo River, took service under King Leopold in 1879, and during the next five years established a practicable land and water transport system from the head of the Congo estuary to Stanley Falls, more than a thousand miles upstream, by the modern Kisangani (once Stanleyville).

Leopold, meanwhile, was deftly preparing the way for international recognition of his rule over the whole area of the Congo basin. Although his real intention was to develop his colony on the basis of a close-fisted commercial monopoly, he was successful in persuading a majority of the European powers that it would be preferable to have the Congo basin as a free-trade area under his 'international' regime than to let it fall to any of their national rivals. The skill of King Leopold's diplomacy has been widely recognized. What has received less notice is the extent to which it sharpened the mutual suspicions of the European powers about their activities in Africa as a whole. Probably it was Leopold, more than any other single statesman, who created the 'atmosphere' of scramble.

The next power to enter the African scene was Germany. Acting with stealth and swiftness in the eighteen months from the end of 1883 to the beginning of 1885, Germany made extensive annexations in four widely separated parts of the continent – South-West Africa, Togoland, Cameroon and East Africa. It was this German action which was really to let loose the scramble on a scale bound to continue with ever-increasing intensity until the whole continent was partitioned. It is therefore the more remarkable that historical research has tended to show that Germany entered Africa, not primarily in order to satisfy a desire for empire there, but rather as part of a much wider design to deflect French hostility against her in Europe by fomenting rivalries in Africa and by creating a situation in which Germany would be the arbiter between French and British ambitions.

The key to this situation lay in Egypt. Here in 1881 the joint Anglo-French financial control had broken down in face of the revolt of the national army, led by one of its most senior Egyptian officers,

'Urabi Pasha, with the tacit sympathy of the puppet Khedive Taufiq. France and Britain planned to act in concert to destroy 'Urabi, but on the eve of the operation a domestic crisis prevented the French government from participating. In consequence, the British invaded Egypt alone in 1882, and remained there, despite promises of withdrawal, as the *de facto* though not *de jure* rulers of the country until the declaration of a British Protectorate in 1914. The continued British occupation of Egypt angered the French and encouraged them to develop their formal empire in West Africa. This suited Germany, and it also gave Germany the means of twisting the British arm without openly supporting France, for British rule in Egypt was only possible with the support of a majority of Egypt's creditors represented on the international Caisse de la Dette, and this majority was controlled by Germany. Throughout the vital years of partition Germany supported British rule in Egypt, but at the price of British acquiescence in German actions throughout the rest of the continent. The German annexations were intended to incite the French to further action in Africa, but to action directed more against Britain than against Germany. In this way the painful subject of Alsace and Lorraine would be forgotten in the Anglo-French rivalry over Africa.

Such then was the motivation for the scramble. To the three powers already engaged on the African coastline – Britain, France and Portugal – there were now added two more, one of them a European sovereign in search of a personal empire, the other the strongest state in continental Europe, seeking to induce the most recent victim of its aggression to wear out its resentment in colonial adventure. In the circumstances, partition was bound to follow. Of the five powers mainly concerned, only King Leopold was positively anxious for a widespread territorial empire. Of the others, however, none was prepared to stand aside and see the continent swallowed by its rivals. And it was only a matter of time before Italy and Spain would likewise each claim a share. Deeply as it was to affect all the peoples of the continent, the partition was in its origin essentially a projection into Africa of the international politics of Europe. The new map of Africa which emerged from partition bore little relation to the activities of Europeans in Africa during its earlier periods.

As it happened, the first to secure international recognition of a large African empire was King Leopold. In 1884, after the British merchants engaged in the Congo trade had opposed their government's intention of recognizing Portuguese claims to the Lower Congo region, Portugal changed tack and instead appealed to France and Germany for support. France, seeing a chance to embarrass Britain, agreed to Bismarck's suggestion of determining the Congo question by an international conference in Berlin. And even before this conference could meet, France (having made a deal with King Leopold by which she secured the reversion of his Congo empire in case its development became too much for his resources) had joined Germany and the United States in granting recognition to the 'Congo Free State'. When the conference met in December 1884, the other powers had no option but to follow suit.

The Berlin Conference passed many high-sounding resolutions on the slave trade, on free trade, and on the need to prove effective occupation before fresh annexations were declared. In fact, however, the six months during which the conference was being prepared had seen the most flimsily supported annexations in the whole partition, those of Germany herself. While the conference was actually sitting, Bismarck announced his government's protectorate over those parts of East Africa where Karl Peters and his associates had obtained dubious treaties from bemused and often bogus 'chiefs' in the course of a single expedition lasting a few weeks. It was now clear to all that a quick partition of the whole continent was inevitable, and the delegates went home from Berlin at the beginning of 1885 to consider where further claims for their own countries could most usefully be developed.

The logic of earlier interests made it inevitable that the French African empire should expand first within the western bulge of the continent. By 1883 their war against Ahmadu, which they had begun in 1879, had brought the French to the Upper Niger. It was natural that they should think first of expanding along the internal line of communications offered by this great river, and then of connecting their conquests with their spheres of influence on the coast. But their advance down the Niger was slow: Timbuktu was not reached until 1893. The French right flank was threatened by an adventurous soldier-trader, Samori Toure, who was building up an empire on traditional Mande lines. This was a much more formidable obstacle than Ahmadu's conquest state. Samori was not finally overcome until 1898, and it was not till some two years before this that the French were able to resume their westward advance.

During the 1880s, the future of the French Gabon remained less certain. Although King Leopold's activities in the Lower Congo had stimulated the French to develop a treaty network in the area explored for them by an adventurous naval officer, de Brazza, it was not until the nineties that they began to drive expeditions northwards to meet the expanding frontiers of French West Africa at Lake Chad, and north-eastwards up the Ubangui to threaten the Upper Nile.

For Britain the strategy of expansion was by no means so obvious as for France. Southern Africa was one possible growing-point. It was also, however, a region where Britain had already been compelled to recognize the independence of the Boer Republics, and where it was now faced with extensive German annexations on the south-western side of the subcontinent. Northward expansion from the Cape had therefore to take place through the bottleneck of Botswana, hastily annexed in 1885 to counter the Germans. Moreover, although the British government had to handle the diplomacy of partition and to acquire the nominal sovereignty, this was a region where the practical initiative lay with the Europeans of the Cape Colony. Among these the most active figure was Cecil Rhodes, a British settler who had made a vast fortune out of the amalgamation of the diamond mines at Kimberley in Griqualand West. In response to his pressure, the British government in 1888 declared the existence of a British sphere of interest between Botswana and the Zambezi. In 1889, by Royal Charter, it delegated the functions of government in this region to Rhodes's British South Africa Company.

In Africa north of the Zambezi, wider options had to be exercised. Commercially the most valuable region lay in West Africa, and there were many who thought that other interests should be sacrificed for the sake of an advantageous partition of this part of Africa between Britain and France. It is in fact probable that at any time during the eighties there would have been terms on which the French would have left the British an unbroken sphere from Sierra Leone to Cameroon; and a British withdrawal from East Africa could probably also have produced a German withdrawal from the west coast. The first of any such terms, however, would have been a British with-drawal from Egypt, and this was a thing which no British government after 1885 would even contemplate. Indeed, Lord Salisbury, who as Prime Minister and Foreign Secretary handled the British side of partition during the decisive years from 1886 to 1892, built the whole of his African policy around the retention of Egypt. This meant in the first place a deliberate encouragement of French expansion in the west, to the point of doing nothing to prevent the encirclement of the four well-established British spheres along the coast. It meant, there-fore, looking for the main British share in the partition on the eastern side of the continent, even though it was commercially almost valueless, and even though it must in the long run prove expensive to occupy. The Germans were already entrenched on the mainland op-posite Zanzibar, but in 1886 Salisbury was able to demarcate the rough limits of a British sphere of influence in what is now Kenya, while holding open the possibility of a British Uganda and of a 'back door' to the Sudan and Egypt. In East Africa, as in Zambezia and in central and northern Nigeria, a Chartered Company's willingness to take the responsibility for administration lay at the back of Salisbury's decision to negotiate at the international level.

There remained only the additional claims to what is now Zambia and Malawi, formulated in 1889–90, and Salisbury's design was complete. In 1890 and 1891 he proceeded to delimitation with Germany, France, Portugal and Italy. The most important of these agreements was that with Germany. Though often described as the exchange of Heligoland for Zanzibar, Britain in fact ceded Heligoland to Germany as part of a settlement which defined most of the new Anglo-German frontiers in Africa in a manner satisfactory to Salisbury. The agreement with Italy fixed the frontier between the British East African Protectorate and the newly claimed Italian colony in Somalia. The two Anglo-Portuguese agreements of 1890 and 1891, though imposed in a high-handed way by a strong power upon a weaker one, definitively settled the frontiers between British Central Africa and its Portuguese neighbours. It was the Anglo-French agreement which was the least satisfactory of the four, since it left the inland frontiers in West Africa undecided, and since it failed to touch upon the all-important question of the Sudan.

*

The most remarkable aspect of the first ten years of the scramble for Africa was the extent to which almost everything of importance happened in Europe. Statesmen and diplomats met in offices or country houses and drew lines across maps which themselves were usually inaccurate. Often the lack of geographical detail was such that frontiers had to be traced along lines of latitude and longitude. In Africa itself the reality of partition was slight indeed. A dozen over-worked men could make up the local representatives of a Chartered Company. A consul and two assistants might well form the government of a Protectorate. Such establishments were apt to be too busy keeping themselves alive to engage in military collisions with neighbouring governments. Even if rival teams were racing for a treaty in the same area, it was most unlikely that their paths would cross. The conflicting claims would be sorted out a year later round a table in some European capital.

As the scramble passed into its second decade, however, the activities of the men on the spot assumed a new significance. The position of interior frontiers often depended upon which of two neighbouring powers was able to create something like effective occupation. En-counters between the nationals of different European powers became increasingly frequent. They happened especially along the western frontiers of Nigeria, where (after the French had conquered the kingdom of Dahomey in 1893) fairly substantial military forces threa-tened to collide in the disputed territory of Borgu. The hurry to reach Borgu before the French also involved Goldie's Royal Niger Company in its first military clashes with the African states lying within its chartered sphere; to forestall the French in Borgu it was necessary to conquer the emirates of Nupe and Ilorin. The need to preserve British interests, coupled with the risk that troops of a British com-pany might clash with soldiers of the French Republic, led a forceful new British Colonial Secretary, Joseph Chamberlain, to institute an official West African Frontier Force in 1897. It was with imperial troops that Ashanti was invaded, and protectorates declared over it and its northern marches, in order to keep some hinterland for British interests on the Gold Coast, and that the kingdom of Benin was conquered.

Again, by the later nineties French expeditions were converging on Lake Chad from three directions, from the French Congo, from

Algeria and from the Upper Niger, and for a brief time the dream of a vast French empire linking the Mediterranean, the Atlantic and the Indian Ocean caught the imagination of the French public. A French occupation of the Upper Nile would strike a vital blow at the British in Egypt. From 1896 until 1898, therefore, Commandant Marchand pushed a painful passage with a small company of black soldiers all the way from the Gabon to Fashoda on the White Nile, some 400 miles south of Khartoum. Britain in 1885 had compelled Egypt to abandon its former dominion in the Nilotic Sudan to the forces of the Mahdi, Muhammad Ahmad, on the grounds that Egypt could not then afford the expense of reconquest. Salisbury, however, had never lost sight of the Sudan; in 1896, after a disastrous defeat inflicted upon the Italians by the French-armed troops of Menelik of Ethiopia, the new Egyptian army trained by Kitchener was ordered to begin the southward advance. The province of Dongola fell the same year, Berber in 1897, Khartoum itself after the battle of Omdurman in September 1898. A week later Kitchener heard of Marchand's presence at Fashoda, and hastened to confront him with a vastly superior force: the 'Fashoda incident' brought France and Britain to the brink of war. This well-known fact of history has tended to obscure another, which is that Kitchener's reconquest of the Sudan, at a conservative estimate, cost the death in battle of 20,000 Sudanese. The partition of Africa, as it approached its logical conclusion, was beginning to be a bloody business.

The crowning bloodshed, however, was that inflicted by white men on white in South Africa. Here the discovery of the vast gold wealth of the Witwatersrand in 1886 had given enormous potential power to the Transvaal, hitherto the poorest and weakest of the European communities. And this was clearly appreciated by both the titans of the South African scene – by Paul Kruger, President of the Transvaal from 1883 to 1902, and by Cecil Rhodes, who had extended his mining interests from Kimberley to the Witwatersrand and who, from 1890 to 1896, was also Prime Minister of the Cape Colony. To Kruger's ambition of creating a united white South Africa under Boer republican leadership, Rhodes opposed a larger dream. He envisaged a federation of South Africa, where Boer, Briton and even conceivably the Bantu might achieve the closest harmony. Such a federation would be internally self-governing but would maintain a strong connection with Britain and the British Empire, the extension of which Rhodes once described as his only religion. Kruger, then, represented a seventeenth-century Afrikaner ethos making belated attempts to adapt itself to new circumstances; Rhodes was the local embodiment of the new capitalist imperialism of the late nineteenth and early twentieth centuries, which in South Africa had a predominantly British colouring.

In the opening stages of the conflict, as we have seen, Rhodes had concentrated on turning the Transvaal flank; he had helped to manoeuvre the British government into Botswana, and had obtained a Royal Charter to govern the region to the north of it. In 1890 he sent a pioneer column of policemen and settlers to occupy the Shona territories to the east and north-east of Matabeleland. In 1891 the operational sphere of his Company was extended to include most of what became Northern Rhodesia (the modern Zambia).[1] Rhodes believed that these measures, as well as being the first steps in the northward expansion he sought for British rule, would encircle the Transvaal and so drive it into closer cooperation with the Cape Colony. He hoped that the minerals of the new territories in the north would enable the Cape to match the wealth of the Transvaal. But before the new settler colony of Southern Rhodesia could begin to take root in Zimbabwe, Rhodes's men had first to engaged in unofficial war with the Portuguese from Moçambique, then to conquer a Matabele nation bitterly resentful of their presence, and finally to overcome a rising of both Matabele and Shona occasioned by the settlers' demands for land and labour. Fighting did not cease until 1897. Even then, the promised gold of the Monomotapas' former empire proved disappointing, and also (until the coming of the railways from the Cape and from Beira in 1899) very costly to extract.

In relation to the Transvaal, all Rhodes had succeeded in doing was to convince Kruger that the very existence of his country was at stake, and to determine him to cut loose from the rest of South Africa by securing the completion of the Transvaal's own railway to the Portuguese port at Delagoa Bay. He was thus able to keep out of the customs union and the integrated railway system from the ports

---

1 In exchange for this extension of the Charter, Rhodes provided for a few years a subsidy of £10,000 a year to pay for the administration of Nyasaland.

in the Cape and Natal, with which Rhodes had been hoping to enmesh him. Meanwhile, the integrity of Kruger's Boer republic was being menaced from within by the growing numbers and wealth of the Uitlanders, the foreigners drawn to the Transvaal by its mining industry. The old informal Boer ideas of government had given way before a new administrative machine, staffed by educated Netherlanders, which insisted on the Uitlanders subscribing to Afrikaner ideals before sharing in political rights. Rhodes, always an impatient man,

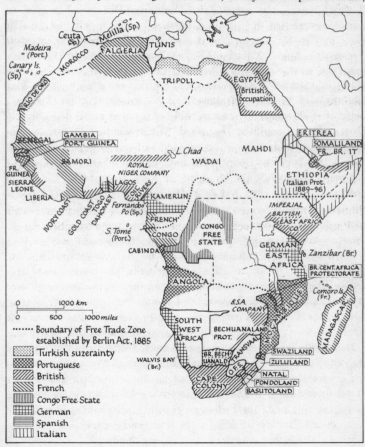

16   Africa in 1891

retaliated by mounting the Jameson Raid of 1896, in an attempt to replace Kruger's government by an Uitlander regime more amenable to his designs for South Africa.

The ignominious failure of the Jameson Raid ruined Rhodes politically. He forfeited all claim to Afrikaner support, even in his own Cape Colony. Indeed, he convinced Afrikaners throughout South Africa that British South Africans, supported by Britain, were aiming at the overthrow of the republics and the ideals for which they stood. This was indeed the case, for the direction of British policy in South Africa now passed to Chamberlain, who had been privy to the Raid plan, and to his nominee as British High Commissioner in South Africa, Sir Alfred Milner. Whereas Rhodes, for all his faults and mistakes, was as much South African as British, or more so, in his aims and outlook, Chamberlain and Milner cared nothing for local feelings, and Milner even more than his master was impelled by a belief that all South Africa had to be conquered and ruled until the Dutch element could be anglicized. Milner deliberately pressed the Uitlander cause to the point of conflict, and war came at last in 1899. The help Kruger had hoped for from Britain's European rivals did not materialize. Only the Orange Free State stood by the side of its brother republic against the might of Britain and her empire. Independent Boer commandos continued the struggle long after the British armies had taken formal possession of the two republics, but by 1902 the majority of the Boers had had enough, and sought peace.

With the British conquest of the Boer republics, the European scramble for African colonies was virtually complete. Over large areas of the continent it was still mainly a paper transaction negotiated in the chancelleries of Europe, and it was only much later that its significance became apparent to most of the Africans concerned. Here and there, however, it had already provoked bitter resistance. For Ahmadu and Samori in the western Sudan, for Ashanti and Dahomey and Benin, for the Arab and Swahili slave-traders of east and central Africa, for the Mahdists on the upper Nile and for the Matabele in Zimbabwe, and not least for the Afrikaners in the extreme south, the coming of the European governments could only mean the destruction of their traditional ways of life and the imposition of new orders in which they could see no place for themselves. All these had fought to the best of their abilities, and lost.

Of the peoples of Africa who still remained independent by 1902, the Moroccans were sheltered for a space by the mutual jealousies of the European powers. But in 1904 Britain and France settled their differences in the Entente Cordiale, and in 1911 France bought off the German interest by surrendering a large slice of her Congo territory to the German colony of Kamerun (Cameroon). Morocco could thus at last be partitioned by France and Spain. Only the Ethiopians had succeeded in holding back the flowing tide of European material power, forcing the Italians to limit themselves for some time to the dry and torrid coastlines of Eritrea and Somalia. In 1911, however, Italy sought her compensation in the conquest of Libya from the dying Turkish empire. Liberia also had precariously preserved her independence, from all but the European money-lenders. Elsewhere there could be no doubt that Africans were to enter the twentieth century under the firm control of one or other of the European colonial powers.

17   The Colonial Period: First Phase

Nothing so well demonstrates the element of unreality in the scramble for Africa as the thirty-five years of almost total obscurity which followed the limelight of partition. For as long as the international rivalry lasted, African questions were the most important in the world. Prime ministers spent time on them. Cabinets met over them. They coursed through almost every channel of international diplomacy; and from one point of view, it is a remarkable tribute to those involved that the partition of Africa was accomplished without involving the world in war. The international tension grew in intensity as the unclaimed areas in Africa diminished; but no sooner was the new map of Africa complete than the excitement, just as suddenly, died down. Even while the scramble was in progress, no sooner was a new colony or protectorate added to the dependencies of one or other of the colonial powers than interest in that territory dried up. The colonial powers had partitioned Africa as an insurance for the future, not because they had any present plans for its exploitation. Thenceforward, their main concern was that the annual premium should not be too high.

The ideal colony was one which was economically self-supporting. Whether it produced much or little, whether its people progressed fast or slowly, whether its economic development was undertaken by the people themselves under the guidance of the colonial government or by European settlers or mining companies, all these things mattered little in comparison with how nearly the budget could be balanced, how small the grant-in-aid could be. Early-twentieth-century Europe was in no need of an increase in African products, and African markets accounted for a negligible proportion of European exports. One day the position might be different.

Till then, the less heard of the African colonies the better.

This attitude on the part of the colonial powers, which lasted until after the First World War, was one which threw responsibility squarely upon the young colonial governments, and it is astonishing to remember that colonial governments at this period consisted of mere handfuls of men. Johnston was sent out to found a colonial administration in Nyasaland with his own salary and £10,000 a year. Colvile started the protectorate administration in Uganda with a grant-in-aid of £50,000 a year. Lugard in Northern Nigeria had a little over £100,000 for a territory containing about 10 million people. French patterns were a little less niggardly, but not basically dissimilar. In relation to Africa, France soon had to abandon her normal doctrine that the colonies should trade only with the metropolis. Any form of revenue which would reduce the financial drain on the metropolis was welcome.

With such attitudes prevailing, colonial occupation had of necessity to be a slow process. Johnston, with his £10,000, could just afford an armed force of seventy Indian soldiers under two British officers. Any further increase in his civil or military establishment had to be paid for out of the local revenue – when there was one. Lugard set out to rule Northern Nigeria with a staff of five European administrative officers and a regiment of the West African Frontier Force, consisting of 2,000 to 3,000 African soldiers under about 120 European officers and N.C.O.s. Any one of half a dozen of the powerful emirs in Hausa-land could have put many times that number in the field against him. In these as in many other comparable cases, the colonial forces were of course much better armed and disciplined than those who tried to contest their authority. Still, forces of this size always had to be used with the greatest caution. One serious defeat, or even a successful ambush, could have wiped out the entire armed force of most early colonial governments. The Marxist stereotype, of brutal imperialists riding to power over the machine-gunned corpses of defenceless Africans, is far further from the truth than its opposite, which would maintain that colonial occupation was a bloodless process.

Clearly the first task of every colonial government was to establish its authority over its own subjects. The touchstone of such authority was the power to tax. For as long as a colonial adminstration merely wished to live in the country at its own expense and without getting too much in the way of the local inhabitants, fair words were often sufficient; and in some colonies this arrangement lasted for many years. It was when a colonial government wished to recover the costs of occupation that the real test came. What every colonial government tried to do was to establish a nucleus around the capital, and to extend its influence slowly outwards as its resources increased. What every colonial government learned from experience was that the inhabitants of the peripheral areas did not simply wait peacefully until their turn to be brought under administration arrived. They traded their ivory and built up their supplies of arms. They started to form alliances against the colonial government, or to annoy the governments of neighbouring territories. They cut telegraph wires. They attacked caravans. They harboured refugees from the administered areas. Expeditions had to be sent against them long before the appointed time, and while the troops were absent on these forays, the areas within the nucleus seized the opportunity to revolt. Such was the life of a young colonial administration.

In nearly every territory of every colonial power only a serious military crisis brought forth reinforcements and forced up grants-in-aid to a level which permitted some rough policing of the whole territory. By 1900, for example, Nyasaland's £10,000 grant had risen to £100,000, and Uganda's £50,000 to £400,000. The situation in most colonial territories showed a comparable development five to ten years after the start of colonial rule. This was usually the high peak for metropolitan grants-in-aid, which from then onwards tended to decline annually as the local revenues rose, until by about 1914 they were virtually extinguished. Basically, it was because he could not provide the capital outlay represented by the period of grants-in-aid in more conventional colonies that King Leopold's personal rule in the Congo sank to such appalling depths of maladministration. Faced by the failure of revenue to meet expenditure, he employed an ill-controlled and barbarous native soldiery to levy arbitrary amounts of tribute in rubber and ivory for the benefit of the state and the concessionnaire companies in which it held interests. Even these measures, however, failed to produce the necessary funds, and when news of the worst atrocities leaked abroad, international opinion at length forced the King to surrender his private empire to the Belgian government in 1908.

Throughout tropical Africa the termination of grants-in-aid more or less coincided with the bringing of all but the most remote of the peripheral areas under civil administration. In a sense, therefore, the grant-in-aid can be regarded as the cost of the unremunerative military policing of areas as yet unadministered. On the face of it, financial self-support was a simple product of the progress from military to civilian rule. For this reason, early colonial historians often talked of a stage called 'pacification' as preceding another stage called 'law and order'. In fact, however, the progress was very closely related to the growth of communications. Before taxes could be paid in any district, there had to be something which the people could grow and sell. But before there could be economic crops, there had to be communications to get them to market.

The supreme example of this thesis on the one hand was the Oil Rivers Protectorate in eastern Nigeria, where (with palm-oil as an economic crop and with the Delta waterways for communication) colonial administration was set up and paid for out of customs duties without any grant-in-aid. As an example of the opposite sort, there could be no taxation in Uganda until the railway from Mombasa began to approach Lake Victoria about 1900. Before that date, the only economic export was ivory. With the railhead at Kisumu and a couple of steamers on the lake, however, hides and skins, wild rubber, beeswax and a number of other natural products at once became marketable, while the way was opened for the introduction of cotton and coffee, the two staple crops of the Lake Victoria basin in modern times. Thenceforward there was no problem of taxation in the nucleus of the Protectorate; but it was not for another decade, with the construction of roads and the arrival of the motor lorry, and with extensions of the railway and steamer system, that the inhabitants of the northern half of the country were able to offer to the collector anything more than their own labour services in commutation of tax. Until about 1910, therefore, this remained an area controlled mainly by military patrols, and civil administration was not finally established there until about 1919.

One of the most difficult questions about which to generalize is the degree to which the lives of ordinary people were changed by these early proceedings of European colonial governments. It is here that we encounter the apparently basic distinction between the territories where Europeans were in search of land and minerals, and those where they were seeking merely to trade and govern. The former group of territories included not only Southern Rhodesia, Northern Rhodesia, Nyasaland and Kenya, but also the Portuguese territories in East and West Africa, the German territories in East Africa, South-West Africa and Cameroon and also those parts of the French and Belgian Congo where the state and commercial companies held large territorial concessions. Here there were many hundreds of thousands of Africans who in one way or another lost the lands they had previously cultivated. Many were forced to move to new and perhaps inferior land in 'native reserves'. Many others were left in possession of the lands they were cultivating at the time of the occupation but lost the surrounding uncultivated land which in a sense was their 'fallow'. Accordingly, when they moved, in the course of shifting cultivation, they found themselves rent-paying 'squatters' on alienated land.

It would, however, be a great mistake to imagine either that all Africans who lived in colonies of settlement or land concessions suffered in this way, or that such suffering was confined to territories where land was alienated to Europeans. In Southern Rhodesia it may well be that most of the African population suffered some disturbance in their land use as a result of European immigration; in all the territories to the north of the Zambezi, however, the numbers of people affected were a very small proportion of the total. In German East Africa these were confined to one small corner of the northern province. In Kenya peoples as numerous as the Luo and the Baluyia were virtually untouched by European settlement, while even among the Kikuyu, who later came to nurse a special grievance on this score, it is likely that those directly affected constituted less than one per cent. Most of the land alienated in Kenya was taken from the pastoral tribes – the Masai, the Nandi and the Kipsigis. All that white settlement did to the agricultural peoples was to block their natural expansion into land previously held at the spear's point by the pastoralists.

An indirect effect, which was somewhat more widespread, was the wage-labour demand by settlers, and above all by plantation and mining companies in all these territories. During the early part of the colonial period, such demands were almost invariably satisfied by political pressure of one kind or another. Here, however, one must remember that in all colonial territories a very large part of the demands made by governments upon their subjects were demands for labour – labour for the construction and maintenance of roads and railways, labour for the building and clearing of government stations, and (above all in the early days) labour for porterage. Nominally such labour might be given in commutation of tax. In practice, however, it was compulsory labour, imposed not upon all alike but upon those who were detailed by their chiefs to give it, in response to the demands of government officers. Africans of this period did not perceive the difference, so clear to European minds, between compulsory labour for public and for private purposes; they were merely aware that one of the most immediate and unpleasant consequences of European rule was that the able-bodied might be enlisted for arduous labour of a kind previously considered suitable only for women and slaves.

For the African peoples the most important factor at this stage of colonial history, however, was probably not the issue of European settlement or its absence, not the relatively concrete issues of land and labour, certainly not the difference between the policy of one colonial power and another, but the far more intangible psychological issue of whether any given society or group was left feeling that it had turned the colonial occupation to its own advantage, or alternatively that it had been humiliated. To a large extent this was a result of the accidents of occupation in each particular territory. Every occupying power inevitably made both friends and enemies. Every occupying power, before it could train a local army or police force, needed native allies and was prepared to accord substantial privileges to those who would play this part.

According to the value judgements of modern Africa, such peoples were traitors and quislings; but these categories hardly fit the circumstances of a century ago. Then, the primary choice lay not with individuals but with their political leaders. If these were far-sighted and well-informed, and more particularly if they had had access to foreign advisers such as missionaries or traders, they might well understand that nothing was to be gained by resistance, and much by negotiation. If they were less far-sighted, less fortunate or less well-advised, they would see their traditional enemies siding with the

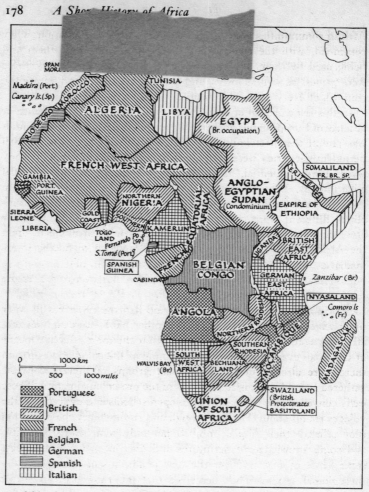

17   Africa in 1914

invader and would themselves assume an attitude of resistance, which could all too easily end in military defeat, the deposition of chiefs, the loss of land to the native allies of the occupying power, possibly even the political fragmentation of the society or state. In trying to see the early effects of the colonial occupation upon the African peoples, it is essential to realize that the rivalries and tensions between

African communities did not end with the colonial occupation. They continued, with the colonial administrations both using them and being used by them. As with the slave trade in earlier times, there were gainers as well as losers, and both were to be found within the confines of every colonial territory.

In this issue of gain or loss, there is no doubt that the presence or absence of European missionaries as precursors of the colonial regimes was one of the most important factors. At the start of the colonial period missionaries were frequently more numerous, and in many ways more influential, than the representatives of the colonial governments. They knew the language of the people among whom they had been working, and although they often belonged to nationalities different from that of the colonial power in any particular area, they understood the new forces which were breaking in upon the African world. They were thus well qualified to be the intermediaries between the one and the other, and from now on were so not merely as the advisers of African rulers but even more as the teachers of their subjects.

No colonial government of this period had the resources to enter upon education. Missionaries, on the other hand, were finding that all over pagan Africa the school was by far the most effective means of Christian evangelism. By the beginning of the colonial occupation there were already in existence small groups of literate converts gathered around the mission stations of the pre-colonial period. These early converts were now sent out to open schools and churches in the villages round about. However rough and rudimentary the education they offered, their pupils imbibed not only some Christian faith, and some knowledge of Scriptures and doctrines, but also at least some sense of mastery over the new conditions of life created by the colonial system. They perceived that the knowledge and skills of the newcomers were communicable. They found that for those who would learn, the new age could spell not servitude but renascence.

The first third of the colonial period, therefore, almost throughout tropical Africa from the Sahara to the Zambezi, was a period when the colonial powers had no positive policy and when colonial governments were concerned first and foremost to make their own territories economically self-supporting. Some small immediate steps

in this direction could be taken by the imposition of import and
export duties, by the granting of concessions and by the lease or sale
of lands and mineral rights. Essentially, however, the problem was
one of creating for the inhabitants the opportunity to earn cash
incomes which could then be taxed. This could be done either by
stimulating them to grow economic crops on their own land or
alternatively by encouraging European settlers or companies to establish plantations, or to develop mining industries, in which Africans
would be employed as wage labourers. Either way, the imposition of
direct taxation would be the incentive; but such taxation could not be
imposed until governments had provided the necessary basic structure
of civil administration, law and order, and communications. In consequence, it usually took between twenty and thirty years before self-
support could be achieved, even on the most meagre scale of revenue
and expenditure. Throughout this initial period deficiencies in
revenue had to be met from imperial grants-in-aid, grudgingly
given.

Where any particular colonial government placed the emphasis in
its economic development, whether on immigrant enterprise or on
indigenous peasant production, followed partly from local circumstances, but also largely from the personal views of individual
governors. France pursued one policy in West Africa, another in
Equatorial Africa. British colonial governments encouraged European
plantation agriculture in Kenya and to some extent in Nyasaland, but
discouraged it in Uganda and disallowed it altogether in the West
African territories. The imperial governments in France and Britain
were not especially concerned one way or the other about such issues.
Nor did the various policies pursued at this stage make much difference to any but a small minority of Africans living in the territories north of the Zambezi. It was only later, when settlers tried to
consolidate their political influence in the face of the rising aspirations
of the African majority populations, that the difference between
European-settled territories and the rest became profound and
serious. For the African populations of all these territories, the vital
issue during the first thirty years of colonial rule was the way every
particular people came to terms with its colonial government, whether
early or late, whether by agreement or by force, whether advan-
tageously or disadvantageously in relation to its African neighbours.

It was within the framework of these communal changes and of changes caused by the coming of colonialism that individual choices of cooperation or resistance had to be exercised.

18 · The Colonial Period: Second Phase

In the years immediately preceding the First World War, colonies throughout Africa south of the Sahara and north of the Zambezi began to assume the classic forms which they were to retain until the eve of independence. The colonial governments, whether British or French, German or Italian, Belgian or Portuguese, were now the real masters of their territories. The period of resistance by traditional tribal communities was over, that of opposition by emancipated nationalism had not yet begun. Military garrisons, consisting almost entirely of African troops under European officers, were adequate to deal with any small emergencies, while sea and rail communications were so far developed that reinforcements could now be brought from one territory to another in a matter of weeks if not of days.

Civil administration was now the rule for all but the remotest districts, and under the governors and their small central secretariats the regular hierarchies of provincial and district officials were developing. These were now recruited on a professional basis, and were no longer, as their predecessors had been, seconded army officers or locally engaged traders and big game hunters. Great strides had been made in medicine and in hygiene, in so far as these affected the lives of Europeans in the tropics, and even the wives of expatriate officials were now occasionally seen in Africa. With the wives came the clubs and the social colour bar. The second generation of colonial rulers was much more firmly dug in, not only in security but also in outlook, than the first.

By the outbreak of the First World War, expatriate officials in most of the African colonies had grown in numbers from the original dozens to a few hundred. The functions of colonial governments, however, were still extremely limited. Almost all the increase in staff made possible by the gradual growth of the revenues had until now been absorbed in building up the general administrative services. The only technical departments which had been seriously developed were those dealing with public works like railways, roads, waterways and government buildings, including the housing of expatriate officials. Medical services were in general sufficient only for government employees. Education, as a function of government, was practically non-existent. Agricultural and veterinary services, though important results had been achieved at the level of research and experiment, had no machinery other than the occasional help of administrative officers for getting new plants and techniques into circulation.

The district administrative official, therefore, was the linch-pin of the whole system, but even his influence had narrow enough limits. His primary duties, as the local representative of the colonial government, were to maintain law and order and to supervise the collection of the tax. In practice this meant that he exercised some control over the way local communities governed themselves. How much control, and at what level, was a thing which varied greatly not only from territory to territory but also from one part to another of the same territory. French and Belgian colonial governments had quarrelled with and deposed almost all their African kings and big chiefs. They had broken up the larger indigenous political units, ruling the divided sections through nominated chiefs. British and German governments had tended to respect the integrity of larger units, where these existed, and to rule such areas indirectly through the traditional rulers and chieftainly hierarchies. But there were many areas where political units were small and where power was divided among ill-defined groups of elders. In such areas British and German practice approximated to that of the French and Belgians.

While there were differences in the degree of interference, however, for ordinary purposes most Africans continued to be ruled by Africans. Most criminal and all civil cases were tried in native courts and according to customary law. European administrators acted as magistrates in a few more serious cases, but most of their judicial work consisted in revising and modifying the sentences and procedures of native courts. Questions of land occupation, inheritance, marriage, birth, sickness and death were still (apart from the Christian influences emanating from the missions) treated very much as they had been in pre-colonial days. For those who lived in the rural areas, and most areas were rural, the prohibition of warfare and the imposition of tax were the two principal innovations of the first phase of the colonial period; but the tax was usually small, and there were many who were never called upon to pay it, and many more for whom the obligation was commuted into a few days or weeks of road-making or porterage, undertaken at the bidding of the village chief. In most colonies all that had happened was that a light form of overall policing and administrative control was being undertaken by the alien governments, which after twenty years of annual deficits were now able to recover the running costs from the governed. There was no sense of any need to hasten change, however. The assumption on the part of all the colonial powers was that the colonial system would operate for hundreds of years to come. It was for governments to maintain peace and the rule of law, leaving education, morality, and even health, to the missions, and economic development to the initiative of individual producers and traders.

In the period between the First and Second World Wars, colonial governments were still essentially unhurried. There was, however, a marked change in their conception of the functions of government. In part this was the result of the first war. Having been locked for four years in internecine combat, the colonial powers were less arrogantly self-confident as to the innate superiority of the western world and in particular as to the unfettered sovereignty of its national units. In the metropolitan countries it began to be felt that colonialism needed a goal and a justifying philosophy. This need was made urgent by the decision of the victors to break up the German colonial empire. In Africa the former German colonies of Togoland and Cameroon were each divided into French and British spheres; South-West Africa was allocated to the Union of South Africa; and German East Africa was partitioned between Great Britain and Belgium. But the allies, though they arranged the details among themselves, did not just baldly annex these territories in the peace treaty. From the newly constituted League of Nations they accepted the duty of governing them as 'a sacred trust of civilization' until such time as they were able 'to stand on their own feet in the arduous conditions of the modern world'. The arrangement no doubt contained a large element of hypocrisy, but among those who made it there were a few men of great integrity and influence who were genuinely concerned to develop a new and more creative kind of colonialism, suited to the third and fourth generations of colonial rule.

The idea which was new and important in the Mandates system of the League of Nations – it was elaborated alike by Britain's greatest African administrator, Lord Lugard, in his *Dual Mandate in British Tropical Africa*, and by the French Colonial Minister, Albert Sarraut, in his *Mise en valeur des colonies françaises*, during the years immediately after the war – was that the colonial powers had an obligation, not merely to govern justly but also to carry the colonial peoples decisively forward both economically and politically. Both Lugard and Sarraut still visualized a long future for colonialism; but their conceptions were dynamic, not static. Moreover, both authors reached the pleasing conclusion that what was best for the colonies was also in the best material interests of the colonial powers. The time was past when Africa's productive capacity and potential markets could be held in reserve. From Europe's point of view as from Africa's the time for economic development had arrived.

Allégé désormais des obligations de la conquête, le labeur français aux colonies peut maintenant se consacrer à l'organisation du plein rendement de sa patrimoine. L'intérêt souverain de la France, en effort de relèvement après une guerre où son héroisme a sauvé le destin de ses colonies, est aujourd'hui d'accord avec les intérêts de chaque possession coloniale, pour dégager avec sûreté les plans directeurs, les principes dominants, l'unité des vues, qui doivent guider et ordonner la tâche de mise en valeur.[1]

The main implication of Sarraut's doctrine, very ably stated for the British African territories in the two Ormsby-Gore Reports, for East Africa in 1924 and for West Africa in 1926, was that economic development throughout tropical Africa must be centred on the indigenous peoples, and that it must start with the development of medical services, educational services and agricultural services. This

1 Relieved henceforward of the obligations of conquest, French effort in the colonies can now be dedicated to the full development of its heritage. The sovereign interest of France in her struggle for recovery after a war in which her heroism has safeguarded the destiny of her colonies, is today at one with the interest of each colonial possession to lay down the secure guiding plans, dominant principles, and unity of views which must direct and control the task of development.

would open to every African the possibility of bringing up a healthy family, with eyes open to the need to improve living standards. Furthermore, help and instruction would be available in the rural areas to enable African peasant proprietors to become producers for the world market and buyers of imported goods. The Ormsby-Gore plan was not in the least a matter of starry-eyed idealism, but rather

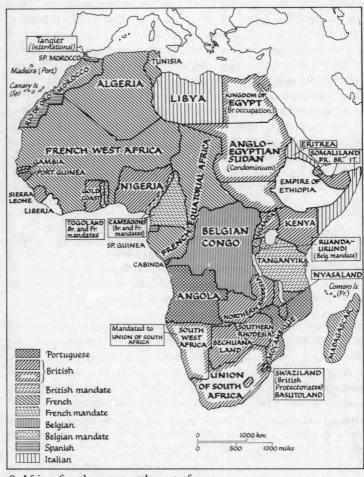

18 Africa after the peace settlement of 1919

one of enlightened self-interest. It did not advocate large-scale metropolitan aid for the tropical colonies. It did, however, at a time when
colonial revenues were just beginning to outgrow the needs of law
and order, suggest a broad extension of the accepted functions of
government in a way which most colonial governments would hardly
have advocated of their own accord.

The outstanding example in British territories was that of education, a field in which, if left to themselves, colonial governments were
apt to be particularly apathetic. In 1925 the British governments
created an Advisorship and a powerful Advisory Committee at the
Colonial Office; the governors of the African colonies were
summoned to a conference, and a practicable and far-reaching education policy was agreed whereby colonial governments would spend
their limited funds in subsidizing, inspecting and improving the
schools already operated by the Christian missions, not in founding
rival and far more expensive systems of state education. In the following ten or fifteen years, therefore, most of the territories in British
tropical Africa witnessed the development of educational systems
capable of providing perhaps a quarter of their young citizens with
two to four years of schooling, and a select few with eight years or
even twelve. Belgian policy in the Congo was similar, but with the
emphasis on primary education. The French, on the other hand,
made no use of the pre-existing missionary foundations, but set up
state schools in which a very small minority of Africans followed the
curricula of metropolitan France. Numbers, however, were hardly
the most significant issue at this stage. What was of overriding importance was that all over tropical Africa it was being shown that
Africans were as capable as anyone else of becoming educated, efficient and responsible, able to carry out the most exacting tasks that
have to be performed in any modern state. From this moment the
ultimate future of the African in most of his own continent was
never in serious doubt.

At the theoretical level, during these inter-war years, there appeared
to be a fundamental difference between British colonial policy and
that of all the colonial powers of continental Europe. France, Belgium,
Portugal and Italy all in theory maintained the doctrine of assimilation. Despite the rise and fall of earlier French empires in Canada
and India, French Africa was bravely known as France Outremer. In

theory, Senegalese were to be taught to think of themselves as Frenchmen, Congolese as Belgians, Angolans as Portuguese and Somalis as Italians. In theory Africans in French and Portuguese territories, whenever their economic and educational attainments justified it, could aspire to transfer from the status of subjects to that of citizens, bound by metropolitan and no longer by customary law, and with representation in the metropolitan governments as a right more essential than representation in the local councils of the colony. In none of these continental countries was there, between the wars, any serious proposal that the African colonies should at any stage become independent of the metropolitan countries; their inhabitants would merely grow into citizens of a greater France, a greater Belgium, a greater Portugal and an Italy more reminiscent of the Roman Empire. In contrast, Britain between the wars was not thinking in terms of a greater Britain. Even the Commonwealth was a new idea, formulated for the first time in the Statute of Westminster in 1930, and it was by no means certainly envisaged that it would come to include India, much less the African colonies. There was no feeling that Africans should be turned into Britons. On the contrary, talk was all of allowing them to 'develop on their own lines', though in the absence of any clear idea about what those lines should be, the patterns that emerged were apt to be British.

While the centralizing and assimilationist policies of the continental powers were just as unrealistic as the empirical and decentralizing practice of the British, the continental Europeans were at least spared the constitutional wrangles over the political rights of white settlers in Africa which occupied so much of the surface of British relations with the African colonies from the 1920s until the eve of independence. The doctrine that a colony was, or was destined to be, politically integrated with the metropolitan country was sure to prove fallacious; but while it lasted it assuaged the worst anxieties of European residents in the colonies. British empiricism, however, encouraged British settlers in East and Central Africa to believe that their political future depended on their own efforts, and that if they could gradually manage to take over control of the colonial governments from the expatriate colonial civil service, they would be able to guide their own and their African fellow citizens' destinies for an indefinite period. In fact, of course, this was a complete illusion. Everywhere north of the

Zambezi, British colonists were so thin upon the ground that, whether they realized it or not, their position depended entirely upon the presence in the background of British imperial power. Had they succeeded in removing that power, they would have been quite incapable of controlling the vast African majorities among whom they lived. Nevertheless, British African policy, following the example of the older colonies rather than that of British India, gave them votes and representatives in the legislative councils of the colonial governments. It encouraged them to embark on their hopeless struggle for power, perhaps without any clear idea of where that struggle would lead.

The Union of South Africa apart, it was only in Southern Rhodesia that there occurred a full devolution of political power to a local European minority. This followed from the special circumstances of Southern Rhodesia's occupation, in which private settlers had from the very beginning been the strong right arm of the Chartered Company. When the Charter expired in 1923, therefore, it would have been difficult to institute a colonial government in its place. The white Southern Rhodesians were offered either amalgamation with the Union of South Africa or internal autonomy on the basis of an income suffrage high enough to exclude all but the merest handful of black voters. They chose autonomy, and by concentrating all their policies during the next thirty years on the promotion of further white settlement, they succeeded in building up their power and their economic predominance to a point from which it needed more than an ordinary nationalist movement to oust them.

Elsewhere in Central and East Africa, by comparison, settler politics presented no more than a temporary façade. Their first centre was in Kenya, where in the period before 1914 a handful of wealthy and well-connected settlers, led by Lord Delamere, had acquired considerable influence in the government of the territory. British settlers were to remain prominent in Kenyan politics until the late fifties, but the real turning-point of their influence came in the early twenties. An attempt at a substantial increase in white settlement in the years from 1919 to 1922 overreached itself and was successfully attacked by those who believed it was hindering the development of the African population. In 1923 the British government stated that in Kenya, as in Uganda and Tanganyika, African interests were to be treated as paramount, and that while European interests would be respected, responsible government on the Southern Rhodesian pattern was not to be expected. From that time onwards, settler influence entered a slow decline.

In East Africa, as in Nigeria, the Gold Coast and the more prosperous French territories such as the Senegal and the Ivory Coast, the really significant factor for the future was the small but growing number of Africans entering secondary schools and thus approaching the educational standards of many of the immigrants and expatriate officials. North of the Zambezi, it was only in Northern Rhodesia, with the growth of the copper-mining industry in the late twenties and early thirties, that immigrant Europeans were able to gain any considerable increase in political power. Their opposite numbers in the older-established copper industry of the Katanga had already been firmly told by the Belgian government that they might expect privileges but not political rights.

Superficially, the period between 1914 and 1939, between the two world wars, was the time when all important initiatives in Africa were taken by Europeans. During this period there were hardly any Africans in positions of real responsibility in their own countries. In 1936 even the ancient kingdom of Ethiopia went down before the invasion of Mussolini's Italy. Everywhere colonial governments were at the zenith of their power. African kings, where they survived at all, had been reduced to the position of either figureheads or subordinate civil servants. Even the successful battles fought in defence of African interests against those of immigrant communities were fought not by Africans but by European missionaries and colonial officials, as well as by liberal forces in the metropolitan countries. Such people were staking their judgement on a belief that the inhabitants of 'darkest Africa' were potentially as capable as any other set of human beings, and therefore that what was required in the long run was not to bring in more masters but to train up more men. During this period a new generation of Africans was putting itself to school, and from it a few were to emerge equipped not merely for participation but for leadership in the new Africa. Some white men in Africa began to speak scornfully of 'trousered blacks' and 'handfuls of examination-bred students'; yet during this second phase of the colonial period their appearance was the most important event in African history.

Until the 1920s the theory of the colonial powers, and until the 1940s
their practice, did not include any financial assistance to stimulate the
economic development of the colonial territories from the outside.
Essentially this was a projection into the colonial field of the limited
view of their economic responsibilities in their own countries taken
by most European governments, a view which lasted until about the
same period. In Africa the colonial powers had been prepared to
subsidize the primitive colonial revenues until such time as these were
sufficient to cover the bare minimum of administrative expenses. In
the way of capital expenditure metropolitan governments had here
and there made outright grants towards the cost of strategic railways
– the Uganda Railway was an early example, and the railways of
German East and South-West Africa were greatly extended in the
years immediately before 1914 – but only after the failure of other
methods of financing them had been clearly demonstrated. With these
exceptions, colonial governments were expected to live on their own
meagre revenues, and to limit their borrowing to the measure of the
security provided by those revenues.

Considering these limitations, it was remarkable how much was
achieved. By the 1920s, for example, the railway map of Africa had
virtually assumed its modern shape. The resulting economic development, though occasionally impressive, was, however, not as great
as it should have been. In the first place, systems of transport designed
to meet the needs of government were not always efficient for
commerce. Thus government launches could navigate the Senegal
and Niger rivers between railheads, where boats carrying useful
amounts of cargo could not. The rail and water transport system of
the Congo required a vividly uneconomic amount of unloading and

reloading from train to steamer and steamer to train. Again, for want of funds, the construction of ocean ports capable of handling any substantial amount of trade engendered by the railways tended to lag far behind the railways themselves. Even in the comparatively wealthy colony of the Gold Coast, for example, the deep-water harbour necessary to serve the Ashanti Railway was not opened until 1928, although the railway had been completed in 1903.

Railways, moreover, were not an automatic means of promoting economic growth. Obviously, such growth followed most easily and naturally in areas already initiated into the business of production for trade. Railway-building produced greater results more rapidly in West Africa than in East Africa. Within West Africa the results were more appreciable in the coastal colonies than in the remote territories of the western Sudan. The peoples of the southern Gold Coast and Nigeria soon realized the advantages of the new transport systems for the exportation of cocoa, timber and palm produce. Senegal and northern Nigeria were not far behind with groundnuts, and the economies of the Ivory Coast and French Guinea were also among the first to stir. In East Africa one of the greatest obstacles to development was that the railways had to run through hundreds of miles of arid and sparsely inhabited country in order to tap the agricultural produce of the well-watered and densely populated Lake Victoria basin. A partial solution was found to the economic problem of the Uganda Railway by settling white farmers in the Kenyan highlands. In German East Africa, the Tanganyika of 1919–63, not even this solution was possible for its vast desiccated central area, and railway development reaching to the south of the Lake Victoria basin was in consequence delayed by twenty years. South-West Africa offered perhaps the prime example of an extensive railway system, built for largely strategic reasons across vast tracts of barren underpopulated country, which could never pay its way commercially.

At the time of the scramble for Africa, high hopes had been placed on the economic stimulus of private European settlers. After thirty or forty years, however, the results were seen to be meagre. Although nearly 50 million people emigrated from Europe to other continents between 1880 and 1930, few of these migrants found their way to Africa, and most of those who did settled either in Algeria or in South Africa. North of the Limpopo and south of the Sahara the European population of Africa amounted in the early thirties to a mere 60,000. Most of Europe's emigrants were surplus labourers possessing few skills and no capital. There were few openings for such people in tropical Africa, which needed capital and technical skills but had plenty of indigenous unskilled labourers. Many mistakes were usually made, and many lean years experienced, before the European farmer with capital, working with an African labour force, learned what crops could be grown and what animals reared; and the same considerations militated against collective European investment in plantation agriculture. With some exceptions – such as tobacco in Southern Rhodesia, tea in Nyasaland and sisal in Tanganyika – the most successful plantation crops could be produced almost as well, and usually more economically, by African farmers working on their own account and on their own lands. If Europeans wished to invest their money in Africa – and, until the 1920s, investment in other continents usually promised less risk and better returns – it was more profitable to support companies engaged primarily in buying from and selling to African producers rather than those which themselves engaged in agricultural production.

The great exception to this rule, both as a foundation for European settlement and as an attraction for private European capital, was mining. It was the diamond and gold discoveries of the 1870s and 1880s which caused the emergence of a considerable urban and industrial community in South Africa. It was the promise of gold and other minerals which enabled this community to expand into Southern Rhodesia in the nineties, and into the copperbelt astride the Zambezi-Congo watershed in the first three decades of the twentieth century. The importance of mineral wealth, and of the industrialization which followed in its train, was graphically illustrated by Professor S. H. Frankel in 1938, when he published figures for the capital so far invested in Africa south of the Sahara. Of the estimated total of £1,222,000,000 – a sum almost equally divided between private investment and public loans – no less than £555,000,000 had been invested in South Africa. A further £102,000,000 had been invested in the Rhodesias and £143,000,000 in the Congo. In other words, two-thirds of the European investment had been in territories whose economies were based on mining.

In southern Africa the economic momentum was such that even

costly installations like railways could be financed and built by private enterprise. Private enterprise also created the towns which grew up around the mining-camps and deeply affected the lives of whole populations in these areas. Only in the Belgian half of the Katanga did the mining companies pursue a policy of stabilized labour, encouraging all their employees to bring their families to the mining towns and to settle down there as a permanently urbanized class. In South Africa and the Rhodesias, the existence of European settlement before the establishment of the mining industry made it impossible for the mining companies to develop a stable African labour force. White trade unions feared lest the Africans should acquire experience and training which would enable them to challenge the white monopoly of technical skills. Most Africans in the mining industry were therefore 'migrant labourers', recruited on a temporary basis from rural areas for hundreds of miles around, who left their families on the land and came for a year to live in the 'native compounds' established by the mining companies. Unsatisfactory though this was socially, and in the end economically too – for short-term contract labour, though paid low wages, was inefficient and therefore not cheap – it did mean that experience of urban life became very widespread. By the late 1930s there were probably few African families between the Cape and Malawi who did not have some of their members away at work in the towns.

Moreover, although in Southern Africa there was an enormous differential between the earnings of African labourers and those of European managers and skilled artisans, African cash incomes became significantly higher on the average than anywhere else in black Africa. Together with the presence of a sizeable European population, this made it possible for European enterprise to develop secondary industries producing for the local market. Such industries became a feature of the South African scene in the 1920s and of the Southern Rhodesian in the late 1940s. This growing industrialization greatly increased the flow of African labour to the towns, and also tended to make its urbanization permanent. The European masters of southern African society had never envisaged the development of a black proletariat on this scale, and hundreds of thousands of Africans were eventually living in appalling shanty towns round the fringes of the major European centres.

This genuine industrial revolution, though creating grave new tensions, gave southern Africa a very different economy from that of the rest of black Africa. By the mid-1930s, the Union of South Africa alone was responsible for more than half of the whole international trade of Africa south of the Sahara; the Union's foreign trade amounted to some £22 per head of population, while that of Tanganyika was only £1½ and that of all French West Africa even less. Elsewhere, only the larger British West African territories, which possessed some mineral wealth as well as expanding communities of peasant farmers producing for export, had really even begun to join the world economy. Before the world slump of the 1930s severely depressed the demand for their agricultural exports, their share of a sub-Saharan Africa's trade had been as high as a sixth. Even in 1936, the richest of them, the Gold Coast, still had trade worth £7 per head of population.

It was indeed the world slump which first suggested to the European powers that they could not expect the economies of their African territories to expand usefully through the efforts of their inhabitants themselves, with the sole aid of private European investors and settlers. In 1929, for example, the British government for the first time took general powers to lend or even give money to colonies in order to help stimulate their economic development. This was not altruism but self-interest. During the depression, Britain had a pressing need to increase her own foreign trade, and the stagnant colonial economies seemed a suitable outlet conveniently within her reach. But in those years money was naturally scarce, and the results were not spectacular. By 1938, the British dependencies in Africa had received only £4,000,000 from the new Colonial Development Fund, a sum equivalent to the addition of only about 1 per cent to their combined annual revenues.

A real understanding of the extent to which the potentialities of colonial Africa had remained undeveloped came only with the Second World War. Older lines of supply were disrupted by transport and currency difficulties; there was a greatly increased demand for the strategic raw materials Africa could supply; and postwar shortages of foodstuffs and of many raw materials were to be expected. The colonies suddenly became of immense economic value. For Belgium and France during 1940–44 the African territories held almost the only resources which could be contributed to the war effort.

The consequences of this new situation were often remarkable. The mining industries of Northern Rhodesia and the Belgian Congo, whose earlier development had been greatly frustrated by the depression, entered upon a fantastic boom. By 1953 the value of the Congo's exports had increased fourteenfold, and her government revenue had been multiplied fourfold. Northern Rhodesia experienced a ninefold increase in her exports – almost entirely of copper – and a twentyfold increase in revenue. From being, with Nyasaland, the Cinderella of British Central Africa, she suddenly became by far the richest territory. In British West Africa, the establishment of government purchasing agencies for vital produce like oil crops and cocoa broke the hold the European trading companies had so far maintained on the peasant economies. These agencies paved the way for post-war marketing boards under local control, which guaranteed the farmers a price for their produce free from world market fluctuations, and were able to build up substantial reserves to cover lean years. These reserves in fact were soon so substantial that it became possible to lend or grant large sums from them for local schemes of economic and social development. Moreover, during the war and up to the 1950s, European industry was unable to supply the African territories with all the manufactured capital and consumer goods their greatly increased purchasing powers could command. Many colonies were therefore enabled to build up substantial credit balances in Europe.

After the war, then, it became possible for the richer colonies to embark on ambitious development schemes which they knew they could to some extent finance from their own resources. Nor was this all. Throughout Africa there was a great stepping-up in private European investment, which was now shut out from many of its former profitable fields in the Americas and Asia. North American capital also became increasingly available. Moreover, the governments of Europe sometimes attempted to meet their own particular needs by embarking directly on ambitious African projects, which if undertaken at all in former years would have been left to private enterprise – though some of these, most notably the over-ambitious scheme for the mechanized production of groundnuts in East Africa, were not always very well conceived.

The Atlantic Charter and the concept of the United Nations demonstrated a change in the political climate also, and the rapid economic and social development of the African territories came to be pursued, not only because backward colonies were of no value to the powers possessing them but also because the powers felt a moral obligation towards their colonial subjects. By the end of the war, in the words of Sir Keith Hancock, one of the foremost advocates of a progressive colonial policy, 'vigorous State action to promote colonial development and welfare' had become 'the new orthodoxy'. In Britain, the colonial development principle initiated in 1929 was extended to cover schemes for social as well as economic advancement. The permissible annual expenditure rose from a maximum of £1,000,000 to £5,000,000 a year (1940), and then to £12,000,000 or even more (1946). With this available to supplement local resources, even the weaker British territories were able to join with the more fortunate in development plans providing for the expenditure of a total of some £210,000,000 during 1946–55. For French Africa, where the rate of investment, especially from private sources, had so far been much lower, the change was even more startling. The development plans for the nine West African territories alone totalled £277,000,000 for the same period, with a much higher proportion of the funds provided by the colonial power. In the Congo, the Belgian colonial government was hard put to it to expend all the money which by the end of the war Belgium had come to owe to her colony.

In many ways, the most striking results of this new approach to colonial development were social rather than economic. At least for the richer territories, much of the economic advance, even where consciously planned by governments, followed naturally enough from the new economic circumstances. But it was not so in the social field. The European governments had been awakened to the extent to which their African subjects needed more doctors, welfare workers and trade unionists, better water supplies, sanitation and housing, and above all many more and better schools. The new development plans, therefore, were very consciously aimed at social as well as economic betterment. The need for expansion in education was especially stressed. In 1943, for example, the British government even began to contemplate the goal of universal literacy in its African empire. Shortly after the war it embarked on the establishment of colonial universities, a step which necessarily involved the strengthening of all the lower rungs in the educational ladder. The French and Belgian governments were little if at all behind, though their methods were often different. For the French, and equally for the French Africans, the peak of educational advance remained attendance at a university in France. Almost throughout colonial Africa, an educational and social revolution began to accompany the economic revolution.

The consequences of this revolution were by no means the same throughout the continent, and some of them were quite unexpected. They varied in accordance with the ultimate aims of the colonial powers, and also with the extent to which local administrations were subject to European settler influence. In British Central and East Africa, therefore, where settlers often had a considerable voice in the conduct of affairs, and also in the Belgian Congo, where there was no plan to accompany the often very impressive economic advance with political progress, the stress in educational policy lay on the improvement of African primary and vocational schooling. In both regions it was thought dangerous to allow the African to advance too far or too quickly.

In view of the earlier shortage of educational facilities for Africans, it was possible to implement the extensive plans for social and economic advancement only by greatly increasing the numbers of Europeans in the field. Hitherto – apart from settlers, where they existed – the Europeans in Africa had been engaged in only three major activities: trade and other economic exploitation, missionary work (which of course covered almost all the early work in education) and the administration of government and the services essential to it. It was now necessary to import large numbers of school teachers, university lecturers, social welfare officers, labour organizers, rural water engineers, surveyors, builders and so on, as well as innumerable sorts of researchers and planners and advisers. All these people drew large salaries and generous travel allowances to enable them to enjoy regular leaves in Europe. They also had to have houses and services provided for them, so that they and their families could live in as good conditions as they were used to in their own countries, or better. Thus a sizeable proportion of the moneys made available for African development seemed to disappear into European pockets.

In West Africa, by and large, the Africans were able to take this in

their stride. Shortly after the war they could already see the way to
control of their own territories opening before them, and they knew
that before long they would be able to replace many of the new
European 'experts' while keeping the remainder under due control.
Elsewhere, however, the new European invasion of Africa always
widened and sometimes deepened the tensions between Africans and
Europeans, especially when the newcomers came to swell an already
established settler population. At best the invasion might help to
encourage or even create African demands for political advancement.
Sometimes, and especially towards the south, it unfortunately tended
to do little more than make the gulf in wealth and education between
the Africans and their European masters seem even wider and more
difficult to cross than ever before.

It is clear that colonial Africa in the 1940s and 1950s was moving very
quickly away from the stagnation of the previous half century. The
increase in wealth combined with a great improvement in communications – symbolized by the new roads which began to reach even
the smallest and remotest villages – and with the growth of education to
promote a new social mobility which weakened old tribal cohesions and
created many fresh problems for the future. Both the physical face of
the continent and the outlook of its peoples were changing on a scale
and at a rate unprecedented in previous history. Unevenly, and often
with serious growing-pains, Africans were once more catching up with
the rest of the world. They still had a long way to go. African
economies were still far too dependent on the export of only a few
major primary products. National incomes per head, so far as they
could be calculated in territories where most people were still producing
mainly for subsistence, were still very low by European standards, if
not by those of some Asian countries. As against typical western
European figures of more than £300 per annum in the mid-1950s, the
figures for Tanganyika and Nyasaland were only £17 and £7 respectively, while for territories like Somalia or Upper Volta they were
still hardly measurable. The best Africa could show was a mean of
£115 a year very unevenly divided between the different races in South
Africa, and £75 a year for the Africans of the Gold Coast. Nevertheless,
in innumerable ways a climate was being created in which the continued
political domination of Africa by Europe was bound to be challenged.

20 The Road to Independence

The general disintegration of the colonial system in Africa – initiated in 1957 when the British colony of the Gold Coast became independent Ghana – was essentially a feature of the *tropical* African scene, following from the economic and social developments just discussed. At the two ends of the continent, the timing and the circumstances of independence tended to be different. Thus the four British colonies of European settlement in South Africa had come together as early as 1909, in a Union which was a self-governing Dominion of the British Commonwealth, and in 1923 a status not far short of this was accorded to the other major settlement colony in the south, Southern Rhodesia.

The self-government gained by the Union of South Africa and by Southern Rhodesia, however, was in effect self-government for their white inhabitants alone. The South African war of 1899–1902, which converted the two Afrikaner republics into British colonies, had been an attempt to resolve the issues between the two white stocks. Indeed, when white South Africans then talked about 'race relations', they nearly always meant merely the relations between Briton and Boer. One of the terms on which the Boers had accepted peace in 1902 was that votes for the Bantu inhabitants of the ex-republics would not be raised as an issue until the two territories had once again become self-governing. Local autonomy was in fact granted to the Transvaal and to the Orange Free State as early as 1906 and 1907, mainly because the British Liberal government that took office in 1905 was dominated by men who had bitterly opposed Chamberlain's South African policy, and the resultant war, as an unjustifiable attack on the liberties of the small Afrikaner nation. These Liberals were so obsessed by this Gladstonian principle (which was astutely exploited by the new

Boer leaders of the Transvaal, Generals Botha and Smuts) that they forgot the obligations Britain had towards the non-European inhabitants of South Africa, Bantu, Coloured and Indian. The new constitutions for the Transvaal and Orange Free State colonies enfranchised only white men.

When, therefore, the political leaders of the Cape Colony, Natal, the Transvaal and the Orange Free State combined in 1908–9 to argue out the terms of Union, all except the Cape delegates represented only white electors. The Cape utterly failed to persuade the others to accept its tradition of voting-rights for men of all races who satisfied a given income or property qualification. Although the need for a common 'native policy' was one of the factors which had led to the constitutional convention in the first place, agreement on a Union was reached only on the understanding that 'the native problem' would be left till later. One consequence of this was that the three British protectorates, Basutoland (the modern Lesotho), Bechuanaland (Botswana) and Swaziland, remained outside the Union. Another was that there was no common franchise for elections to the first Union parliaments: the status quo was preserved, with no vote for Africans outside the Cape Province. Moreover, although Cape statesmen, Afrikaans- as well as English-speaking, thought that their tradition of granting this franchise to 'civilized' non-whites was right and should prevail, it was necessary to protect this tradition by one of the 'entrenched clauses' in the Union constitution, alterable only by a two-thirds majority of both houses of parliament sitting together.

The subsequent political history of South Africa revolves around the campaign of Afrikaner nationalism to redress the defeat of 1902 and to re-establish the principles of the Great Trek. The franchise for all non-whites in the Cape was first whittled away and then abolished, while from 1948 onwards the majority of electors repeatedly voted for apartheid, the theory that black and white in South Africa should be totally separated (or separated as totally as is practicable). The South African Republic which came into existence in May 1961 was committed to the exclusion of all non-whites from any share in its political life, and to the relegation of the Bantu to separate areas ('Bantustans'), where it was supposed that they would one day form separate nations.

The establishment of the Republic was manifestly the apotheosis of Afrikaner nationalism. The development of mining and industry, followed by Union, involved the economic and political leadership of white South Africa passing from the Cape to the Transvaal, from a relatively outward-looking community which could afford liberal principles since – for most of its history – there were relatively few Blacks in it, to the land in which the most diehard trekkers had struggled to create their own society in the interior of Bantu Africa. For the Afrikaners, politics were an inbred tradition; most English-speaking whites were content to enjoy the fruits of a developing economy, and the franchise was slanted against the towns in which they lived. All South Africa's premiers from Union onwards were Afrikaners, and so too were the bulk of their ministers. Avowedly Nationalist governments held office during 1924–33 under General Hertzog, and, after 1948, were led successively by Malan, Strijdom, Verwoerd, Vorster and P. W. Botha. The other major white political grouping, first called the South African and later the United Party, never opposed the Nationalists on the basic goal of segregation. Rather it urged the advisability of proceeding with caution, of not wholly alienating the Coloured population, or of securing a closer understanding between Afrikaners and English-speakers. Its leaders were also Afrikaners, notably Generals Louis Botha (Prime Minister, 1910–19) and J. C. Smuts (Prime Minister, 1919–24 and 1939–48), while in 1933–9 it joined under Hertzog in a coalition government.

The division between the Afrikaners and the English-speaking whites, which had engrossed the attention of politicians throughout the nineteenth century, ceased to be a major issue and by the 1960s was disappearing altogether. This trend first became apparent in 1924, when Hertzog's first Nationalist government secured power only with the support of the white trade unionists, at this time predominantly English-speakers. They wanted to preserve their jobs from competition by non-Europeans, who could do the same work for lower wages, as much as the Afrikaners wanted to preserve white control of land and the franchise. From this time on, self-interest always led some English-speakers to give at least tacit support to the Nationalists. As black opposition to increasingly severe policies of segregation in land, urban residence, mobility, employment and education began to become more active and violent, so the two sections of the white community drew closer together in the one *laager* mentality.[1]

African opposition to white policies was of course originally tribal and military, and warfare between black and white continued until the suppression of the major Zulu rebellion which took place in Natal in 1906–7. By this time, however, the South African Asians, led by Mahatma Gandhi, were already demonstrating the possibilities of organized, non-violent opposition. In both the Cape and Natal, appreciable numbers of Africans had received education from Christian missions; some indeed had shown their desire for independence of white control by founding their own 'Ethiopian' churches. Pioneers like J. T. Jabavu and John Dube were beginning to form African opinion through Bantu-language newspapers. The Asian example and the complete disregard for non-European opinion in the formation of the Union were obvious incentives for African political organization.

An African National Congress was founded in 1912. For nearly half a century the leaders of the A.N.C. believed that discussion and negotiation would suffice to improve the African lot. However, as early as the 1920s, the brief success of the Industrial and Commercial Workers' Union (I.C.U.), led by Clements Kadalie, demonstrated that there would be increasing support for more direct action. The conditions of life for Africans were being radically altered. The native reserves, the basis for the future Bantustans, were only 13 per cent of the total land area, and were ever less capable of supporting the African population, which outnumbered the whites by more than three to one, and which by 1960 would have grown to nearly 10 million. Though these Africans were apparently better off than the 1,360,000 Coloureds and 440,000 Asians, who had no 'tribal homelands' at all, the majority of them were bound to seek work in the white economy, and increasingly in its towns and industries. Indeed, their labour and, increasingly, their aggregate purchasing power were essential if the European economy was to prosper and the whites were to maintain their living standards. But in this white South Africa, non-Europeans came to be treated as total strangers. They were subjected to humiliating pass laws which restricted their freedom of movement and employment, and they could legally reside only in

1 *Laager* means camp, and more specifically the circle of trek-waggons formed to resist attack on the trekkers.

locations or distressing shanty towns outside the towns proper and often miles from their places of work. Violence could never be far below the surface in this situation in which black and white became economically ever more dependent on each other and yet politically and socially ever more apart. Even when black resentments were expressed passively, violence could readily arise through white actions based on fear of it. When, in 1943, it became apparent that African trade unions were not to be recognized, and when in 1948 the Native Representative Council (a palliative instituted in 1936 when the assault on the non-European franchise began) ceased to function, there were really no milder alternatives for the non-Europeans than active non-cooperation, and for the whites than the erection of a police state.

The attempts of liberally minded people to establish political parties with philosophies more progressive and humane than those of the Nationalists or of the bulk of the United Party members secured no significant support from an all-white electorate. The A.N.C. became involved in a policy of boycotts, strikes and mass protests, but even so it seemed too moderate for many Africans; in 1959 a radical alternative appeared in the form of the Pan-African Congress, which chose pass-burning as its first weapon. This led in 1960 to the massacre at Sharpeville and a massive African demonstration in the centre of Cape Town. For a brief moment the whites seemed to hesitate. But their ranks were quickly closed; any dissent from the majority white opinion by men of any colour was viewed as treason. Many dissentients chose to emigrate or were forced into exile; those who remained in South Africa were subjected to various forms of arrest or prohibited from public expression of their opinions. The whites settled down in their *laager*, taking good care that they were adequately armed and organized to resist any attack on it.

One consequence of the increasingly nationalist, republican Afrikaner trend in South African affairs was to confirm the growing white and predominantly British population of Southern Rhodesia in its wish to stay out of the Union. On the other hand, however, this white minority was determined that power in central Africa should remain in the hands of 'civilized' men, which for the foreseeable future meant themselves. Thus they largely frustrated the vote for non-whites which they had inherited from the Cape, and embarked on a segregationalist policy. The Southern Rhodesian whites thought that both their objectives would be secured if they could engineer a

British Central African Dominion incorporating the two Rhodesias and possibly Nyasaland also. This, they hoped, would at once rid them of the British government's nominal surveillance of native policy, which was enshrined in their 1923 constitution, and create a bloc strong enough to withstand the political and economic strength of the Union. The Southern Rhodesian settlers soon received support from the white community which was developing along the Northern Rhodesian copperbelt and which had become alarmed by the British government's 1930 declaration of the ultimate paramountcy of African interests in its Central and East African dependencies. Initially, the settlers' plans were frustrated by the British government's recognition (in the Bledisloe Report of 1939) that the Africans of the two northern territories were steadfastly opposed to any closer association with Southern Rhodesia and its segregationalist policies. After the war, however, the campaign was renewed, with stress on the economic advantages of a federation. It was pointed out that both Rhodesias looked to Nyasaland for much of their labour force; that Northern Rhodesia's copper mines were dependent on Southern Rhodesian coal, and that the new wealth flowing from them could be used to help develop the poorer territories; that Southern Rhodesia's new industries regarded the northern territories as a natural market for their growing output. It was asserted that a central African federation would integrate all these resources and would attract more capital (and settlers) for their further development, to the advantage of Britain, of the Commonwealth and of its own peoples.

This argument, forcefully presented by settler representatives and their allies in Britain, was accepted in 1953 by the British government, and the Federation of Rhodesia and Nyasaland came into being. But African opposition had grown even more intense and outspoken than before. It was in no way assuaged by the provision of a minority of seats for Africans in the Federal parliament, by the exclusion of affairs touching on African interests in the two northern territories from the competence of this parliament and the government responsible to it, or by the British government's retention of a theoretical final control over general native policy in the Federation. The federal constitution thus fell considerably short of settler ambitions, yet provoked strong African nationalist movements committed to its destruction and to the establishment of independence for the two northern territories.

The fundamental demand of the African nationalists in the Federation was that governments should be responsible to legislatures that were elected by the whole adult population, with the votes of black men and women counting equally with those of whites. In Southern Rhodesia almost all the electors continued to be white throughout the 1950s and, although the politicians they elected to power, like Garfield Todd (a former missionary) and Sir Edgar Whitehead, proclaimed multiracial ideals, most whites were not in the last resort willing to accept the principle of 'one man, one vote'. Their state was therefore obliged to take increasingly severe police measures to restrain the activities of the black nationalists, and it possessed the resources to do this with success. But in the two northern territories of the Federation, with smaller and less well-established white populations, serious strains became evident following the uncompromising stands of non-cooperation taken up by Kenneth Kaunda's Zambia National Congress and Hastings Banda's Malawi Congress Party. These strains led the British government in 1960 to appoint a Commission under Lord Monckton, which recommended that African political representation should be rapidly increased and also that each territory should be given the right to secede from the Federation. Following this, new constitutions were negotiated for all three territories. For Nyasaland and Northern Rhodesia this led to the control of the administration by the elected representatives of the African majority, and to their emergence in 1964 as the independent republics of Malawi and Zambia, with Banda and Kaunda as their first presidents.

The new constitution which Southern Rhodesia received in 1961 was euphemistically described by the British government as a first step towards complete multiracial government. The white Rhodesians agreed to a second electoral roll with lower qualifications, which for the first time enfranchised some thousands of Africans. But there were only fifteen seats guaranteed to African members in a legislature of sixty-five, in which the right to amend the constitution rested with a two-thirds majority – in effect with the Europeans. For this reason, the African nationalists in Rhodesia would have nothing to do with the new constitution, pressing instead for full equality on the basis of 'one man, one vote'. But with the break-up of the Federation bringing independent black African states all the way to their Zambezi frontier, the white Rhodesians became virtually solid in their opposition to the African claim for advancement. They swept aside any leader who showed the slightest sympathy towards multiracialism, and demanded complete independence on the basis of the 1961 constitution. In 1965, when it became clear that Britain would not agree to independence without evidence of at least substantial and continuing progress towards true majority rule, a new Prime Minister, Ian Smith, with the greater part of the settlers solidly behind him, unilaterally and illegally proclaimed a Rhodesian 'declaration of independence'.

In northern Africa the course of events was coloured by two currents of virtually no significance elsewhere in the continent: first, the direct political and military conflicts between European states, and second, and even more importantly, the growth of Arab nationalism.

During 1940–43, British, French and American armies fought those from Italy and Germany over almost the whole length of the North African coastlands, while the British also encompassed the destruction of the Italian empire in North-East Africa. The more senior members of the imperial club, notably Britain and France, had regarded Mussolini's conquest of Ethiopia in 1935–6 as an anachronistic display in very bad taste, made even worse by the fact that Ethiopia, even if regrettably uncertain in her attitude to such matters as slavery, was a fellow-member of the League of Nations, just as much as Italy or themselves. By 1941, Italian soldiers and administrators had been evicted from all their East African territories. Ethiopia resumed its status as an independent state and its Emperor, with a renewed sense of urgency, returned to the problems of how to modernize his medieval kingdom without thereby losing control over it. At first Eritrea and Italian Somaliland remained under British military administration; in 1952, however, it was possible to federate Eritrea with Ethiopia. The traditional and active hostility of the Somali nomads forbade any such solution for Somalia, and in 1950 the United Nations entrusted its administration for ten years to the Italians (who had indeed done much to provide the material groundwork for a modern state in Eritrea and Ethiopia). At the end of this period, Somalia joined British Somaliland in the independent Somali Republic.

The Italian colony of Libya was also involved in the Anglo-Italian conflict. It passed under British military administration in 1942, and nine years later its three component parts, Tripolitania, Cyrenaica and the Fezzan, were federated into a united kingdom under King Idris al-Sanussi, the spiritual leader of the Sanussi, a Muslim brotherhood which had been the main cohesive element in indigenous opposition to Italian rule.

Elsewhere in North Africa, the effects of the European fighting were more indirect but none the less important. The British protectorate over Egypt, declared because in 1914 Britain had found herself at war with Egypt's nominal suzerain Turkey, had been concluded in 1922. The country had then become a nominally independent monarchy under King Fuad, a son of the Khedive Ismail, though British troops remained in occupation to guard the Suez Canal. This occupation was naturally not to the liking of the Egyptian nationalist party, the Wafd, which had developed from student opposition to British rule, already manifest in the pre-war years. This opposition in turn was largely a consequence of the fact that although, under Lord Cromer's autocratic guidance, British officials had done much to reform and modernize Egypt's administration, army and police – as well as her whole economy – little had been done to develop an educational system capable of training young Egyptians to take over from the British.

Whenever free elections were held after 1922, the Wafd was returned to power, only to find its aspirations blocked either by the British or by Fuad, who liked to rule as well as reign. The Egyptian government would then pass into the hands of 'moderates', the rich property-owning interests, who in turn would fail because they commanded neither popular nor royal confidence. A period of palace rule would then ensue, until the Wafd and the moderates could combine to force free elections again. During the 1930s, however, both the Wafd and the British began to moderate their views, and the result was the Anglo–Egyptian treaty of 1936. The two countries became partners in an alliance under which British troops were to be withdrawn to a narrow zone on either side of the Suez Canal. Long before this withdrawal could be completed, however, the whole of Egypt had become a vital base for the British armies in their campaigns of 1940–43. Initial Axis victories suggested to the new young king, Faruq, and his palace clique that the final liberation of Egypt was at hand. In 1942 Britain used force to impose a Wafd government on Faruq. But by 1945 the positive energies of the Wafd were devoted to the formation of the Arab League and the problem of Palestine. At home it had become as corrupt and self-seeking as the palace party or the other parliamentary groups. The incompetence and corruption revealed in the political direction of the Arab war on Israel at length persuaded a group of young army officers, inspired by Colonel Gamal Abdul Nasser, to assume the inheritance of Muhammad Ali and 'Urabi Pasha. During 1952–3 they finally swept away the old parliamentary and monarchical regime.

Nasser's military government undertook basic reforms over the whole field of Egyptian life, especially in land tenure, which secured him the wholehearted support of the Egyptian masses. Externally his career was more chequered. His ambition to lead a united Arab world was frustrated by the continued existence of Israel and by the fraternal jealousies of the Arabs themselves. Moreover, his foreign policy inevitably annoyed western powers slow to forget the past or to recognize the moral strength of Arab nationalism. All the same, Nasser finally succeeded in ridding Egypt of the last legacies of European domination. In 1953 he was successful in securing an agreement with Great Britain on the future of the Sudan and, with this issue out of the way, in the following year the British agreed to withdraw their remaining forces from the Suez Canal zone. But Nasser's desire to balance western interests in Egypt by developing relations with, and securing military and other aid from, Communist countries led the Western powers in 1956 to withdraw an offer of finance for the High Dam at Aswan on which he was counting for the increase of Egyptian productivity and wealth. Nasser retaliated by nationalizing the essentially Franco-British Suez Canal Company. In the following year, in secret collusion with an Israel whose armed forces had invaded Egypt and were overrunning all its troops east of Suez, the British and French retaliated in their turn with a military landing in the canal zone – attempting to justify their action with the excuse that they were protecting the canal from the Israelis!

However, the British and French were quickly forced by world opinion, more particularly by the United States, to withdraw, thus giving Nasser a moral victory to offset his defeat by the Israelis and making him momentarily the hero of the anti-colonialist movements throughout Africa and Asia. But he was now face to face with a militant Israel in a continuing contest of great danger for the peace of the world. In 1967 the Israelis mounted another pre-emptive strike, the Six Day War, which almost totally destroyed the armed forces of Egypt and which resulted in their occupation of all Egyptian territory up to the east bank of the canal. Russia rearmed Egypt – the United Arab Republic as it had been called since 1958 – and provided the assistance needed to finance and build the Aswan High Dam, but Nasser was no longer the major world figure that he once had been.

Because of its dependence on Nile waters, Egypt had always had a vital interest in the Sudan. This had been reconquered from the Mahdi by a combined British and Egyptian force, and in 1899 it had been agreed that it should become an Anglo-Egyptian Condominium. The Governor-General was appointed by the Egyptian government on Britain's recommendation, and had Egyptian as well as British officials and troops under him. But in 1924, in reprisal for the assassination in Cairo of Sir Lee Stack, who was both Governor-General of the Sudan and Commander-in-Chief of the Egyptian army, Britain had barred Egyptians from any responsibility for the government of the Sudan. From this time onwards, the Sudan was ruled by an efficient bureaucracy, British in its higher direction though increasingly Sudanized from below, in what the British conceived to be the Sudanese interest, and with scant regard for the interests of Egypt. Part of the Nile flood was devoted to the Gezira scheme, an impressive exercise in cooperative agriculture, and the success of its cotton crops gave to the Sudan the foundation of a viable economy. With the growth of wealth and education, a professional class with nationalist aspirations emerged. This soon split between those who aimed at simply taking over control from the British and those who thought it necessary to call in Egypt to get the British out. Both the old Egypt of King Faruq and the new Egypt of the young officers were prepared to fish in this troubled stream. However the Anglo-Egyptian agreement of 1953 provided that the Sudanese should be allowed to decide their own future after a three-year transitional period of self-government under international supervision. And when the time came in 1956, the Sudan voted to become an independent republic.

*

By the time France was engulfed in the Second World War, her policy in North Africa had shown itself to be completely sterile. Algeria was considered part of metropolitan France; but 8 million out of Algeria's 9 million people enjoyed little or no say in its government, since Muslims could not then acquire the status and rights of French citizenship unless they agreed to abandon their own Islamic law. Therefore, in so far as the territory was not governed in the interests of France, it was governed in the interests of the European settlers. Nor had the settler presence brought an increase in the economic opportunities available to the Muslims sufficient to compensate for the loss of their best lands; there was, in fact, a steady flow of Algerian emigrants seeking work in France.

Tunisia and Morocco were still protectorates, which France claimed to administer on behalf of their traditional rulers. The administration of both territories was essentially absolutist; even the 400,000 Europeans in Morocco and the 250,000 in Tunisia had no political rights. In Tunisia this absolutism had by 1934 occasioned the formation among the French-educated Tunisians of a movement for national liberation, the Néo-Destour,[1] led by Habib Bourguiba. Within four years, Bourguiba was in jail and his party proscribed.

The issues in Morocco were not at first so straightforward. When the French arrived in 1911 the Sultan's writ hardly extended beyond the plains, and until 1934 they were primarily occupied with the conquest of the mountain tribes. An effective nationalist movement could hardly exist until there was an all-embracing French administration to conspire against and until the structure of a modern state to be taken over had itself been built. Even as late as 1953 it was still politically possible for the French to use the traditional hostility of the Atlas Berbers towards any Moroccan government as an excuse to secure the deposition of the Sultan, who then seemed unduly sympathetic to the aspirations of the Istiqlal, the independence party formed in 1944.

Of the three territories, Morocco was the least affected by the war and by the loss of prestige which the French incurred through their collapse in 1940 (though Spain seized the opportunity to take over

1 *Destour* means constitution. There had been an earlier Destour Party formed by educated Tunisians, who resented the way French rule was subverting the constitution which the Bey of Tunis had granted to his people in 1857.

the international city of Tangier, and doubtless hoped that an ultimate German victory would later give her the whole of Morocco). Algeria and Tunisia, however, were extensively fought over, and French opposition to the Anglo-American landings in 1942 finally convinced North Africans of the obscurantism of French policy. For a short time it appeared as though Germany and her allies would serve as liberators; during the brief German occupation of Tunisia, Bourguiba was released and the Bey was allowed to appoint Néo-Destour ministers. But by 1943, despite the Atlantic Charter, despite the Casablanca conference and the interest of Roosevelt, the local victory of the Allies had put the French firmly back in the saddle. With the formation of the Arab League, the North African nationalists naturally began to look to Egypt for help in their struggle. In 1945 Bourguiba established the pattern, which the Algerians were shortly to follow, of organizing propaganda and resistance against France from Egyptian soil.

Active hostilities first developed in Tunisia in 1952, after French moves towards a compromise with the nationalists had been sabotaged by the local Europeans. After two years of guerrilla warfare, the French agreed that Tunisia should have local autonomy, and in 1955 Bourguiba returned to head the government. In Algeria, the Front de Libération Nationale (F.L.N.), an eventual coalescence of parties of opposition to European rule – all of them consistently oppressed by France since their first appearance in the 1920s – declared open war on the French in 1954. In the following year, another movement of revolt demanding the return of the Sultan, whose deportation had made him a national hero, broke out in Morocco. With Tunisia already on the way to independence, the French saw the futility of fighting to maintain their position in Morocco. It seemed desirable to concentrate their efforts on Algeria, whose considerable settler community possessed an effective voice in French politics. The Sultan was therefore returned to his throne and in 1956 full sovereignty was granted to Morocco, which shortly afterwards secured the accession of Tangier and the Spanish protectorate. Tunisia could not lag behind, and so asked for and received her independence. In 1957 the Bey was deposed and Tunisia became a republic with Bourguiba as President.

France now had only one war to fight, but it proved her most bitter African struggle since her original conquest of the Algerian people during 1840–79. She was, in fact, fighting that war all over again. But the circumstances were now very different. The F.L.N. had moral support from the whole Muslim world and from all independent black Africa, and it received aid from Egypt, Tunisia and Morocco. Only the employment of close on half a million troops could enable France to hold her own. But the cost of this effort was great, politically as well as in men and money. In 1958 the French army in Algeria rose against the conduct of affairs there by the French parliamentary regime and placed General de Gaulle at the head of the French state. But, contrary to the expectations of some army officers, de Gaulle was as convinced as most metropolitan Frenchmen had become that it was futile to try and continue to maintain the French hold on Algeria by force. In 1959 he recognized the right of the Algerians to self-determination, and in 1962 his government finally succeeded in negotiating a cease-fire with the nationalists. France's main problem was then one of securing the acceptance of her policy by the Algerian colonists, among whom there were extremists prepared to use terrorism – against France as well as against the Muslims – in a desperate final attempt to frustrate the setting up of an independent Algeria which the Muslim majority would control. Eventually, however, an Algerian republic was recognized with Muhammed Ben Bella as President.

In tropical Africa the first opposition to European rule was of course that of traditional African societies, resentful of the new moulds into which the colonizing powers sought to force them. This kind of opposition was mainly characteristic of the more remote areas of colonies, and of their early days; but sometimes the cohesion of a traditional society was so strong that in the end colonial government had to compromise with it. In such cases, traditionalism might still be politically relevant, as it was with the Baganda, for example. But generally, as European administrations became more firmly established, and as the economic and social climate also began to change, so new types of opposition began to emerge.

Some of these were not overtly political. Thus in eastern, central and southern Africa, where Christian missions often preceded European administration and where the development of European settlement could lead to severe maladjustments in African society, African opposition sometimes found expression in 'Ethiopianism' – the formation of separate and specifically Black Christian churches in which beliefs and practices learnt from the missions were often coloured to suit local ways. The members of such churches might on occasion break out into blind revolt against the European administrators and settlers, who generally regarded them with suspicion and hostility. One of the best-known examples of this was the 1915 rebellion led by John Chilembwe in Nyasaland. In a different way, the Mau Mau movement among the Kikuyu of Kenya in 1952–6 was perhaps as much a psychological and magico–religious as a political reaction to alien pressures.

Ultimately much more significant, however, were the movements of political protest. In tropical Africa these developed first in the West African coastlands, where the long contact with Europe before the opening of the colonial period ensured that the development of colonial administration took place at more or less the same time as the growth of a European-educated African professional class. As European political control tightened and the pace of colonial development quickened, so that more and more Europeans came to dominate African affairs, this class felt increasingly frustrated and shut out. Its members began to turn their minds to acquiring control over the new institutions of government Europe had imposed on Africa.

The directions initially taken by this opposition were to a considerable extent determined by the nature of the colonial policies pursued by the two major powers concerned. In British West Africa the practical direction of affairs lay in the hands of the local governors advised by executive and legislative councils, the former composed entirely of officials but the latter containing a few African nominees. Here, then, the objectives of the politically minded Africans became first the conversion of the legislative councils into African parliaments, and then the conversion of the executive councils into African ministries responsible to such parliaments. Political associations working towards these objectives had already begun to appear by the 1890s, and this was manifestly the general programme of the West African National Congress, formed in 1918. In the French colonies, however, authority was much more effectively centred in France. Moreover, as early as 1848 the principle that Africans could become French citizens, able to share in elections to the French metropolitan parliaments, had been established in the Senegal settlements. Thus the early political aspirations of French Africans tended to be directed towards securing greater influence in Paris. Political associations of French Africans, affiliated to metropolitan parties, began to be significant during the 1930s.

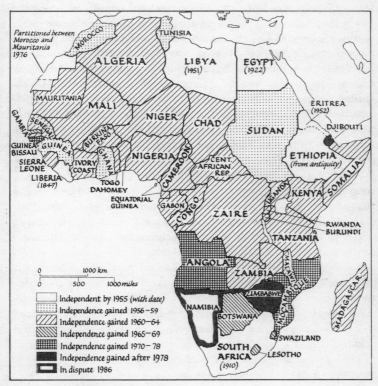

19 Africa: progress to independence

These early political associations, however, carried little weight in either British or French West Africa, mainly because the practical attainment of political freedom for Africans then appeared so very remote. In the French territories, only those few Africans who had actually been born in one of four communes in the Senegal could acquire French citizenship of right, and until 1947 the British had granted self-government only to colonies of European settlement. Against such a background, many of the eventual leaders of the new Africa appeared at first more in the guise of intellectuals than in that of practical politicians. Léopold Senghor, for example, was a notable Senegalese French poet before he became an effective nationalist leader. Fodeba Keita first gained international renown as director of Les Ballets Africains. J. B. Danquah, the first leader of the movement to turn the colonial Gold Coast into the new Ghana (a name which he himself had deliberately chosen), was also the author of books on Akan customs and religion. Such men usually spent a period studying and working in and around universities in France, Britain or the United States. Almost invariably, they became converts to the intellectual socialism current among university students at the time. They were also caught up in the excitement of the Black renascence in America and the West Indies, led by men like W. E. B. DuBois and Marcus Garvey. From this flowed the first ideas of pan-Africanism, though it was not until the last in the series of pan-African conferences held under the inspiration of DuBois – that at Manchester in 1945, which involved the significant conjunction of George Padmore, Kwame Nkrumah and Jomo Kenyatta – that pan-Africanism began to take shape as an effective political movement. The main concern of black leaders on either side of the Atlantic was to establish a respectable intellectual and moral station for their people in a world which seemed excessively dominated by the traditions and values of Western Europeans. The forging of concepts of *négritude*, of *la présence africaine*, of the 'African personality', seemed an essential prerequisite for effective African action in the political field.

This intellectual concentration of the early nationalists was also a consequence of the situation facing them at home, where indeed their first political groups had as much the character of debating societies as of political parties. They could hardly appeal for popular support, since few Africans beyond their own small circles had had much or indeed any opportunity to learn the language, let alone the ideas, of nationalist politics. Moreover, there were as yet few means or none by which an African public could effectively influence a colonial administration. And so the early African politicians addressed themselves as much (or more) to European as to African ears, arguing with and sniping at the local administrators, or trying to mobilize support for their ideas in Europe. This last tactic was obviously appropriate for French Africans; but delegations and cablegrams to London remained a prime political gambit in British West Africa also, even into the 1950s.

The Second World War radically changed the picture. Africans and Europeans alike learnt that European empire was not an immutable monolith in the landscape of world history. This was most drastically demonstrated in Asia, first by the Japanese occupation of many valuable colonial territories, and then by the British, Dutch and French themselves, who recognized in their different ways and at their varied paces, that even though their side had eventually turned the tables on Japan, they could not simply begin again in their Asian colonies where they had been forced to leave off in 1941. Within a few years of the end of the war, a host of South and South-East Asian peoples – Indians, Pakistanis, Burmese, Indonesians, Indo-Chinese – had either secured their independence or were on their way to it. Africans began to ask why they too should not follow into the equal world of the United Nations, where the new Asian states soon became a significant group dedicated to anti-colonialism – a cause already supported, in their several ways, by the American republics and by the Communist states.

There was no comparable direct shock of war for the colonial regimes in tropical Africa. But the German occupation of France in 1940, and the subsequent division of Frenchmen into Vichyites and Gaullists, had important repercussions for the French territories. The policies of Nazi Germany had been widely and unfavourably publicized. The French West African administration's declaration for Vichy therefore led many Africans to suspect it of Nazi racialism. This combined with some of its political actions to create a new sense of unease, which was heightened when the much less advanced Equatorial African colonies, under the inspiration of Félix Eboué, a black West Indian who was then Governor of Tchad, declared for de Gaulle and Free France. Eboué was soon Governor-General, and under his dynamic leadership French Equatorial Africa became a bastion from which African and French soldiers sprang to share in the liberation of

North Africa. By 1942 the French in West Africa appreciated the need to change sides, but the initiative in determining French policy in Africa had already passed from them. In 1944, at Brazzaville, Free French politicians and colonial officials from all over black Africa, inspired by Eboué and his friends, drew up a blueprint for the future of French Africa. Their most vital decision was that African representatives should share in drawing up the post-war constitution for France; the ultimate effect of this, combined with the specific Brazzaville proposals, was the transformation of the colonial empire into the French Union, in which the 'overseas territories' were to be 'partners' with France. All Africans became citizens and were thus able to share in French parliamentary elections. More significantly, perhaps, the empire began to be decentralized, more authority being given to the territorial administrations and elected assemblies possessing some control over finance being introduced.

The emergent African leaders now had an exploitable political status. The most widely supported of the newly emerged parties was the Rassemblement Démocratique Africain, an inter-territorial party which under the leadership of Félix Houphouët-Boigny of the Ivory Coast soon began to play a leading political role, in France as much as in Africa. In 1948–50, however, its militant agitation and close association with the French Communists led to suppressive measures against it by the colonial administrations.

At this point the French Africans were rescued from their political cul-de-sac of regarding France rather than Africa as the main battle-ground by the consequences of what was happening in the adjacent British West African territories. Here the war and its aftermath had induced considerable economic and social tensions, especially in the coastlands of the Gold Coast and Nigeria, the regions most closely linked to the outside world. As has been seen, wartime conditions and post-war shortages of tropical produce had greatly increased the incomes both of African producers and of the colonial governments. At the same time, the war had brought many Africans into much closer touch with events and currents of opinion in the outside world than ever before. Many West Africans had served on terms of equality with British soldiers in other parts of the world, notably in the Burma campaign. Many more had seen the old stereotype of the European as solely an administrator, or a director of African labour, smashed by the presence in their own countries of appreciable numbers of British or American servicemen. Great expectations were aroused by talk of the Atlantic Charter and the new United Nations, by Asian independence, by the new British plans for colonial development and welfare. But both in the personal and in the public sphere the immediate postwar years brought disappointment. West African producers felt cheated because there were serious shortages of the consumer goods they could now afford, and they suspected the European importers of exploiting them through high prices. The development plans both of governments and of private European enterprises were delayed, since capital goods too were in short supply. At the same time, however, they still involved the bringing in of more European advisers, technicians and supervisors. In every direction, the expectations of Africans who had acquired new skills, new outlooks, new wealth and new standards of living were cruelly frustrated.

The tensions boiled over first on the Gold Coast. In 1948 there was a widespread boycott of European traders, and then rioting in the major towns. Effective capital was made of these troubles by the nationalists, for in the previous year Danquah and his colleagues had brought back from England Kwame Nkrumah, in the radical vanguard of the new pan-Africanism, to help in the organization of popular support for a nationwide political party demanding self-government. The official inquiry into the riots reported their underlying cause as growing African frustration, stated that the new constitution which the Gold Coast had received only two years earlier – and in which, for the first time in colonial Africa, Africans had been granted a majority in the legislative council – was 'outmoded at birth', and recommended a rapid advance towards responsible government. In 1949 the Governor appointed an all-African committee to devise a new constitution to this end.

The old school of Gold Coast nationalists shared in the composition of this constitution. Nkrumah and the new vanguard, however, struck out on their own, declaring that nothing short of 'Self-Government *now*' would do. The mass following Nkrumah had built up was soon transferred to himself and his new Convention People's Party, and in the first general election held under the new constitution (1951), the popular vote went overwhelmingly in its favour. By this time Nkrumah was in gaol for sedition, but the new Governor, Sir Charles

Arden-Clarke, assessed the situation correctly. Nkrumah was released and he and his colleagues were given the leading posts in the new administration. By 1957 the combined efforts of Nkrumah, his party and the British had converted the Gold Coast into the independent Commonwealth country of Ghana.

The British government knew that once the colonial dam had been broken in the Gold Coast, it was impossible to maintain it elsewhere in British West Africa. It needed little prompting from local nationalists to place Nigeria, Sierra Leone and the Gambia on comparable paths to independence. If the pace was slower, this was mainly a consequence of particular local circumstances. The size of Nigeria, and the considerable differences among its three major regions in outlook and wealth, necessitated the development, by trial and error, of a federal system with local autonomy for the regions before full independence for the whole could be reached (in 1960). Sierra Leone also had factional differences to be overcome, in this case between the Creoles (the descendants of the liberated Africans), who had hither-to dominated African politics, and the much more numerous natives of the interior. But in 1961 she too secured independence under the leadership of the first of the latter to gain a university education, Milton Margai. Finally, in 1965, it was agreed that, despite their fewness and the poverty of their country's resources, what had been allowed to other West Africans must not be denied to the Gambians.

It is doubtful whether the British government appreciated the radical effect that its new West African policy was to have elsewhere in tropical Africa. The most immediate consequences were in French Africa, since if those West Africans who had been under British rule were to be accounted fit to manage their own affairs, presumably the same was true for their neighbours under the French. This was immediately apparent in French Togoland, where, since some of the people of the former German colony were incorporated in the emergent Ghana, almost complete self-government was granted in 1955. More generally, the aspirations of the French West African nationalists and the direction of French policy both began to change, the latter more slowly than the former. Although the R.D.A. shortly recovered from the disaster brought on it by its earlier tactics and developed a new policy of advance through mutual understanding with the French, it was now facing competition from local nationalist parties in a number of territories. Thus, when Houphouët-Boigny took office in a French Socialist government in 1956, he became instrumental in drafting the *loi cadre*, an outline law which gave the French government power to grant to each territory a considerable degree of local self-government. Territorial assemblies and councils of ministers began to assume many of the powers formerly exercised by the French in Paris, Dakar or Brazzaville.

Both Houphouët-Boigny and the *loi cadre*, however, incurred increasing criticism from those nationalists who felt that French Africa was being broken up into units too small and insufficiently autonomous to be really free of French control. Within the R.D.A., Sekou Toure, a Guinean descendant of Samori and the leader of a strong inter-territorial African trade union movement, began to urge a union of territories much more firmly independent of France. Similar arguments were also presented by Senghor in the Senegal, the one territory where the R.D.A. had never been strong and where his Bloc Populaire Sénégalais had come to power following the *loi cadre*.

The next advance, however, came from the French in 1958, when the new de Gaulle regime, brought into power by events in Algeria and seeking to ride the whirlwind, gave all black African territories the choice of either complete independence or autonomy as separate republics within a French 'Community' dealing with foreign policy, defence and several other common matters. This initiative appeared to succeed, for in the ensuing referendum all the territories except Guinea, where Sekou Toure's influence secured an all but unanimous vote for independence, voted for autonomy within the Community. Guinea's action, however, led to the virtual destruction of the Community as de Gaulle had envisaged it. In 1959, Senegal and the French Sudan asked for complete independence *within* the Community, as the Federation of Mali. When this was granted, the territories still within Houphouët-Boigny's sphere – the Ivory Coast, Niger, Dahomey and the Upper Volta – felt they had to go one better, and secured independence *outside* the Community, as a preparatory step to achieving an understanding with France. By the end of 1960, all the former colonies of both French West Africa and French Equatorial Africa had become technically independent of France.

When Guinea declared its independence, the whole of the French administration was immediately withdrawn and all French financial and economic aid stopped. The greater part of Guinea's consequent need for assistance was met from Communist sources, the U.S.S.R., Czechoslovakia, China and East Germany. The most immediate and dramatic offer of assistance however, came from Nkrumah's Ghana, with whom a form of union was briefly proclaimed. It was now obvious that Nkrumah regarded Ghanaian independence merely as a means to a greater end, the complete liberation of Africa from colonialism and the achievement of the widest possible measure of unity among the African peoples. With this in view, he could tolerate no disunity in Ghana, which he shaped into a monolithic republic under the complete control of his party and dominated by his own personality as President (1960). The total energies and resources of the state were to be directed outwards to the anti-colonial and pan-African cause. In 1958, Accra was the scene both of the first conference ever held between the governments of independent African states and also, perhaps even more significantly, of the first All-African Peoples' Conference, attended by the representatives of the nationalist movements of twenty-eight African territories, many of them still under colonial rule. From now onwards it was abundantly clear that the African revolution would not be confined to West Africa. Indeed, there were at this time many well-informed people who assumed that it would sweep onwards with gathering strength into the strongholds of white supremacy in the far south.

The most immediate consequence of the All-African Peoples' Conference was felt in the Belgian Congo, the rulers of which had scarcely begun to relax a rigid paternalist control which, though often enlightened in its care for African economic advance, allowed no political scope whatsoever to Africans (or for that matter to Belgian settlers). After 1955 the Belgians had begun to take a little note of what was happening elsewhere in Africa, especially in French territories just across the lower Congo and Ubangui. Their cautious reappraisal had permitted the emergence of a number of African political associations, but these – in so vast a land, where few Africans had had any contact with the outside world or any higher education, and where none had held any post of responsibility – were organized for the most part on a regional or even a tribal basis. Independence still seemed a long way off; indeed, when a young Belgian professor,

A. A. J. van Bilsen, published in 1956 a plan for the political emancipation of the Congo in thirty years, he was bitterly attacked for his imprudence. In 1958, however, Patrice Lumumba, the only Congolese leader with any pretence to more than a purely local following, went to the All-African Peoples' Conference in Accra, where his radical and unitary approach to the problem of independence for the Congo secured immediate recognition, so that for pan-Africanists he became the hero of Congo nationalism. 1959 was a year of mounting disturbance in the Congo, and in 1960 the Belgians concluded that their best chance of retaining their great economic interests in the territory lay in the grant of free elections and immediate independence.

Lumumba duly became the first Premier, but his government depended on the parliamentary support of politicians of very different ideas from his own, and he could govern only with the help of the Belgian civil service and the Belgian-led army. When, seeing no independence for themselves in the continued presence of their white officers and N.C.O.s, the soldiers of this army mutinied, the whole edifice collapsed. Fighting broke out between tribes anxious to repay old scores. The Katanga province, vital to the whole Congo economy and itself controlled by an unholy alliance between the Belgian mining interests and local African politicians led by Moise Tshombe, declared its independence. Belgium used force to protect her citizens and interests. At first the independent African states scored a great success through their insistence that order should be restored only by their own soldiers acting under United Nations control. But they soon began to differ among themselves over the extent to which it was legitimate to intervene in the affairs of a fellow African state. One group, including Guinea, Ghana and Egypt, clung to the strict pan-African line that the Lumumba government was the only legitimate government in the Congo, and after Lumumba's murder in Katanga this group became bitterly critical of the United Nations. Other states such as Tunisia, Nigeria and the Sudan saw the need for some compromise – for some coalition of the various contending Congolese factions, able to command a firm majority in the National Assembly and also perhaps, to reach a constitutional adjustment between the unitary demands of Lumumba's supporters and the federalism sought by other influential Congo leaders. The situation was further complicated during 1960 by the attainment of independence by many French territories, which – being nearer to the Congo and more closely allied with the West than other independent African states – thought that both the pan-Africanists and the United Nations were unduly interfering in matters which were best left to the Congolese and themselves.

Ultimately the Katanga secession was ended and a semblance of order imposed on the Congo by the troops and officials brought in under United Nations auspices. But these could not stay for ever (financing their operations all but wrecked the United Nations). When they withdrew, the government under President Kasavubu was faced with armed resistance at a number of points – whether from Lumumbists, or from dissident tribesmen, or from gangsters or would-be war-lords. Kasavubu's most original tactic for dealing with this situation was to invite the hitherto arch-dissident, Tshombe, to become his prime minister. Tshombe's links with the Western world enabled him to secure the resources, including white mercenary troops, to establish a crude control over virtually all the Congo except the remoter rural areas. But neither Tshombe nor Kasavubu inspired political confidence among Africans, whether within or without the Congo, and in 1965 their futile attempts to secure a working form of parliamentary government were swept away by the commander of the Congolese army, General Mobutu Sese Seke, who eventually succeeded, with the financial backing of the U.S.A., in establishing an arbitrary control over the whole country, which he shortly renamed Zaire.

The independence of Zaire in 1960 was shortly followed by that of the four East African territories of Tanganyika (1961), Uganda (1962), Kenya (1963) and Zanzibar (1963). Here, there is no doubt that the British government would have preferred to play a much slower game, using a system of 'multiracial' constitutions to protect the European and Asian minorities until such time as racial distinctions had become blurred by intermarriage. Such a policy was defensible so long as West Africa was the only standard of comparison. With an independent Congo and an independent Somalia (see p. 207), it ceased to be so. Moreover, by the late 1950s the African political parties of East Africa were beginning to show their mettle. The Tanganyika African National Union (TANU), founded by Julius

Nyerere in 1954, rapidly became as effective as Nkrumah's Convention Peoples' Party as a mass party incorporating all earlier political associations. Also Nyerere found in Sir Richard Turnbull a governor of the same pragmatic outlook as Nkrumah had found in Arden-Clarke. Within weeks of his appointment in 1958, Turnbull had ditched the multiracial policy of his predecessors. Where Arden-Clarke had held Nkrumah to an apprenticeship of seven years, Turnbull settled with Nyerere for three.

The other East African territories, because of their internal dissensions, moved just a little more slowly. Uganda, though without European settlers and though much further developed economically and educationally than Tanganyika, had been held back by the unwillingness of Buganda to surrender the privileged position which it had enjoyed under the colonial regime. When the Democratic Party eventually emerged as a nationwide party willing to challenge the colonial government, leading Baganda organized the Kabaka Yekka Party to oppose it. Only when Milton Obote founded a third party – the Uganda People's Congress, based in the less developed northern part of the country – were the Baganda supporters of Kabaka Yekka persuaded to enter a coalition with the U.P.C. against the Democratic Party, and so to create a grouping strong enough to achieve independence in 1962.

In Kenya the main delaying factor was of course the need to smooth a little the withdrawal of British support for the hitherto privileged minorities of Europeans and Asians, who had acquired over the years a considerable stake in the government of the country, and whose peaceful cooperation in the new scheme of things was very much to be desired. In the event it was remarkable that, despite some talk of betrayal, more than half of the Europeans and the great majority of the Asians remained in Kenya when the country passed under African rule in December 1963. Jomo Kenyatta, the veteran East African nationalist who had only recently emerged from eleven years of imprisonment and detention following his conviction for involvement in Mau Mau, proved a singularly unresentful and conciliatory leader of one of the most stable and successful of African successor regimes.

In the same year that Kenya became independent, the British recognized the independence of the Sultanate of Zanzibar, which they had taken under their protection in 1890 and which since 1961 had had a legislature with an elected majority. Early in 1964, however, Zanzibar experienced an armed revolution which killed or sent into exile many of the old Arab ruling and land-owning class. The new radical rulers of Zanzibar were soon receiving appreciable aid, including military aid, from Communist countries, and it was doubtless this that persuaded President Nyerere of Tanganyika that he should try and exert some moderating control over the new island republic that had emerged less than twenty miles from his own shores. In April 1964, therefore, a United Republic of Tanzania was brought into being, in which the President of Zanzibar served as first Vice-President.

By the mid-1960s, the only colonial powers remaining anywhere in Africa were Portugal and Spain. As will be seen in the following chapter, Spain was quick to accept that colonial rule was an anachronism in the later twentieth century, while Portugal had already begun to face large-scale armed revolt in all her colonies. It was clear that the period of formal European political control of Africa and Africans was at an end.

Contrary to many predictions, the actual transfer of power to the first cohort of independent African governments was accomplished smoothly enough. Zaire and Guinea, as we have seen, were exceptions to the general rule. Elsewhere, old flags were lowered and new ones raised, but many white civil servants and military officers remained at their posts and the basic framework of government was little changed. The most active of the pre-independence politicians were rewarded with parliamentary privileges, party posts or directorships of public corporations. The educated élite was creamed off into diplomacy and into the shop-window positions of domestic administration. The first few years of independence presented few problems of internal security. It was therefore a period during which African heads of state and their ministerial colleagues were able to give much attention to foreign affairs. Inevitably, their central concern within this area was with the parts of Africa still under colonial rule. We have seen that within a year of gaining its independence Ghana was playing host to an All-African Peoples' Conference, from which Tom Mboya went home to Kenya to found the Pan-African Freedom Movement of East and Central Africa. No sooner had Tanganyika become independent, than it placed itself at the service of the liberation struggle in Moçambique, offering bases for training and a channel for the supply of arms from Eastern countries. Having gained its own independence by armed struggle, Algeria became an active training ground for insurgency and a major conduit for Russian arms. The Organization for African Unity, established in Addis Ababa in 1963, at once set up a nine-nation Liberation Committee with its headquarters in Dar es Salaam. From about 1965 it was plain that any non-African government still operating in Africa, whether composed of colonial officials or of resident colonists, would soon have to face not merely civil but military opposition.

Of the two colonial powers remaining in Africa after 1965, Spain was the less deeply involved. The government of General Franco, already softening its doctrinal stance in anticipation of his death and the restoration of the monarchy, proved keen to swim with the tide of decolonization. Independence was swiftly granted in 1968 to Equatorial Guinea, that is to the Gulf of Guinea islands of Fernando Po and Annobon and the 10,000-square-mile enclave of Rio Muni on the adjacent mainland. However, the Spanish Sahara – the Atlantic coastlands between Morocco and Mauritania – presented more of a problem. Though thinly peopled, this territory possessed considerable wealth in its deposits of phosphates and in its offshore fishing banks, and both its southern and its northern neighbours laid claim to it. In 1976 the solution was adopted of dividing the territory between the two of them.

Neither act of decolonization did much to improve the lot of the African peoples involved. The president elected in Equatorial Guinea, Macias Nguema, proved to be a cruel tyrant whose most constructive act was probably to rename his two islands, which are now known as Bioko and Pagalu respectively. By 1979, when he was overthrown and killed by his army, his country's economy had been ruined and something like a third of its people had fled to neighbouring territories. His successor (and nephew), Obiang Nguema, was able to secure aid from Spain and elsewhere, but he faced an uphill task in restoring both the economy and more responsible government. As for the western Sahara, when Morocco and Mauritania sought to occupy their new lands, they met with armed opposition from the Polisario Front of the local Sahrawi, which maintained that the Sahrawi should be allowed to determine their own future. The Front received substantial military aid from the more radical African and Muslim governments, Algeria in particular. King Hassan's Morocco was strong enough to fight back, but the war was too much for Mauritania. Its civil government collapsed in 1978, and its subsequent military rulers had no alternative but to recognize Polisario and to accept that this made them vulnerable to military and political pressure from Morocco.

Decolonization was not something that could be embraced by the

Estado Novo of Portugal. In 1951 this had proclaimed that there were no Portuguese colonies, only some provinces of Portugal which happened to be overseas and whose inhabitants might, through assimilation, achieve the same rights as the people of Portugal. But since the *Estado Novo* was a dictatorship, these rights did not include that of self-government and, in any case, less than 1 per cent of the people of the African colonies achieved *assimilado* status. The remainder were seen essentially as cheap and conscriptable labour which should be mobilized to bolster the Portuguese economy, which was the weakest in Europe. From the 1940s onwards, in an effort intended at once to help relieve poverty at home and to develop the 'overseas provinces' by exploiting their land and labour, metropolitan Portuguese were encouraged to settle in Africa. The climate discouraged emigration to Guinea, but by 1960 there were over 200,000 Europeans living in Angola and some 80,000 in Moçambique, where they formed about 4.5 per cent and about 1 per cent respectively of the populations. Their numbers continued to increase until the early 1970s, when they may have touched a grand total of half a million. The European presence had a depressing effect on those Africans, the *assimilados* especially, who were aware of the progress towards self-government and independence being made by their neighbours under other colonial regimes. A *Partido Africano de Independência da Guiné e Cabo Verde* and a *Movimento Popular de Libertação de Angola* were both founded in 1956. In Moçambique, relatively sheltered behind the white regimes of South Africa and Rhodesia, a comparable organization, the *Frente de Libertação de Moçambique*, emerged later, in 1962. But as early as 1959–60, in Moçambique as well as the other two colonies, the Portuguese authorities had shown that they would not hesitate to shoot down strikes and meetings of protest. Very soon afterwards, in Angola in 1961, in Guinea in 1963 and in Moçambique in 1964, armed risings began against their rule.

These risings developed into full-scale revolutions, employing astute guerrilla tactics and adept at mobilizing rural support, and handsomely supported by the training facilities and arms and other aid available in independent African states but commonly originating from Communist countries in other continents. Within a few years, the Portuguese government had been forced to deploy to Africa some three-quarters of its army of conscripted soldiers and a considerable proportion of its air and naval forces. The superiority in number of Portugal's troops, the professionalism of its officer corps, its NATO standard equipment and the eventual expenditure of nearly half the national budget on the African wars were insufficient to restore complete control. In the end, the strain on Portugal's domestic economy and society was such as to lead in 1974 to the overthrow of the *Estado Novo* itself by a junta of disillusioned young army officers.

Immediate independence was granted to Portuguese Guinea, control of which had been virtually lost, and accommodations were sought with the nationalists in Moçambique and Angola. A transfer of power was quickly arranged in Moçambique, where independence was recognized in 1975. In Angola, however, independence had to await the outcome of an armed struggle which had developed between the M.P.L.A. and two other independence movements, the *Frente Nacional de Libertação de Angola*, founded in 1962, and the *União Nacional para a Independência Total de Angola*, founded in 1966. Support for the two latter was essentially regional, but each provided an entry for outside interests seeking to influence affairs in Angola. The F.N.L.A. was based in the north, among the Bakongo, and its main support came from across the frontier in Zaire. U.N.I.T.A.'s strength lay in the south, among the Ovimbundu in particular, and it proved attractive to southern African interests. The issue was decided following the incursion of a South African military column from South-West Africa, ostensibly in defence of the South African position there. This led to a great rallying of active support for the M.P.L.A. from Communist Bloc countries, spearheaded by troops and technicians from Cuba. In the face of this, the South Africans thought it politic to withdraw. The M.P.L.A. was then free to scotch all opposition from the F.N.L.A. in the north and, by extending its control over the greater part of Angola, it received general recognition as the successor to the Portuguese colonial authority.

When Portugal lost control of Angola and Moçambique, the white settler governments in southern Africa became much more exposed to black nationalism. This was particularly the case with that of the much smaller and less strongly established Rhodesian community, whose independence had been recognized by no other country in the world, not even by South Africa. The independent black African countries argued that the settler regime in Rhodesia should be put down and majority rule installed by force of arms, and they expected Britain, the dispossessed colonial authority, to take the lead in this. But it was difficult to see how the British could move sufficiently superior forces into a landlocked country many thousands of miles distant from their nearest bases to ensure military victory over the by no means insignificant military and air forces controlled by the whites in Rhodesia with South Africa in covert support. It was also highly questionable whether public opinion in Britain would countenance the use of force against settlers who were their 'kith and kin'. Eventually, the Africans had to accept that action against Rhodesia would be limited to sanctions against its trade. But as long as Rhodesia had free access to the ports of Moçambique as well as of South Africa – and the governments of those territories were sympathetic to her – such sanctions were difficult to implement.

Once Moçambique had been brought under African rule, the situation changed. It became much easier for effective military attacks to be mounted against the whites in Rhodesia. Earlier guerrilla attacks on them from across the Zambezi in the north had been spasmodic and ineffective. The main effort of the African nationalists, whether within or without Rhodesia, who were seeking to secure the vote for all the people of Zimbabwe (as they had renamed Rhodesia), had remained political rather than military. But after 1975 the Rhodesian authorities had to cope with a long eastern frontier with a territory whose rulers had ten years' experience of successful military action against European imperialism. Guerrilla warfare threatened to become endemic over large areas of Rhodesia outside the larger towns. This placed considerable strain on the human and financial resources of the relatively small white community, which was now also suffering from the world economic recession of the 1970s – exacerbated in its case by the cumulative pressure of sanctions. By 1977, this combination of military and economic difficulties was sufficient to suggest to Ian Smith that he should attempt to secure recognition for the independence he had taken by accepting the principle of majority rule.

There was little chance of his reaching agreement with the two major nationalist movements, the Zimbabwe African People's Union, under the veteran nationalist Joshua Nkomo, and the Zimbabwe

African National Union, led by the younger and more highly educated Robert Mugabe. Indeed, their coming together in 1976 in a Popular Front for the better prosecution of the war against the white regime clearly helped to induce Smith's change of tack, for they were determined to fight for total victory. But there were softer black nationalists with whom Smith did find it possible to negotiate, and during 1978 he and they worked out a new constitution which seemed to concede universal suffrage without threatening white interests. In 1979 a black Prime Minister, Bishop Abel Muzorewa, took office at the head of a multiracial government in what was now called Zimbabwe-Rhodesia. But this new regime proved unable to end the fighting, which became ever more extensive and bloody, or to secure international recognition. However, in the same year it so happened that Rhodesia's northern neighbour, Zambia, was host to one of the regular conferences of Commonweath statesmen, and there the British government was prevailed upon by those African Commonwealth leaders who were friendly to the Popular Front to call a conference at which Mugabe and Nkomo would meet with Smith and Muzorewa. This conference met in December at Lancaster House in London under the forceful chairmanship of the British Foreign Secretary, Lord Carrington. An agreement was secured by which Rhodesia renounced its independence, and all sides accepted a short transitional period of British supervision under which there was to be a ceasefire, the guerrillas were to be disarmed and demobilized, and the first elections were to be held under a constitution which enshrined the principle of 'one man, one vote' but which also, for the first ten years, gave the whites twenty seats of their own in the 100-seat legislature. At the elections held early in 1980, the Z.A.N.U. wing of the Popular Front won a decisive victory, and Mugabe became the first Prime Minister of an independent Zimbabwe.

At first the whites in South Africa felt little threat from the rise of the independent black states further north. By the 1960s their economy was so buoyant that the Afrikaners had ceased to be an impoverished, embittered and exclusively rural community. Brimming with success and self-confidence, they were now able to draw English-speakers into their own concept of one white nation secure in its own destiny. They also possessed incomparably the greatest industrial and military power to be found anywhere in sub-Saharan Africa. In 1960 this white community decided by plebiscite that their land should return to the tradition of the Afrikaners of the Great Trek and become a republic. When at the Commonwealth Conference in the following year the leaders of other African Commonwealth countries raised the issue of whether this reconstituted state could retain its membership, the government of Dr Verwoerd chose withdrawal.

The new confidence brought with it a new and more sophisticated attitude towards the march of black nationalism outside South Africa. There could be little objection to the constitutional advancement of the British South African protectorates, of which Bechuanaland and Basutoland achieved independent status, as Botswana and Lesotho respectively, in 1966, and Swaziland in 1968. The situation of these landlocked territories was such that they had little alternative but to be economically associated with the Republic. In South African eyes, they were little more than a more positive aspect of apartheid as practised by Verwoerd and his successors. This was the policy of 'separate development' by which tribal homelands were to receive local autonomy, and might ultimately become what the South African government would regard as legally independent states, the so-called 'Bantustans'. This road was followed by the Transkei, which accepted its independence in 1976, and it was followed by a number of the other more substantial homelands. But the independence of these little black satrapies was not recognized by any other country, and the leaders of some of the major African ethnicities in the Republic, most notably the Zulu, also thought it a sham and stood out against it.

What was newer was the appreciation by the leaders of white South Africa that European rule was quitting the rest of the continent for ever, and that their country's best interests lay in reaching an accommodation with some at least of the new African rulers. This made sound political and economic sense. Hostility towards the new African states, with their natural leanings towards socialism, might tend to drive them to look for more, and more militant, aid from Russia and China. From the economic point of view, the newly independent African countries, essentially still all exporters of primary products, were now natural trading partners for the prime industrial power on the continent, and increased trade with it should help to strengthen them against involvement with Communist powers.

A vital question arising from this new foreign policy was where to draw the line between white and black Africa. Instinct inclined the South Africans to make common cause with the white Rhodesians and with the Portuguese regimes in Moçambique and Angola. However, a more realistic appraisal of the Rhodesian situation and of the ceaseless warfare which the Portuguese were having to wage against African nationalists, continually supported from independent African states, suggested that the real boundary was not the Zambezi but the Limpopo. The most that could be hoped for between the two rivers was a delaying action while the white bastion in the south made itself even more impregnable. In the 1970s, indeed, it would seem that whatever their innermost feelings, the South African leaders were advising Ian Smith to reach a compromise with the Zimbabwe nationalists before it was too late.

On the other hand, these same leaders were in no doubt that South-West Africa must remain within their sphere. Much of this country was desert, and it was very thinly peopled except along its northern border with Angola, where the Ovambo provided roughly half the total population – which in 1960 was about 500,000, rising to about a million by 1980. But some 70,000 white settlers, predominantly of Afrikaner or of German stock, formed a substantial proportion of the remainder and were entrenched in the relatively well-watered south-central highlands. The territory was additionally valued because it possessed substantial mineral wealth in diamonds and base metals (including uranium).

After the conquest of the German colony by South African troops during the First World War, the League of Nations mandate to administer the territory had been given to the South African government. After the Second World War, South Africa – unlike other mandatory powers – refused to recognize that the new United Nations Organization had inherited a supervisory authority over the territory. Thus South-West Africa, which the United Nations renamed Namibia in 1968, did not become a trusteeship territory to be prepared for self-government. Instead, the South Africans began to incorporate it into their Republic as a fifth province, a process which was complete by 1969. The full apparatus of apartheid was introduced, and the South-West African People's Organization developed as a full-blooded nationalist movement. As the illegality of

South Africa's actions was confirmed in 1971–2 by the International Court of Justice and by Resolution of the U.N. Security Council, so S.W.A.P.O. moved into armed resistance.

When Angola had become independent and was receiving military and other aid from Cuba and other Communist countries, S.W.A.P.O., in which Ovambo were dominant, had a useful ally just across the Namibian border. South Africa therefore extended its military action against S.W.A.P.O. into regular incursions into Angola and to military aid to U.N.I.T.A. in the war against its M.P.L.A. government. These actions, though not unsuccessful from the military point of view, outraged world opinion and could not solve the political problem. From 1978 onwards, the western members of the U.N. Security Council were endeavouring to bring about an agreement by which free Namibian elections might be held under U.N. supervision in preparation for the territory's independence. At the same time, the South Africans were trying to establish a multiracial partnership within Namibia to which they might hand over their responsibilities. Neither of these mutually contradictory policies could succeed, since the South Africans would not join in the first and S.W.A.P.O. would not join in the second.

While the white South Africans were prepared to come to terms with black nationalism outside their borders, they were still unwilling to countenance it within them. It was impossible to maintain apartheid without active repression of all opposition to it and rigid control of the black population. The idea that the Bantustans could provide adequate scope for black economic and political aspirations had never been tenable. They were too small, too poor, too little developed and possessed too little resource potential. Moreover, the number of blacks living in the Republic and the Bantustans was growing extremely rapidly, at about 3 per cent per annum: by the mid-1980s, they would number about 25 million (compared with about 5 million whites, 3 million Coloureds and rather less than 1 million Asians). As long as the great majority of the blacks who had to live outside the homelands continued to face restrictions on their freedoms of movement, employment and education, and were denied political rights, racial tensions were bound to continue, to be exploited by black nationalists (whether operating within or without the laws made by the whites) and to boil over from time to time into violence. Serious disturbances began in 1976 in Soweto and other black townships adjacent to the white cities; by the early 1980s a militant arm of the illegal A.N.C. was engaging in bombing campaigns and its imprisoned leader, Nelson Mandela, had become a nationwide focus of unrest; and by 1985 this unrest was becoming general. The government was forced to declare states of emergency in a number of areas and to call on troops to assist the police; in twelve months, over 1,000 deaths were reported.

This growing unrest and the measures taken against it brought the South African regime into worldwide disrepute. Since the early 1960s, black African states had given open support to the A.N.C. militants and had begun to call for some kind of intervention in aid of the blacks in South Africa. By the mid-1970s more and more was being heard in the developed countries outside the continent of the need for international sanctions against South Africa. But the most that could be achieved was an agreement that its government should not be supplied with arms. As late as 1985, a call for an embargo on trade with or investment in South Africa did not find general acceptance. The Conservative government of the United Kingdom (which, together with the U.S.A., the Federal Republic of Germany and Japan, was one of South Africa's major trading partners) argued, for example, that such an action would not only damage the U.K.'s own economy, but that it would also be harmful to the very people in South Africa who needed help, namely its black majority.

Nevertheless, within South Africa itself, the administrations of B. J. Vorster (1966–78) and P. W. Botha (1978 onwards) thought it advisable to begin to modify the practical application of apartheid. If the economy was to continue to grow and weather the world depression that began in the 1970s, the cooperation of the blacks was essential, particularly those in increasingly skilled employment. Thus black trade unions, which had begun to show their teeth in 1973 in effective strikes, received some recognition, and it became accepted that economic efficiency required that some blacks should no longer be regarded as migrant labourers but should be given security of tenure in peri-urban housing. 'Petty apartheid', that is segregation in public places, was substantially reduced; mixed marriages were no longer forbidden. But the basic principle remained that the direction of affairs could not be entrusted to or shared with the black majority of the inhabitants of South Africa. Nevertheless, since the whites formed an ever-decreasing proportion of the whole population, Botha thought it necessary to try and bring the Coloured and Asian people into government as junior partners of the whites. In 1984 he secured by referendum a new constitution under which he became an executive President at the head of a complicated structure in which, in addition to a national government which included a few Coloureds and Asians alongside the white ministers but which was responsible to a legislature of whites elected only by white voters, there were also lesser governments of Coloureds and Asians responsible for the internal affairs of their own communities to lesser assemblies elected by Coloured and Asian voters. It remains to be seen how meaningful this innovation might be. By bringing other races into government even in this limited way, and by relaxing the laws of apartheid, Botha had alienated the more conservative of the voters who had elected white Nationalist Party governments since 1948. On the other hand, few Coloureds or Asians were happy to participate in the limited roles assigned to them by the new constitution. Above all, for the blacks the new arrangements seemed to be a final closing of the door on their claim to full political rights in their own country.

Apologists for South Africa could at least claim that the people of this most industrialized and urbanized of all African countries were much better off than those in almost any other part of the continent. In the 1960s and 1970s the South African economy had a real per capita growth rate which averaged about 2·5 per cent per year. At the end of this period, G.N.P. per head was estimated to be about U.S. $2,500. In the whole continent only two countries had more income per head, and these were the two oil exporters which happened also to have very small populations, namely Libya, with some $5,000, and Gabon, with about $3,250.

However, the figure for South Africa is deceptive, for two obvious reasons. The first is that its wealth was – and is – very unevenly distributed among the races. For example, whites in mining or industrial employment earned at least five times as much as blacks in such employment; many blacks and virtually no whites were employed in very low-paid jobs, such as agricultural labourers or domestic servants; and while practically all whites belonged to family groups which had measurable monetary incomes, substantial numbers of blacks – especially in the homelands – did not. In the second place, the South African statistics exclude the predominantly black populations living in the 'independent' Bantustans and in the three former British protectorates, which exported wage-earners to the Republic and which were all in some measure satellites of its economy. If allowance is made for these things, it can be suggested that on average each individual South African black's share of the Republic's G.N.P. in 1980 would probably have been less than U.S. $1,000. That this may not be far off the mark is suggested by the 1979 estimates for the two more prosperous of the former protectorates, Botswana and Swaziland, which were some $720 and $650 respectively.

But even so, South African blacks would still seem to have been better off in material terms than the inhabitants of all other black African countries except Gabon and the Ivory Coast (for which the figure was U.S. $1,040). In 1979 twenty-five of the thirty-nine countries south of the Sahara for which data were available were among the world's poorest, with mean annual incomes per head within the range $110–370. A further twelve among the 'middle income countries' had mean annual incomes per head ranging from $380 to $720 (with a median income of $530). Over the twenty year period beginning in 1960, the per capita incomes of some of the poorest countries, particularly those in the semi-arid belt reaching across the continent immediately south of the Sahara, showed little or no real growth. Eight of the thirty-nine are even thought to have had negative growth rates, that is actually to have become poorer, during 1960–79. These included three countries with relatively high per capita incomes, in the range $400–440. Two of these – Ghana and Senegal – had been among the most developed in the colonial period, while in the third – Angola – a major new resource, petroleum, had become available for exploitation. The growth rates of eleven countries over these twenty years were less than 1 per cent per annum. Five others were in the range between 1 and 2 per cent. Only fourteen had growth rates of the same order as, or better than, South Africa's, and four of these – the three former protectorates and Malawi (in which there had been substantial South African investment) – were much influenced by the South African economy and policies.

South Africa's paramount position among the sub-Saharan economies seemed to be associated with two historical factors: it had

entered into world trade and it had successfully developed industry
earlier than the other countries. It was hardly surprising that the
rulers of the newly independent states for the most part should think
that their appropriate economic strategy was at once to encourage the
export of those of their agricultural or mineral products for which
there was a world demand, and to tax the resultant income or to
borrow against it to provide funds to develop their economies and to
improve their societies. In particular, more of a better educated,
healthier and better housed labour force should be employed in industry. As industrial production grew, so there would be less need to
expend wealth on importing manufactures from other countries. The
balance of trade would improve, so that it would become easier to
meet the payments on foreign borrowings and, indeed, to reduce
them, and the new nations would follow the example of South Africa
and of the richer economies generally, and become steadily better
off.

The position of the five African countries north of the Sahara and
the kind of development strategy followed by their governments were
not very different from those in tropical Africa. Egypt, Algeria and
Tunisia had all been touched by currents of world trade and had
attracted foreign investment earlier than was common in tropical
Africa, and they all had some industrialization. But Morocco had
been very isolated before the declaration of the French protectorate
in 1912 and Libya, largely desert and a very thinly peopled territory,
had been poorer and more backward than many countries in tropical
Africa until the exploitation of its oil resources began in 1960. All
depended on the export of primary agricultural or mineral produce
for their foreign earnings; Libya and Algeria would have been very
much poorer had it not been for the oil and gas extracted from
beneath their soils. It was these, of course, that in 1979 gave Libya
the high G.N.P. per head that has already been mentioned, and
Algeria as much as U.S. $1,800. Morocco and Tunisia, with around
$850, were towards the top of the range of middle-income countries,
but were less well-off than the Ivory Coast. Egypt, though advanced
in many respects, was held back by its large population of over 40
million, by the military and other expenditure necessitated by the
wars with Israel, and by a high rate of inflation. At around $500 per
head, it was in the middle of the middle-income range, ranking with a

country like Zambia. If the North African countries were to be distinguished from those further south, it would be chiefly because they tended to have higher growth rates. This would obviously be expected for Libya, but in the 1970s the others were achieving rates as high as 6–8 per cent.

By and large the development strategy adopted by most African governments did not work too badly during the 1960s, when there were positive annual growth rates for all countries south of the Sahara, usually of the order of 3–4 per cent, and substantially higher than this in North Africa. But already there was an obvious problem in sub-Saharan Africa; few of its countries had sufficient inhabitants to provide domestic markets large enough to support more than a few very simple secondary industries. In 1970, indeed, only Nigeria, Ethiopia, Zaire, Sudan, Tanzania and Kenya had populations in excess of 10 million, and there were actually six countries which each had less than a million inhabitants. It must also be said that the newly independent countries were less amenable than the old colonies had been to the solution of joining together in regional economic organizations or customs unions.

In the 1970s, however, the standard development strategy was less successful, and by the 1980s it was experiencing serious difficulties. One reason for this was that any programme of modernization and industrialization was dependent on adequate supplies of energy being available at reasonable cost. Few African countries outside South Africa had substantial deposits of workable coal; there was significant production only in Zimbabwe, Zambia, Morocco, Moçambique, Nigeria and Botswana. At least two dozen had harnessed some hydroelectric power, but the investment – in distribution networks as well as in dams and power stations – needed to secure substantial quantities of power was not easily forthcoming unless large transnational corporations wanted electricity for smelting operations, as they did, for instance, in Ghana, Guinea, Zaire and Zambia. So for the most part African countries looked to petroleum products for anything from 60 to 90 per cent of their supplies of energy for production and distribution (and, of course, for transport generally). From about the 1950s onwards, oilfields began to be developed in a number of African countries. Three of these became major suppliers of the world market, namely Libya and Nigeria, each of which was producing about

2,000,000 barrels per day (b.p.d.) by the end of the 1970s, and Algeria, with about 1,200,000 b.p.d. Other sizeable African producers by 1979 were Egypt (about 500,000,b.p.d.), Gabon (200,000 b.p.d.), Angola (200,000 b.p.d.), Tunisia (100,000 b.p.d.), and the Congo (60,000 b.p.d.). Other African countries had to buy the oil they needed on the world market.

During the 1960s oil was not only an easily portable source of energy but also a very cheap one. But in the 1970s its price began to rise. In 1970–71 crude oil sold for around U.S. $1·80 a barrel (160 litres), and by mid-1973 the price had risen to about $3·00. It then shot up steeply at the end of that year, when the Middle Eastern countries which produced nearly half the world's exports decided to cut production to bring pressure on the Western states that supported Israel in the Yom Kippur War (in which Egypt and Syria sought to recover the territory they had lost, in Egypt's case with some success). By early 1974 the price had steadied around $12. It then remained at about that level until 1979, when the crisis in Iran and its war with Iraq sparked further great price increases, first to $20 a barrel and then, by 1981, to $34 or more.

Thus in the space of ten years the current price of oil had risen nearly twentyfold; it had become an extremely expensive resource. What was worse was that the oil price rise fuelled a great inflation, not only in Africa but also in the developed countries outside the continent, those countries the African nations looked to for manufactured goods and for capital funds. The result was that, whereas in the 1960s African countries had as a rule experienced annual rates of inflation of no more than 2 or 3 per cent, in the 1970s rates of inflation of around 10 per cent per annum were quite usual (and in one or two cases they were over 30 per cent). Moreover, since the African countries which were themselves producing and exporting oil had more money to spend on securing capital and consumer goods from the developed countries, they suffered inflation quite as much as the oil importers.

The oil price rises sparked a depression in world trade which from about 1979 began to have a serious effect on African countries which needed to maximize their incomes from the export of primary agricultural and mineral produce if they were to secure funds for their own programmes of development. The industrial nations reduced their demands for this produce, and the prices gained for it on the world markets tended not to keep place with inflation. In addition, many African countries were experiencing increasing difficulty in growing enough foodstuffs for their own needs, and so they were using more of their static or declining earnings from foreign trade to buy such necessities on the world market. Agricultural production is thought to have been declining in most sub-Saharan countries in the 1970s at rates of around 1.4 per cent per annum, and they began to spend about as much on importing foodstuffs as they spent on importing fuel, each of these things constituting on average something like 14 per cent of the value of a country's imports.

The underlying reason for the growing inability of African nations to feed themselves was that for some time death rates, of young children especially, had been falling and life expectancies had been rising. By the 1970s the result was that in almost every African country population was increasing at rates between about 2·5 and 3 per cent per annum – which meant that populations could be expected to double in about twenty-five years. This might not have mattered had adequate attention been given to improving the yields of domestic foodstuffs, and to providing better distribution facilities and better conditions of life – education, medical services, good water supplies, etc. – for the rural farming communities that grew the food. But the emphasis in agricultural planning and funding had been placed on production for export. This often meant farmers concentrating on the production of non-food crops such as cocoa, coffee, tea, tobacco, rubber and sisal.[1] Earnings from these crops, and taxes on the farmers that produced them, were expected, as has been seen, to help develop the more 'modern' sections of the economy, the extraction of minerals for the world markets and, above all, the development of industry and of the towns that housed the labour and services required by industry and the mines.

Accelerating urbanization was itself a factor in the growing inability of tropical African countries to feed themselves. Labour was attracted away from the countryside, and out of domestic food production, by the lure of the money which might be earned in the towns and the

1 The consumption needs of growing African populations sometimes extinguished the export of agricultural produce, for example groundnuts and palm oil in Nigeria, which could also be consumed locally as foodstuffs.

mines. The concentrations of people in towns made possible the provision of services and facilities – supplies of water and electricity, markets, shops, schools, medical services, entertainments and so on – so much better or more extensive than could be found in the countryside that people were eventually being drawn into the towns irrespective of whether they could find reasonable employment in them. (In any case, the larger the towns, the more opportunities there were for employment in their service activities.) This kind of urbanization had long been a feature of the temperate zones at either end of the continent. In 1945, for instance, there had been ten towns of more than 100,000 inhabitants in Egypt, nine in Morocco, four in Algeria, one each in Tunisia and Libya, and eleven in South Africa and two in Rhodesia, but only eleven in all the rest of the continent (four of which were in Nigeria). By the 1970s, however, there were something like 120 such towns in Africa, and few countries did not have at least one (Nigeria had no fewer than thirty-two). It was estimated that in the short space of twenty years from 1960 to 1979, the urban population of Africa south of the Sahara had doubled, and that by 1980 more than a fifth of the people were living in towns. Capital cities were growing faster than others, with their populations doubling every ten years or so. If urbanization were to continue at such rates, by the 1990s half the people would be living in towns.

Finally, disaster began to strike food production in tropical Africa, particularly but not exclusively in the semi-arid zone immediately south of the Sahara and in north-eastern Africa (the Sudan, Ethiopia and Somalia), when from 1973 onwards there were more years than usual in which rainfall was markedly less than the average. Most African farmers and cattle-herders could survive one year in which the seasonal rains failed, but two or more in succession were another matter. Livestock ate up the grasses on marginal pastures; these could not be renewed and the land deteriorated into desert. Large numbers of cattle died, and the survivors were moved by their owners on to lands which had hitherto supported agriculture and, therefore, a higher level of food production than pastoralism. These lands in their turn would be converted into marginal grasslands to which agriculture could not return unless means could be found, through dams and boreholes, of providing permanent supplies of water. Such dramatic weakening of the traditional mechanisms of food production led to famines which governments were not well equipped to deal with. They could not easily afford to buy the surplus foodstuffs of temperate lands in Europe or America, nor did they readily possess the organization and means to distribute large quantities of food to populations which had hitherto always fed themselves. As well as the animals, millions of people died, especially children and the old and infirm. The survivors camped on the outskirts of towns, or were gathered in refugee camps where they were supplied by international relief agencies with the basic food and medical services needed to enable them to survive both the famines and the epidemics of dysentery and cholera that accompanied them.

Failures of the seasonal rains over two or more successive years, and the famines that resulted, were nothing new in African history; indeed, in the long run they might be regarded as recurrent threats. But in the past populations had been much smaller, so that there was less pressure on the land, and they had fewer unproductive mouths to feed in the shape of children and the aged and infirm. It was therefore easier for them to recover, the more so because the levels of material welfare which could be regarded as acceptable would be lower. The long-term results of the droughts and famines of the 1970s and 1980s have yet to be seen, not least because they occurred in societies which had lost the capacity to feed themselves. The manner in which pastoralists and farmers had reacted to the droughts had further weakened the capacity for domestic food production, and the food relief brought from abroad had increased the taste and the demand for imported foodstuffs.

By the 1980s, a further serious problem had arisen in that, with the worsening of the terms of trade for African countries and with the generally less favourable performance of their economies, the servicing of the foreign debts they had incurred in better days to help finance their development was becoming an excessive strain on their foreign earnings. It was calculated, for example, that nearly two-thirds of Zaire's export earnings in 1982 would be required to meet the service costs due on its external debt in that year together with what was still owed in respect of 1981. The position of the Sudan in 1983 was much the same, and that of the hitherto apparently very prosperous Ivory Coast little better, with over 40 per cent of export earnings needed for debt servicing. In percentage terms the burden on oil-producing countries may not have been so great, but it was growing and the actual sums required were substantial. Thus the cost of servicing Nigeria's foreign debt went up from less than 10 per cent of foreign earnings in 1982 to over 15 per cent in 1983 (when the total debt was thought to be some U.S. $10 billion at the least). In such situations, African states had little alternative but to approach the International Monetary Fund and ask for their debts to be re-scheduled. But such relief was forthcoming only on terms which considerably restricted their freedom of action in economic matters. Even worse was the fact that the credit-worthiness of African countries was at an extremely low ebb at the very time when they needed more help from the richer nations of the world if they were not to lag even further behind in their economic development.

In these circumstances it was hardly surprising that the richer Western nations, and bodies like the I.M.F. and the World Bank which were perceived to be their agencies, should be accused of 'neo-colonialism'. The political independence that African peoples had gained could hardly be considered complete so long as they were economically dependent. But it was not only *economic* dependence that could be found in post-colonial Africa. As will be seen, from time to time African governments might become in some degree dependent on outside military aid to preserve their political position, and such aid could come from Communist countries as well as from the Western industrial democracies.

During the early years of independence, the problems facing the leaders of the new African states had seemed to be predominantly political. The fundamental economic and social problems that have just been outlined had either not become apparent or were still in their infancy. The outstanding political questions were how the small, comparatively well-educated and well-off indigenous groups, which had succeeded to the almost absolute power previously wielded by alien colonial governments, could both maintain their own integrities and retain the confidence of sufficient of the poor and largely illiterate masses to justify their privileged positions. In the last resort the colonial rulers had been able to maintain their positions of privilege by their control of superior force, and it was when they decided that they would no longer employ this force in Africa that power had passed into African hands. The new black leaders had stepped into the positions formerly occupied by the colonial officials in the most literal sense. They moved into the offices and houses occupied by their predecessors, were driven by the same chauffeurs in the same or larger cars, and had the same servants, administrative and technical officials, policemen and soldiers at their command.

The difference was that the new rulers were themselves Africans, and that they had initially acquired their positions not through force but through the votes of fellow Africans. But there was a great gulf between them and the mass of ordinary men and women in the villages and in the fields, for whom life went on much as it had before, except that the District Commissioner now had a black face. All the new African rulers, whether they professed radical socialism or were conservative and empirical in their policies, found difficulty in fulfilling the expectations aroused in their citizens, first by the swelling contact with the developed world that the colonial period had brought through trade and education, and then by the fact that the developed world had cut the colonial guiding strings and declared that they could stand by themselves. Through newspapers and advertising, through the transistor radio, increasingly through television, ordinary Africans were more and more aware of what the twentieth century had to offer and were keen to secure a share of it.

But the relative weakness and lack of development of the ex-colonial economies – sometimes, indeed, their sheer lack of resources – meant that not all the voters could get shares that they would accept as sufficient, at least within a reasonable time. The new rulers were therefore often not keen to submit themselves regularly to competitive elections. They tended instead to argue that party politics were a luxury which developing nations could not afford, and that what was required was a strong single party which would represent the political mobilization of the whole nation, and which could get on with the business of government and development without interference. It was claimed, and with some conviction, that such single-party rule was the modern equivalent of traditional African systems of government, in which the national will was determined not by the periodic counting of votes but by the elders' determination of what the people were saying and wanted.

But what was to happen when the people found that they were not getting what they felt they had a right to expect, or when they – or some of them – felt that too much of the limited resources of the nation were not being used for its general good, but were going to support the panoply of power in the new capital cities, into the presidential palaces, embassies, airlines and armies which sovereign states apparently had to have, or were being used simply to enrich the politicians and their friends and relatives? It was not difficult to find an answer. Like the colonial governments before them or, indeed, governments anywhere, the self-perpetuating African political machines depended in the last resort for their power on their control of the military. In the new African armies there proved to be a rival élite which could if necessary be used, or which might take it upon itself, to challenge and overpower the political élite.

The prototype of such action in Africa – at least in modern times – was the military coup in Egypt in 1952 which swept away the monarchy and brought Nasser to power. By the end of 1985, there had been more than fifty other occasions on which armed force had been used successfully to take over the administration of an independent African state. Sometimes the military leaders kept power for themselves, sometimes they came to share it with civilians, sometimes they arranged for elections to be held and then handed over power to the winning politicians. All these coups, especially if they involved bloodshed, tended to be highlighted in the world media, with the result that it has become a commonly held opinion that the politics of Africa since independence have been generally violent and unstable.

On closer examination, this is too facile a generalization. In the first place, in cases where the military decided to keep power for themselves, and were able to maintain their discipline, their rule might mean no more than government directed by a council of senior officers, with the civil administration and judiciary continuing to operate much as they always had. Only if the military themselves became divided in the course of secondary and tertiary coups might their rule deteriorate into large-scale oppression or into general disorder. Secondly, it must be pointed out that of the forty-four independent states on the African continent in 1985, eighteen (41 per cent) had never experienced a military take-over, and fourteen (32 per cent) had not had more than one.

In the five countries of Africa north of the Sahara, governments had been remarkably stable. The Egyptian regime established by

Nasser, who died in 1970, remained intact despite the wars with Israel and despite the assassination, in 1981, of Nasser's immediate successor, his former Vice-President, General Sadat (who was then succeeded by *his* Vice-President, General Mubarak). In Tunisia, Bourguiba, who had taken his country to independence in 1956, was still president in 1986. Morocco still had its king. In Algeria, Ben Bella was ousted in a coup in 1965 by his military colleague, Colonel Boumédienne. The latter died in 1978, but the regime he had established was still in control twenty years later. In Libya in 1969, young officers led by Colonel Gaddafi had risen to abolish the monarchy and establish a socialist regime on the Nasser model, and in 1986 Gaddafi was still in charge.

The sub-Saharan record is more varied. Nevertheless, some of the new leaders, even if they could not please all of the people all of the time, and sometimes dealt harshly with some of their leading opponents, proved remarkably skilful in manipulating the balance and the rewards of power to maintain both their own positions and national stability. Eight leaders who took their countries to independence in the 1950s and 1960s were able to continue in office for twenty years or more. These were Presidents Sekou Toure of Guinea (independence, 1958; died 1984), Ahidjo of Cameroon (independence, 1960; retired, 1982), Houphouët-Boigny of the Ivory Coast (independence, 1960; still in office, 1986), Senghor of Senegal (independence, 1960; retired, 1980), Nyerere of Tanzania (independence, 1961; retired, 1985), Banda of Malawi (independence, 1964; still in office, 1986), Kaunda of Zambia (independence, 1965; still in office, 1986) and Jawara of the Gambia (independence, 1965; still in office, 1986). President Kenyatta of Kenya might well have been of this number had he not been about seventy years old when his country became independent in 1963; when he died in 1978, power passed relatively smoothly to his successor, Daniel arap Moi. There was also stability and continuity in Botswana (independence, 1966), whose first President, Seretse Khama, died in 1980, and in Swaziland (independence, 1968) under King Sobhuza II, who died in 1982.

There are also a number of states which experienced violent interludes but which otherwise had stable government for considerable periods. Kenya and Tanzania might perhaps be brought into this category since early in 1964 British troops were briefly called in to deal with mutinies in their as yet tiny armies (and also that of Uganda). A parallel but much more serious situation occurred at almost exactly the same time in Gabon. Here President M'Ba was actually ousted by his army but was able to recover his position with the aid of French troops. When he died in 1967, his Vice-President, Omar Bongo, took over and, with the great resources of oil, uranium, manganese and timber available in his small country, had no difficulty in maintaining political stability.

Mali had none of Gabon's advantages. It is large, unwieldy, landlocked, arid and one of the poorest countries in Africa. The architect of its independence, President Modibo Keita, did not deal very competently with its many problems. In 1968, therefore, it was not surprising when he was overthrown by a young army officer, Lieutenant Moussa Traore, who eventually assumed the presidency. Traore was sufficiently successful to be still in command eighteen years later. This was by no means the only case of a new state discarding its founding father after a few years' experience of his administration, and replacing him with a new ruler sufficiently skilful to retain power for a substantial period and to survive until 1986. Thus in Niger, which had the same problems as Mali – though it was marginally less poor – President Hamani Diori was replaced by Colonel Kountche in a military coup in 1974.

Some cases were less straightforward. In Togo, President Sylvanus Olympio, a leading nationalist since the early 1940s, was killed in a military coup in 1963, after which his principal political opponent was invited to become president. But he proved uninspiring, and in 1967 there was a further coup, following which the military leader, Colonel Eyadama, took the presidency for himself. In the adjacent former French colony of Dahomey, three politicians, each with his own regional power-base, found it difficult to provide a stable government at the centre, and the soldiers were constantly intervening. There were no fewer than three coups leading to changes of the civilian government before ultimately, in 1972, General Kerekou decided to retain power. The new President then thought it advisable to find an ideology and to rename his country the People's Republic of Bénin. Sierra Leone became independent under the parliament premiership of Milton Margai. After he died in 1964, he was succeeded by his brother, Albert Margai, who was moving towards a single-party state when in 1967 he lost an election. The Army commander then mounted a coup in order to keep out Margai's more populist opponent, Siaka Stevens; but his officers took over power for themselves until, in 1968, some of the ordinary soldiers mutinied and brought in Stevens. In 1971 Stevens faced a further coup and thought it wise to bolster his position with troops from Guinea. In the same year he became President, and in 1978 he instituted a one-party state.

In Sierra Leone's neighbour Liberia, a President elected as early as 1943, W. V. S. Tubman of the True Whig Party, did much to give the indigenous Africans a share in government alongside the descendants of the Afro-Americans who had settled in the country from the 1820s onwards. When he died in 1971, he seemed to have passed on a settled inheritance to his Vice-President and successor W. R. Tolbert. But intellectuals, students and soldiers had caught a radical fervour from the adjacent ex-colonial territories. In 1980 young soldiers destroyed a political and social pattern that had endured since at least 1860, when the True Whigs had first been elected, and set up a People's Redemption Council led by a former sergeant appropriately called Samuel Doe. How stable the new form of government would be was still an open question in 1986.

The True Whig regime in Liberia was in many respects akin to the monarchies which had been swept aside in Egypt and Libya. The oldest monarchy in Africa – and one of the oldest in the world – disappeared in 1974. Except for the five years of Italian occupation, Ethiopia had been ruled since 1916 by Haile Selassie, first as regent and then, after 1930, as Emperor. He had striven to modernize a feudal government and society, but by the early 1960s he was seventy years old and his administration was running into increasing difficulties. In 1962 it was decided that the federated territory of Eritrea should be no more than a province of the empire, and this quickly brought active resistance from an Eritrean Liberation Front which was backed by neighbouring Muslim countries. By 1972 this had developed into open warfare. In the 1960s also there began to be open armed conflict with Somali tribes over grazing lands in the Ogaden border territory. In 1972–3 there occurred the first of the famines which were ultimately to decimate populations in large areas of Ethiopia. None of these problems was confidently dealt with, and this was in part because of Haile Selassie's greatest failure, his reluctance to give adequate power and responsibility to the young people for whom training had been provided in schools, colleges and universities at home or abroad. Open discontent with and criticism of his regime became increasingly manifest from the mid-1960s onwards in student demonstrations and workers' strikes. By 1974 the army had been affected and in that year young officers, encouraged by diplomatic representatives of Communist countries, deposed the Emperor (who died shortly afterwards) and set up a Provisional Military Administrative Council (the *Dergue*) to rule what was declared to be a socialist state.

There followed a dreadful period of three years in which there was an open and bitter struggle for supremacy between various groups, each with its own idea of the appropriate socialist ideology and strategy; many thousands of lives were lost. By 1977, however, a single leader for the revolution had emerged, Colonel Mengistu, who set about the enormous task of rebuilding a shattered country with aid from the U.S.S.R. and other Communist countries, for whom the strategic position of Ethiopia commanding the Red Sea oil-routes was doubtless an important consideration. An invasion from Somalia was repulsed in 1978, but many difficulties remained. There was continuing rebellion in Eritrea and disaffection spread to other northern provinces, and this, together with widespread resistance to land reform, made it almost impossible for the Ethiopians to deal effectively by themselves with the overriding problems of drought and famine.

However, except for the short period 1974–7, it would hardly be correct to say that the central government in Ethiopia was unstable. Its problem was rather that from about 1960 onwards its writ did not run over all the lands it claimed to administer. In similar fashion, although General Mobutu became head of state in Zaire in 1965 and was still in office twenty years later, his administration's control over some of the parts of his country away from his capital was by no means always secure. Other large states with this problem were the former Portuguese territories of Angola and Moçambique. Here South Africa gave active support to those who were prepared to challenge the authority of Marxist central governments in the hope that these would be destabilized. In Angola this secured the revival of U.N.I.T.A. despite the substantial military aid, in men as well as material, received by the M.P.L.A. government from Communist countries.

Of course, small states could run into problems as well as large ones. The Gambia, one of the poorest as well as smallest, with not much more than half a million people and all but surrounded by Senegal, was always a problematic entity. Nevertheless, under President Jawara it was a working democracy with regular elections and had every appearance of stability. In 1981, however, a small group of conspirators joined with members of the tiny defence force to stage a rebellion. Jawara's government was restored only with the aid of troops from Senegal, who were then invited to stay to maintain order. The Gambia went on to resume its democratic practices but also began to join with its larger neighbour in a Confederation of Senegambia.

Rwanda had had a moment of intense communal violence when, on the eve of independence, the Hutu majority of the population rose and slaughtered many thousands of the Tutsi ruling caste, driving the survivors as refugees into Uganda. The military take-over of President Kayibanda's government by General Habyarimana in 1973 was by comparison an almost peaceful event. Neighbouring Burundi, on the other hand, has had a deplorable record of communal violence, culminating with the events in 1972, when around 100,000 Hutu – more than 3·5 per cent of the entire population – were wiped out within a few weeks by the Tutsi government of General Micombero. More than 150,000 Hutu took refuge in adjacent countries.

French colonial administrators had always been uncertain how best to deal with the medium-sized, rather densely populated but very poor territory which they called the Upper Volta and which, in 1984, was to adopt the African name of Burkina Fasso. At one time they treated it as part of their French Sudan, at another as part of their richer colony of the Ivory Coast. In 1960, however, it happened to be a colony in its own right and so became an independent state. But even before it was hit by famine, its resources seemed inadequate to allow stable government, whether by civilians or the military. There were no fewer than four successful coups between 1966 and 1983. After the last of these, a radically minded junior officer, Captain Sankara, began to act in the spirit demonstrated immediately to the south in Ghana by Flight-Lieutenant Rawlings, and even contemplated integrating

Burkina Fasso with its more developed southern neighbour.

Ghana, of course, had been the original standard-bearer for the cause of independence in sub-Saharan Africa. Kwame Nkrumah was very proud of this and, after his country had become independent in 1957, he devoted a major share of his energy and eloquence, as well as some part of Ghana's resources, to the wider promotion of the pan-African and anti-colonial causes. At home he tended to favour expensive but unremunerative prestige projects and did little to curb the self-interest of many members of his all-embracing political party. The consequences may not have been as extreme or as brutal as those which afflicted the Central African Republic under General Bokassa, who seized power in 1965, had himself crowned Emperor in Napoleonic splendour in 1976, and was finally rejected by his people in 1979 with the aid of French troops. But this was because Ghana was a much more developed country, in terms of education and skills as well as in matters material. Nevertheless, by 1966 Nkrumah's government had squandered a large part of the resources it had inherited at independence, and there was widespread rejoicing when he and his colleagues were ousted by a military coup. The soldiers then engineered a return to democratic, parliamentary government and the election to office of more conservative politicians. But the administration that was elected in 1969 under Dr Busia was unable to show whether it was more efficient and honest than Nkrumah's single-party government because, at a time of declining cocoa prices, its economic measures were unpopular and impatient soldiers became inspired to take power again. In 1972 General Acheampong and a National Redemption Council set out to show that they could do better. They failed, the economic situation worsened, and the people showed that they could dislike a military dictatorship as much as they had disliked Nkrumah's. So in 1978 General Acheampong gave way to General Akuffo, who promised a return to civil government. In the event this was precipitated in 1979 by a coup of junior officers and N.C.O.s led by a charismatic young air force officer, Jerry Rawlings; they thought their seniors bumbling and corrupt and executed many of them. When by 1981 a renewed parliamentary system was not fulfilling their hopes, Rawlings and his supporters seized power again and instituted a Provisional National Defence Council with the aim of revivifying the whole Ghanaian society.

Chad is statistically the poorest country in Africa – if not in the world. It has fewer people than Burkina Fasso in a vast territory five times the size, even more arid and prone to famine in the north, where it stretches halfway across the Sahara to the southern frontier of Libya, while in the south it reaches to the fringes of the Congo basin. This situation has produced a fatal political division between the nomadic Muslim cattle-herders of the north and the agriculturalists of the south, for the most part pagan but also touched by Christian education. By 1967 the north was in open revolt against rule by a single party based in the south. In the 1970s Libya began to give military assistance to the Muslims in what had become a civil war, advancing its own interest by annexing a supposedly mineral-rich strip of territory along Chad's northern border. During 1975–80 a northern faction and its Libyan allies were kept out of the south only by the interposition of French troops, and by the end of this period various combinations of African states were vainly trying to stabilize the situation, whether by diplomacy or by installing a security force drawn from their own armies. But the French were called in again in 1983–4 when the Libyans renewed their advance. The division in Chad seemed not to be bridgeable by any native politician or soldier.

The Republic of the Sudan, Chad's neighbour to the east, is an even larger country – the largest, indeed, in all Africa – but it has about twice as many people to the square mile, and it is at the top rather than at the bottom of the range of low-income African countries, with G.N.P. per head more than three times that of Chad. But it suffers from the same division between north and south, although in the Sudan it is the Muslim north that has more education and political experience, and in 1955 it was the poorer, part-Christianized south that rose in revolt. In 1958, when parliamentary government was proving incompetent even in the north, there was a military takeover under General Abboud. He was able to restore effective administration in the north, but virtually the whole weight of the army failed to give him control of the south. A return to parliamentary government in 1964 produced no better result, and in 1969 the military resumed power under a group of young officers led by Colonel Nimeri. A renewed attempt to subdue the south by force led only to more bloodshed and chaos, and to mounting international criticism, especially from Christian churches. In 1972, therefore, peace was negotiated with the south, which was promised local autonomy. After this, however, Nimeri's regime lost its way and became increasingly conservative. Opposition to it steadily increased when foodstuffs became in increasingly short supply and prices rose. This reached a peak following Nimeri's declaration in 1983 that the law of Islam was the law of the state, and in 1984 of martial law. In 1985 he had begun to moderate his policy when he was replaced by a minister he had newly appointed, General Swar al-Dahab.

Major regional and cultural divisions also presented serious post-independence problems to two other territories, Uganda and Nigeria, which – together with Ghana – had been thought of as among the major successes of British colonial policy. Uganda's troubles stemmed from the fact that during the colonial period education and economic development had been rather concentrated in the Bantu-speaking southern provinces, whereas soldiers had always been recruited from the 'martial races' of the poorer north. At independence in 1962 the government rested on a precarious alliance between the mainly northern party of Milton Obote and the party of the traditionalist Baganda, whose Kabaka Mutesa was also the President of Uganda. In 1966 Obote felt strong enough to topple the Kabaka and to seize the presidency for himself. But he did not use his new power well, either in his country's interest or his own, and in 1971 he was overthrown by the military commander who had led the assault on the Kabaka's palace, General Amin, another northerner. This change was initially welcomed both at home and abroad. But Amin had even less idea than Obote as to how to employ power constructively. He gained local popularity by expelling the Asian community, but this hardly helped the economy, which steadily deteriorated. As more and more individuals and groups began to criticize Amin, so he became more and more free in the brutal use of force to rid himself of real or imagined foes. By 1978 the army itself was beginning to come apart in the disorder that it had helped to create, and Amin sought some relief for himself and distraction for his soldiers by invading Tanzania. But when the Tanzanian army counter-attacked, his own army collapsed into lawless bands, and within five months Tanzanian troops had occupied most of Uganda, including its capital, and Amin had been forced to flee the country.

However the Ugandans did not find it easy to agree among themselves on how best to govern their liberated land. Eventually, Obote, who was supported by Tanzania on the grounds that he had been unlawfully deposed in 1971, won an election and became President for the second time. But as the Tanzanian troops were withdrawn, so public order – never wholly restored – dissolved into chaos. By 1983 Obote's 'Ugandan' army was but one band competing with other guerrillas for booty as well as power. Although by the end of 1985 a military victor had emerged in the shape of the National Resistance Army, a much more disciplined and purposeful force led by Yoweri Museveni from the west of the country, it was not easy to see how stability and prosperity might be restored to Uganda, especially to its northern districts.

Nigeria, a substantially larger country than Uganda, had comparable regional and ethnic divisions and rivalries, but these never occasioned a complete, nationwide breakdown of law and order of the kind that had beset Uganda. This was not so much because it had a greater range of resources, including the substantial oil wealth that began to be exploited from the end of the 1950s onwards, for rich though Nigeria was, its wealth had to be shared among by far the largest number of people in any African country; by 1985 the population was thought to exceed 80 millions (twice that of Egypt). Rather, it would seem a consequence of the fact that in 1967 its divisions were to lead it into a major civil war which was bitterly fought out for two and a half years between two large armies, perhaps half a million soldiers all told, a war which resulted in at least a million deaths, with civilian losses from starvation and disease probably outnumbering military casualties by something like ten to one. Tragedy on this scale made it imperative for soldiers and politicians alike to try and evolve forms of government for the future which would be acceptable to all sections of the country.

Nigeria became independent as a federation of northern, eastern and western regions. The north had as many or more people as the two southern regions combined, and it had rather more seats than they did in the federal legislature. A single party had an overwhelming majority in the assembly of each region and formed its government. In the south, where there was more development and education, these were typical nationalist parties, albeit with ethnic bases, Ibo in the east, Yoruba in the west. In the north the ruling party was an association of the conservative Muslim Fulani-Hausa emirs. No government could function at the centre without its support, and at independence power passed to a coalition between the northern conservatives and the eastern, and more radical, nationalists. When this collapsed, as it did in 1964, the northerners retained control with the support of the voters of a mid-west region that had just been created and of a puppet government in the west. The consequences were a general breakdown of order in the west and increasing dissatisfaction among civil servants and army officers – who were for the most part southerners, from the east in particular – at the disingenuousness of the federal politicians. In January 1966 young army officers staged a coup in which the federal prime minister, the leader of the northern party and the prime minister of the west were all killed. A military government was set up under General Ironsi, an Ibo. Peace returned to the west, and it was decided to replace the four regions with a larger number of more evenly balanced states. But the military government was not to the liking of northerners, whether they were its traditional élite or the soldiers who constituted the bulk of the rank and file in the army; both thought it too much dominated by Ibos. In July Ironsi and many other Ibo officers were killed in a mutiny. Military discipline was restored under General Gowon, a Christian northerner, but he had to face a wave of hatred in the north directed against the southerners, Ibos in particular, who had come to play major roles in its trade, administration and technical and other services. Large numbers were killed, and perhaps a million fled south, mainly into densely populated Iboland. Led by the military governor of the east, Colonel Ojukwu, the Ibos came to fear that the new state system would perpetuate northern domination. At the end of May 1967, Ojukwu proclaimed the secession of the east as the independent state of Biafra, and a month later the civil war began.

The Biafrans created an army of unusual ingenuity and enterprise, but in the long run they could not prevail against the superior numbers and military equipment that the federal government could mobilize and the blockade it imposed on them. A disastrous shortage of food, as well as of munitions, eventually brought Biafra to heel. Ojukwu fled in January 1970, and the remaining secessionists agreed to surrender. They were generously treated by Gowon and his government; much was done to make them feel at home in the new Nigeria that was to be built. But a vast amount of reconstruction – material as well as political – was needed before there could be any hope of democratic government functioning again. Gowon found increasing difficulty in turning aspirations into reality, and in 1975 he was replaced by a more active northern officer, General Murtala Muhammad, who quickly achieved popularity by producing a timetable for the restoration of civil administration by 1979. Despite his assassination in 1976, this timetable was adhered to. A second Nigerian republic was inaugurated with an executive president, no fewer than nineteen component states, each with its own assembly and government, and five-tier elections. But this new federal scheme was no more successful than the old one in promoting good government. There were too many political wills to be accommodated and nests to be feathered. Ambitious development plans were too often tailored to political ends, and by 1983 even the substantial funds accruing from oil revenues had been overcommitted. Most ordinary Nigerians experienced a sense of relief when, at the end of the year, the military resumed control.

The recent history of many of the new African states does not always seem to fulfil the high hopes of the time of independence. But that would have been too much to expect. Nevertheless, in a world in which violence and disaster is increasingly commonplace, it is important that these states have all survived. Despite the great increase in population throughout the continent, despite the disasters of drought, famine and disease which have affected many areas, despite the problems with food production, most African countries are materially somewhat better off than they were at the end of the colonial period. It is true, of course, that most of them are also still desperately poor, that in half of the countries the mean income per head in 1980 was less than U.S. $380 per year (and in four instances less than $200), and that there were only five countries in which it was more than $1,000. (In the United Kingdom – by no means any longer a particularly rich country – per capita G.D.P. in 1980 was about $7,250.) One might have expected poverty to have been a major cause of political unrest and disaster, but in fact it would seem that Africans have found it equally easy to quarrel within a context of relative affluence as, for example, in Nigeria, Ghana or Uganda.

If there was less instability than is sometimes thought, it must be admitted that political stability does not necessarily mean that the populace was always happy and content; Sekou Toure's Guinea, for example, was not a very comfortable place to live in unless one was a member of the ruling party – and not always then. Nor did it mean that all problems were being solved; thus the 'economic miracle' by which – after oil-rich Gabon – the Ivory Coast under Houphouët-Boigny became by far the wealthiest state in black Africa may prove to have been to the benefit more of French and other Western businesses than to the average Ivoirean, who was certainly saddled with an appreciably higher per capita foreign debt to service than most other black Africans. However, it does seem that the stability that has been achieved is due at least as much to statesmanship and good sense as to dogma. The ideologies and political outlooks of the longer-lasting political leaders embrace a very wide spectrum from formal Marxism (for example Sekou Toure), through various brands of 'African socialism' (Nasser, Nyerere) and of pragmatism (Kaunda, Kenyatta), to full-blooded capitalism (Houphouët-Boigny) and, even, cooperation with white South Africa (Banda). There has also been much flexibility within each of such categories. For example, although in Guinea Sekou Toure started by seeking aid from Communist states, his country's economy was always dependent on the sale of bauxite and alumina to the Western industrial nations, and he was moving towards closer cooperation with them when he died. Or again, a ruler like Senghor in Senegal sometimes appeared to be an African socialist and sometimes to be essentially pragmatic; moreover, he was always looking to the former colonial mentor, France, for help to make good the economic loss to his country caused by the break-up of the French West African Federation. Yet again, Angola, while depending on the Soviet Union for arms and on Cuba for military assistance, relies for the exploitation of its oil resources on Gulf Oil, a U.S. company.

In more general terms, what has been seen in many cases has been a shift from parliamentary and single-party regimes towards personal government, in which more and more decisions are taken by a single individual who assumes the role of fountainhead of goodness for the whole people. These individuals tend to be surrounded by courtiers rather than cabinets – courtiers who are rewarded less by salaries than by the opportunity to take their cuts from the various projects which they sponsor for public contracts, planning permission, import licences, foreign exchange and such like. The system would have been perfectly familiar to any monarch of sixteenth- or seventeenth-century Europe. If some of the decisions do not work out for the best, then it is not the leader who is to blame but institutional defects or less god-like individuals in the party or the bureaucracy that link the leader to the people at large. Nevertheless, it is apparent that it is possible to reach a point beyond which such a shifting of responsibility is no longer acceptable, and this has often been the point at which the military would intervene in civil affairs, arguing that things had gone so wrong that it was necessary to make a completely new start. It was quite another matter, however, whether the soldiers would be able to achieve such a new start. If they chose to restore parliamentary or party government, it was always possible that it would develop the same faults of inefficiency, indiscipline and corruption that had originally provided a justification for the development of personal rule. Then there would follow the dilemma that further interventions by the military would only serve to encourage much the same faults in their own ranks. Alternatively, of course, a military commander might see fit to develop his own personal government.

The importance of soldiers in the recent political history of Africa is plain to see. It might be said, indeed, that they have spent more time and energy trying to set governments right than they have in fighting wars. Nevertheless, there have been wars in Africa – though it is questionable whether they have been more common or savage that those in some other parts of the world. Some of these wars have been substantial, for example that involving Morocco, Mauritania and the Polisario Front, or the struggle in southern Angola involving the M.P.L.A. government and its Cuban supporters, S.W.A.P.O., U.N.I.T.A. and South Africa. There were major civil wars too, such as those in Nigeria and Zaire, and there was also great and extensive disorder amounting to civil war in substantial parts of such countries as the Sudan and Ethiopia. Nevertheless, it is probably fair to say that complete breakdowns of peaceful order over whole countries for substantial periods have occurred only in Zaire, Chad and Uganda.

Some wars were at least in part inheritances from the colonial period when, for example, there were unresolved uncertainties about the boundaries between the Italians in Libya and the French in Chad, and between Italian Somaliland and Ethiopia. But post-independence quarrels over boundaries were really exceptional. In general it is remarkable how sacrosanct the former colonial boundaries became for African statesmen, despite their earlier nationalist criticisms of them as artificial and ethnically divisive. The principle that each state should respect the sovereignty and the territorial integrity of the others was indeed enshrined in the constitution of the Organization of African Unity which encompassed all the independent states except the Republic of South Africa. It is worth remarking that President Nyrerere of Tanzania, characteristically among the least militant of African leaders, was heavily criticized for his army's invasion of Uganda in 1978, even though its purpose was clearly to remove a cruel tyrant who had wantonly attacked his own country. On the more positive side, it is also noteworthy how African states have increasingly shown willingness to help their neighbours in times of difficulty, for example Guinea and Sierra Leone, Senegal and the Gambia, Ghana and Burkina Fasso, and also, of course, many countries with Zaire and with Chad. By the mid-1980s there were hopes that such actions could lead to the more general and permanent kinds of cooperation that were so badly needed if some of the smaller and weaker countries that were denied the largesse of oil or some other valuable resource were not to stagnate for ever.

In many ways the Africa of the later 1980s was a more westernized continent than that which had entered upon independence in the 1960s and 1970s. Cities and towns were more prominent, and their centres more international in character. In most countries there was a recognizable middle class of fairly affluent town-dwellers, anxious for improvement and concerned to secure the best education for their children, saving money and investing in land and buildings, owning motor cars and glued to television in the evenings. Of the population at large, far more were literate in a European language or else in Arabic. Three or four times as many people belonged to Christian churches, and Muslims had also increased significantly in number. At the same time memories of direct dependence on the Western world were fading. There were hardly any Europeans left in government or education, and even fewer in the churches. For those under thirty or forty years of age the colonial period was no more than a vague childhood impression or an idea learned at school. Even among older people colonial rule was becoming a distant memory, and no one sighed for its return. By and large, Africans had come to feel responsible for the failures as well as the successes of their own societies. Slowly but surely, the sense of nationhood was growing at the expense of more local loyalties. On the larger scale, pan-Africanism as a political programme had receded, but there remained a strong sense of African community. In part, of course, this came from the Africans' common experience of colonialism, and it was further cemented by their community of opposition to the continuance of white domination in South Africa. Nevertheless, to a historian it is apparent that the African sense of community has much deeper roots than those of its temporary tutelage to Europe. Before Arab or Portuguese sailors and merchants had opened up the African coastline, Africa's lines of communication were interior ones, and it is along these ancient established interior lines that there have travelled the essential influences which have resulted in this sense of an African community.

Suggestions for Further Reading

CHAPTERS 1 TO 4

The general reader who wishes to go deeper into African history may need first to widen his knowledge of the African peoples, their geographical environment, their cultures, their languages and their social institutions. A convenient all-purpose reference work is Michael Crowder and Roland Oliver (eds.), *An Encyclopaedia of Africa*, 1983. The many times reprinted (e.g. 1966) *Races of Africa* by C. G. Seligman is unfortunately based on a totally misleading understanding of African history. Cautious use may be made of G. P. Murdock, *Africa – Its Peoples and their Culture History*, 1959 which is at once stimulating and contentious. H. Baumann and D. Westermann, *Völkerkunde Afrikas*, available in French as *Les peuples et les civilisations de l'Afrique*, 1948, is solid and reliable if now a little old-fashioned, while J. L. Gibbs (ed.), *Peoples of Africa*, 1965, is perhaps the best introduction in English though, unlike the other works, it does not attempt to be comprehensive but consists of a number of selective studies. Though his classification is by no means universally accepted, the most modern general work on the languages, and one which is historically very important, is Joseph H. Greenberg, *The Languages of Africa*, 1963; there is also a useful collection of papers edited by David Dalby, *Language and History in Africa*, 1970. There are two useful historical atlases: J. F. A. Ajayi and Michael Crowder (eds.), *Historical Atlas of Africa*, 1985, is on the grand scale, with contributions from many hands; J. D. Fage, *An Atlas of African History*, revised edn, 1978, is handier.

The fundamental work of reference for the African prehistory outlined in Chapters 1 to 3 is *The Cambridge History of Africa*, Vol.

1, 1982, edited by J. Desmond Clark. For those who require a shorter survey, the same ground is covered by David Phillipson, *African Archaeology*, 1985. The *UNESCO General History of Africa*, Vol. 1, edited by J. Ki-Zerbo, and Vol. 2, edited by G. Mokhtar, both 1981, contains some excellent contributions, notably those by L. Balout and Y. Coppens, J. Yoyotte, N. M. Sherif, A. A. Hakem, and J. E. G. Sutton.

Ideas about the food-producing revolution have changed very radically in recent years, and the modern interpretation is best illustrated in J. Desmond Clark and Steven A. Brandt (eds.), *From Hunters to Farmers*, 1984, which contains an up-to-date bibliography. The progress of research on the Iron Age in Africa is regularly monitored in the *Journal of African History*, which also publishes surveys of the results of radiometric dating. A synthesis of recent research on the Early Iron Age by an archaeologist and a historian working in collaboration is *Africa in the Iron Age*, by Roland Oliver and Brian Fagan, 1975. R. Mauny, *Les siècles obscurs de l'Afrique noire*, covers some of the same ground, while P. L. Shinnie (ed.), *The African Iron Age*, 1971, is a collection of shorter regional syntheses for sub-Saharan Africa. A more extensive collaborative work on the period from 500 B.C. to A.D. 1050 will be found in *The Cambridge History of Africa*, Vol. 2, edited by J. D. Fage, 1978.

For the origins of Egyptian kinship and political institutions W. B. Emery's *Archaic Egypt*, 1961, is of great interest and should be compared with Chapter V of V. Gordon Childe's classic *New Light on the Most Ancient East*, revised edn, 1954. The best short account of ancient Egyptian civilization is Cyril Aldred, *The Egyptians*, 1961. For Egyptian colonization up the Nile valley and the subsequent history of Nubia, the outstanding work is W. Y. Adams, *Nubia Corridor to Africa*, 1977. For the Ptolemaic period, Edwyn Bevan, *A History of Egypt under the Ptolemaic Dynasty*, 1927, is still unrivalled. For Ethiopia during the pre-Axumite and Axumite periods Sergew Hable Sellassie, *Ancient and Medieval Ethiopian History*, 1972, provides a useful conspectus of the main sources, while for the background to Monophysite Christianity in Egypt, Nubia and Ethiopia, W. H. C. Frend, *The Rise of the Monophysite Movement*, 1972, is a work of fundamental importance.

CHAPTERS 5 TO 7

The reader interested in ancient North Africa cannot do better than to start with Herodotus: there is a Penguin Classics translation by Aubrey de Selincourt. Thereafter, the long sequence of colonization by Carthaginians, Greeks, Romans, Vandals and Byzantines is best studied in C.-A. Julien, *Histoire de l'Afrique du Nord*, Vol. I, 1951, for the Maghrib, and in H. Idris Bell, *Egypt from Alexander the Great to the Arab Conquest*, 1948, for Egypt and Cyrenaica. Donald Harden, *The Phoenicians*, 1962, is the best book in English on Carthage. B. H. Warmington, *The North African Provinces*, 1954, is a study of Roman colonization in Africa. For early Christianity in North Africa, C. P. Groves, *The Planting of Christianity in Africa*, Vol. I, 1948, is useful, and W. H. C. Frend, *The Donatist Church*, 1952, is essential. For the intriguing question of Jews and Judaic influences, H. Z. Hirschberg, *A History of the Jews in North Africa*, 1968, is invaluable. For Roman influences in the Fezzan and beyond, Mortimer Wheeler, *Rome beyond the Imperial Frontiers*, 1954, makes an alluring introduction.

For the background to the Arab conquests, a start might be made with two classic essays, H. A. R. Gibb, *Mohammedanism*, 1949, and Bernard Lewis, *The Arabs in History*, 1950. An important large-scale work of synthesis is *The Cambridge History of Islam*, 2 vols., 1970, edited by P. M. Holt, Ann K. S. Lambton and Bernard Lewis, of which Vol. I deals with the central Islamic lands, which include Egypt, and Vol. II with the further Islamic lands, including the Maghrib and Africa south of the Sahara. Two very useful volumes appeared in 1986 in the series 'A History of the Near East' under the general editorship of P. M. Holt, *The Prophet and the Age of the Caliphates* by Hugh Kennedy, and *The Age of the Crusades* by Holt himself; between them they run from the sixth Christian century to 1517. Y. F. Hasan, *The Arabs and the Sudan*, 1967, is a standard work on the Arab penetration and settlement of Christian Nubia. E. F. Gautier, *Le passé de l'Afrique du Nord: Les siècles obscurs*, second edn, 1952, is a stimulating discussion of the changes in the Maghrib between Roman times and the Hilalian invasions, while Vol. II of Julien's *Histoire*, revised edn by Roger Le Tourneau, 1952, provides a general narrative and good bibliographies for the period up to 1830; an English translation, edited by Charles Stewart, was published in

1970 under the title *History of North Africa: Tunisia, Algeria, Morocco from the Arab Conquest to 1830*. J. Abun Nasr, *A History of the Maghrib*, 1971, offers a shorter, though well-reflected synthesis. H. Terrasse, *Histoire du Maroc*, 1949–50, and R. Brunschwig, *La Berbérie orientale sous les Hafsides*, 2 vols., 1940–49, are useful, while S. Lane Poole, *The Barbary Corsairs*, 1890, is still valuable for its narrative.

The development of trans-Saharan relations during the early centuries of Islam is intimately linked with the growth of states in the savanna belt of West Africa. The subject is attractively introduced by E. W. Bovill, *Caravans of the Old Sahara*, 1933, and *The Golden Trade of the Moors*, new edn with Robin Hallett, 1968. On the economic side, the widest survey of both archaeological and documentary evidence is R. Mauny, *Tableau géographique de l'ouest africain au moyen âge*, 1961, although its layout as a work of historical geography presents some difficulties for historians; for this reason the same author's chapter in Vol. 2 of *The Cambridge History of Africa*, edited by J. D. Fage, 1978, will be found useful. N. Levtzion, *Ancient Ghana and Mali*, 1973, though very concise, is the most authoritative study of the western part of the region, while his chapter on 'The Western Maghrib and Sudan, 1050–1591' in *The Cambridge History of Africa*, Vol. 3, edited by Roland Oliver, 1977, provides the most detailed account of the Songhai empire and offers a new and exciting synthesis of events on both sides of the western desert. The same volume contains a parallel chapter on 'The Eastern Maghrib and Central Sudan' by H. J. Fisher. For the early history of states in Kanem-Bornu and Hausaland, the chapters by M. Last and B. Barkindo in J. F. A. Ajayi and Michael Crowder (eds.), *History of West Africa*, Vol. I, 3rd edn, 1985, should be consulted. Earlier problems relating to both the accessibility and the understanding of the Arabic sources which are so vital to the early history of the western and central Sudan have largely disappeared since the publication in 1981 of the extremely well-translated and comprehensively edited *Corpus of Early Arabic Sources for West African History* by J. F. P. Hopkins and N. Levtzion.

CHAPTERS 8 TO 11

The best introduction to the medieval history of Ethiopia and the Horn is the chapter by Taddesse Tamrat in *The Cambridge History of Africa*, Vol. 3, edited by Roland Oliver, 1977. The same author's *Church and State in Ethiopia, 1270–1527*, 1972, is a work of outstanding merit. Richard Pankhurst, *The Ethiopian Royal Chronicles*, 1968, provides an anthology in English translation of the most important indigenous historical writings from the late medieval period onwards. C. F. Beckingham and G. W. B. Huntingford (eds.), *The Prester John of the Indies*, 2 vols., 1961, is an English translation of Alvares's narrative of the Portuguese embassy to Ethiopia of 1520–26; this gives a unique glimpse of the kingdom in its late medieval glory, before the Muslim invasions which began in 1527. Richard Pankhurst, *An Introduction to the Economic History of Ethiopia*, 1961, is largely concerned with the period from the 16th to the 18th century. M. Abir, *Ethiopia: The Era of the Princes*, 1968, concentrates on the period 1769–1885. Donald Crummey, *Priests and Politicians*, 1972, is a study of the impact of European missions on the Ethiopian Church during the period 1830–68.

For East Africa in pre-colonial times there are two well-established collaborative works: the *History of East Africa*, Vol. I, edited by Roland Oliver and Gervase Mathew, 1962, and *Zamani: A Survey of East African History*, edited by B. A. Ogot and J. A. Kieran, revised edition, 1974. G. S. P. Freeman-Grenville, *East African Coast*, 1962, is a useful anthology of the main written sources in English translation. The archaeology of the coast and islands is surveyed by H. N. Chittick in *The Cambridge History*, Vol. 3, and more briefly in *Zamani*; his *Kilwa*, 2 vols., 1975, and *Manda*, 1984, are the definitive records of his work at the two most important coastal sites. Edward A. Alpers, *Ivory and Slaves in East Central Africa*, 1975, is a study of wide significance, while Justus Strandes, *The Portuguese Period in East Africa*, first published in German in 1899, English translation, 1961, is still a standard work. The interior of East Africa from about the 15th century until the 19th is known mainly through studies of oral tradition, for which the accepted methodological guide was J. Vansina, *Oral Tradition*, English translation, 1965; however, now see his *Oral Tradition as History*, 1985, and his magisterial study of

Bakuba history, *The Children of Woot*, 1978. Vansina's *L'évolution du royaume rwanda des origines à 1900*, 1961, was among the earliest of a series of monographs based on fieldwork, which now includes B. A. Ogot, *History of the Southern Luo*, 1967; D. W. Cohen, *The Historical Tradition of Busoga*, 1972; S. K. Karugire, *A History of the Kingdom of Nkore*, 1971; M. S. M. Kiwanuka, *A History of Buganda*, 1972; Godfrey Muriuki, *A History of the Kikuyu*, 1974; I. N. Kimambo, *A Political History of the Pare*, 1969; Steven Feierman, *The Shambaa Kingdom*, 1974; Aylward Shorter, *Chiefship in Western Tanzania*, 1972; and Derek Nurse and Thomas Spear, *The Swahili*, 1985.

For the Guinea coastlands, J. D. Fage, *A History of West Africa: An Introductory Survey*, 1969, can be compared with J. F. A. Ajayi and Michael Crowder (eds.), *A History of West Africa*, Vol. I, and with the relevant chapters of H. Deschamps (ed.), *Histoire générale de l'Afrique noire*, Vol. I, 1970. A. G. Hopkins, *An Economic History of West Africa*, second edn, 1975, is the first work by an economic historian to establish its base firmly in the pre-colonial period. The Iron Age archaeology of the region is in general little developed and obscurely published, but there are notable exceptions in Frank Willett, *Ife in the History of West African Sculpture*, 1967, and Thurstan Shaw, *Igbo-Ukwu*, 2 vols., 1970. In the field of traditional history there are some important collections by amateur historians, such as Samuel Johnson, *History of the Yorubas*, second edn, 1956, and Jacob Egharevba, *A Short History of Benin*, revised edn, 1960, and also a few modern professional studies such as Michel Izard, *Introduction à l'histoire des royaumes Mossi*, 2 vols., 1970, Claude H. Perrot, *Les Anyi-Ndenyi et le pouvoir au 18ᵉ et 19ᵉ siècles*, 1982, and Robert Smith, *Kingdoms of the Yoruba*, second edn, 1976. However, the main thrust of research has so far been in European archival sources. A list of the major monographs would include: Walter Rodney, *A History of the Upper Guinea Coast, 1545–1800*, 1970; K. Y. Daaku, *Trade and Politics on the Gold Coast 1600–1720*, 1970; R. A. Kea, *Settlement, Trade and Politics in the Seventeenth-Century Gold Coast*, 1982; Ivor Wilks, *The Northern Factor in Ashanti History*, 1961, and *Asante in the Nineteenth Century*, 1975; Robin Law, *The Oyo Empire,c. 1600–c. 1836*, 1977; Alan Ryder, *Benin and the Europeans, 1485–1897*, 1969; David Northrup, *Trade without Rulers; pre-Colonial Economic De-*

velopment in South-Eastern Nigeria, 1978; and A. J. H. Latham, *Old Calabar, 1600–1891*, 1973. Thomas Hodgkin's *Nigerian Perspectives*, new edn, 1975, is an excellent anthology from the sources up to 1900. There are also some excellent chapters in Vols. 3 and 4 of *The Cambridge History of Africa*, 1975, 1977.

For West-Central and Southern Africa, the introductory synthesis provided by Roland Oliver and Brian Fagan, *Africa in the Iron Age*, 1975, is amplified by the same authors in Vol. 2 of *The Cambridge History of Africa* and continued by David Birmingham and Shula Marks in Vols. 3 and 4. The period 1400–1870 is covered in greater detail for the lands between Cameroon and the Limpopo in the first volume of the cooperative *History of Central Africa* edited by David Birmingham and Phyllis M. Martin, 1983. Brian Fagan, *Southern Africa during the Iron Age*, 1965, deals with Zambia, Zimbabwe and South Africa. Peter S. Garlake, *Great Zimbabwe*, 1973, is the most up-to-date work on this outstanding site, while D. N. Beach, *The Shona and Zimbabwe 900–1850*, 1980, provides the most complete survey of the traditional history of this region. J. Vansina, *Kingdoms of the Savanna*, 1966, deals with the emergence of states to the south of the Congo forest, while Joseph Miller, *Kings and Kinsmen*, 1976, traces the same process in central Angola. The pioneering studies of the Kongo Kingdom by Jadin and by Cuvelier can now for many purposes be replaced by two modern studies, Anne Hilton, *The Kingdom of Kongo*, 1985, and J. K. Thornton, *The Kingdom of Kongo: Civil War and Transition 1641–1718*, 1983. Richard Gray and David Birmingham (eds.) *Pre-colonial African Trade*, 1970, is a collection of essays on early long-distance trade routes. The best overall account of Portuguese contacts with this part of Africa is Ronald L. Chilcote, *Portuguese Africa*, 1967, while V. Magalhaes Godinho, *L'économie de l'empire portugais du XV et XVI siècles*, 1969, is of great importance for the economic background of Portuguese imperialism. More particular studies of the Afro-Portuguese contact are Phyllis M. Martin, *The External Trade of the Loango Coast, 1576–1870*, 1972; David Birmingham, *Trade and Conflict in Angola*, 1966; Eric Axelson, *The Portuguese in South-East Africa 1488–1600*, 1973; and *The Portuguese in South-East Africa 1600–1700*, 1960; M. D. D. Newitt, *Portuguese Settlement on the Zambezi*, 1973; and Allen F. Isaacman, *Mozambique: The Africanization of a European Institution, the Zambezi*

Prazos, 1750–1902, 1972. The most important studies of oral tradition for peoples not directly in contact with Europeans are M. Plancquaert, *Les Jaga et les Bayaka du Kwango*, 1932; E. Verhulpen, *Baluba et Balubaïsés*, 1936; I. Cunnison, *The Luapula Peoples of Northern Rhodesia*, 1959; A. D. Roberts, *A History of the Bemba*, 1973; and D. P. Abraham, 'Ethno-history of the Empire of Mutapa' in J. Vansina, R. Mauny and L. V. Thomas, *The Historian in Tropical Africa*, 1964, pp. 104–21. For the southern part of the region, Monica Wilson and Leonard Thompson (eds.), *The Oxford History of South Africa*, Vol. I, 1969, is important; see also the collection of essays edited by Thompson, *African Societies in Southern Africa*, 1969.

Finally, there is a growing literature dealing with slavery in African societies and with the impact on these of the export slave trades, important subjects in their own right as well as for their effect on the thinking of the Europeans whose infiltration into Africa is discussed in Chapters 12 to 15. There is a general study with a comprehensive bibliography by Paul Lovejoy, *Transformations in Slavery: A History of Slavery in Africa*, 1983, and some useful collections of papers, such as J. E. Inikori (ed.), *Forced Migration: The Impact of the Export Slave Trade on African Societies*, 1982; Suzanne Miers and Igor Kopytoff (eds.), *Slavery in Africa: Historical and Anthropological Perspectives*, 1977; and Henry A. Gemery and Jan S. Hogendorn (eds.), *The Uncommon Market: Essays in the Economic History of the Atlantic Slave Trade*, 1979.

CHAPTERS 12 TO 15

The changing European attitudes to Africa described in Chapter 12 are part of European history as well as of the history of Africa. A recent study is Roger Anstey, *The Atlantic Slave Trade and British Abolition, 1710–1810*, 1975. Philip D. Curtin, *The Atlantic Slave Trade, a Census*, 1969, is a definitive assessment of the volume of the trade at different periods, while his *Image of Africa: British Ideas and Action, 1780–1850*, 1965, is an important study of the changing attitudes referred to above. Another important synthesis for the whole European approach to Africa in the nineteenth century is H. Brunschwig, *L'avènement de l'Afrique noire*, 1963. An overall guide to

European missionary expansion is C. P. Groves, *The Planting of Christianity in Africa*, of which Vol. I (1948) goes up to 1840, Vol. II (1954) covers the period 1840–78 and Vol. III (1955) covers 1878–1914. M. Perham and J. Simmons, *African Discovery*, first published in 1942 and often reprinted, is a most readable anthology of the principal British explorers, for whom it supplies the main bibliographical details. A. Adu Boahen, *Britain, the Sahara and the Western Sudan, 1788–1861*, 1964, and two books by Robin Hallett, *Records of the African Association, 1788–1831*, 1964, and *The Penetration of Africa* (Vol. I, to 1815), 1965, are important studies. For the southern half of the continent the career of David Livingstone is crucial. A good short study is J. Simmons, *Livingstone and Africa*, 1955. Livingstone's own *Missionary Travels and Researches in South Africa*, originally published in 1857, and the edition of his *Missionary Correspondence* by I. Shapera, 1961, may be read with pleasure and profit.

For 19th-century Egypt, there is P. M. Holt, *Egypt and the Fertile Crescent, 1516–1922*, 1966, which has an excellent bibliography. H. H. Dodwell, *The Founder of Modern Egypt: Mohammed Ali*, 1931, and John Marlowe, *Anglo-Egyptian Relations, 1800–1953*, 1954, are still useful. For North Africa, there are excellent chapters by A. Raymond and A. Nouschi in *The Cambridge History of Islam*, Vol. II. C.-A. Julien, *Histoire de l'Algérie contemporaine*, 1964, is a work of major importance covering the period 1827–71. C. R. Ageron, *Histoire de l'Algérie contemporaine 1830–1965*, 1966, and Y. Lacoste, A. Nouschi and A. Prenant, *L'Algérie passé et présent*, 1960, deal with the colonial period as a whole. For Morocco there is J. L. Miège, *Le Maroc et l'Europe, 1830–1894*, 1961–4, and for Tunisia, J. Ganiage, *Les origines du protectorat français en Tunisie, 1861–1881*, 1969. For 19th-century West Africa, the best general work is J. F. A. Ajayi and M. Crowder (eds.), *History of West Africa*, Vol. II, 1974. The second volume of Deschamps's *Histoire générale*, 1971, is clearly the leading work in French, with excellent bibliographies for every chapter. John D. Hargreaves, *West Africa, the Former French States*, 1967, and his anthology of documents, *France and West Africa*, 1969; Bernard Schnapper, *La politique et le commerce français dans le Golfe de Guinée 1838 à 1871*, 1961; R. Cornevin, *Histoire du Togo*, 1962, and *Histoire du Dahomey*, 1962; C. W. Newbury, *The Western Slave Coast and its*

Rulers, 1961; and F. Fuglestad, *A History of Niger, 1850–1960*, 1983, are all useful. There are two major studies of *jihads* and their results: Murray Last, *The Sokoto Caliphate*, 1967, and David Robinson, *The Holy War of Umar Tal*, 1985. For the exceptionally industrious reader, Yves Person, *Samori, une révolution dyula*, 3 vols., 1968–75, and Ivor Wilks, *Asante in the Nineteenth Century*, 1975, will be correspondingly rewarding. For Gambia and Sierra Leone there are J. M. Gray, *A History of the Gambia*, reprinted 1966 and Christopher Fyfe, *A History of Sierra Leone*, 1962. For Ghana a brief reading-list would include J. D. Fage, *Ghana: a Historical Interpretation* reprinted 1983; G. E. Metcalfe, *Maclean of the Gold Coast*, 1962; and David Kimble, *A Political History of Ghana, 1850–1928*. And for Nigeria a comparable list would include Michael Crowder, *The Story of Nigeria*, fourth edn, 1978; K. Onwuka Dike, *Trade and Politics in the Niger Delta, 1830–85*, 1958; S. O. Biobaku, *The Egba and their Neighbours, 1842–72*, 1957; J. F. Ade Ajayi, *Christian Missions in Nigeria, 1841–91*, 1965; E. A. Ayandele, *The Missionary Impact on Modern Nigeria, 1842–1914*, 1966; J. F. Ade Ajayi and Robert Smith, *Yoruba Warfare in the Nineteenth Century*, 1964; S. A. Akintoye, *Revolution and Power Politics in Yorubaland, 1840–1893*, 1971; R. A. Adeleye, *Power and Diplomacy in Northern Nigeria, 1800–1906*, 1972; and T. G. O. Gbadamosi, *The Growth of Islam among the Yoruba, 1841–1908*, 1979.

For Zaire and Angola the later chapters of J. Vansina, *Kingdoms of the Savanna*, should be supplemented with the chapter on 'West Central Africa, 1800–1880' in Roland Oliver and Anthony Atmore, *Africa since 1800*, second edn, 1972, and with the chapter by David Birmingham in *The Cambridge History of Africa*, Vol. 5 (edited by J. E. Flint), 1976. On a larger scale, there is the cooperative *History of Central Africa* edited by David Birmingham and Phyllis M. Martin which has already been mentioned. Roger Anstey, *Britain and the Congo in the Nineteenth Century*, 1962, and Richard J. Hammond, *Portugal and Africa 1815–1910*, 1966, are also useful.

For southern Africa, in addition to the cooperative history edited by Monica Wilson and Leonard Thompson listed above, C. W. de Kiewiet, *A History of South Africa; Social and Economic*, 1941; E. A. Walker, *The Great Trek*, 1934; and J. D. Omer-Cooper, *The Zulu Aftermath*, 1966, are essential reading. Also to be recommended are

E. A. Ritter, *Shaka Zulu*, 1955; W. M. Macmillan, *Bantu, Boer and Briton*, 1929; C. W. de Kiewiet, *The Imperial Factor in South Africa*, 1937; and S. D. Neumark, *Economic Influences on the South African Frontier*, 1957. M. V. Jackson Haight, *European Powers and South-East Africa*, reprinted 1967, examines the interacting influences of British, French and Portuguese in South-East Africa from 1796 till 1856.

The standard works on the East African coast are still those of R. Coupland, *East Africa and its Invaders*, 1938, which covers the period to 1856, and *The Exploitation of East Africa, 1856–90*, 1939. The *History of East Africa*, Vol. I, edited by Roland Oliver and Gervase Mathew, 1962, contains three substantial chapters by J. M. Gray, Alison Smith and D. A. Low on the period 1840–84 which treat the history of the East African peoples and the Muslim penetration of East African much more fully than Coupland, whose work will, however, remain of importance for the study of British policy in this region. For the Nilotic Sudan in the 19th century there is Richard Hill, *Egypt in the Sudan, 1820–81*, 1959; P. M. Holt, *The Mahdist State in the Sudan, 1881–98*, 1958; and J. R. Gray, *A History of the Southern Sudan, 1839–89*, 1961.

CHAPTER 16

There is not as yet a single satisfactory modern study of the partition of Africa. The nearest to it is perhaps *Africa and the Victorians* by Ronald Robinson and John Gallagher, 1961, but this is weak on the aims and diplomacy of some of the continental European powers. In this connection, the work of H.-U. Wehler is important but, since all that is available in English is his article 'Bismarck's Imperialism' in *Past and Present* for 1970, reference may be made to older works such as W. L. Langer, *The Diplomacy of Imperialism*, revised edn, 1951, the chapters by F. H. Hinsley and R. E. Robinson in *The Cambridge History of the British Empire*, Vol. 3, 1959, or the summary written by Robinson for *The New Cambridge Modern History*, Vol. 10, 1963. Other important studies are Henri Brunschwig, *French Colonialism: Myths and Realities*, 1966; G. N. Sanderson, *England, Europe and the Upper Nile*, 1965; and Eric Axelson, *Portugal and the Scramble for Africa, 1875–1891*, 1967.

For West Africa alone, there are John Hargreaves, *Prelude to the Partition of West Africa*, 1963, and *West Africa Partitioned*, Vol. I, *The Loaded Pause, 1885–89*, 1975, and Vol. II, *Elephants and the Cross*, 1985; A. S. Kanya-Forstner, *The Conquest of the Western Sudan*, 1969, and from another point of view altogether, the essays edited by Michael Crowder under the title *West African Resistance*, 1970. A study for another region is D. M. Schreuder, *The Scramble for Southern Africa*, 1980. Other aspects of the scramble are best appreciated in biographies, such as J. G. Lockhart and C. M. Wodehouse, *Rhodes*, 1963; Margery Perham, *Lugard*, 2 vols., 1956 and 1960; J. E. Flint, *Sir George Goldie and the Making of Nigeria*, 1960; John S. Galbraith, *Mackinnon and East Africa 1878–1895*, 1972, and Roland Oliver, *Sir Harry Johnston and the Scramble for Africa*, 1957. The best study of the origins of the South African War is J. S. Marais, *The Fall of Kruger's Republic*, 1961; for the war itself, Thomas Pakenham, *The Boer War*, 1979; and for its immediate political consequences, L. M. Thompson, *The Unification of South Africa, 1902–10*, 1960. For North-East Africa, an important work is Harold G. Marcus, *The Life and Times of Menilik II of Ethiopia, 1844–1913*, 1974.

CHAPTERS 17 TO 19

Readers who wish to form a comprehensive view of the colonial period in Africa south of the Sahara cannot do better than to steep themselves in Lord Hailey's great *African Survey*, using and comparing the editions of 1938 (reprinted 1945) and 1957. S. H. Frankel, *Capital Investment in Africa*, 1938, is an important special study that was undertaken in connection with the Hailey *Survey*. R. L. Buell, *The Native Problem in Africa*, 2 vols., 1926, although old, is invaluable for its carefully documented account of publications of colonial governments in Africa prior to its date of publication. The best modern overview is probably that by J. Ganiage, H. Deschamps and Odette Guitard, *L'Afrique au XXᵉ siècle, 1900–1965*, 1966. W. K. Hancock, *A Survey of British Commonwealth Affairs*, Vol. II, Part 2, 1942, subtitled 'Problems of Economic Policy 1918–39', is a brilliant analysis of problems aroused by the expansion of white settlement in southern Africa and by the expansion of trade in West Africa. Among collaborative works, Prosser Gifford and William Roger Louis (eds.), *Britain and Germany in Africa*, 1967, and *France and Britain in Africa*, 1971; Robert I. Rotberg and Ali Mazrui (eds.), *Protest and Power in Black Africa*, 1970; and the first four volumes of L. H. Gann and Peter Duignan (eds.), *Colonialism in Africa*, 1969–75, contain many excellent chapters by leading authorities, while Vol. 5 of the last series has the best bibliographical information for the colonial period. More recent studies of value are H. S. Wilson, *The Imperial Experience in Sub-Saharan Africa since 1870*, 1977; Bill Freund, *The Making of Contemporary Africa: The Development of African Society since 1800*, 1984, which concentrates on the period from 1900 to 1960; and J. Forbes Munro, *Britain in Tropical Africa, 1880–1960: Economic Relations and Impact*, 1984.

South Africa is largely anomalous with the rest of the continent both in periodization and historiography, and we confine our suggestions to a few items of outstanding interest for the history of the 20th century. First and foremost is Vol. II of *The Oxford History of South Africa*, 1971, edited by Monica Wilson and Leonard Thompson, which was the first comprehensive work to attempt an approach comparable to that of other modern African historians. Significantly, the chapter on African nationalism from 1910 till 1964 had to be omitted from the version sold in South Africa. Wilson and Thompson's work can now be supplemented with T. R. H. Davenport, *South Africa: A Modern History*, second edn, 1978. W. K. Hancock, *Smuts*, 2 vols., 1962 and 1968, is a great biography by a great historian, which covers most of the period, while Alan Paton, *Hofmeyr*, 1964, is also outstanding. D. W. Kruger (ed.), *South African Parties and Policies, 1910–1960*, 1960; W. H. Vatcher, *White Laager: The Rise of Afrikaner Nationalism*, 1965; and Peter Walshe, *The Rise of Nationalism in South Africa: The African National Council, 1912–1952*, 1970, are all useful. Edward Roux, *Time Longer than Rope*, reprinted 1964, and Mary Benson, *The African Patriots*, 1963, are sympathetic and scholarly studies of the African struggle for equal rights. B. G. M. Sundkler, *Bantu Prophets in South Africa*, 1948, is a famous study of the effects of white rule upon African Christianity, while Shula Marks, *Reluctant Rebellion*, 1970, is a detailed study of the Zulu revolt of 1906–7. Gwendolen M. Carter, *The Politics of Inequality*, 1958, is a classic analysis by a first-rate political scientist. In recent years a school of younger South African historians has begun to look in depth at the social history of their multiracial society; an excellent example is Charles van Onselen, *Studies in the Social and Economic History of the Witwatersrand, 1886–1914*, 2 vols., 1982. For South-West Africa, there is Helmut Bley, *South-West Africa under German Rule*, 1971, and Ruth First, *South-West Africa*, 1963.

Africa south of the Sahara and north of the Limpopo, but excluding East Africa, is covered for the period 1870–1980 in Vol. 2 of the cooperative work edited by David Birmingham and Phyllis M. Martin, *A History of Central Africa*, 1983. A. J. Wills, *Introduction to the History of Central Africa*, 1964, will serve as a regional survey of British Central Africa in the colonial period, but should be supplemented by territorial studies such as L. H. Gann, *A History of Southern Rhodesia*, 1965; Philip Mason, *The Birth of a Dilemma*, 1958; Richard Gray, *The Two Nations*, 1960; Robert I. Rotberg, *The Rise of Nationalism in Central Africa: The Making of Malawi and Zambia, 1873–1964*, 1965; T. O. Ranger, *Revolt in Southern Rhodesia, 1896–7*, 1967; and Andrew Roberts, *A History of Zambia*, 1976. For Portuguese Africa in the colonial period, there are two comprehensive modern studies, Malyn Newitt, *Portugal in Africa, the Last 100 Years*, 1981, and Gervase Clarence-Smith, *The Third Portuguese Empire, 1825–1975: A Study in Economic Imperialism*, 1985, to which may be added D. L. Wheeler and R. Pelissier, *Angola*, 1978.

For East Africa regional studies include *A History of East Africa*, Vol. II edited by Vincent Harlow and E. M. Chilver, 1965, and Vol. III edited by D. A. Low and Alison Smith, 1976; *Zamani*, edited by B. A. Ogot and J. A. Kieran, 1968; K. Ingham, *A History of East Africa*, 1962; Roland Oliver, *The Missionary Factor in East Africa*, second edn, 1965; J. Spencer Trimingham, *Islam in East Africa*, 1965; F. Welbourn, *East African Rebels*, 1961; and J. S. Mangat, *A History of the Asians in East Africa, c. 1886–1945*, 1969. For Kenya, during the colonial period there is G. H. Mungeam, *British Rule in Kenya*, 1968; Elspeth Huxley, *White Man's Country* (the life and times of Lord Delamere), second edn, 1953; George Bennett, *Kenya: A Political History*, 1963; Carl G. Rosberg and John Nottingham, *The Myth of Mau Mau*, 1967; and Anthony Clayton and Donald C. Savage, *Government and Labour in Kenya, 1895–1963*, 1974. For

Uganda there are K. Ingham, *The Making of Modern Uganda*, 1958; Walter Elkan, *The Economic Development of Uganda*, 1961; David E. Apter, *The Political Kingdom in Uganda*, second edn, 1967; James Barber, *Imperial Frontier*, 1968; D. Anthony Low and R. Cranford Pratt, *Buganda and British Overrule, 1900–1955*, 1960; and H. G. Hansen, *Mission, Church and State in a Colonial Society, Uganda, 1890–1925*, 1984. For Tanzania the key work is John Iliffe, *A Modern History of Tanganyika*, 1979. The German period is studied in Fritz Ferdinand Müller, *Deutschland-Zanzibar Ostafrika*, 1959, while John Iliffe, *Tanganyika under German Rule, 1905–12*, 1969, is a brilliant monograph on the governorship of Rechenburg; Wm Roger Louis, *Ruanda-Urundi , 1884–1914*, 1963, deals with that province of German East Africa and Ralph A. Austin, *Northwest Tanzania under German and British Rule*, 1968, is a valuable local monograph. Kathleen M. Stahl, *History of the Chagga People of Kilimanjaro*, 1963, though beginning before the colonial period, is of special interest for the adaptation of tribal politics to the colonial situation. For colonial Zanzibar there is L. W. Hollingsworth, *Zanzibar under the Foreign Office, 1890–1913*, 1953, and Michael F. Lofchie, *Zanzibar: Background to Revolution*, 1965. I. N. Kimambo and A. J. Temu (eds.), *A History of Tanzania*, 1969, contains some useful essays on different aspects of the colonial period by various hands.

For North-East Africa, I. M. Lewis, *The Modern History of Somaliland*, new edn, 1979, deals with both the Italian and the British territories. Richard Greenfield, *Ethiopia*, 1965; Margery Perham, *The Government of Ethiopia*, 1948; and Christopher Clapham, *Haile Selassie's Government*, 1964, are all useful for pre-revolutionary Ethiopia.

For West-Central Africa Ruth Slade, *King Leopold's Congo*, 1962, and Roger Anstey, *King Leopold's Legacy*, 1966, provide between them an excellent introduction to the Belgian Congo. P. Ceulemans, *La question arabe et le Congo, 1883–1892*, 1958, is a special study of great interest, as are R. O. Collins, *King Leopold, England and the Upper Nile, 1899–1909*, 1968, and Ruth Slade, *English-speaking Missions in the Congo Independent State*, 1958. René Lemarchand, *Political Awakening in the Belgian Congo*, 1964, and Crawford Young, *Politics in the Congo*, 1965, are both useful studies of the period leading up to independence. For the former French Equatorial Africa,

C. Coquéry-Vidrovitch, *Le Congo au temps des grandes compagnies concessionnaires 1898–1930*, 1972, is an outstanding work of scholarship, which may be supplemented by Pierre Kalck, *Histoire de la République Centrafricaine*, 1974, and by Brian Weinstein, *Eboué*, 1972. For Cameroon Harry R. Rudin, *Germans in the Cameroons, 1884–1914*, 1938, is still the best book in English, though superseded by Karin Hausen, *Deutsche Kolonialherrschaft in Afrika: Wirtschaftsinteressen und Kolonialverwaltung in Kamerun vor 1914*, 1970. For Equatorial Guinea, there is René Pelissier, *Les territoires espagnols d'Afrique*, 1963.

The coverage of the colonial period in the history of West Africa is somewhat patchy. Michael Crowder, *West Africa under Colonial Rule*, 1968, is the only general work, and provides a valuable comparison between French and British systems. Robert W. July, *The Origins of Modern African Thought*, 1968, is a unique and valuable study of the intellectual history of English and French-speaking West Africa during the colonial period. R. Delavignette, *Freedom and Authority in French West Africa*, English translation, 1950, has an excellent discussion of French colonial policy between the wars; but readers who want more general accounts of the French territories during the colonial period are probably best advised to look in the relevant volumes of the *Encyclopédie de l'empire française*, published during the later 1940s, or the highly critical Marxist work by Jean Suret-Canale, available in English as *French Colonialism in Tropical Africa, 1900–1945*, 1971. V. Thompson and R. Adloff, *French West Africa*, 1958, and *The Emerging States of French Equatorial Africa*, 1960, are encyclopaedic surveys of these two areas from the time of the Brazzaville Conference in 1944 until shortly before the dates of publication, though for political history the former has been largely superseded by Ruth Schachter Morgenthau, *Political Parties in French-speaking West Africa*, 1964. For English-speaking West Africa the stituation is better only in relation to Nigeria, for which the works by Flint on Goldie and Perham on Lugard listed in the previous sections are both relevant; Margery Perham's baptism of fire is well presented in her *West African Passage: A Journey through Nigeria, Chad and the Cameroons, 1931–32*, 1983. E. D. Morel, *Nigeria: Its Peoples and its Problems*, reprinted 1968, is a survey of the country in 1911 by a leading authority and colonial reformer. E. A. Ayandele, *The Missionary Impact on Modern Nigeria, 1842–1914*, 1966, and

J. B. Webster, *The African Churches among the Yoruba, 1888–1922*, 1964, are both important monographs. F. D. Lugard, *The Dual Mandate in British Tropical Africa*, 1922, the classic statement of the indirect rule policy, was written with Nigeria mainly in mind, while Margery Perham, *Native Administration in Nigeria*, reprinted 1962, examines that system as it was operating in the middle of the 1930s. Another perspective is provided in the collection of essays on *West African Chiefs*, 1970, edited by M. Crowder and O. Ikime. Recent monographs by Nigerian historians include A. I. Asiwaju, *Western Yorubaland under European Rule, 1889–1945*, 1976; P. A. Igbafe, *Benin under British Administration, 1897–1938*, 1979; Fred I. A. Omu, *Press and Politics in Nigeria, 1880–1937*, 1978; and Akinjide Osuntokun, *Nigeria in the First World War*, 1979. For Ghana, there is David Kimble's *Political History* mentioned above, to which may be added W. Tordoff, *Ashanti under the Prempehs, 1888–1935*, 1965; R. E. Wraith, *Guggisberg*, 1967; F. M. Bourret, *Ghana: The Road to Independence, 1919–57*, 1960; David E. Apter, *The Gold Coast in Transition*, 1955; and Dennis Austin, *Politics in Ghana, 1946–1960*, 1964. For Sierra Leone there is little other than Arthur Abraham, *Mende Government and Politics under Colonial Rule, 1890–1937*, 1978; for Liberia J. Gus Liebenow, *Liberia: The Evolution of Privilege*, 1969.

For Egypt and the Sudan in the first half of the 20th century, a select reading list would include P. J. Vatikiotis, *A Modern History of Egypt*, revised edn, 1980; John Marlowe, *Arab Nationalism and British Imperialism*, 1961; J. N. Ahmed, *The Intellectual Origins of Egyptian Nationalism*, 1960; J. S. R. Duncan's *The Sudan's Path to Independence*, 1957; and L. P. and G. N. Sanderson, *Education, Religion and Politics in the Southern Sudan, 1899–1964*, 1981. For North Africa west of Egypt, there are Nevill Barbour, *A Survey of North West Africa*, 1959; Jacques Berque, *French North Africa: The Maghreb between Two World Wars*, 1967; R. le Tourneau, *Evolution politique de l'Afrique du Nord musulmane, 1920–1961*, 1962; E. E. Evans-Pritchard, *The Sanusi of Cyrenaica*, 1954; Dwight Ling, *Tunisia from Protectorate to Republic*, 1967; Pierre Bourdieu, *The Algerians*, 1961; Mostefa Lacheraf, *L'Algérie: Nation et société*, 1965; Franz Fanon, *A Dying Colonialism*, 1970; Douglas Ashford, *Political Change in Morocco*, 1961; Albert Ayache, *Le Maroc: Bilan d'une colonisation*, 1956; and J. L. Miège, *Le Maroc*, 1962.

There are a number of works which look back at decolonization with some perspective. These include W. H. Morris-Jones and Georges Fischer (eds.), *Decolonisation and After; The British and French Experience*, 1980; Prosser Gifford and W. R. Louis (eds.), *The Transfer of Power in Africa: Decolonization, 1940–60*, 1982; John Hargreaves, *The End of Colonial Rule in West Africa*, 1978; and R. B. Collier, *Regimes in Tropical Africa: Changing Forms of supremacy, 1945–75*, 1982.

A considerable literature was engendered at the time. Ronald Segal, *Political Africa*, 1961, and Colin Legum (ed.), *Africa: A Handbook to the Continent*, 1961, are still valuable guides to the politics and personalities of the late 1950s. Thomas Hodgkin, *African Political Parties*, 1961, and his earlier *Nationalism in Colonial Africa*, 1956, are excellent and may be supplemented with Edward Mortimer, *France and the Africans 1944–1960*, 1969; Ruth Schachter Morgenthau, *Political Parties in French-speaking West Africa*, 1963; William Foltz, *From French West Africa to the Mali Federation*, 1965; James Coleman and Carl G. Rosberg (eds.), *Political Parties and National Integration in Africa*, 1964; William H. Friedland and Carl G. Rosberg, *African Socialism*, 1964, and Aristide Zolberg, *Creating Political Order: The Party States of West Africa*, 1965. Immanuel Wallerstein, *Africa: The Politics of Independence*, 1961, and *Africa: The Politics of Unity*, 1967, are both of value, as are Gwendolen M. Carter (ed.), *African One-Party States*, 1962, *Five African States*, 1964, and *Politics in Africa*, 1966. Two particular studies of great merit were James S. Coleman, *Nigeria: Background to Nationalism*, 1958, and Dennis Austin's *Politics in Ghana, 1946–1960*, 1964, mentioned in the previous section. Colin Legum, *Pan Africanism*, revised edn, 1964, is a useful introduction to this subject, which can be supplemented by Immanuel Geiss, *Panafricanism*, English translation, 1974. W. F. Gutteridge, *The Military in African Politics*, 1969, and *Military Regimes in Africa*, 1975; Ruth First, *The Barrel of a Gun: Political Power in Africa and the Coup d'Etat*, 1970; and Basil Davidson, *The People's Cause: A History of Guerrillas in Africa*, 1981, are all contributions to the study of the use of force in modern Africa.

A selection of general studies of the politics of African states since independence might include: William Tordoff, *Government and Politics in Africa*, 1984; R. Hodder-Williams, *An Introduction to the Politics of Tropical Africa*, 1984; Roger Tangri, *Politics in Sub-Saharan Africa*, 1985; Crawford Young, *Ideology and Development in Africa*, 1982; Gwendolen M. Carter and Patrick O'Meara (eds.), *African Independence, the First Twenty-five Years*, 1985; John Dunn (ed.), *West African States, Failure and Promise: A Study in Comparative Politics*, 1978; and C. G. Rosberg and T. M. Callaghy (eds.), *Socialism in Sub-Saharan Africa: A New Assessment*, 1979. Robin Cohen (ed.), *African Islands and Enclaves*, 1983, is valuable for the smaller and often neglected territories. Mention should also be made of two stimulating works by Basil Davidson, *Africa in Modern History: The Search for a New Society*, 1978, and *Modern Africa*, 1983.

Some of the territorial histories mentioned in previous sections (e.g. Vatikiotis on Egypt, I. M. Lewis on Somalia) cover events up to the 1980s or later. In addition, among books dealing specifically with recent history in particular territories, the following may be found useful. For North and North-East Africa: R. W. Baker, *Egypt's Uncertain Revolution under Nasser and Sadat*, 1979; Virginia Thompson and R. Adloff, *The Western Saharans*, 1980; John Wright, *Libya: A Modern History*, 1982; I. M. Lewis (ed.), *Nationalism in the Horn of Africa*, 1983; and René Lefort, *Ethiopia: An Heretical Revolution?*, 1983.

For East and Central Africa: John Saul, *State and Revolution in Eastern Africa*, 1979; R. Cranford Pratt, *The Critical Phase in Tanzania, 1945–68*, 1980; W. H. Morris-Jones (ed.), *From Rhodesia to Zimbabwe*, 1980; D. Martin and P. Johnson, *The Struggle for Zimbabwe*, 1981; and Ian Linden, *The Catholic Church and the Struggle for Zimbabwe*, 1980.

For South Africa: Leonard Thompson and Andrew Prior, *South African Politics*, 1982; Leonard Thompson, *The Political Mythology of Apartheid*, 1985; Tom Lodge, *Black Politics in South Africa since 1945*, 1983; and R. Green and M. and K. Kiljunen, *Namibia: The Last Colony*, 1981.

For West Africa: Walter Schwarz, *Nigeria*, 1968, J. de St J. Jorre, *The Nigerian Civil War*, 1972, and A. Kirk-Greene and Douglas Rimmer, *Nigeria since 1970: A Political and Economic Outline*, 1981, between them cover two decades of Nigerian history; B. A. ten

Tuinder, *Ivory Coast: The Challenge of Success*, 1979; Christopher Clapham, *Liberia and Sierra Leone: An Essay in Comparative Politics*, 1976; Sheldon Gellar, *Senegal: An African Nation between Islam and the West*, 1983.

For the former Portuguese territories: Patrick Chabral, *Amilcar Cabral: Revolutionary Leadership and a People's War*, 1983; J. Marcum, *The Angolan Revolution*, 2 vols., 1969 and 1978; Allen and Barbara Isaacman, *Mozambique: From Colonialism to Revolution, 1900–82*, 1983; and Barry Munslow, *Mozambique: The Revolution and its Origins*, 1983.

The World Bank report, *Accelerated Development in Sub-Saharan Africa*, 1981, provides essential data for the economic history of the 1960s and 1970s. It may be fleshed out by such works as Douglas Rimmer, *The Economies of West Africa*, 1984; I. Livingstone and H. A. Ord, *An Introduction to Economics for Eastern Africa*, 1980; or the series of case studies edited by P. A. Robson and D. A. Lury, *The Economies of Africa*, 1969. Robert H. Bates, *Markets and States in Tropical Africa: The Positive Basis of Agricultural Policies*, 1981, is an influential study of an important topic; René Dumont, *False Start in Africa*, 1966, is an older book which, though opinionated, presented a fundamental critique of the economic policies of the new African states. More specialized studies of value include Rita Cruise O'Brien, *The Political Economy of Underdevelopment: Dependence in Senegal*, 1979; Nicola Swainson, *The Development of Corporate Capitalism in Kenya, 1918–77*, 1980; Colin Leys, *Underdevelopment in Kenya, the Political Economy of Neo-colonialism, 1964–71*, 1975; Tony Killick, *Development Economics in Action: A Study of Economic Policies in Ghana*, 1978; Robert Palmer and Neil Parsons (eds.), *The Roots of Rural Poverty in Central and Southern Africa*, 1977; and Robin Cohen, *Labour and Politics in Nigeria*, 1982.

A number of books touching on religion in Africa have already been mentioned. Two handy general surveys are I. M. Lewis (ed.), *Islam in Tropical Africa*, 1966, and C. G. Baeta (ed.), *Christianity in Tropical Africa*, 1969. D. B. Barret, *Schism and Renewal in Africa*, 1968, is an important study, while Adrian Hastings, *A History of African Christianity, 1950–1975*, 1979, is constantly stimulating.

Finally, it should be said that it is not easy to follow the ever-changing circumstances of each of the independent countries of

Africa. Those who want really up-to-date information would do well to consult the volumes of *Africa South of the Sahara* and *The Middle East and North Africa*, which are published annually in London by Europa Publications. Between them these contain excellent and regularly updated surveys by recognized authorities of the recent histories and changing economies of all the African states, together with some useful general surveys.

Index

FOR THE BEST IN PAPERBACKS, LOOK FOR THE

In every corner of the world, on every subject under the sun, Penguin represents quality and variety – the very best in publishing today.

For complete information about books available from Penguin – including Pelicans, Puffins, Peregrines and Penguin Classics – and how to order them, write to us at the appropriate address below. Please note that for copyright reasons the selection of books varies from country to country.

In the United Kingdom: For a complete list of books available from Penguin in the U.K., please write to *Dept E.P., Penguin Books Ltd, Harmondsworth, Middlesex, UB7 0DA*

In the United States: For a complete list of books available from Penguin in the U.S., please write to *Dept BA, Penguin, 299 Murray Hill Parkway, East Rutherford, New Jersey 07073*

In Canada: For a complete list of books available from Penguin in Canada, please write to *Penguin Books Canada Ltd, 2801 John Street, Markham, Ontario L3R 1B4*

In Australia: For a complete list of books available from Penguin in Australia, please write to the *Marketing Department, Penguin Books Australia Ltd, P.O. Box 257, Ringwood, Victoria 3134*

In New Zealand: For a complete list of books available from Penguin in New Zealand, please write to the *Marketing Department, Penguin Books (NZ) Ltd, Private Bag, Takapuna, Auckland 9*

In India: For a complete list of books available from Penguin, please write to *Penguin Overseas Ltd, 706 Eros Apartments, 56 Nehru Place, New Delhi, 110019*

In Holland: For a complete list of books available from Penguin in Holland, please write to *Penguin Books Nederland B.V., Postbus 195, NL–1380AD Weesp, Netherlands*

In Germany: For a complete list of books available from Penguin, please write to *Penguin Books Ltd, Friedrichstrasse 10 – 12, D–6000 Frankfurt Main 1, Federal Republic of Germany*

In Spain: For a complete list of books available from Penguin in Spain, please write to *Longman Penguin España, Calle San Nicolas 15, E–28013 Madrid, Spain*

A CHOICE OF PENGUINS AND PELICANS

The Second World War (6 volumes)   Winston S. Churchill

The definitive history of the cataclysm which swept the world for the second time in thirty years.

1917: The Russian Revolutions and the Origins of Present-Day Communism
Leonard Schapiro

A superb narrative history of one of the greatest episodes in modern history by one of our greatest historians.

Imperial Spain 1496–1716   J. H. Elliot

A brilliant modern study of the sudden rise of a barren and isolated country to be the greatest power on earth, and of its equally sudden decline. 'Outstandingly good' – *Daily Telegraph*

Joan of Arc: The Image of Female Heroism   Marina Warner

'A profound book, about human history in general and the place of women in it' – Christopher Hill

Man and the Natural World: Changing Attitudes in England 1500–1800
Keith Thomas

'A delight to read and a pleasure to own' – Auberon Waugh in the *Sunday Telegraph*

The Making of the English Working Class   E. P. Thompson

Probably the most imaginative – and the most famous – post-war work of English social history.

FOR THE BEST IN PAPERBACKS, LOOK FOR THE 🐧

A CHOICE OF PENGUINS AND PELICANS

The French Revolution   Christopher Hibbert

'One of the best accounts of the Revolution that I know . . . Mr Hibbert is outstanding' – J. H. Plumb in the *Sunday Telegraph*

The Germans   Gordon A. Craig

An intimate study of a complex and fascinating nation by 'one of the ablest and most distinguished American historians of modern Germany' – Hugh Trevor-Roper

Ireland: A Positive Proposal   Kevin Boyle and Tom Hadden

A timely and realistic book on Northern Ireland which explains the historical context – and offers a practical and coherent set of proposals which could actually work.

A History of Venice   John Julius Norwich

'Lord Norwich has loved and understood Venice as well as any other Englishman has ever done' – Peter Levi in the *Sunday Times*

Montaillou: Cathars and Catholics in a French Village 1294–1324
Emmanuel Le Roy Ladurie

'A classic adventure in eavesdropping across time' – Michael Ratcliffe in *The Times*

Star Wars   E. P. Thompson and others

Is Star Wars a serious defence strategy or just a science fiction fantasy? This major book sets out all the arguments and makes an unanswerable case *against* Star Wars.

FOR THE BEST IN PAPERBACKS, LOOK FOR THE 🐧

A CHOICE OF PENGUINS AND PELICANS

The Apartheid Handbook   Roger Omond

This book provides the essential hard information about how apartheid actually works from day to day and fills in the details behind the headlines.

The World Turned Upside Down   Christopher Hill

This classic study of radical ideas during the English Revolution 'will stand as a notable monument to . . . one of the finest historians of the present age' – *The Times Literary Supplement*

Islam in the World   Malise Ruthven

'His exposition of "the Qurenic world view" is the most convincing, and the most appealing, that I have read' – Edward Mortimer in *The Times*

The Knight, the Lady and the Priest   Georges Duby

'A very fine book' (Philippe Aries) that traces back to its medieval origin one of our most important institutions, marriage.

A Social History of England   New Edition   Asa Briggs

'A treasure house of scholarly knowledge . . . beautifully written and full of the author's love of his country, its people and its landscape' – John Keegan in the *Sunday Times*, Books of the Year

The Second World War   A J P Taylor

A brilliant and detailed illustrated history, enlivened by all Professor Taylor's customary iconoclasm and wit.

The Penguin English Dictionary

Over 1,000 pages long and with over 68,000 definitions, this cheap, compact and totally up-to-date book is ideal for today's needs. It includes many technical and colloquial terms, guides to pronunciation and common abbreviations.

The Penguin Reference Dictionary

The ideal comprehensive guide to written and spoken English the world over, with detailed etymologies and a wide selection of colloquial and idiomatic usage. There are over 100,000 entries and thousands of examples of how words are actually used – all clear, precise and up-to-date.

The Penguin English Thesaurus

This unique volume will increase anyone's command of the English language and build up your word power. Fully cross-referenced, it includes synonyms of every kind (formal or colloquial, idiomatic and figurative) for almost 900 headings. It is a must for writers and utterly fascinating for any English speaker.

The Penguin Dictionary of Quotations

A treasure-trove of over 12,000 new gems and old favourites, from Aesop and Matthew Arnold to Xenophon and Zola.

The Penguin Wordmaster Dictionary   Manser and Turton

This dictionary puts the pleasure back into word-seeking. Every time you look at a page you get a bonus – a panel telling you everything about a particular word or expression. It is, therefore, a dictionary to be read as well as used for its concise and up-to-date definitions.

FOR THE BEST IN PAPERBACKS, LOOK FOR THE

PENGUIN REFERENCE BOOKS

The Penguin Guide to the Law

This acclaimed reference book is designed for everyday use, and forms the most comprehensive handbook ever published on the law as it affects the individual.

The Penguin Medical Encyclopedia

Covers the body and mind in sickness and in health, including drugs, surgery, history, institutions, medical vocabulary and many other aspects. 'Highly commendable' – *Journal of the Institute of Health Education*

The Penguin French Dictionary

This invaluable French-English, English-French dictionary includes both the literary and dated vocabulary needed by students, and the up-to-date slang and specialized vocabulary (scientific, legal, sporting, etc) needed in everyday life. As a passport to the French language, it is second to none.

A Dictionary of Literary Terms

Defines over 2,000 literary terms (including lesser known, foreign language and technical terms) explained with illustrations from literature past and present.

The Penguin Map of Europe

Covers all land eastwards to the Urals, southwards to North Africa and up to Syria, Iraq and Iran. Scale – 1:5,500,000, 4-colour artwork. Features main roads, railways, oil and gas pipelines, plus extra information including national flags, currencies and populations.

The Penguin Dictionary of Troublesome Words

A witty, straightforward guide to the pitfalls and hotly disputed issues in standard written English, illustrated with examples and including a glossary of grammatical terms and an appendix on punctuation.